M. R. G. Davies abandoned a successful career as a newspaper editor to write fiction. As an author, he completed Desmond Bagley's thriller *Domino Island* for posthumous publication and has written two sequels, *Outback* and *Thin Ice*, both published by HarperCollins. His debut play *Rasputin's Mother* won the Bristol Old Vic playwriting competition and subsequent work for the stage includes *The Seagull Has Landed* (Power Plays festival winner), *MacHamLear* (UK tour), *Reality* (Royal & Derngate) and the book and lyrics for *Tess – The Musical* (workshopped at the RSC). He has written narrative non-fiction for worldwide television, had short stories and poetry commissioned and published, and contributes regular essays for theatre programmes.

www.mrgdavies.com

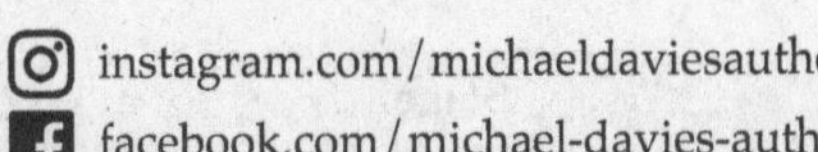

Also by M. R. G. Davies

Novels

THE BILL KEMP TRILOGY:

Desmond Bagley's *Domino Island* (as curator)

Outback

Thin Ice

A COSY CRIME CLUB MYSTERY SERIES:

Murder by the Book

A Game of Murder

Licence to Murder

Stage

The Seagull Has Landed

MacHamLear

Tess – The Musical (with composer Michael Blore)

South Sea Bubble

Reality

Rasputin's Mother

Television

Meet, Marry, Murder

A Killer's Mistake

Made for Murder

MURDER BY THE BOOK

A Cosy Crime Club Mystery

M. R. G. DAVIES

One More Chapter
a division of HarperCollins*Publishers*
1 London Bridge Street
London SE1 9GF
www.harpercollins.co.uk
HarperCollins*Publishers*
Macken House, 39/40 Mayor Street Upper,
Dublin 1, D01 C9W8, Ireland

This paperback edition 2026
3
First published in Great Britain in ebook format
by HarperCollins*Publishers* 2026

A catalogue record of this book is available from the British Library

ISBN: 978-0-00-875504-1

Printed and bound in the UK using 100% Renewable Electricity
by CPI Group (UK) Ltd

For Richard and Trina,
who will understand why.

I caught him, with an unseen hook and an invisible line which is long enough to let him wander to the ends of the world, and still to bring him back with a twitch upon the thread.

The Queer Feet, G. K. Chesterton

MILO: Oh yes, the police are always stupid in your kind of detective stories, aren't they? They never solve anything. Only an amateur sleuth ever knows what's really happening. But that is detective fiction. This is fact.

Sleuth, Anthony Shaffer

Lord Quaint put his cocktail glass on the mantelpiece, tapped out his pipe in the grate and turned his back to the fire. In the hushed stillness of the room, apprehension cut the atmosphere like a bejewelled sgian dubh *– coincidentally the very weapon that had been used to murder the Dowager Duchess of Crompton. Quite where the killer had managed to lay their hands on an ornamental Scottish blade in this remote corner of the West Country was just one of the many mysteries that had surrounded her death and confounded Chief Inspector Watkins of the local constabulary. It was, in fact, the unusual nature of the fatal instrument which had prompted the policeman to call on his old sparring partner for the kind of unofficial assistance which, Watkins had discovered to his chagrin, often brought such cases to a resolution. Where the boys in blue were constrained by the niceties of procedure, an amateur with a nose for adventure could often upturn some nugget that might be forbidden to, or concealed from, the professionals.*

Now Lord Quaint observed Watkins at the back of the room, moustache twitching and notebook in hand, near the door where Constable Flanchberry was stationed, awaiting his Lordship's signal.

Quaint took a moment to survey the company assembled in varying degrees of repose between him and the inspector. Towards the furthest corner – one might almost say lurking – perched the Hon. 'Biffy' Blyth and his irritating fiancée Lady Victoria. Despite their titles, their impecunious state meant that they had much to gain from the death of the Dowager Duchess and they had been, early on in the investigation, two of the inspector's leading suspects. Looming over them from behind was Margeson, the butler, whose indifference to intimidation had irked the police but whose quiet insubordination had endeared him enormously to Lord Quaint. To his left and slightly behind him – as was only proper in the order of these things – stood Mrs Pemberton the cook, two indistinguishable maids, the gardener Ferris and an under-butler whose name Quaint had never been able to pronounce, but who had come to England as a refugee after the war and inveigled himself into a berth in the servants' quarters at Crompton Hall. The numerous other lower staff had been excused attendance, written off by Quaint as incidental to his enquiries, and were even now preparing the dining room for a repast of freshly murdered game.

Nearest to the fireplace was an array of titled personages, every one kin in some degree to the victim. The ages of the six relatives ranged from older than sixty to just thirteen – she had proved a particular thorn in Quaint's side – and their likeness could not fail to be mistaken. To a man (and woman), they matched the fading portraits that climbed the stairs in the hall outside; densely thatched brows overhanging dark eyes set deep in faces more luxuriously rotund than any Quaint could recall seeing in a single family. If they had suffered any post-war privations, as the rest of the country certainly had in the wake of such a long and barbaric conflict, then he was hard-pushed to identify where the budgetary axe had fallen among the expenditures of Crompton Hall.

The Duke himself sat stage-centre, shrouded in thick blue cigar smoke and scowling with all the vehemence of a wounded panther. His petite wife retained a measure of demure disinterest but was blinking rapidly – whether against the acrid smoke or as a natural idiosyncrasy Quaint could not tell. Beside her, the next generation of aristocratic delinquents was laid out for Quaint's perusal: the three children of the Duke and Duchess, the heir haughty, his debutante sibling anxious, their young sister decidedly mischievous. Finally, a little apart from the rest of the family, the Duke's uncle Lord Arthur Kettering looked thoroughly miserable in his raggedly mustered dinner wear. Quaint had known Kettering slightly at Cambridge and had always marvelled at his ability to remain utterly disgruntled by his lot as younger brother to the old Duke, inheriting nothing from his brother's death save the continued opprobrium of the now deceased dowager. If ever there was a man with motive to murder his relations, Lord Arthur was he.

'Your Graces, your Lordship, honourable and esteemed guests,' began Quaint, not caring whether his honorifics were accurate: he was here not to flatter but to accuse.

'Yes, yes,' grumbled Lord Arthur from the wings. 'Our pigeon is getting cold in there.'

Quaint's look withered Lord Arthur's complaint in an instant. 'The pigeon will have to wait, I'm afraid, until I have identified quite another kind of bird – a jailbird.'

The maids quivered audibly. Thirteen-year-old Lady Petunia giggled. Her father grunted.

'Are you saying you have found your man, Lord Quaint?' he asked, his thick breath cutting a swathe through the smoke.

Quaint smiled peaceably. 'And what makes you think it is a man, your Grace?'

The Duke harrumphed in surprise and looked accusingly at his wife.

'No, no,' Quaint continued. 'It is too easy to jump to such a conclusion without first addressing the considerable quantity of evidence which the murderer inadvertently left behind them – evidence which my colleagues from the constabulary kindly compiled but whose significance they inevitably neglected to notice.'

Chief Inspector Watkins gave a loud sigh of annoyance from the back of the room, which Quaint ignored with equanimity.

'Let us take, for example, the sgian dubh*. As you know, this is a traditional Scottish knife that is nowadays chiefly worn for ceremonial and dress occasions north of the border. Its appearance at Crompton Hall has been one of the most mysterious aspects of the case, until one considers the personal history of the Dowager Duchess in her years before coming out. It became quickly apparent to me that the rest of the family were ignorant of this personal history, yet a simple exploration of* Debrett's *reveals that her predecessors were ancient custodians of a long-lost tribal seat somewhere to the west of Dunglochan. This morsel led me to wonder if she had ever paid a visit to her ancestral home.'*

The Duke blustered again. 'What are you talking about, man? There's no Scottish blood in the Cromptons.'

'On the contrary, your Grace. If my deductions are correct – and I have no reason to doubt their veracity – you are descended maternally from Robert Bruce himself.'

'Poppycock,' erupted Lord Arthur. 'The dotty old bat was no more Scottish than you or I.'

Quaint pierced him again. 'Regardless of your opinion of the Dowager Duchess and her mental faculties, the facts remain.'

The Duke stood up and moved towards Quaint. 'Even if that's true, what does it have to do with her murder? How does it help to know she had Scottish ancestry?'

'I'm coming to that. It has a particular pertinence to the weapon, of course, but there is another vital piece of the puzzle that has so far remained out of sight.'

'What piece? It seems pretty clear-cut to me – always has. Everyone knows Uncle Arthur hated her because she snubbed him in favour of my father, and he finally saw his chance to be rid of her while we were all out on a shooting trip. He was the only one left in the house, and when we got back she was dead.'

Quaint invited the Duke to return to his seat before resuming his narrative. 'Lord Arthur may have been the only member of the family left in the house, but he was far from the only person here.'

'Stop talking in riddles, man.'

Quaint waved a hand in the direction of the servants, ranged along the wall behind the family. 'At least twelve other people were in or near Crompton Hall at the time of the murder.'

The Duke jumped to his feet again. 'Are you telling me that one of these … heathens killed my mother?' He made a start towards the line-up of staff but found himself immediately impeded by his wife's voluminous skirts.

'Your Grace, I beg you, please sit down,' said Quaint, a note of exasperation in his voice. When the Duke had subsided into his chair once more, Quaint continued. 'I am merely illustrating the limitations of a view which refuses to recognise the existence of the lower orders as full participants in the human experience.'

'Well, they're not, are they?' muttered Lord Arthur.

'If I am correct, it will not be very many years before such an

observation will be deemed unacceptable in society. Some of the lower classes already have the vote – rightly or wrongly – and it may well be that the move towards emancipation for females gains sufficient ground that they, too, will be permitted to express opinions publicly.'

'Damn fool progressives,' began the Duke, but stopped again at the insistence of his wife's elbow in his ribs.

'As I was saying, when subject to one limited perspective, a host of possibilities is excluded from view. As soon as one opens one's eyes to the wider picture, other prospects become possible – likely, even. And so we ask ourselves, which of our potential cast of characters becomes visible in this wider view? We have the close family, of course'—he gestured towards the six seats nearest him—'along with the more obscure relations.' Here, he nodded at Biffy and his baffled bride-to-be. 'But there are also the supporting players from below stairs, each of whom had their own reason for despising the Dowager Duchess. Margeson and Mrs Pemberton, for instance, whose secret affair was discovered by her Grace and who have lived for years in enforced penury for fear of being exposed by her. Or her chambermaids, Alice and Lily, whom she treated with almost sadistic contempt. Or Ferris, there, who once hoped for promotion to head footman but was relegated by the Duchess to the garden after an indiscretion with a scullery maid, and who has never forgiven her. And finally, our foreign friend, about whom we know so little, whose connection to her Grace can only be surmised and whose swarthy looks betray an inner darkness – one might even say hatred.'

The Duke coughed loudly. 'So you're saying it could be anyone in this room? The question is, which one?'

'Aha!' said Quaint, giving his signal at last to Constable Flanchberry. 'Not necessarily in this room.'

With a flourish, the policeman threw open the door he was

guarding, revealing another constable with one hand cuffed to a very strange individual indeed. All eyes turned to look at the squat, rat-faced man, dressed all in white and with a small peaked cap perched on his forehead, who was now growling at them from the doorway. His long, lank hair framed a face that was filthy with grime, sporting several days' worth of beard growth and considerably fewer than the conventional number of teeth.

Mrs Pemberton let out a small cry—'Oh, it's Mac, the milkman'—and fainted dead away.

'Mac, the milkman, indeed,' said Lord Quaint, indicating to the constable to bring his charge to the fireplace. There he stood beside his Lordship, nose twitching for all the world like a verminous rodent, manacled to his captor and staring defiantly at the room.

'Or should I use your full name … Mr McMorran?'

The Duke leaped to his feet again. 'McMorran? But that was Mama's maiden name. You're not telling me this man was a relative of hers?'

Lord Quaint allowed a smile to crease the corners of his mouth. 'Not just her Grace's, your Gruce, bul your Grace's father, his Gracc, as well. Meet your brother Dougal.'

It took several minutes for the pandemonium in the room to die down. The Duke had to be restrained by Constable Flanchberry and forcibly held in his seat, flexing his fisted hands towards the becuffed milkman, while the Duchess was only revived from her state of shock with a large balloon of brandy delivered by Margeson, who then returned to minister lovingly to the recovering Mrs Pemberton now that their liaison had been revealed. Biffy and his fiancée moved seats to get a better view of McMorran; Lord Arthur sat chuckling into his whisky glass, eyeing first his nephew, then the new interloper, apparently the Duke's illegitimate older brother. When some semblance of order had at last been restored, Lord Quaint stepped forward to speak once more.

'Every one of you in this room had good reason for wanting the Dowager Duchess out of the picture. Please note that I am not condoning her murder in any shape or form, merely establishing the possibility of a motive for each of you. Fortunately for you all, your desire for her demise has become a reality, thanks to Mr McMorran here. If you look at things from his point of view, he might think that you all owe him a debt of gratitude.

'One could certainly argue that Mr McMorran has every right to feel aggrieved. I'm sorry to have to inform the family that the Dowager Duchess had a secret: she was, I regret to say, rather better acquainted with her future husband than she led the vicar at their wedding to believe. She had, in fact, given birth to their first child a year earlier, when she enjoyed a lengthy stay with her ancestral family in Scotland for the purposes of obscuring her confinement. The boy was quietly adopted by one of them and she returned to her former life, with nobody any the wiser. But on reaching adulthood, the young man was determined to learn the truth about his lineage and embarked upon an arduous journey of discovery – a journey that ultimately led him here, to Crompton Hall. That young man has become the unfortunate destitute you see before you.'

The Duke wrestled one arm free from Flanchberry and wagged a finger dangerously in Quaint's direction. 'You can't tell me that this … this … bastard is anything other than a murderous criminal. He killed my mama!'

'Thus freeing you from a lifetime of humiliation at her hands,' replied Lord Quaint.

The Duke let his finger drop and subsided into his chair.

Lord Arthur piped up, a tone of amusement in his voice: 'I have a question – if I may?'

Quaint nodded his permission.

'How did this man, this McMorran, actually do it? He's the village milkman, after all. How did he hope to get away with it?'

Quaint turned to the servants at the back wall. 'Mrs Pemberton, how long has McMorran been the village milkman?'

Margeson helped his lover to her feet and she straightened her pinny before replying. 'Oh, not long, sir – about three weeks.'

'Three weeks,' said Quaint. 'About the same time that this little party gathered for the summer holidays. And did he, like other tradesmen from the village, have access to the house at any time?'

'Oh yes, sir. Whenever they called. He could easily have slipped through into the main house without anyone knowing.'

'Which is precisely what he did, armed with his familial sgian dubh, *while the rest of you were out hunting on the day the Dowager Duchess died. Tell me, Mrs Pemberton, what do you know about Mac, the milkman?'*

'Not much, sir. He told me he was from a little place down in Cornwall, and he spoke in that funny way they do down there, so I had no reason to doubt him.'

'Ah, dear Mrs Pemberton. That "funny way" of talking was not, as you suspected, a Cornish burr, but a poorly concealed Scottish accent from somewhere to the west of Dunglochan. Am I right, Mr McMorran?'

The rat-faced man lurched towards Quaint but was quickly halted by the constable. 'Damn you, Quaint!' he spat. 'If it hadn't been for you and your meddling, I would have got away with it too. That malicious old hag got everything she deserved after dumping me with her Presbyterian missionary third cousin when I could have had all this.' He waved a hand vaguely at the luxurious surroundings.

'Sadly, I'm afraid you could never have had all this,' said Quaint, resting a hand on the miscreant's shoulder. 'The Duke was correct in

his terminology: you were born a bastard and could never hope to inherit the title or the estate. And now your vengeful greed will bring you to the gallows. It is the only possible reward for the evil you have wrought in the guise of a milkman. It is the price you must pay for the delivery of death.'

THE END

Tuesday

Chapter One

She may have been the newest member of the bookshop's reading group, and five feet four in her tallest heels, but Bella Bourton was developing *views*. Opinions. Notions of her own.

'Well, that was brilliant,' she opined as the final words of the King of Crime's magnum opus died away in the vaulted echoes of the space. 'I'd never have guessed it was the milkman.'

'And therein lies the problem,' said Professor Stone, his rich voice cutting across hers. He leaned forward in the institutional armchair he was occupying and looked at her as if he was lecturing to a class full of his students. 'It was entirely impossible to guess, and therefore a deeply unsatisfying *dénouement*. It came out of nowhere.'

The flamboyantly dressed man sitting next to Bella on the worn settee chipped in. 'In the trade, we call it a *deus ex machina*. Although I'm never sure whether it's pronounced *mackina* or *mashina*. Hard or soft "c", Professor – what do you think?'

Bella could feel her confidence ebbing away like gin down a plughole. 'What does *deus ex* ... thingy ... mean?'

'Just what I said,' the Professor replied. 'A deeply unsatisfying *dénouement*.'

From the other armchair, Lauren smiled warmly at Bella. 'It's all right, love – I didn't know what it meant either.'

'Literally, "God from the machine",' said the Professor, tilting his head backwards and steepling his fingers under his chin in a gesture that prompted Bella to suppress a giggle. He was obviously aiming for intellectual; to Bella, he made it just about as far as comically pompous. 'In ancient Greek tragedies, actors playing gods would be winched onto the stage using elaborate mechanisms to bring about a swift, although often unconvincing, resolution.'

'You learn something new,' said Lauren, nodding again in Bella's direction.

'Or old, in this case,' said the Professor.

'If you say so,' mumbled Bella, then instantly regretted it, fearing she might have annoyed the Professor. She might be starting to spread her analytical wings but she had no desire to upset anyone in the process. Such an approach probably didn't make her a shoo-in as the chief literary critic at *The Times*, but at least she could feel good about herself.

'What did you think, Harrison?' asked Lauren.

The stylish man shifted on the settee to face her, waving his copy of *Delivery of Death* to emphasise his point. 'I'm with the Professor on this one. I mean, this is supposed to be the pinnacle of the golden age of detective fiction, and he's coming up with a ridiculous plotline like that? There should have been much more foreshadowing, for a start.'

Lauren nodded. 'I think I agree, although the milkman was mentioned in Chapter Five.'

'That's nowhere near enough,' said the Professor. 'If you're going to drop in a hint to the identity of the killer, they've got to appear more than once in a passing reference. He didn't even use McMorran's name to give the reader a clue. And where did Lord Quaint get all that background information about the Dowager Duchess? Why didn't the family know she had Scottish ancestry when her maiden name was McMorran? No, no – it's really disappointing.'

Bella stayed silent. She was captivated by the discussion but felt that any contribution she might make would appear childish and naïve to this smart bunch who formed the reading group of The Quaint Bookshop. Professor Stone was a senior academic, after all, Harrison's weather-beaten features gave the impression of being worldly wise, and Lauren was clearly much more widely read than her tender years suggested. Bella was definitely the odd one out in the quartet. On the other hand, she found it difficult to understand how someone could be disappointed by the ending of a mere book. The last person she would have described as disappointed was her husband after Norcester United got knocked out of the World of Parsnips (Midlands Division) Trophy in the second round, but then they had been up against the inferior opposition of Nether Buckton Albion and were optimistic for a decent cup run before the Albion striker put five past their keeper. Disappointed hadn't really covered it, to be honest. Trevor had been apoplectic.

'What about you, Bella?'

Lauren's voice wandered in through her musings and she looked up into the expectant, generous eyes of the thirtyish young woman in the armchair, her long Rapunzel hair falling carelessly around her shoulders. Bella knew she had a job in a nearby infants' school as a teaching assistant, but now she tried to picture her at home. Was she married? Was she gay? Who would be there to meet her when she got back from the bookshop? She had answers to none of these questions but found that she wished she had.

'What about me?' she asked.

'The book? You were saying you thought it was brilliant.'

'Oh, what do I know? I'm just trying to expand my horizons a bit. I don't know anything about how murder mysteries work. I should really be at home making Trevor's tea.'

'Definitely not,' said Harrison, thrusting out a hand as if to stop a car. 'I don't know who Trevor is – never met him, never heard of him – but whoever he is, he should undoubtedly be making his own tea if you're here at the reading group. Why should you go putting yourself out on his account if you've got something better to do?'

Bella felt a tremor of vindication at this little speech on her behalf, even though her knight in shining armour knew next to nothing about her. It was only the second time she had met him, after the first group meeting she'd attended the previous week, and she hadn't intended to reveal much about her private life. She'd surprised herself by even mentioning Trevor but she was beginning to realise that a shared interest in literature and the overwhelmingly welcoming attitude of her fellow group members had won her confidence easily and quickly. She was feeling distinctly comfortable, even if she was hopelessly out of her depth. Now Harrison's intervention had made her feel justified, validated – significant, even. She had a sudden urge to go out into Norcester High Street and proclaim that she had every right to be there.

She wouldn't tell Trevor that, though.

'Trevor's my husband,' she said, dropping her chin in almost embarrassment. 'I make his tea every day.'

'Then maybe it's time he learned how to make his own,' said Harrison without a hint of irony. 'How long have you been married?'

'Nineteen years. And three months.'

'Not that you're counting?'

Bella laughed limply. She absolutely was counting.

The Professor cleared his throat. 'I fear we may be straying from our central theme here. We'd be very interested to hear why you enjoyed *Delivery of Death*.'

Bella wasn't sure she believed him, but it was another example of their warmth towards her. She felt entitled to offer her verdict, however inferior it might be.

'Look, I know you three have got a lot more experience in reading this kind of thing than I have, but I've got to say I really liked everything about it – the characters, Crompton Hall, the time period. Even the ending. I love the way Lord Quaint ties up all the loose ends in a neat bow and tells everyone whodunit, as if they should have known all along.' She cast a glance at the Professor. 'In spite of the *deus ex* whatnot.'

'Well, I suppose it's a classic for a reason,' said the Professor. 'Personally, I find that kind of thing irritating beyond belief, but if it works for you…'

Bella was feeling … what was the word? Resilient – that

was it. Maybe it had something to do with Lauren's generosity, Harrison's pep talk or even the Professor's less-than-graceful climbdown, but the truth was that she didn't really care. She was feeling more like herself than she had in years, and she made a mental note to thank the bright, enthusiastic bookshop manager who had alerted her to the existence of the reading group and encouraged her to come along the previous week.

'They love their murder mysteries,' the woman had told her, 'but I'm sure they could be persuaded to try other things too, if you ask them.'

'Oh no, murder mysteries'll be fine,' Bella had replied, peering at the official badge on the young lady's lapel to remind herself of her name. 'Thank you, Felicity. I'll definitely give it a go.'

The Professor dropped his book on the table and began to haul himself out of his armchair.

'All right, that's another one off the list. Now all we have to do is decide what to read next. Do we continue with our expedition through the golden age or shall we try something a little more up to date?'

'What are the options?' asked Lauren, showing no inclination to move.

The Professor sat back again and took out a sheet of paper from his inside jacket pocket. Inspecting it over the top of his glasses, he said, 'Well, we could stay in the countryside with the death of a poultry farmer – *Murder Most Fowl* – or try a locked-room mystery, *The Mystery of the Locked Room*.'

'Ooh, that sounds like a Sherlock Holmes story,' said Lauren excitedly. 'I love Sherlock Holmes.'

'Any particular reason?' asked Bella.

'There is, actually. When I was a child, our family doctor

was called Watson. I couldn't help getting into Conan Doyle after that, could I?'

Harrison and the Professor laughed, and Bella joined in tentatively so as not to look stupid. She'd heard of Dr Watson, of course – she remembered the old Basil Rathbone black-and-white films – but Conan Doyle might as well have been Conan the Barbarian for all she knew. She had quite a bit of catching up to do, she could tell.

'I fancy something a bit more theatrical,' said Harrison. 'Something with an epic sweep to it.'

'You can take the actor out of the theatre…' said the Professor, inclining his head indulgently towards Harrison.

'I haven't retired yet, you know. It's called "resting".'

Bella was curious. 'How long have you been resting, Harrison?'

In her peripheral vision she noticed Lauren wince.

'Yes, well, I need to think about changing my agent,' said Harrison darkly. 'Anyway, an epic sweep?'

'I might have just the thing,' said the Professor, still studying his list. 'A body in the basement of a convent sparks an investigation that threatens to bring down the entire edifice of the Roman Catholic Church.'

'Sounds like my kind of drama. What's it called?'

'*And Then There Were Nuns.*'

'Is it very long?' asked Bella. 'Only I've always been a slow reader and I wouldn't want to get left behind in the weekly discussions.'

'About a thousand pages.'

'I'll never read that by next week,' she said, panicking slightly and looking to Lauren for back-up. 'It's taken me all my spare time to get through the last book, and that was only three hundred pages.'

'Don't worry – we'll only talk about the first hundred or so. The boys like to show off with the doorstop books but they never get any further through them than me.'

Harrison got to his feet decisively and tapped the cover of his book twice with his middle finger. 'Well, I must admit I'm quite glad to see the back of *Delivery of Death*. It seemed to take for ever to unmask the killer.'

'Agreed,' said the Professor. 'I'd like to think that if I ever found myself mixed up in a real-life murder, I'd do a damn sight better job of solving it than Lord Quaint.'

A shadow passed across the opaque Perspex wall that separated the reading room from the main body of the shop. A moment later, Felicity's head appeared round the door. She picked out Bella and gave her an enquiring look.

'How are you getting on, Mrs Bourton?'

'Fine, thank you. I'm being looked after very well.'

'These old-timers making you feel welcome, I hope?'

Lauren looked affronted. 'Who are you calling old?'

Bella laughed – for real this time – and was glad the others did too.

Felicity indicated the watch on her wrist and spoke to the Professor. 'Five minutes to lock-up.'

He nodded and put on his best teacher-in-charge expression. 'On our way out now, Felicity. Thank you, as always, for your hospitality.' He slipped the list back inside his jacket and gathered up his overcoat from where it was draped over the back of the armchair. 'The nuns it is, then. I'm sure Felicity can find four copies to put aside for us.'

'My pleasure,' said Felicity, stepping inside the room to allow the others to leave.

Bella was the last to reach the door. 'Thank you so much for recommending this group to me,' she said, placing a hand on Felicity's arm, and squeezing it gently. Not for the first time, she was grateful for having found the courage to open up a conversation when she'd picked up a couple of Colleen Hoovers a few weeks earlier. It had been a spur-of-the-moment decision, not like Bella at all, but its apparent success was now leading her to think she might indulge in spur-of-the-moment decisions a little more often. 'With what I'm going through just now, I think this is going to be a real life-saver for me.'

'Think nothing of it,' said Felicity, smiling broadly. 'Whatever doesn't kill you makes you stronger.'

Bella hesitated. 'What do you mean?'

'Oh, just an expression.'

In the street outside the bookshop, a few passers-by were enjoying the last remnants of dusk. Felicity said a cheerful 'Bye' and closed the heavy door behind them. One of the things that had first drawn Bella to The Quaint Bookshop was its previous history as a Methodist chapel. She could remember it in the days when it had inspirational messages posted outside, exhorting passers-by to 'Prevent truth decay – brush up on your Bible' or 'Come inside for a faith lift'. Its pews had long since been exchanged for shelf stacks and its hymn books for (mainly) crime novels, but the essential architecture and imposing grandeur of the vast place remained, and now Bella heard the sound of the original iron bolts being pushed home and a key turning in a lock.

The Professor made a quick getaway, disappearing up an alley beside the shop towards the town's main multi-storey car park, while Harrison waved breezily and marched off down the hill towards the nearest tram stop. Lauren stood with Bella for a few moments more.

'I'm so glad you've joined the reading group,' she said. 'Those two are great fun but it'll be nice to have some female company for a change. And maybe we can get them to read something different once in a while.'

Bella didn't mind. As she watched Lauren turn a corner to the street where she'd parked her car, Bella could sense things were already different. She rather fancied she might have found a new tribe. Maybe their friendliness and support would help ease her ongoing domestic struggle against the overbearing clutches of Trevor. Yes, it was early days but perhaps she could make out a hint of light at the end of that nineteen-year tunnel. Maybe there would come a time when she would no longer have to make his every meal. She hardly dared imagine it, but perhaps she might refuse to accompany him to a football match to listen to the inane, insulting chants on the terraces around her. Just two weeks at the reading group had sparked a new feeling deep inside her: she was her own woman.

Now all she had to do was persuade Trevor.

She was walking towards the bus stop, mulling over exactly what she would say to him, when a stomach-churning scream from the bookshop pierced the evening gloom.

Chapter Two

Professor Stone stared at the Perspex, willing the dark shapes on the other side to come into focus. When they met as the reading group, the privacy offered by the wall's opacity was a welcome separation from the tiresome types who often frequented the bookshop. Now it was a barrier that prevented him from seeing what was going on.

He guessed at some of the silhouettes. The taller, more immobile ones were likely to be uniformed officers performing sentry duty; the shufflers and amblers could be forensics, impeded by body suits and plastic galoshes and edging their way around the crime scene; one shorter figure, almost certainly female, moved briskly between them. Stone thought this was probably the senior detective who'd corralled them into the reading room, efficient but cold and very much giving off the vibe that they were a nuisance to her and her newly instigated investigation. She'd asked them to wait – directing her instructions primarily at Stone himself, apparently the most authoritative of the group – and told them someone would be over to speak with them when they were free. She had given no indication of timescale and walked off without answering any more of their questions.

Stone thought she'd been rather rude.

Now there was a uniform outside the door and the four of them were essentially prisoners in their own hobby room.

He turned away from the Perspex to face the small, comfortable space where the group met each week. Surveying the scene, he imagined himself as Lord Quaint, upright and imposing in front of a country-house fireplace. The saggy armchairs and faded covers on the settee didn't quite match his mental image of Crompton Hall's opulent drawing room but they would have to do. Stone's visceral queasiness about what had happened in the bookshop less than half an hour earlier was starting to dissipate and his calculating mind was shifting into gear. With their lovely Felicity slumped between the shelves, there was evidently an attacker on the loose and Stone felt his senses tingling – less Spider-Man and more distressed friend furious at his own impotence. Already he was trying to decipher the mechanics of the crime – but which of the assembled company had the means and motive? Well, none of them, clearly, since at least two of them constituted the people he could reliably call 'friends' in Norcester, and he wasn't prepared to throw them under the bus purely in the name of crime-fighting. Not without some firm evidence, at least. Besides, logic told him he'd only recently parted company with them all in the street outside, with Felicity locking the doors behind them. The means were surely beyond any of them. But a little thing like that wasn't going to stop him speculating, and he eyed each of them in turn, wondering what his suspicions would be if they actually were potential suspects.

Bella Bourton was, naturally, the blankest page: she'd only joined the reading group the week before and he knew precious little about her. A housewife, he surmised from her rather prim outfit of skirt and old-fashioned blouse, and she'd mentioned making Trevor's tea. Nineteen years they'd been married, so that would put her ... what, in her forties? She certainly had the air of a downtrodden spouse, with her innate timidity and hint of subservience, but he had been gracious in allowing her opinion about the book and his ability to listen, honed from years of students moaning about trivial problems, meant he would give her a fair hearing. He could stand to know more about this mousy new addition to their group and made a mental note to find some quiet time to speak to her in more depth.

Lauren Sherwood was a different matter altogether. There was no way Stone would get the chance to quiz her gently about her life – at least a decade younger than Bella, she was far too forthright to indulge anyone in that kind of buttering up. In any case, Stone already knew more about her than he did Mrs Bourton, and what he knew led him to believe she could never seriously be a suspect in a murder case. The closest she would ever get to skulduggery was the cosy crime novels she kept starting then abandoning when she realised there was more to writing a bestseller than bashing out some words on a keyboard and hoping some kind of plot would emerge. Stone was aware of four attempts at least, each begun in a lively spirit of literary entrepreneurism that carried Lauren through the first five thousand words or so before running out of steam and dumping her latest amateur sleuth as too dull or too clever or too obvious. As for her private life, she had never let slip any details about a partner: her great loves appeared to be her two cats, Romulus and Remus, with whom she lived in a small terraced house on the far side of the railway bridge. Stone had seen pictures on her phone – of the cats, not the house – and had politely agreed that they did indeed look like 'cute little fluff balls'.

And then there was the actor, all exaggerated utterances and mannered gestures, but underneath it all just a boy playing at being a grown-up. Even his identity was made up: he'd adopted the stage name Harrison Fforde – 'two fs and an e', he would proclaim grandly at first introduction – when he joined the actors' union Equity, hoping the jocular confusion with the film star might make him stick in the memory of a hungry casting director. It seemed to have worked for a while, but when things went from joke name to just joke, Fforde's progress in the industry had stalled. Now in his early fifties, Stone guessed, there was little hope of his landing a major television role or Hollywood movie, and it would be character parts all the way to the pension counter. That's if he could find work at all. Smaller actors might have grown bitter about the trajectory of their career but, in spite of his long periods 'resting' and the apparent ineptitude of his agent, Fforde seemed unhampered by pessimism, confidently expecting a call from Steven Spielberg or Russell T. Davies at any moment. Stone liked that about him. He had a curious sideline in conspiracy theories, which Stone was less impressed by, and could be immensely irritating apparently without even trying, but Fforde's disposition was predominantly sunny and the conspiracies unerringly upbeat, so maybe he could be permitted the odd foible.

After all, didn't everyone have their little quirks?

'What's going on out there?' asked Lauren, her voice quivering. She looked up at Stone from the settee where she sat with Bella Bourton holding her hand, forehead creased with a frown and eyes wet with tears.

'No idea,' Stone replied grimly. 'We'll just have to wait until they're ready to talk to us.'

Fforde was pacing behind the armchairs but the room was too small to get to more than four so he was turning almost as much as he was pacing. It was starting to become annoying, so Stone sat down in one of the armchairs and addressed the women opposite.

'I'm sure they won't be too long. We are key witnesses.'

Stone heard Fforde stop behind him. 'Yes, but key witnesses to what?' There was a strong dose of anxiety in his voice. 'Poor Felicity is lying out there among the books and we don't have a clue what happened. Was it a tragic accident or was there someone else in here? And if so, how did they get in? As far as I knew, we were the last people here and she locked the door behind us. I didn't see anyone else – did you?'

Stone wasn't sure who the question was aimed at but chose to ignore it anyway. 'We all heard her scream, didn't we? And we all arrived back at the front door at about the same moment. Now, let's focus – it's important we get our stories straight.'

Lauren let out a little cry and pulled her hand away from Bella's to wrench a tissue from the box on the table in front of her. Dabbing at her nose, she said, 'What are you talking about, Professor? Get our stories straight? We don't have any stories. We're just the reading group at the bookshop where Felicity worked. We don't have to make sure there are no plot holes in our narrative, do we? You're talking as if we've got something to hide.'

Stone was quick to cover himself.

'No, of course not. I didn't mean it in the sense of colluding to deceive the police or anything like that. It simply occurs to me that since we were the last people to see Felicity, as Harrison has pointed out, we're bound to be high on the list for questioning by the detectives. If they were to uncover – how shall I put it? – any little discrepancies between our versions of what we saw and heard, that might cast suspicion on us.'

A look of utter horror passed across Bella's face. 'Suspicion? Us? But I've only just joined the group.'

'Don't worry, Bella,' said Fforde, resuming his pacing. 'The Professor's just gone a bit Lord Quaint.'

Stone stiffened as he recalled his imaginings from a few minutes earlier and resented the fact that Fforde was spot-on. 'I'm thinking more of Sherlock Holmes's dictum, that when you have eliminated the impossible, then whatever remains, however improbable, must be the truth.'

Lauren's voice rose again. 'Are you seriously suggesting that the police will think one of us killed Felicity – no matter how improbable that is?'

'I can't be a suspect,' said Bella, reaching for a tissue herself. 'I've got to make Trevor his Horlicks.'

Lauren switched her attention back to the older woman beside her. 'He doesn't know you're here, does he?'

Bella shook her head and sniffled. 'He wouldn't like it. I made it home last week before he got in from the late shift, and I was hoping to do the same tonight. Not now, though.'

She suddenly caught herself and looked round the room, horrified.

'Oh no – I'm so sorry. What a selfish thing to say. My domestic concerns are the least of our worries after what's happened to…'

Stone had always prided himself on being a calming influence in most situations but this one was starting to get out of hand. He decided to wheel out his avuncular persona in an attempt to diffuse the anxiety choking the room. Hoping he'd put enough gravity into his tone to settle everyone, he said, 'Look, I think we're all getting ahead of ourselves. We don't even know for sure that Felicity is dead.'

Everyone fell silent for a moment, contemplating.

Stone wound back time and tried to recall the precise sequence of events since he'd pulled out his mobile phone and dialled 999. It had taken a little persuasion to get the call handler to take him seriously when he reported the blood-curdling scream they'd all heard, but after he'd put Lauren on the line to give them the full histrionics, the message seemed to get through. Within minutes, there were sirens in the air and blue flashing lights casting their weird pallor over four desperate faces. It had taken two burly coppers five more minutes to get inside the building, one of them turning back to open up the main door for their colleagues, and by the time the reading group reached the vaulted central hall, the place was swarming with officers and paramedics and they were being herded to one side. Stone had managed to catch sight of a crumpled heap, clearly recognisable as Felicity, between two avenues of books in the Noir section, and he knew the others must have seen her too, because both Bella and Lauren gave involuntary cries, while Harrison froze, muttering, 'Good God!'

They had been kept in the Children's section, across the aisle from Noir, for the next ten minutes while a series of officers established who they were and what they were doing there. By the time Stone had given his name and address to a rather harassed-looking WPC – he couldn't bring himself to drop the 'W' from the outdated abbreviation, no matter how passive-aggressive her correction had been – they were being pointed at from across the room by the first officer to have arrived on the scene, indicating their presence to a woman of commanding authority. She wasn't in uniform and Stone guessed she was the detective in charge of what was now likely to be an extremely high-profile case. He'd watched her approach, noting the straight back, brisk pace and fierce haircut, and wondered momentarily if she had served in the armed forces. Or maybe she was born terrifying.

'Right, who are you and what are you doing in the shop?' she barked from a distance.

Stone stepped forwards, adopting the mantle of group leader without seeking, or being given, permission by the others.

'We're The Quaint Bookshop reading group and we were the last people to see Felicity.' He checked himself. 'Actually, that's an assumption on my part. As far as we know, we were the last to leave the shop.'

'Felicity? That's her name?' The woman cast a glance back towards the crumpled heap, now shrouded in heavy-duty PVC and surrounded by all-in-one white romper suits.

'Felicity Penman,' volunteered Lauren, rather nervously.

'Good name for a bookshop owner,' said the woman.

'Oh, not the owner,' corrected the Professor. 'Felicity was the manager. To be honest, I've never really been sure who actually owns the place.'

He looked round to see if any of his colleagues could offer some enlightenment. They couldn't.

The woman didn't seem particularly interested in any case.

'Right, we'll need to speak to you all but we haven't got the manpower at the moment. Is there somewhere you can wait? Away from … all this?' She waved a hand vaguely behind her, where an officer was starting to unroll striped tape around the bookshelves.

'There's the reading room,' replied Stone. 'It's where we usually meet.'

'Fine. Wait in there and we'll get to you as soon as we can. And no sneaky shots on your mobiles – understood?'

Harrison edged forward half a pace. 'Are you with homicide?'

The woman gave him a filthy look up and down, as if she'd found him unconscious in an alley with an empty whisky bottle in his hand. Her voice dripped with disdain. 'This isn't America, you know. And I'm not Columbo.'

Pondering their current situation in the reading room, Stone realised he couldn't imagine anyone less like Columbo. Where the fictional detective had a scruffy tan mac, this woman looked like she meant it: sharp suit, cropped brown hair, and an overwhelming sense of efficiency that left her Stateside counterpart looking precisely the chaotic shamble he purported to be. But, Stone knew, Columbo's image was all a façade, and he wondered if the same was true of this woman.

It was another twenty minutes before the door crashed open and the not-Columbo non-American detective marched into the room. She took one look at Fforde, still to-ing and froing behind the armchairs, and pointed silently at the empty one beside Stone. Without a word, Fforde stepped over to it and sat meekly down.

'Have you all given your names to one of my officers?' she began without any preamble.

Bella and Lauren nodded, Fforde muttered something inaudible, and Stone answered with a clear, deep 'Yes.'

'Right. My name is Detective Chief Inspector Miranda Carlton and this'—she moved slightly to one side to reveal a rather dishevelled figure Stone hadn't noticed before—'is Detective Sergeant Muir.'

'Geoffrey,' said the man, raising a pencil as if in diffident greeting.

He wore a scruffy tan mac.

The senior officer appeared unimpressed. '*Sergeant Muir,*' she said pointedly, 'will be taking some notes.'

Fforde lifted a tentative hand. 'Excuse me – are you going to interview us all together? Shouldn't you be questioning us individually?'

'Why? Have you got something to hide?'

'No, it's just that the protocol in this kind of situation—'

'Protocol?' DCI Carlton's voice was withering. 'Oh, so you want to play it by the book, do you? All right, that's fine by me. I was simply trying to save you all a little time and effort, but if you want to do things the hard way, be my guest. I'll require each of you to come into Norcester Police Station tomorrow – Sergeant Muir will arrange a specific time with you – and we'll interview you separately.' She threw an ugly look at Fforde. 'As per the protocol.'

Stone silently cursed the actor's idiotic eagerness. Why had he opened his big mouth? The last thing Stone wanted to do was spend a wet Wednesday at the police station. Much better to have got the whole unpleasant business over and done with tonight.

He realised Carlton was still talking.

'And if any of you so much as breathes a word of this to anyone – and I mean anyone; no boyfriends, girlfriends, elderly mothers or cats – there'll be hell to pay.'

She turned dramatically, about to stride out of the room, when she stopped abruptly and looked back.

'Oh, one quick question.'

Stone wondered what was coming next.

'I don't suppose any of you had a grudge against Felicity Penman?' She didn't wait for an answer. 'No, thought not. Now pop off out of my crime scene.'

Muir gave them a glance that Stone could not begin to interpret – was it abject pity, silent apology, utter contempt? – and followed his superior out of the room, his scruffy tan mac fluttering in the draught. For a fleeting moment it reminded Stone of an empty bin bag being blown up a back alley, and he wondered if he should read it as a metaphor for a similar kind of hollow uselessness in Muir's role.

'Right, who's up for meeting again tomorrow after our interviews?'

He stared at Fforde, still ebullient even in the face of the most horrific of circumstances.

'Didn't you hear what she just said?' asked Bella, visibly quaking on the settee. She and Lauren were holding hands again. 'We're not allowed to talk to anyone.'

Fforde threw his hands up in a dismissive gesture. 'Oh, she didn't mean us. If she hadn't wanted us to talk to each other, she wouldn't have left us on our own in here, would she?'

Grudgingly, Stone conceded that Harrison Fforde might have a point. Not only had they been stashed away in the reading room for the past half-hour but they'd also been abandoned now, free to expound all manner of theorems, conspiracies and hypotheses between themselves. It scarcely fitted with the chief inspector's moratorium on talking to anyone about the night's business.

'I'm not sure,' said Bella, looking down at the floor.

'Besides,' Fforde went on as if Bella hadn't spoken, 'we'll all have been interviewed by then, so we won't be in a position to influence each other, will we?'

Lauren patted Bella's hand. 'He's right, you know. I don't think the inspector meant us.'

'And I don't know about you, but I've got questions.' Fforde certainly looked like he meant business. Stone just wasn't sure if it was the kind of business Fforde would be any good at.

It was Lauren who took the bait. 'Such as?'

'Such as who would want to attack Felicity Penman, for starters.'

The foursome fell silent once more. Stone found himself picturing the efficient, enthusiastic bookshop manager he'd grown so fond of, and he suspected the others were doing the same..

'And how did they get into the shop? Was it an inside job?'

Bella sounded morose. 'I just want to know if she's going to be all right. It looked pretty horrible from where I was standing.'

Stone closed the door and leaned his back against it.

'There's something else,' he said quietly, staring into the middle distance with an intensity he'd reserved in the past for misdemeanours ranging from a late dissertation to a colleague's wayward drinking habits. He'd convinced himself it lent gravitas and it was just the aura he needed when he was trying to convey seriousness.

Three faces turned expectantly towards him.

'I think we owe it to Felicity,' he said.

'What do you mean?' asked Lauren.

'Look, we're all in the same boat, the four of us. Until the police rule us out, we're all going to be potential suspects for the attack, and that puts us in a corner. But nobody outside this little circle will understand our situation – it's just us. Whether we like it or not, we're in this together.'

He paused, eyeing up the others to gauge whether they did indeed like it. Or not.

'Felicity is our friend, isn't she? We're all part of this group because of her, ultimately. Now we're a team and we have to trust each other. All right, so there's a mystery surrounding this attack on her. And maybe right now we're in the sights of the police. But let's face it: who is there better than a group devoted to mysteries to help solve this one?'

Chapter Three

As she eased her Mini carefully through the dark, damp streets of Norcester, Lauren Sherwood's mind was racing considerably faster than the engine.

There were a thousand unanswered questions from the events of the evening but only one kept surfacing, like the corpse of a fish in a polluted reservoir: was Felicity Penman actually dead? It was the Professor who had put the thought into her head. When she first saw the body she'd automatically assumed Felicity had been killed. The activity of the forensics team they'd glimpsed from afar in grotesque fascination seemed to confirm the idea. And while DCI Carlton had not officially commented one way or the other on the matter, she had certainly offered them no firm reason to be optimistic about their friend. But now that she was alone, turning things over for herself, Lauren kept coming back to that one uncertainty. She didn't know enough about police procedure to be able to tell if the arrival of a chief inspector was normal, or whether the DCI's appearance on the scene did indeed signify a fatality. She had certainly turned up pretty sharpish, and her manner towards the members of the reading group had been abrupt, to say the least, but Lauren expected she often had to deal with the more unpleasant aspects of human nature and probably spent much of her time among the dead: perhaps that explained her shortage of empathy when it came to the living.

There had been something about Miranda Carlton that Lauren found intriguing. It wasn't just that she was a woman with obvious resources and power at her disposal – Lauren had met women like that before and thought them distant and aloof – but she also seemed to have a vulnerability that leaked out through her terse, barked orders. If you knew what you were looking for. Lauren was sure that the others hadn't spotted it, but she had recognised in the detective a subtle brittleness that resonated with her. Indeed, it was probably her own sense of inner strength mismatched with chronic imposter syndrome that enabled her to see it in other people. The mask was well constructed and particularly well fortified in the course of official duties; nonetheless, a mask it was.

She jumped as a noisy BMW with souped-up exhausts and laughable spoilers roared past her towards the railway bridge.

'Hurry up, darling!' shouted a boy of about sixteen, waving a gesture from the passenger-side window that she suspected was faintly obscene but was grateful she couldn't precisely identify.

Then they were gone.

Mildly disturbed by the encounter, Lauren concentrated on her driving for the next few minutes until the matter of Felicity's current status intruded once more and her thoughts were off again. It was horrifying enough that the poor woman should have been attacked: she wasn't far off Lauren's age and the possibility that she was, in fact, dead hardly bore thinking about. Which made it all the more odd that it wouldn't leave her head.

By the time she pulled up at the back of the delineated parking bay near her house – still some walk away but as near as she was likely to find at this time of night – Lauren was no closer to answering the question.

But she had made a decision.

In the hall, she took off her coat, hanging it on one of the empty pegs behind the door, and bent down to caress the cat that had come out of the living room to meet her.

'Hello, Remus,' she said, stroking from the cat's shoulders to the tip of its tail, enjoying the way it arched its back and tucked its head against her shin. Romulus wouldn't bother to drag himself away from his comfortable chair by the radiator, she knew, but she'd find him and make a fuss of him whether he liked it or not. First, though, she went through to the kitchen at the back of the house and poured herself a generous glass of white wine from the fridge.

She wasn't ready for bed yet, and there was work to be done.

'You soppy old thing,' she said sombrely to Romulus when she went into the living room. He was exactly where she'd expected him to be, nose curled under his tail, but he opened out into a curved stretch at her approach, offering his warm belly for her attention. She tickled him for a moment, then turned to Remus, who was shouting at her from the rug in front of the fire.

'Yes, you're a soppy old thing too,' she said, kneeling down beside him and cradling his skull with one hand, the other occupied with her glass. 'Have you missed me?'

The cat gave a little grunt as if in answer then lay down on its side, the fussing evidently over. In spite of her mournful mood Lauren smiled, loving the mercurial inconstancy of her boys, and went over to the desk by the back window.

She fired up the computer and sat down, swinging the rotating chair from side to side and sipping at her wine as the digital jiggery-pokery did its thing. When the prompt window popped open, she put the glass down on her Isle of Man souvenir coaster and typed in a sequence of letters and numbers with the rapidity that only constant repetition can bring.

I really should change my password, she thought for the umpteenth time, then clicked open the file she wanted.

It took the word-processing program thirty laborious seconds to load the document, its ancient mechanism scrolling to the end with gentle inefficiency. Lauren picked up the glass and sipped again, then flicked the mouse with her free hand, working her way backwards through the pages until she found the passage she was looking for.

The second murder, a good two-thirds of the way into the novel.

Lauren had only caught a glimpse of Felicity Penman in the bookshop but the image had made a deep impression on her. She hadn't realised just how deep until it had struck her, driving home in the dark, that it would make a perfect scene in her book. She'd always considered that second death a little too unreal, too melodramatic to be credible, but in the months since she'd written it she hadn't been able to come up with a better alternative. She'd considered poisoning the victim, throwing him off a cliff, recently even stealing the fatal *sgian dubh* from *Delivery of Death*, but nothing had been quite right.

There must be at least half a dozen rewritten versions of this chapter tucked away in archived folders on the computer, never to see the light of day. But now she had it: he would be crushed by a falling bookcase in his own library.

She was halfway through her latest rewrite, the abandoned wine seeping up to room temperature, when she realised she was herself acting like a character in detective fiction. Wasn't this exactly the kind of situation Jessica Fletcher always found herself in: deep into the writing of her latest novel when a murder happened right under her nose? The crimes would then find their way into her books and that would be another bestseller under her belt, the authenticity of real life adding verisimilitude to an otherwise implausible narrative.

Oh, for the popularity of just one of Jessica Fletcher's novels. And the sales, naturally.

Now Lauren was writing fast – faster than she'd ever written before. Up to now, she'd always found it a chore, slogging away at the keyboard, searching for the most appropriate word or phrase to convey her meaning and frequently stretching for the well-worn thesaurus from the bookshelf beside her. In darker moments, when her characters evaded her and the sparkling dialogue remained frustratingly out of reach, she wondered why she put herself through it at all. Weren't there enough mediocre novels out there already? Did she really need to add to the destruction of the world's trees to satisfy her own ego? It was at times like this that the imposter syndrome really kicked in hard, and it took all Lauren's strength not to highlight the entire research folder for her latest masterpiece and hit 'Delete'.

But there was something about this one that had prevented her from doing so, and now she was glad of it. Her fingers tapped keenly as the prose flowed and she found her melancholy at the evening's trauma morphing into something more like intensity. She wondered if it was a little twisted to think that if Felicity was indeed dead, at least her memory could be immortalised in print, if only Lauren could find a publisher for her book.

Yes, she decided, it probably was.

And then her mobile went off.

The shrill old-fashioned telephone ringtone, selected from the mobile's menu as a fond reminder of her parents' prehistoric landline, made her start, almost upending the wine. She grabbed the glass before it toppled, then snatched up the mobile from the desk and accepted the call, even though the number showed up as unrecognised.

'Hello, Lauren Sherwood speaking,' she said in the sing-song voice she'd been taught to use as a child. As an unequivocal Millennial, she couldn't be doing with Gen Z's cavalier attitude to unknown calls – no leaving it to voicemail for her – and she'd happily adopted the more prosaic style of her Boomer parents, greeting the caller and formally introducing herself out of politeness.

This time she would regret it.

'Oh, hi Lauren,' said a cheery but slightly forced woman's voice on the other end. 'I'm so glad I caught you. Sorry it's a bit late.'

Lauren looked over at her grandmother's clock in the middle of the mantelpiece and was surprised to see it reading 11.45 p.m. She'd had no idea it had got so late and now she wouldn't get in her requisite eight hours' sleep before the alarm roused her the next morning. It being the school holidays, there was no work to go to, but she did like regularity when life permitted.

'Who is this?' she asked cautiously, wondering now just who could be calling her at this time of night, from a number she didn't know.

'I wanted to get hold of you tonight, before everything breaks tomorrow,' said the woman. Lauren noticed she hadn't answered her question.

'I'm sorry,' Lauren replied. 'I'm afraid I don't know what you mean.'

'Oh, my bad,' said the voice.

Lauren's mood sank a little lower: a Zoomer. The younger generation. No wonder she didn't understand her.

'It's just that the story is going to be all over the news in the morning and I wanted to get in first. If that's OK with you, I mean?'

Lauren felt a lurch in the pit of her stomach, as if an overripe prune had reached her digestive tract and was trying to beat a retreat.

'What story is that?' she asked, trying to sound nonchalant.

'Oh,' said the caller, uncertainty creeping into her tone for the first time. 'You did say this was Lauren Sherwood, didn't you?'

'I did, but you didn't tell me who you are.'

'Didn't I?' The fake nonchalance matched Lauren's own. 'I'm sorry. It's Nicki Bailey here. From the *Echo*.'

She clearly thought this should be enough information to satisfy Lauren.

It wasn't.

'And how exactly can I help you?'

'I was led to believe you were at The Quaint Bookshop this evening. When the murder took place.'

The prune descended a little lower into Lauren's gut. So it was confirmed: Felicity was dead.

The sickening feeling was joined by a growing sense of outrage. Outrage at what had happened to the lovely, helpful girl who looked after the reading group and enabled their meetings. Outrage at the perpetrator, whoever he was, who had committed such a devastating crime. And outrage at this reporter, calling her up late at night to go digging blithely about for an angle she could use to sell more newspapers.

'Hello? Lauren? Are you still there?'

Lauren collected up all the impoliteness she could muster and hung up the call.

For several minutes she stared at the cats, relaxed and sleepy in their respective spots, and wrestled with her emotions. Then she picked up her mobile, clicked through to the Contacts page, and pressed on a name.

Wednesday

Chapter Four

It had been touch and go but Bella thought she might have got away with it.

Trevor had gone to bed by the time she got in, evidently not waiting for his Horlicks, nor to catch the local news headlines at ten-thirty, and he was snoring noisily when she tiptoed into the bedroom. Shaken by the evening's events, she'd got off the bus one stop early on her way home, by the car park of the Pulp Beater on the corner of Lambton Avenue and Beech Street. Her intention had been to revive herself with a half-pint of shandy: she hadn't had shandy in years but the circumstances had generated a thirst for something sharp and restorative. When it came to it, she had changed her order at the last moment, after the tattooed barman asked which type of lager she would like and she couldn't decide between Schnabelwörter and Nasseswasser. Persuaded finally by the fact that she could pronounce neither, she settled for a plain lemonade (no ice) instead. It was probably for the best: if Trevor were still awake, he might detect the scent of beer on her breath – although how he'd have got close enough to do that she wasn't sure – and that would have taken more explaining than she felt up to at half past ten with a brutal attack on her mind.

No, she concluded, it was enough to stop at the pub for a lemonade.

She'd turned on the television, making sure to mute the volume before the picture came properly to life, and managed to work the remote control so that the subtitles came on. She heard the theme music for the news bulletin in her imagination as it played out silently on the screen, the dramatic drum thumps accentuating each headline, but the subtitles were being typed live so they were a full fifteen seconds behind the presenter, and when they cut away to footage from the top stories, the words were still scrolling from the previous item.

Never mind, she thought, *it's that nice lady who does the house-swap programme in her spare time. I'll pretend I can hear her voice.*

Once she'd convinced herself that a possible murder at Norcester's leading independent bookshop hadn't made the news, she switched off the television, slipped out of her clothes to avoid waking Trevor in the bedroom, and tiptoed upstairs.

It was a different matter over breakfast.

'Egg's hard,' Trevor had said, stabbing the offending item with the unsliced end of a sausage.

It was par for the course these days, and at least he hadn't quizzed her about last night. Yet.

'Do you want me to do you another?' she asked, then worried that she'd put a little too much confrontational attitude into the question.

'Doesn't matter,' he said sullenly. 'Haven't got time

anyway. The boss wants to see us all for ten minutes before we start shift.'

'What's that about?' she asked, her natural timidity returning unprompted.

'I don't know, do I? If I knew what it was about I wouldn't need to be there, would I?'

Bella presumed the questions didn't require an answer so went back to stirring the porridge she was brewing for her own breakfast. If Trevor was going to an early meeting before work, he'd have to be leaving within the next few minutes, and that suited her just fine. It looked as if she might have the day to herself after all. There was a mountain of housework she needed to do, from collecting up Trevor's discarded 'grunties' – she hated the euphemism for underwear that she'd only ever heard him use – and putting them on a heavily soiled wash, to tidying up the front garden after Mrs Morris from the church wives had called round unexpectedly yesterday on a quest for jumble and found a used tissue nestling in the undergrowth by the path.

But all of that could wait. Bella had an important, if moderately alarming, mission to undertake, and it wasn't going to stand being put aside for the sake of a few boring chores.

Bella had a police interview.

She was feeling the oddest sensation as she switched her domestic servility from the hob to the sink, where her yellow Marigolds dripped bubbles onto the mat while she mused. On one hand, she was on heightened alert for the backlash she feared from Trevor. On the other, she couldn't deny that her fibs were making her feel ever so slightly rebellious. They weren't exactly white, her lies, but they could hardly be described as anything darker than magnolia, surely? And now she came to think of it, she hadn't actually said anything directly untruthful. Her fault – if it could even be labelled as a fault – was that she hadn't said anything at all. If she spoke, she was terrified of incriminating herself; if she didn't, that in itself might be enough to make Trevor suspicious.

Was this what a midlife crisis felt like?

Then, one foot already in a work boot and the other sporting a bedraggled old sock, Trevor had asked The Question.

Bella dreaded The Question. She had done for several years now, but even the familiarity of repeated usage had not dulled its power to instil in her a sense of guilt. For being found out. Or for not being completely honest. Or for deceiving her husband. Or in this instance, all three.

She'd thought today she might evade its grippy tentacles. But Trevor had other ideas.

'Where were you last night?'

In normal circumstances, there was only one excuse that would satisfy Trevor: she had been visiting her sister for the evening and got back slightly later than she'd meant to. These were not normal circumstances, but Trevor didn't know that. The problem for Bella was that she had, in fact, visited her sister the evening before, and two visits on consecutive nights was not only stretching the truth, it was beyond the realms of credulity. Ronnie, who worked as a volunteer in the gift shop at Abbots Chantry, a dusty country house in the depths of the remote Norcester hinterlands, could be hard work. Even Bella couldn't imagine wanting to spend two nights in her company. She loved her sister, of course, but her stream-of-consciousness conversation about everything from immigration policy (ineffective) to the exact shade of the Princess of Wales's fascinator at the Cheltenham Gold Cup (arguably teal but in all likelihood viridian) could be more than a little tiring, and Trevor was only too aware that there was a limit to how much Bella could stand.

Bella had lain awake, listening to Trevor's heavy breathing, and pondered exactly how she would address this moment if it came. She'd considered a range of possibilities – trapped by a traffic light failure in the roadworks on the ring road, stopping to console an injured badger, that kind of thing – and had finally drifted off to sleep trying to grasp hold of one particular lie. By morning, whatever the slippery tale had been had already vanished from memory, and she was left floundering for an excuse.

The truth had not occurred to her.

There was no way Trevor would have permitted her to join the reading group. She could imagine his response if she casually mentioned she was off to spend the evening in the company of like-minded strangers whom Trevor had never met, could not understand and would never be able to communicate with. While he had never actually been physically violent towards her, he could certainly be intimidating enough to stop her leading her own life and having her own friends. In fact, he'd probably have laughed at her, which would have been worse. The irony was that her secret assignations at the bookshop – just the two of them so far – had already shifted her attitude towards their domestic situation, and not in Trevor's favour.

No, she would have to come up with something else. And fast.

It was exhausting, all this subterfuge.

'Didn't you find your tea in the oven?' she asked, hoping she might be able to divert his questioning by subtly reminding him of the attention she paid to her wifely duties. On the off-chance that he'd finish his shift early and get home before her, she'd left a vague note directing her husband to the large cuboid kitchen appliance and indicating that she would be out late and not to wait up, but she'd been decidedly cagey about the reason for her absence, and she knew it would have been a miracle for him to let it lie. It wasn't unprecedented for her still to be out after he went to bed – her visits to Ronnie were a regular case in point – but he was hardly overjoyed about it. For all her forethought, she still hadn't come up with a decent alibi to cover the reading group meetings.

'I did, but that doesn't tell me where you were,' he said, pulling on the other boot.

Bella wondered if he'd been planning this moment, delaying it until just before his departure for maximum impact. Had he really been awake when she crept into bed? The crisis began to overwhelm her again. What did she think she was doing? How on earth had she found herself embroiled in a serious crime investigation? That wasn't Bella Bourton's style; that wasn't for the likes of her. Maybe the whole reading group idea had been a terrible mistake after all. The only thing she could do now was to confess everything to Trevor and face the consequences. She would only have herself to blame if he went off on one and took his fury out on her.

And then, in a moment of recklessness for which she could find no rational explanation, she opened her mouth and a blatant lie rose up from the depths of her consciousness like a kraken from the Mariana Trench.

She'd read somewhere – those books could be treacherous

allies – that to carry off a lie successfully, you needed three critical elements: scale, bravado, and as near adjacency to the truth as could be managed without giving the game away. Scale was obvious. The bigger the lie, the easier it was to believe. Bravado, ditto. The more confidently you could push your fake line, the more you were likely to carry people with you. It was the third one that was really smart. Concealing your lie among a narrative that was otherwise perfectly and demonstrably true not only made it harder to spot but also easier to defend if you ever were to get found out.

Oh no, I never suspected for a moment – after all, everything else they said was true!

'There was a huge police operation in the middle of town and they stopped the buses for hours,' she said boldly. 'I don't know what happened but it must have been something big. There were blue lights everywhere.'

'You never said anything,' said Trevor, heaving his donkey jacket onto his shoulders.

'Well, you were asleep last night and I didn't think to mention it this morning.'

'You could have phoned.' He sounded more hurt than angry, and Bella softened a little towards him.

But not much.

'I didn't want to bother you. I knew you wouldn't worry.'

That was true enough.

Bella was delighted that Trevor chose not to pursue the matter any further. He picked up his shoulder bag containing the lunch that Bella had made as she fried his bacon, and walked down the hall towards the front door.

'Bye, love,' she called after him. 'See you later.'

He grunted something indecipherable and banged the door behind him.

Not even a peck on the cheek.

After she'd eaten her porridge, leaving the bowl rebelliously unwashed beside the sink, she followed in his footsteps down the hall to put on her best shoes for her appointment at the police station. She saw immediately that there was something lying in the cage that hung behind the letterbox to catch the mail. It was a brown parcel, only just small enough to fit through the gap in the door, and well taped up at both ends.

When she turned the package over to look at the address, she was astonished to see her own name staring back at her.

The chief inspector's interview would have to wait for a few minutes. Standing over the kitchen table with a pair of scissors ready to do their worst on the package's taped-up edges, she felt a new thrill of danger. She never got mail, and this was a hand-addressed parcel for her. Not for her and Trevor, or one of Trevor's rather sad online purchases of model figurines that he would take to the shed to assemble and paint.

This was just for her.

She dug the point of the scissors into the packaging and got to work.

Chapter Five

Harrison Fforde was feeling significantly braver than he had been the previous evening, when the terrifying detective chief inspector had put the fear of God's angrier older brother into him. He'd gone straight home, made himself a Whisky Mac rather stronger than his usual, and tucked himself up under his Tintin duvet, where belligerent officialdom could not reach him. Despite – or perhaps because of – the appalling events at the bookshop, he slept heavily.

The interview with DCI Carlton and Sergeant Muir – 'Geoffrey, please,' he'd insisted again that morning – had been brief but ultimately unproductive.

As he'd told the chief inspector, Felicity Penman was one of the few people in Norcester he could legitimately call a friend. The attack on her had, in a way, if it wasn't too melodramatic to put it like that, also been an attack on him.

'How did you meet her?' she asked, her official lanyard banging against the table as she leaned towards him.

Fforde had never been involved in a police interview

before. He'd once roleplayed a suspected burglar in a training exercise for the Metropolitan Police and found it incredibly hard to maintain his sole line of dialogue – 'No comment' – for more than a few minutes in the face of professional inquisitors. He'd declined further invitations to repeat the experience on the grounds that he felt intimidated almost to the point of humiliation and he hadn't gone into the entertainment business to suffer that kind of indignity, so he had no real barometer for what the actual process involved. In his head, it was all defiant lags being hauled over the coals by gruff, macho officers. And the male ones were even worse.

He must stop watching reruns of *The Bill*.

Quelling the nervousness in his belly, he told her, 'I think it was actually during her first week at The Quaint Bookshop. About eighteen months ago.'

Carlton nodded at Muir, sitting beside her with his pencil poised. 'That tracks.' She turned back to Fforde. 'Anything between you?'

For a moment Fforde didn't understand what she was asking. Then his face betrayed the outrage that matched his surprise at the question. At one point, a few months after they first met, he had in fact invited Felicity out for a drink – not with any foolish notions of romance or anything like that, but to spend some pleasant time with a bright, educated woman who didn't treat him like an imbecile. There were precious few of those, after all. Yes, she'd declined his invitation, but she'd done so in a way which left him feeling oddly better about himself, and their friendship had gone from strength to strength, albeit limited to the precincts of the bookshop. Perhaps she'd noticed his quiet loneliness; perhaps that was what inspired her to invite him to join the reading group not long afterwards. Either way, knowing her had somehow made Norcester that little bit more tolerable for him.

DCI Carlton's question made all that sound sordid.

'No,' he'd said meekly. 'Nothing like that.'

Now, back in the messy, unkempt surroundings of what he grandly called his apartment but was in reality a poky two-room flat in a crumbling Edwardian house, he wondered yet again how he had wound up here, in a seamier part of this unremarkable place, and decided that in another version of his life, Fate might have been kinder to him. Having played a wide and challenging selection of roles in one of the last proper repertory seasons at the grandly named Theatre Royal and Opera House, he had found himself one grey April without an acting job or anywhere else he needed to be. He'd negotiated a very favourable rate for a longer-term stay in his theatrical digs and had remained in Norcester ever since, in and out of a marriage, snapping up the infrequent bit parts his superannuated and formidable agent managed to truffle out for him but otherwise making ends meet with odd jobs. Over the years he'd been a cinema usher, a seasonal postie and even a part-time dog-walker, but his favourite had been working as a town guide the summer before last, entertaining sparse groups of visitors with an overblown Brian Blessed delivery and half-scripted anecdotes. He'd amused himself by making facts up with abandon, dramatising historical events with invented quotations and interacting overzealously with the tourists – the latter ultimately bringing about the termination of his employment after an American complained he'd assaulted her when all he'd done was poke her with a balsa broadsword in a quasi-Shakespearean re-enactment of the Battle of Norcester (1483).

She was meant to be playing the Earl of Plumpton.

'You can't just go about stabbing the guests,' his whining boss had told him at the disciplinary hearing. 'They don't like it. And if you look at the small print in your employment contract, you'll see that clause twenty-seven (b) expressly forbids physical contact with anyone other than a fellow employee of Norcester Borough Council, and then only when they have given their prior written consent. I've had to speak to you about this before, Fforde, and the last time was your final warning, so I'm afraid this time you're out the door. Sorry and all that, but you've only got yourself to blame.'

Some people had no sense of humour.

And with that thought, he returned neatly to Detective Chief Inspector Miranda Carlton. As he'd left the station that morning, she had offered a final, decisive observation to the effect that if he could add nothing further to her investigation into the attack on Felicity, he should therefore leave her alone to get on with her job.

In the safety of his own living room, where his private domestic ineptitude sat incongruously at odds with his public-facing sartorial efforts, Harrison Fforde determined to prove her wrong. Every hubristic detective needed the lone outsider to set them straight every now and then, didn't they? Inspector Japp had his Poirot, Commissioner Gordon his Batman – even the Sheriff of Nottingham had a nemesis. The lone outsider was a part Fforde would need little research to play to perfection.

And if they got lucky, he and the rest of the newly assembled team of bookish crimefighters might just solve this case themselves.

On his way home from the station, he'd suppressed his

rising melancholy and called in at B&Q. There, he bought himself a large corkboard. If there was one thing he knew from watching all those police procedurals on the telly, it was that you had to have a large corkboard if you were going to solve a crime. Time and again he'd seen it, usually adorned with string of differing colours wound between items on the board that were pinned there for easy reference. There might be a map, some mugshots of suspects, photographs of bloodied footprints or vital clues, and probably a list of names with some of them crossed out.

Fforde realised he had a marked shortage of this kind of stuff.

He would have to improvise.

He looked round the room for a suitable place to stand the corkboard and settled on the little dining table that stood in front of the window. He liked to think of his apartment as a bachelor pad, uncontaminated by a feminine hand of any kind, and this frequently meant that he was having to shift portions of uneaten food, old newspapers and used tissues to find any space. Personally, he didn't care except when it came to moments like this, when he desperately needed some room but a few months without tidying had meant the only flat surfaces were hidden several inches beneath the crap. In this instance, a quick scan of the table suggested there was nothing fragile buried in the mess, so he swept it aside with one majestic, if foolhardy, movement of his arm.

As the pile crashed to the floor, there was the unmistakable sound of crockery breaking, and Fforde guessed there must have been a mug under there somewhere after all. Never mind: he would pick up the pieces later. There was no danger of any liquid spillage. Anything that might once have graced the mug would have dried up days ago.

He propped the corkboard on the table, leaning its top edge against the central strut of the sash window. He was sacrificing his only view – of the service entrance to the Taj Mahal Tandoori in the next street – but the corkboard took priority. Stepping back a couple of paces, he surveyed the wide-open orangey-brown frame in front of him and thought hard.

It wouldn't do.

At about three feet off the ground, the table was too low for him to be able to pin things on the board without needing to bend down to it, and he badly wanted to be able to stand, looking pensive and staring at the board at the level of his own head. He turned to look at the wall behind him, where the flat's lone picture was hung: a poor-quality print of *The Scream* by Edvard Munch. It was the only picture Selina had allowed him to remove from the marital home when he left. She'd always hated it, saying it reminded her of their worst holiday together on a rainy, miserable city break in Oslo that had culminated in her tripping on an ornamental cannonball and falling into the freezing fjord. By contrast, Fforde found it oddly comforting: at least, he would tell himself when staring at it, there was always someone worse off than him.

Now he took it from the wall and allowed himself a small outburst of exhilaration.

'Get in!' he shouted at the nail that poked out from the discoloured lavender paintwork.

Fforde spent the next fifteen minutes detaching the length of string that had held *The Scream* in place from the back of its frame, unscrewing the tiny round eyelets – swearing in the process as his fingernails snagged on the tightly fastened ironmongery – and positioning them on the back of the corkboard instead. He had a bradawl somewhere that would have made short work of the job, but Fforde had no idea where it was, or even when he might last have seen it, and none of the random assorted implements that passed for cutlery in the kitchen drawers was quite right for the job. He tried the tine of a fork, slipping it into the closed loop of one of the eyelets, but the ancient metal snapped before it even began to turn the hook, leaving Fforde with either another piece of rubbish or some frankly lethal tableware.

Eventually the eyelets were fitted to the back of the new board, and Fforde wound the string into the loops, stretching the cord across the rear of the board before lifting it into place on the nail. At the third attempt, the string found the nail and Fforde was able to let go of the board and watch it swing serenely from side to side before coming to a halt at a jaunty angle.

When he tried to straighten it, it fell off the nail.

After a few more minutes of fettling, Fforde was finally able to back away from the corkboard and stand, as he had wanted, looking pensive and staring at it at the level of his own head.

He knew it was a bit silly but he felt insanely proud of himself.

Now all he needed was something to pin on it. Inspired by a sudden recollection, he ran out of the flat, down the stairs and out into the street, where he turned left and headed for the corner. Turning twice more, he found himself at the door of the Taj Mahal. Unsurprisingly for this hour of the day, the takeaway was empty.

'Afternoon, Ravi,' he called to the owner with whom he had long since established first-name acquaintance.

'Mr Harrison, very good to see you,' said the man, picking up a pen as if in readiness for Fforde's order, although it would undoubtedly be the same chicken tikka masala and poppadoms that his customer had ordered every Wednesday and Saturday for the past four years.

'Sorry. No time,' said Fforde determinedly, and grabbed a menu from the counter.

'You want to try something new for a change?' asked Ravi, but his voice was lost to Fforde as he ran back out into the street.

In front of the corkboard once more, he unfolded the menu, turned over the one hundred and fourteen listed Anglo-Indian food items, cramped together in tiny point size, and nodded appreciatively at the map of the delivery area that was printed on the reverse. Most of Norcester lay before him – certainly enough of it to make a realistic start on his evidence board – and he held it up against the cork to position it across the centre of the frame.

It looked great, but Fforde had one major problem. He owned no drawing pins.

He balanced the map carefully against the raised edge of the frame, lifting his fingertips away from the glossy paper so as not to dislodge it, and decided he would have to settle for its off-kilter positioning until he could nip to the newsagent's later. For now, the precarious perch would have to do.

In another lightbulb moment, he remembered there was a Sharpie stashed somewhere in one of his jacket pockets. He went through to the bedroom and began rifling through the coats until his hand alighted on the pen. When he approached the map, the draught of air he created immediately swept it from its tenuous position and he caught it in mid-air as it dropped floorwards.

'Bugger.'

Fforde resumed his *Line of Duty* re-enactment at the table, kneeling in front of it because the two dining chairs were heaped with papers and books. Laying the map as flat as he could on the collected flotsam, he scanned it for the High Street, working out after a few moments that the map was highly stylised and not drawn to scale. When he found what he was looking for, he swirled the pen in a bold circle around the rough location of The Quaint Bookshop and drew a heavy cross in the middle of it.

'X marks the spot,' he said aloud, then peered closer again.

It didn't take him long to identify the central police station and he boxed it off with a neat square of his Sharpie. The map featured near its centre the Taj Mahal Tandoori itself, so Fforde was able to figure out where his own flat stood in relation to it, but he decided the two were so close together that there wasn't much point in marking it.

After that, he ran out of things to put on the map.

He'd replaced it gingerly on the corkboard and was staring at it from the settee, a cup of tea in hand, when the doorbell buzzed.

'I've been trying to find one of you all night,' the young girl announced as she perched on the settee and took out a notebook and pen.

Fforde eyed the platinum-blonde cropped hair, black leather jacket and exceedingly short tartan skirt and decided he was getting old. On the intercom, the girl had declared herself to be Nicki Bailey, crime reporter of the *Norcester Echo*, enquiring about 'the incident at the bookshop', and Fforde had expected someone of much more mature years for what he assumed was quite a prestigious post. He'd suppressed his original instinct to send her away with a flea in her ear, figuring he might instead be able to harness the flea and work it to his advantage. It was quite likely that the crime reporter of the local paper, with her police contacts and journalistic expertise, would know more about the events of last night than he did, and if he was to fulfil his resolution to solve the mystery, a little help from the press might not go amiss.

He would just have to be careful not to step beyond the proscriptions of DCI Carlton's order.

'It's very good of you to talk to me,' Nicki continued brightly, her voice revealing a trace of estuary accent. 'The duty sergeant said something about there being people in the building when it happened – you're a book club, aren't you?'

That information seemed safe enough to confirm. 'Reading group, yes,' said Fforde.

'I thought so. I managed to track down someone last night'—she flicked through some pages in her notebook—'a Lauren Sherwood, is it?'

Fforde tried to give nothing away but the girl must have noticed something in his eyes.

'Unfortunately we got cut off before she could tell me anything, so yours'll be the only first-hand account we've got. The police have given us the bare bones, but it'll be much stronger coming from someone who was actually there.'

She turned over a virgin page and looked at Fforde, pen poised expectantly.

'Give us the gory details, then.'

As he stared, mouth half-open, at the girl's keen young face, Fforde found himself on the horns of a cleft stick without a paddle. He could hardly deny he was there, and yet he was explicitly prohibited from talking about it.

'I'm afraid I can't…' he trailed off, not knowing how to finish the sentence.

'You were at the bookshop last night, though?'

'Yes.'

'And somebody did attack the owner?' She checked her notes again. 'Felicity Palmer?'

'Penman,' he corrected her, then regretted it. 'But she's not the owner.'

Nicki seemed to spot his awkwardness because she put down the notebook beside her on the settee and leaned back.

'Look, I don't want to make things difficult for you, but I imagine you've been through a horrible experience.'

Fforde felt a surge of relief. Some empathy, at least. Maybe what they said about journalists wasn't completely true.

Nicki waved a hand at the corkboard on the wall opposite. 'This looks impressive.'

'Oh, it's nothing. Just a bit of idle research.'

She stood and went over to the board, creating a waft that blew the takeaway menu to the floor once more. Fforde leaned to pick it up and found himself face-to-face with the girl, who was also bending down to retrieve it.

She giggled and he flushed.

'Nothing idle about it, from the look of it. You seem to be right on top of the investigation. You must be pretty sharp to be able to put all this together.'

Fforde's blush deepened. 'That'll be all those detective novels we read at the bookshop.'

The smile was still spread across her face and Fforde found he was enjoying being buttered up by a pretty girl.

Especially one who seemed so interested in his corkboard.

'There's more to it than that,' she said, the smile never wavering. 'You're not telling me there isn't a healthy dollop of natural brilliance in that brain of yours?'

They were standing a little too close to each other, Fforde noticed, but she was making no move to change things.

Sauce for the goose, and all that…

'No, no,' he stuttered, trying to remember how to talk to a person of the female variety without sending them running for the hills. 'I assure you it's the books.'

'I don't believe a word of it,' she said, and finally stepped past him to resume her seat on the settee. 'Were you reading one last night?'

'*Delivery of Death*,' said Fforde, warming to the topic. 'Do you know it?'

Nicki shook her head. 'What's it about?'

Twenty minutes later, when Fforde finished enlightening the *Echo*'s crime reporter on the golden age of detective fiction with particular reference to the Lord Rivereaux Quaint novels that had provided the bookshop with its quirky name, he realised that the tour guide in him had bubbled to the surface: he'd also told her everything he knew about Felicity Penman, last night's attack and even this morning's interview with DCI Carlton, all of it accompanied by his usual flair for dramatic embellishment and hyperbole.

Nicki Bailey sat before him, notebook and pen restored to her hands and a giant smile on her face.

'Jerry'll love this,' she said.

'Who?'

'My editor,' she replied, standing up and heading towards

the door. 'Shame it's too late for today's edition. Still, it'll make a terrific splash for tomorrow.'

Fforde felt his face drain of blood.

'Just one more thing,' said Nicki, her pen poised once more. 'How do you spell your name?'

He could feel panic rising. 'Oh, you can't use my name. I'm under strict instructions from the inspector in charge of the case not to talk to anyone.'

'Bit late for that, I'm afraid.'

Fforde's voice rose to match his panic. 'What about "off the record"?'

She waved her notebook at him. She sounded sterner now. 'What did you think I was doing? *Recording* it. "Off the record" only works *before* you go spouting off about blood-stained floorboards and a rictus grimace. There's no moving the goalposts now.'

'But I didn't know where the goalposts were in the first place,' protested Fforde. 'You can't quote me; the inspector will kill me.'

'Sorry, Harrison. It's a done deal. Now do you want me to get the spelling right or not?'

As a dejected Fforde – 'two fs and an e,' he'd finally confessed to the journalist – went to see her out, his neighbour appeared at the door opposite his on the landing.

Mrs Fitch was eighty-five if she was a day but moved with the stealth of one of the cats she would sometimes foster from the local vet. Fforde knew it was against the landlord's strict embargo on animals in the flats but he wasn't going to squeal on her if it gave her some contentment in her waning years. She could be crabby with him but underneath it all he suspected she was an old softie, and the fact that she was as deaf as a deaf post with additional hearing loss meant that she could be a very tolerant neighbour, something Fforde appreciated when he played his Pink Floyd records late at night to make himself feel melancholic, like a true tortured artist.

'Mrs Fitch,' he said, greeting her with a dismal look.

'Pardon?' she said.

'Never mind.'

'You were out this morning,' said the old lady. Her refined vowels always suggested to Fforde that she must have had elocution lessons in her younger days and he sometimes imagined her, knuckles frequently rapped by some fierce tutor, with a book balanced on her head traipsing round in a circle with a classful of other beskirted girls in a Dickensian montage from a black-and-white B-movie.

'I was,' he said, careful not to reveal anything else about the murder of Felicity Penman, even though Mrs Fitch fell into none of Carlton's specified categories. Come to think of it, neither did Nicki Bailey, but he didn't imagine DCI Carlton would see things the same way. He was going to be in enough trouble as it was.

'The postman asked me to take this in for you,' said Mrs Fitch, and she brought a hand from behind her back containing a small paper-wrapped parcel. As she turned back towards her own front door, she called out, 'I'm not your personal delivery service, you know.'

'Thanks, Mrs Fitch,' shouted Fforde, not knowing if she heard him or not.

Back inside, he dropped the parcel on top of the pile of debris on the table and stared at it disconsolately. He felt utterly and understandably sick.

Chapter Six

The temptation to rip the whole thing up and start again was strong, but Lauren was doing her utmost to resist. It was already the third draft of this particular beast, and she'd got much further with this one than she had with any of the others, so she was reluctant to trash it completely. On the other hand, the juicy – if marginally distasteful – possibilities of injecting real-life events into her fictional fantasy world meant that, at best, there was a total rewrite on the cards.

Lauren found it hard to work out exactly what she was feeling. She'd known Felicity Penman for several months thanks to the reading group to which the bookshop manager had personally invited her, and their similarity of age and outlook had made them warm rapidly to each other. They quickly discovered they shared a taste in music and films as well as literature, and would often exchange a knowing smile when the men in the group selected yet another golden age detective story for their next book. Much as she loved a good murder mystery, and notwithstanding her passion for Sherlock

Holmes, Lauren fancied that her own taste extended more widely than the obvious choices: she was a sucker for Jeffrey Archer and Jilly Cooper and suspected Felicity might feel the same, although they had never actually confessed their guilty pleasures to each other.

With a jolt, Lauren realised that now they never would.

She knew from the frequent first-aid updates she underwent at school that shock could easily be delayed, showing up much later in bizarre ways, both physically and mentally. For now, though, she felt remarkably composed. At one level, of course, she was devastated by the attack on a woman she regarded as a friend. But she'd reviewed her own state of mind and found herself to be surprisingly calm, despite the horrors of the previous evening. Was it really so callous to think about mining those horrors? Couldn't that be justified as a creative way of dealing with the trauma? Or was it simply exploitative to work such a terrible circumstance to her own advantage?

She stopped asking herself questions on the grounds that she was starting not to like the answers, and turned back to the manuscript.

She scrolled back to the start of the document and picked up her coffee cup in both hands. As she looked at the opening lines, she tried to work out if she could incorporate any of her existing material. It seemed unlikely.

The body was riddled with bullet holes, the blood seeping across the parquet floor making the elegant hallway look like a busy abattoir on the cleaner's day off. The victim's limbs were spread at an awkward angle, as if the fall from the minstrels' gallery above had contorted him into a broken marionette. All that was missing was the strings.

When homicide detective Danny Esposito walked in, a raven-haired beauty was standing over the body with a Beretta Bobcat in her hand, the muzzle still quietly smoking. She wore nothing but stilettoes and a smile.

Lauren settled for a compromise and saved the draft in a new subfolder, available to be cannibalised as and when the fourth draft required it. She wasn't sure how her naked, wronged heroine in 1980s Chicago might fit into a modern-day murder mystery in the semi-industrial English Midlands but you never knew.

Maybe Felicity Penman had had a secret alter ego.

She was saving a new document under the working title *The Archive Assassin* when a sharp rap at the door startled her. She glanced at her watch and realised she'd been mulling her manuscript much longer than she thought.

'You're on time for once,' she said as Simon strolled past her into the house, a bundle of technical equipment under one arm and a sandwich between his teeth.

When he didn't answer she tapped him on the shoulder, making him jump. As he spun round, the sandwich flew out of his mouth, scattering chunks of cheese across the hall floor. He lifted one side of his headphones away from his ear and stared at Lauren, who could now clearly hear thumping trance music.

'What did you do that for?'

'Sorry. I thought you were ignoring me.'

Simon let the headphones fall back into place, cutting off most of the insistent rhythm, and raised his voice above the sound that only he could hear.

'Just chilling with the latest Armin van Buuren. Never interrupt a guy when he's chilling.'

'Well, come and chill in the living room,' said Lauren, moving in front of him to lead the way. She then repeated the phrase, mouthing it in an exaggerated way to get the message past the music, and pointed at an armchair she'd already prepared for him. A couple of plump cushions created a little nest in the body of the seat, while an upright dining chair beside it provided a workable surface for his laptop.

When she returned from clearing up the cheese sandwich in the hall, she found Simon slumped happily into the nest, his kit resting on the dining chair. As she entered, he tapped his phone and the annoying background beat stopped.

'How's things?' he asked, whipping the headphones off and looking up at Lauren with a smile. 'Sounds like you've got stuff going on.'

Lauren didn't feel able to return his smile. Aside from the gnawing feeling of sickness deep down in her soul, she owed it to Felicity to convey the gravity of the situation to her brother. 'Thanks for coming over. I really need your expertise. How are the wrinklies, by the way?'

Simon pulled a face. 'Annoyingly conventional yet strangely lovable. Same as always. Are you ever going to make me a cup of tea?'

As Lauren went into the kitchen she could hear Simon firing up his music again and the familiar sound of fingers on little square buttons. It had only been a few weeks since she'd seen him but he always brought such a sense of youthful energy when he called that she realised she'd missed him. Not as much as when he'd been 'away', as their mother so politely called it, for six months, the result of his semi-official employment at a self-described security firm that seemed to have involved securing information from other people's computers and telephones in a way that had been deemed rather on the wrong side of legal. Simon's particular skill set was well-suited to this kind of work but the authorities took an understandably dim view of its proximity to criminality, and Simon – as the person who had actually tapped the keys – had been the one in the firing line when it came to handing out sentences. As a white-collar malefactor, he'd been spared the worst excesses of penal retribution but the experience had changed him nonetheless. To the attentive eyes of a loving sister, however, there was fortunately still plenty of the old Simon left behind the wary looks and cautious phrases.

'Your tea,' she said, handing him the second-least-battered mug from her cupboard. It was adorned with stylised pink cats but she didn't think Simon would mind, and if he did he could just go and make himself a cup of tea.

'Cheers,' he said without looking up. 'Your wifi's desperate.'

'I know, but I don't really use it much so I can't justify upgrading.'

Romulus appeared in the doorway, sized up the room and made straight for Simon, jumping up onto his knee where he was balancing the mug.

'Bloody cats,' he said, but Lauren knew he loved them.

'I can't see a thing past your fluffy bumhole,' Simon told the cat, nudging him to move away. 'How do you expect me to get any work done?'

Lauren reached over and picked up the cat under its shoulders. Romulus sagged pathetically, his back legs hanging feebly down and his tail swishing aimlessly behind him. As she cradled him to her neck, she gurgled some babyish noises and took him away to the other end of the room. She sat by the desk and plonked the cat on her knees.

'So, what's this stuff you've got going on?' Simon said, pausing his tapping and looking over at Lauren. 'You were a bit vague on the phone last night.'

'I know. Sorry about that. It's just that I've got involved in something and I'm not quite sure how I feel about it yet.'

Simon looked worried. 'What do you mean, involved?'

'Oh, nothing dodgy. Not like—' She stopped herself just in time.

'What then?'

'I don't know if you've heard the news this morning?'

He shook his head. 'Don't like doing that if I can avoid it. You never know what you're going to find out.'

Lauren stroked Romulus, who was making signs of settling on her lap. Remus was probably out hunting birds somewhere, failing to catch them and getting grumpy. He'd be in later for his fussing.

'There was an attack at The Quaint Bookshop last night. I was there.'

'What?' Simon seemed astonished.

'Well, not actually there when it happened. I go to my reading group there and we'd just left when we heard the scream. Turns out the manager, Felicity, had been … murdered.'

The finality of the word hit hard, and she suddenly burst into tears. The night she'd spent turning over that reporter's announcement in her sleepless mind now caught up with her at last and she could do nothing to stop the flow. It was as if fourteen hours of grief had been accumulating behind her eyes, waiting for the most embarrassing moment they could find before triggering the waterfall.

To his credit, annoying as he could be, Simon stepped up immediately and crossed the room to give her one of his familiar brotherly hugs.

'My God, sis, that's awful.'

'Isn't it?' She was relieved he seemed to understand so readily. 'Sorry about the waterworks but I haven't really had a chance to let it all out yet.'

'Don't worry about it. That's what family's for, isn't it?'

He waited beside her as the river ran dry, pulling frequent tissues from the box on the desk and handing them to her. She tried returning the first used one to him in exchange but he declined to take it from her, reaching for the nearby waste paper bin and placing it by her feet as a more hygienic alternative.

When the sobbing eventually stopped, he returned to his chair and picked up the laptop again.

But he wasn't ready to go back to the keyboard just yet.

'So…' he said slowly. 'You're a key witness?'

'I suppose so,' Lauren replied without thinking. Then it occurred to her. 'But you can't tell anyone. I'm not even supposed to be talking to you.'

'Says who?'

'Says this terrifying chief inspector in charge of the case. She interviewed me earlier and made it very plain. For the second time.'

Disappointingly mundane. That was how Lauren would have characterised her encounter with DCI Carlton if she were writing it in her novel. No more than twenty minutes of basic personal information, every last scrap of detail she could recall about the book discussion – including Stone's dismissal of its lame conclusion – and the memory of the interminable minutes between hearing Felicity's scream and the first police car arriving. Carlton seemed to have heard it all before and Lauren guessed that she wasn't the first reading group member to be making their statement.

Simon didn't have to know the boring truth, though, and she beefed it up for dramatic effect.

'Imagine Clarice Starling crossed with a Doberman.'

Simon turned immediately to his laptop. 'What's her name?'

'No!' said Lauren, so quickly and forcefully that Romulus leaped off her knee and scampered for the door. 'You can't go digging about for stuff on her.'

'Why not?'

'I don't know. They'll probably be able to tell somehow.'

'Look, Lauren, I know most people think they're being spied on every moment they've got their computer switched on, and it's true, they are, but someone would have to be actually looking for evidence that you've been digging about. They're not going to stumble across it by accident.'

'Can't they trace searches through the wifi or something?'

'They could if I was using it, but your wifi's so bad I'm on my 5G. Fully encrypted.'

Lauren frowned. 'I'm not sure, Si. Couldn't they locate you from a satellite?'

Simon sighed. 'Relax, sis. This is my area of expertise, remember? I know what I'm doing.'

But he didn't ask again for the police officer's name.

Lauren picked up her mug of tea and sipped, watching her younger brother do his stuff. Nearly a decade her junior, he'd always been more of a child to her than a sibling, and their parents had been happy for her to step into the role, figuring that it would be good practice for real life when she finally left home. That had all worked out just fine until the moment she finally left home, when Simon kicked into full stroppy teenager mode with no big sister to temper his outbursts. Their parents – out of practice themselves, apparently – had not known what to do with him and he'd spent five years in his bedroom, venturing out only for compulsory education and comfort breaks. In the confines of his black-painted room, he'd honed his computer skills to perfection, learning from the dark web how to hack accounts and upload viruses with impunity. When the truth eventually emerged, Simon was given a stern telling-off by a community support officer so far out of her depth that she could barely see the shore. He'd nodded implacably then gone back upstairs to crash the intranet of a large oil corporation, just for fun. Prison had been the inevitable conclusion of this period of instability in his life, but it seemed to have had the intended remedial effect, as on his release Simon had vowed to Lauren that he would no longer use his know-how for unlawful purposes. She wasn't entirely certain he had kept his word over the intervening three years, but she could hardly keep tabs on him twenty-four hours a day, and he did at least seem to have found a profitable sideline in consultancy for some of the very businesses he'd been ruining just a few months earlier. He'd moved back into his old room – repainted in his absence a more soothing pastel green – and was forging a day-to-day existence alongside their parents, each side treading carefully in the other's presence, with conversation kept to a wholly acceptable level of meaningless pleasantries. Once or twice he'd asked Lauren if he could move in with her instead but there was no spare bed and she wouldn't have coped with him taking over the living room. Romulus and Remus, while they put up with his visits and tested him out for snuggles, would also have found him a difficult housemate to tolerate.

'Right,' he said after a few minutes of focused attention. 'That's everything set up nicely. Now, what exactly are we looking for?'

It dawned on Lauren – rather too late in proceedings to be much use – that she didn't actually know. Mulling it over before Simon had arrived, she'd harboured a vague notion of coming up with something useful and tangible to take to the reading group's spontaneous meeting that evening, but what that thing might be she had no idea.

'I don't know, really. I called you last night on a bit of a whim, but after speaking to the police today I have to say I'm rather worried.'

'About what?'

'About them. They don't seem to have any sense of urgency. You know how they say that the first twenty-four hours of an investigation are the most important?'

'I didn't know that, no. Are you sure that's not just what they say in detective fiction?'

Lauren wasn't sure but she didn't want to admit that to Simon.

He smiled cheekily at her again, the pre-pubescent boy appearing momentarily behind the mask of the cyber mastermind. 'Look, give me everything you've got and I'll see what I can find.'

Lauren was already having second thoughts. Not only had she broken DCI Carlton's injunction not to talk to anyone else about the attack on Felicity, she'd also potentially exposed her little brother to a world she desperately wanted him to leave behind. The less he had to do with police enquiries the better. On the other hand, he was the expert in this kind of thing. And at least she hadn't done anything really stupid, like blabbing to the local paper.

Simon was tapping his fingers impatiently on the laptop keyboard.

'I'm a coiled spring here, waiting to leap into action.'

She looked doubtfully at him. 'I don't think coiled springs can leap.'

'All right,' he said. 'While you work out the applied physics, I'll see if anyone's posted about the murder on social media. Oh, by the way'—he reached into a crevice of the armchair and pulled something out—'I found this on your doorstep.'

He put just enough spin on the package to carry it across to where Lauren sat. She caught the little parcel, neatly taped up at both ends, and stared blankly down at it.

Chapter Seven

It was a close-run thing but on balance Professor Stone suspected he was more irritated by Sergeant Muir's gormlessness than by DCI Carlton's chilly demeanour. It was certainly true that she really didn't have much in the way of interpersonal warmth, but her junior officer's apparent determination to misunderstand every little nuance of what he was telling them was testing his patience to the limit. Occasionally he'd lost his temper with students in stochastic dynamics lectures when they struggled to get their heads round concepts such as probability distribution and random variables; Muir evidently found it hard to grasp the clock.

'About nine-fifteen,' Stone repeated. 'We're usually finished by nine, but there was some additional chit-chat going on about Mrs Bourton's domestic arrangements.'

Muir bowed his head closer to his notebook, squinting as he scratched his blunt pencil across the surface. Stone took him to be in his mid-thirties but he looked older, his shorn hair revealing a lumpy scalp and the skin around his throat wrinkling distastefully. The Professor guessed he had already been promoted to the summit of his aspirations.

'Domestic arrangements,' the sergeant muttered. 'Interesting. And what would those be?'

He looked up eagerly at Stone, who glanced in mild desperation at Carlton, pacing back and forth along the wall of the interview room, listening intently but giving nothing away. He wished he could mouth 'Help me!' at her but he knew it would be fruitless.

'I'm afraid I don't know,' he replied, putting as much restraint into his voice as he could. Someone with a keener understanding of body language would have detected his exasperation in a moment but it soared majestically over Muir's head without being troubled by the policeman and splattered against the back wall, where Carlton opted to leave it unmentioned.

'She said something about her husband Trevor. Actually, no,' he corrected himself. 'She didn't say he was her husband. That was my assumption.'

DCI Carlton stopped pacing.

'You make a lot of assumptions, don't you?' she said slyly.

Stone was affronted: what was she getting at?

'I don't know what you mean.'

'That's the second time you've confessed to making assumptions.'

Confessed? Stone caught his breath. 'Is it?'

'In the bookshop last night, when you said the reading group were the last people to see Felicity Penman, you checked yourself then as well. Do you often change your story, Professor Stone?'

She'd been watching too much *Prime Suspect*, Stone

thought. Fancied herself as Jane Tennison. But if she planned on trapping him with his own propensity to get things right, then she was in for a surprise.

'Accuracy, Chief Inspector. As a mathematician, I pride myself on it.' He risked a dig. 'It's probably not something you're overly concerned with.'

She looked at him for a long moment, her steely eyes skewering him uncomfortably. She seemed to be weighing up her next statement.

'You're welcome to your frivolity, Mr Stone.'

'*Professor* Stone.'

She ignored him.

'But we're going to take things a little more seriously, if you don't mind. You might be interested to know that this is now officially a murder investigation. Felicity Penman died in the ambulance on the way to hospital.'

She waited a moment for the news to sink in, then resumed her pacing.

Stone felt as if he'd been thumped about the head with the kind of ironwood truncheon that had passed into the realms of history three decades ago.

Felicity was dead. The sweet-faced girl who'd suggested to him a year earlier that he might like to start a reading group at The Quaint Bookshop was dead.

But she'd still been technically alive when they last saw her, her body slumped in the aisles of the store.

Something inside him withered a fraction and he suddenly felt cold.

'Not so frivolous now, are we?' said Muir, something resembling a grimace on his face.

Honestly, Stone thought, these people might just be doing

their job, going through the motions of the early stages of a murder investigation, but they really had no idea about humanity. He'd just lost a friend, for God's sake. As the founder member of the reading group, he had definitely come to regard Felicity as that, even though they only met through the semi-official channels of the bookshop, and now he was feeling the strange detachment that mourning an acquaintance of indeterminate closeness brings. It wasn't the painful sting of losing a family member, or the curious indifference to the unexpected death of a member of the university faculty, both of which he had experienced personally, but something in between: a melancholy heaviness at the idea that he would never see Felicity again, and a grim sadness at realising how much that mattered to him.

DS Muir twisted round in his seat to look at his boss, presumably for guidance through the uncharted waters of an interviewee insulting her. At least he'd managed to spot that.

'Tell me about your career in mathematics, Professor,' Carlton said eventually, a studied evenness in her tone.

Stone suspected the change of subject might be another trap and he didn't want to play her game. From the back of his mind he dredged something from John le Carré's first George Smiley book about how to survive interviews. The Chameleon-Armadillo technique, Smiley had called it. The idea was that one either mirrored one's questioner perfectly in order to flatter their vanity or, if they were too stupid to fall for that, shielded oneself by imagining them in any number of incongruous situations – stuck in a sash window and naked at a Masonic banquet were the two that had stuck particularly in Stone's memory.

Given the respective physiques of the two police officers in front of him, he opted to place Muir in the window.

'What would you like to know?' he asked, smiling sourly at Carlton.

Muir was now watching tennis, his head flicking back and forth between the two of them.

'All right. For starters, where do you teach?'

Stone felt his smile fade. 'I don't teach. Not any more.'

'Oh? Why's that?'

'I took early retirement.'

'From where?'

'From the university where I worked.'

'And where was that? Norcester?'

Stone had a strong suspicion that she already knew the answer to that. Quite how she'd picked up such knowledge in the space of a few hours was beyond him – unless she had a mole somewhere – but the warning glint in her eye was a real giveaway.

'No. I didn't work at the University of Norcester. I retired here.'

She stopped pacing again and pulled out a chair beside Muir. She took her time about sitting in it, then peered enigmatically at Stone across the table.

'Why Norcester?'

Stone felt his hackles rise. How much did she know?

'Family connections. My mother was born here and we made frequent visits when I was a child so it had a kind of draw for me, I suppose. It felt like the natural place to retire to.'

'Hardly traditional retirement territory, I'd have thought. A nice bungalow by the sea I could understand. Maybe somewhere overlooking green fields or a lake. You could certainly afford it on your professorial pension, couldn't you? But no, you decide to return to your mother's birthplace and buy a rather humble house on a nondescript street out of the way of prying eyes. Quiet. Unassuming. One might even say secretive. You're the mathematician, Professor: tell me why that doesn't add up.'

Stone shrugged. 'Maybe I want a bit of privacy in my retirement.'

'Or maybe you have something to hide.'

Stone had had enough. He stood up, calmly but assertively, and leaned forward on the table, his fingers splayed dramatically.

'I thought you were investigating the murder of Felicity Penman in her own shop,' he said, holding Carlton's gaze steadily. 'Not winding up her friends. Now if you and Uncle Fester here ever decide to track down her killer, I and the rest of the reading group would be very interested to hear from you. Otherwise, we might just have to go out and do it ourselves. I'll bid you a good morning.'

He'd half-expected her to try to stop him, to call him back and start the interview over again in a more conciliatory tone, but she let him leave the room and he didn't look back. He was crossing the foyer of the central police station on his way towards the exit when his phone pinged a notification.

It was a text message from DCI Carlton.

> If you or your bookshop chums interfere with my investigation, I'll be bringing charges of obstruction against you all. Keep out of my way.

Stone's finger hovered over the delete button but

something prevented him from pressing it. He had a vague sense that he might want this message somewhere down the line. He had no real desire to cross swords with the detective but she'd riled him with her questioning – and her underling with his unimpressiveness – so maybe he should stockpile any weaponry that was to hand. It wasn't much, but the text felt like something worth keeping.

What he couldn't figure out was why DCI Carlton had taken such vehement exception to the reading group. She'd met them for a few minutes last night and now was interviewing them in turn about the little they knew of the murder but he couldn't for the life of him explain her animosity, which seemed sudden and severe. Maybe the others had said or done something in their interviews to upset her. Bella Bourton wasn't the smartest cadet on parade, and on poor form Harrison could be as irritating as a wasp under a duvet, but he found it hard to believe that they could have ticked off the inspector so comprehensively that she was now threatening them all. Her clear lack of compassion notwithstanding, there had to be a better explanation than the fact that she hated having to deal with civilians. That was her job, after all.

Unless…

Could the chief inspector really believe they were suspects? That couldn't be it, could it?

No, he chided himself, putting the idea firmly into a box in the darker recesses of his mind, fixing a padlock to it, covering it with a thick blanket and standing something large and heavy in front of it to screen it from view. Having stashed away the appalling line of thought, Stone looked out through the police station's revolving front door at George Street. There was the usual steady stream of harried passers-by going about their business in this office-heavy part of town. So it was unusual to see a young woman in a black leather jacket leaning against a low wall directly opposite the station, tapping a notebook against her cheek and never taking her eyes off the revolving door.

He didn't need to be introduced to the woman to know that she was a reporter, and for all his reservations about DCI Carlton, her warning not to talk to the press made good sense all round. Not only might it attract interest from the kind of cranks and weirdos who followed this sort of case with a morbid fascination, it also left the witnesses themselves open to approaches that might ultimately prejudice the trial of someone charged with Felicity's murder. On top of that, Stone had been maintaining a low profile in Norcester and a conversation with a journalist was never going to end well in that regard.

Stone pulled a baseball cap from the pocket of his overcoat, turned up his collar and pushed at the door. With his head down and an abnormally rapid pace to his gait, he stepped into the stream of people and hurried away from the police station.

A hundred yards down George Street he ducked left into an alley that would take him up to the High Street, then stopped. He waited five minutes to check that he wasn't being pursued by the reporter before resuming his walk at a more gentle speed, breathing in the fresher air as he approached the park and cutting a corner to restore his soul with the greenery before heading home.

Walking through the trees, he wondered if DCI Carlton had broken the news to the others at their interviews: if not, it was a burden he'd have to shoulder at their meeting tonight. His mood sank a notch lower at the prospect.

He was beginning to formulate a speech for them as he eased open the porch door, and was surprised to find that he felt resistance. It couldn't be a huge parcel – it would have had to fit through the letterbox – so Stone pushed harder and stepped inside, looking down at the tiled floor as he did so.

There, brushed aside from the mat by the opening of the door, lay a small package, about the size of a paperback book, with his address and an inscription in scrawled ink.

Professor E. Stone. Private and confidential.

Chapter Eight

Inevitably there were more tears, and Lauren was unsure how to handle them. Bella's she could cope with, two empathic women sharing a common distress at the murder of their mutual friend. Lauren had already spent much of the afternoon wringing plenty out of herself after hearing the tragic news from DCI Carlton, and she'd been grateful for the presence of her brother for a shoulder to drench, but they began again when the reading group met in The Quaint Bookshop at seven that evening. Tissues and platitudes had cleared up most of the leakages, along with a nice strong cup of tea in the traditional manner.

Harrison Fforde's weeping was a different matter.

It was as if decades of emotion that had been suppressed in the interests of actorly introspection was suddenly allowed to erupt, the dam of years of sentiment breaking its bounds and cascading a waterfall of tears that seemed impossible to stem. Even Harrison himself couldn't really explain what was going on: while he publicly regretted his outpouring of emotion and apologised for his conduct, which he fervently hoped would not make them think any less of him, the news appeared to have hit him particularly hard now that the group Felicity created had reassembled.

It had come as something of a surprise to Lauren to discover that the shop was even open. After the events of last night, she'd fully expected it to be cordoned off, with uniformed police stationed at every entrance and hordes of journalists camped out in the High Street ready to pounce on the latest utterance from the officer in charge.

But then, she reflected, life probably wasn't like *Broadchurch*.

As it was, an officer was positioned inside the store, preventing the ghouls from going into the section where Felicity's body had been found. The arched opening through to Noir was sealed off with striped tape – at least that much was accurate from the television programmes – but otherwise the shop seemed to be open for business as usual, and a handful of people were milling about for one of the evening activities that Lauren knew took place most weekdays, even during the school holidays. One or two were hanging about near the stripy tape but the presence of the young policeman, who wore a luminous yellow vest over his dark clobber and had handcuffs and a baton conspicuously on show, deterred too much rubbernecking.

In the hours since she'd opened her mysterious package, Lauren had been able to think of little else but the attack on Felicity and was keen to be there early for the impromptu meeting. She clutched the brown paper parcel as she made her way across the nave of the old chapel.

'Sorry, madam – this area's closed to the public.'

Lauren found herself confronted by a weaselly man dressed in tweed trousers, a sleeveless maroon V-neck pullover of the type she imagined was worn by schoolboys and bicyclists in the 1930s, and a bow tie that had seen better days. He peered at her over the rim of his wire spectacles and held forth one hand in the universally accepted sign for 'Stop!'

Lauren stopped.

The man was blocking her path to the reading room. She was sure she could hear the Professor's resonant voice coming from inside, so she knew that was where she was supposed to be, and she was in no mood to be hindered.

'I don't know who you are, but I'm going to a meeting in that room,' she said, gesticulating towards the Perspex-walled room.

The man sighed, deflating like a dying helium balloon. 'Oh, you're one of them, are you? Well, I'll have you know I'm Maurice Stapleton, and I'm the interim bookshop manager while this ... business is being dealt with.'

So he had stepped into the still-warm shoes of Felicity Penman. Lauren quietly hoped they might pinch a bit.

'Are you new here?' she asked.

Maurice Stapleton looked affronted. 'Certainly not. I've worked here for twenty-five years. Everybody knows me.'

That was self-evidently untrue, but Lauren was too polite to make the point. In any case, her own familiarity with The Quaint Bookshop was largely focused on the reading room, so it was possible she might have failed to notice him. He did look decidedly insignificant, after all.

'Oh, Lauren – I'm glad I'm not the last.'

The voice behind her was friendly but concerned and Lauren detected more than a hint of stress about it. She turned to find Bella hurrying towards her from the entrance, her flustered countenance in keeping with her middle-aged clothes and uncombed hair. She looked troubled, with a shadow across her face that suggested more than lateness: yes, Lauren decided, she was anxious.

'Are you all right?' she asked, plumbing the same maternal instinct that had served her so well with Simon in the years before she left home and he left the rails.

'Not really,' admitted Bella. 'I wanted to be here on time. I hate being late.'

'Me too,' said Lauren. 'And if we can just get past this gentleman, we won't be.'

She linked her arm through Bella's and turned back to face Maurice Stapleton, whose eyes blinked in a bewildered fashion that wouldn't have looked out of place on Bambi just after his mother had been shot.

'Half an hour,' he blustered eventually. 'That's what I told the Professor. I can't allow you any more time than that. We've had police swarming all over the place, and they're very demanding about their coffee and biscuits. Without Felicity'—there was the tiniest catch in his voice at the mention of her name—'we're extremely short-staffed and I can't spend my time keeping an eye on you lot too.'

Maurice Stapleton took a half pace backwards, allowing just enough room for Bella and Lauren to pass, still arm in arm, then scurried off towards the tills.

'Do you know him?' Bella asked as they headed for the reading room.

'Never seen him before in my life.'

Lauren's intention to be early was misplaced. They were the last to arrive. Harrison Fforde, however, had apparently reserved his collapse especially for them and let out a huge sob before Lauren could even open her mouth in greeting. It took nearly ten minutes of their allotted thirty to get him settled to a point where they could talk.

When Stone finally thumped his parcel dramatically down on the table, Lauren stared first at it and then at Stone himself, looking grave and imperious as he towered over them.

'Oh,' she said, allowing the disappointment to seep out in her voice. 'You've got one too.'

'Erm…' Bella sounded uncertain.

Lauren turned to the older woman beside her and saw that she was holding up another parcel wrapped in brown paper. As she watched, Bella put it down on top of the Professor's.

A moment later, Fforde scrabbled in his inside coat pocket and pulled out a third package.

'Full house,' said Lauren simply, taking out her own parcel and resting it gently on the top of the pile.

The door of the reading room swung open and Maurice Stapleton stuck his head round to look in.

'Everything all right?' he asked in a forced, jolly voice.

'Fine, thank you, Maurice,' said the Professor, verbally attempting to shoo him from the room.

'It's just that I heard a crash and I wanted to make sure you were all OK.'

'Only me, Maurice. I dropped something.'

'Ah, I see,' said the little man, turning his gaze to the pile on the low table. 'I hope you're looking after the bookshop's property?'

'Taking extra-special care,' said Stone.

'Good, good,' said Maurice, and removed himself.

Lauren looked at Stone again and thought she detected a

slightly deflated air about him. Presumably he'd imagined, like her, that his parcel was unique.

'I don't suppose there's any possibility they're unconnected?' she ventured.

'Coincidence?' Stone responded. 'The four members of the bookshop reading group all receive an anonymous package on the same day? Not a chance. This has something to do with Felicity's murder, no question. I assume they did all arrive on the same day? When did you get yours, Lauren?'

'It was delivered sometime today.'

'And the others?'

'Mine came at breakfast time,' said Bella. 'I found it when Trevor went out to work.'

'Could it have been last night?' asked Lauren.

Bella thought for a moment. 'I don't think so. I'm sure I'd have noticed it when I got in after … well, you know.'

'And you, Fforde?' The Professor was clearly finding it difficult to keep his irritation at Harrison's histrionics out of his voice.

'Be gentle with him,' said Lauren, resting a hand on Stone's arm.

'I don't know,' said the actor, rousing himself from his wallowing. 'My neighbour took it in and gave it to me this morning. Could have arrived any time.'

'Did they say who'd delivered it?'

Lauren was getting impatient. 'What difference does it make? Surely the important thing to know is what's in them all.'

The Professor paused. 'Yes. Of course. I mean, it might be useful to know who delivered them at some point, but you're right – that's of secondary importance just at the moment. So, what did everyone get?'

They each picked up their respective parcels from the table and began tipping out the contents. From each package emerged a book and a slip of paper containing a single typed line. Lauren leaned over, examining them carefully, and saw that they were identical.

'*The Secret of Father Brown*,' the line read.

Lauren was about to pick them up when Fforde suddenly leaped into life.

'Don't touch them,' he said excitably. 'They could have fingerprints.'

Lauren withdrew her hand and pointed at Bella's book instead.

'*The Body in the Library*.'

Bella nodded.

'Agatha Christie, eh?' said Stone. 'A classic, if a little obvious.'

'Well I got this,' said Fforde, indicating a hefty volume whose cover revealed it to be *The Girl with the Dragon Tattoo*. He seemed to have recovered his emotions. 'No idea what that means.'

'What about you, Lauren?' asked Bella.

'*A Study in Scarlet*. The first Sherlock Holmes novel.'

'I haven't heard of that,' said Bella. 'I know *The Hound of the Baskervilles*, of course, but only from the Basil Rathbones.'

'The … what?' asked Lauren.

'Basil Rathbone. You know, the old black-and-white films?'

'No, sorry.' Lauren shook her head. 'Robert Downey Junior plays Holmes on film, but the real one is Benedict Cumberbatch in the TV series.'

'Oh, please,' said Fforde, evidently back to his usual self. 'Everybody knows Jeremy Brett was the archetypal Holmes. Benny is just a modern-day cypher. It's like saying Branagh's Poirot is more true to the stories than David Suchet's.'

'Benny, is it?' queried Stone. 'You know him, then?'

'Well, I've never actually met him,' flustered Fforde. 'But I've worked with plenty of people who have.'

'And they all call him Benny, do they?'

Lauren could see Fforde was beginning to lose control all over again. Her mother had often praised Lauren's ability to calm churning waters: it was time to bring some of that churn-calming capacity to bear.

'I think we're getting off the subject. Professor, what's your book?'

A look passed across Stone's face suggesting that the academic was prepared to let the matter of Fforde's acquaintance – or otherwise – with double-Oscar-nominated celebrities drop for now. If Lauren knew him like she thought she knew him, she didn't imagine it would be gone for ever, but Fforde seemed quite happy for everyone's attention to shift away from the planet's leading thespians.

'Archimedes,' said Stone gravely, looking down at a slim volume entitled *On Floating Bodies*.

'Bloody hell,' said Fforde. 'Looks a bit heavy.'

'You could say that.'

Lauren took out yet another tissue from her bag but this time used it to turn the book over, glancing at the rubric on the back. She understood about one word in five, gathering that the tome was supposed to be one of the great mathematical works of all time, its author renowned for his extraordinary mind and almost superhuman abilities.

'Isn't he the one who jumped out of the bath shouting *Eureka*?' asked Bella, peering over Lauren's shoulder.

Stone sighed. 'I can't begin to tell you what a tiny part of his story that is, never mind the fact that it's purely anecdotal and probably never happened.'

'I remember that from school,' said Lauren, ignoring the Professor's objection to the tale. 'Something about the volume of water displacement when he sat down in the bath.'

Fforde joined the chorus. 'And didn't he invent weapons and levers and stuff?'

'Oh God,' groaned Stone. 'Right, sit down, all of you, and I'll give you a potted history of the greatest scientist in all antiquity.'

In five minutes flat, the Professor delivered the skeleton of a lecture he told them he'd managed to condense to ninety minutes for his students, leaving out all the words longer than eight letters and all the theorems more complex than the famous hydrostatic principle to which the scientist gave his name. He skated rapidly over Archimedes' screw, block-and-tackle pulley systems, his work on catapults, shipbuilding and astronomy, lingering briefly – Lauren suspected mainly for Fforde's benefit – on the Sicilian inventor's supposed heat ray, which purportedly used mirrors to focus the sun onto enemy ships, before settling on the primary academic subject of mathematics.

'In short, he was the most brilliant mathematician in the ancient world – some would say ever,' the Professor concluded with a flourish. 'That's why he's known as the father of mathematics.'

Lauren was relieved to see that Fforde and Bella looked as baffled as she felt.

'And what's that got to do with Felicity's murder?' she asked tentatively.

'I haven't a clue,' said Stone, and sat down.

Silence descended on the group as they stared at the volumes on the table between them: two classic detective mysteries, a dense academic treatise and the book that launched the Scandi-noir genre, all of them stickered with the shop's distinctive price tickets featuring a line drawing of the chapel frontage and the initials TQB. Lauren racked her brains but could see no pattern that connected them to each other, let alone to the case.

'Anyone got anything?' she asked eventually.

Three heads shook in dismal acceptance of the dawning reality.

'So we're actually no further forward,' said Fforde.

'What about *The Secret of Father Brown*?' asked Lauren.

'Yes,' said Bella. 'What on earth is that about?'

'I don't know,' said Stone. 'Has anyone read it?'

Three heads shook again.

'G. K. Chesterton, of course,' said Stone in a tone that Lauren assumed meant everyone should know that. 'But what does it all mean?'

'It must mean something,' Lauren continued. 'The books can't just have been selected at random. Whoever sent them knows I'm a big fan of Sherlock Holmes, and presumably that the Professor's subject is Maths. So what's the significance of the *Dragon Tattoo* for you, Harrison?'

Fforde could offer no explanation, and the bafflement seemed to lower his spirits again. There seemed to be no clear link to Bella's title either.

Bella seemed to be the only one willing to grapple with the reality of their situation.

'For a reading group whose speciality is murder mysteries, we don't seem to be doing very well, do we?' she said. 'Shouldn't we be channelling our inner sleuths?'

'Invoke the spirit of Lord Quaint, you mean?' asked Stone.

'Or Sherlock Holmes,' said Bella, nodding towards Lauren.

Lauren felt decidedly unHolmesian in the face of their clues and said so.

Fforde sounded morose. 'Don't take it personally, Lauren. I'm not exactly playing the role of Maigret here.'

Stone was beginning gingerly to manoeuvre the wrappers that had encased the parcels.

'If the books themselves aren't helping, what about the packages they came in? Perhaps they hold a clue.'

Four pairs of eyes stared at the wrappers as Stone laid them out in a neat square on the table. Allowing for the obvious differences in the handwritten addresses, they looked pretty similar to Lauren.

'I feel as if I know that writing,' she said, scratching an itch at the back of her mind. 'Like it belongs to someone I went to school with or something.'

Fforde shrugged. 'Nothing here, I'm afraid.'

'If only we had some idea of who sent them,' said Stone. 'One thing we do know, though.'

Lauren felt a tiny surge of optimism, as if she'd been told bad weather had cancelled lessons for the day and her class would be going out to build snowmen instead.

'What's that?'

'It's somebody close to the bookshop. Someone who knows about the reading group.'

'Sorry to piss on your strawberries,' said Fforde, his tone still somewhere south of miserable. 'Details of the reading group are plastered all over the shop – on noticeboards, on leaflets at the reception desk. We're even mentioned in Felicity's activity pack she gives to new customers. Sorry – *gave*.'

'Are we?' said Stone, looking surprised. 'Can't think why we haven't recruited more members then.'

'There's Bella,' said Lauren brightly. 'Handpicked by Felicity, as I understand it.'

'Yes,' said Stone, flashing a warm smile at the new recruit. 'There's Bella. Our first new member in more than six months. It's not exactly a ringing endorsement, is it?'

'Oh dear,' muttered Bella, and slumped back in her seat. 'Sorry.'

'Whoever it is doesn't just know about the reading group,' said Fforde. 'They know where we live.'

'Oh dear,' said Bella again, an added note of anxiety in her voice.

'Customer records?' wondered Lauren aloud, knowing that nobody was equipped to answer.

Instead, Fforde's comment plunged them all into a glum silence.

'Right,' said Lauren eventually. 'In the absence of any collective meaning for the books, or God forbid a clue to the killer, we're going to have to park the packages for now. I suggest we concentrate on the next thing we all have in common.'

The Professor looked at her curiously. 'And what's that?'

'Felicity herself,' said Lauren briskly. 'Someone wanted her dead and we seem to be holding the only clues as to why.'

'Oh God,' said Bella, her face blanching suddenly.

'What is it, Bella? Are you all right?'

'I've just had the most awful thought.'

Lauren glanced at the Professor for guidance but his internal satnav seemed to have self-destructed.

'Bella?'

She stared round the three of them slowly, as if speaking her thoughts might somehow bring them into being.

'Felicity's been murdered and now we've been sent these anonymous packages. Do you think they mean that we could be next?'

Lauren gasped. 'What, like a warning? That we're targets on someone's hit list?'

'That's ridiculous,' said Stone, although Lauren thought she heard a distinct note of uncertainty. 'Why would anyone want to kill us?'

In a small but chilling voice, Fforde said, 'Why would anyone want to kill Felicity?'

It was a question none of them could answer.

'Oh God,' said Bella, her face blanching suddenly.

'What is it, Bella? Are you all right?'

Everyone had the most awful thought.

Lauren glanced at the Professor and guessed that her mental radar seemed to have been activated.

'Bella?'

She stared round the group of them slowly, as if speaking her thoughts might somehow bring them into being.

'Rachel's been murdered and now we've been sent these anonymous packages. Do you think they mean that we could be next?'

Lauren gasped. 'What, like a warning? That we're on someone's hit list?'

'Don't be ridiculous,' said Stella, although Lauren thought she heard a distinct note of uncertainty. 'Why would anyone want to kill us?'

In a small but chilling voice, Fiona said, 'Why would anyone want to kill Rachel?'

It was a question none of them could answer.

Thursday

Chapter Nine

'After everything I said to you at the station yesterday? Are you wilfully obstructing police enquiries or just stupid?'

Harrison Fforde didn't really know how to answer that. It was a closed question with only two options. Or was it 'alternatives' when there were only two? He could never remember – and neither properly fitted his position. DCI Carlton's instructions not to talk to anyone hadn't specifically included the press, so that put him in the clear as far as wilful obstruction was concerned. Unless recklessness counted. Equally, he didn't consider himself stupid. He could occasionally do stupid things, he knew from bitter experience. That time he'd sacked his one-from-last agent after six months without an audition, only for her other client to land the job of a lifetime at the National in a role that could have been written for Fforde: that had been pretty stupid. The day he'd asked Ian McKellen to fetch him a cup of tea after taking him for the assistant stage manager: that had been very stupid. The night he'd tried to kiss a director in the green room when he mistook her effusive note for flirting: that had been monumentally stupid. But they were just stupid things he'd done. They didn't make him stupid.

'Um,' he said stupidly.

DCI Carlton was struggling to maintain her air of professional chilliness, he could tell. Her face had darkened a couple of shades and there was a definite twitch going on with a vein in her forehead.

Fforde had to admit he was a little disappointed by the inspector's reaction, not least as he'd been feeling surprisingly buoyed by the coverage the *Echo* had given to his elaborate tale. Having given himself a stern talking-to about his inexcusable lapse into emotional incontinence in front of the others at the reading group the previous evening, he'd made sure he was early at the newsagent's that morning to pick up a copy and found himself relishing the front page. Under a large red slab advertising the paper's *EXCLUSIVE*, vast lettering announced: *The man who saw bookshop owner die.* Nicki Bailey obviously hadn't registered that Felicity was the manager, not the owner, and the headline was more than a little elastic with the truth, but then so had he been, and at least they'd used a decent headshot from one of the plays he'd done at the Theatre Royal a few years back, when his hair was still more pepper than salt and the lines weren't quite so deeply engrained in his forehead. In black and white, he looked almost distinguished.

'It's bad enough that you spoke to the papers at all, but the worst thing is that you gave them a description of the crime scene.'

'Why?' Fforde was genuinely confused. 'Why is the fact

that I said Felicity's feet were sticking out from a row of shelves in the Noir section the worst thing?'

Carlton sighed dramatically – not a bad actress, Fforde thought – and leaned towards him menacingly.

'Because, Mr Raiders of the Lost Brain Cell, knowledge of the crime scene is something that only the four of you and the killer will have, and could be crucial when it comes to questioning any suspects. Unless they've all read about it in the *Norcester Echo*, of course.'

Her shoulders slumped, her contempt for Fforde painfully obvious from the other side of the room. Even DS Muir managed a look of distaste as he tucked his pencil behind his ear and stared at Fforde with what he probably imagined was a dark look.

Fforde had sensed even before he picked up the internal phone a few minutes earlier to buzz them in that it was the police. He'd been on the back foot ever since. The fact that he was standing in his untidy living room wearing grubby pyjamas and slippers with holes in their toes added nothing to his sense of self-worth.

When the two officers walked through the door he'd left open for them, he knew he was in big trouble.

Carlton shook open a copy of the *Echo* that she'd been carrying under her arm and displayed it towards him, as if he'd never seen it before.

'What the hell do you call this?' she demanded.

Fforde's natural inclination for humour got the better of him.

'A newspaper?'

Carlton's reaction was sudden and violent. She screwed up

the paper – ruining his headshot in the process, Fforde noticed – and hurled it to the floor.

'Don't get smart with me, you little turd. You know exactly what I'm talking about. And if you can't remember, my sergeant here has a record.' She turned to Muir beside her.

Muir fished a small black notebook from an inside pocket and flicked over a few pages. 'Er, boyfriends, girlfriends, elderly mothers … or cats,' he read aloud.

'I don't think that could be any clearer, could it, Sergeant Muir?'

The sergeant shook his head, pursing his lips at Fforde.

Fforde felt sick.

'That,' she went on, pointing at the crumpled ball on the floor, 'is not my idea of not talking to anyone. It's not even a quiet indiscretion over a pint with a trusted friend. You're on the front page of the *Norcester Echo*, spouting the most unbelievable rubbish about the murder of Felicity Penman, devoid of facts and making up stuff you couldn't possibly know. Unless there's something else you haven't told us?'

She let the implication of her words seep menacingly through the already chilly atmosphere in the room.

'So what did you think you were playing at?'

Fforde wondered if he should offer them a cup of tea but he had serious doubts about being able to find two clean mugs. It probably wasn't the moment anyway.

'I'd forgotten I said all that.'

The pitch of Carlton's voice remained in a register higher than Fforde was comfortable with, and he suspected he hadn't quite got the knack of giving her the answers she wanted.

'You'd forgotten you fed them a load of old cobblers you invented on the spot, probably committing half a dozen offences in the process? I'm presuming it was cobblers, of course. Because it reads very differently from the statement you gave us yesterday. So it's either cobblers and you shot your mouth off to the press in direct contradiction of my instructions, or you lied to us at your interview and you know much more about Felicity Penman's murder than you let on. Either way, that makes me very unhappy right now.'

Fforde didn't know what to say. It was at times like these – although to be fair he'd never actually experienced a time even remotely like this – that he truly understood the benefit of a good scriptwriter. With some clever dialogue woven by a master craftsman into a screenplay, he'd be able to talk his way out of this mess and maybe even end up persuading the ice maiden DCI Carlton to go on a date with him. Left to his own devices in a situation that demanded coolness, calmness and clarity of thought, he was up shit creek.

'When you say "half a dozen offences"...' he began.

'Oh, I don't know – fraud, wasting police time, giving false information. That's just off the top of my head. I could probably come up with at least three more if I really put my mind to it.'

Fforde was starting to feel decidedly jittery. Weighing up the respective merits of admitting talking to the *Echo* or facing a senior officer's suspicion in a murder enquiry, he opted for the inevitable bollocking.

'All right, I'm sorry. I may have embellished a few facts for that reporter.'

Carlton appeared to take that at face value, although the outcome still wasn't pretty.

'Sorry doesn't begin to cover it,' she stormed. 'You've jeopardised my whole investigation, wasted our time this morning and potentially put yourself in line for criminal prosecution. So I refer you to my earlier question: what the hell did you think you were playing at?'

Fforde was out of his depth. The full implications of his talking to the paper had clearly escaped him, but now that Carlton had explained the delicacy of the situation, he knew it was bad and he wondered if he really had soured the investigation by giving away vital clues to the perpetrator. The thought that this might derail the hunt for her killer, letting Felicity down appallingly in the process, sparked a rising sob in his throat and he grasped at straws to somehow twist things to his advantage. Maybe the invented details could be used to weed out false suspects who'd only read the newspaper report? He popped that thought in his back pocket, in case he needed something to win over the chief inspector down the line.

In the meantime he had another card to play. The only thing was, he didn't really know how to approach the topic.

He decided to do it cautiously, from the side, so as not to alarm it.

'Erm, you'll probably think I'm trying to change the subject, Chief Inspector, but I might have some new clues for you.'

The vein in her forehead throbbed.

'What are you talking about?'

He glanced down at the coffee table, where a canvas bag lay, adorned with a giant version of the Royal Shakespeare Company's logo. He'd bought it on a visit to Stratford-upon-Avon several years earlier, liking its chunky typography and bright colours. Now its vibrancy appeared to be mocking him, but he had the last laugh. (Was this what things had come to? Reduced to scoring points over a canvas RSC bag?) For inside its contours lay the four delivered books, given over to Fforde's charge by the Professor, Lauren and Bella the evening before.

'The reading group met last night. We've all been sent anonymous packages. We think the killer could be threatening us.'

He picked up the bag and handed it to Carlton.

'I haven't touched any of them directly. I wore my driving gloves to put them in the bag.'

Carlton peered inside, a frown camouflaging the throbbing vein.

'What are they?'

'Books. We each got a different one. Oh, and there's a typed message in there too – although that was the same to all of us.'

Carlton stopped peering and thrust the bag towards Muir. 'I don't have time to look at this now. We'll add it to the pile. Someone will be in touch for the details, I imagine.'

'Are we in danger?'

The vein reappeared. 'I very much doubt it, Mr Fforde. The nearest you'll get to violence is from me if you ever try a stunt like this again.'

She'd taken two steps towards Fforde and he didn't like the look of her. Although she was several inches shorter than him, he was supremely confident in her ability to take him in a fight, and on top of that she had the full force of the law behind her. He retreated towards the wall and, as he did so, his shoulder made contact with the corkboard that was hung there.

His carefully constructed evidence fell crashing to the floor.

It took a moment for Carlton to react. When she did, it was not in the way Fforde would have expected.

DCI Carlton laughed.

She laughed, turned to Sergeant Muir and directed his attention to the corkboard, then laughed again.

It was only when she stopped that Fforde realised he was smiling along with her in the way that people do when others are laughing, whether they get the joke or not. In his case, he didn't.

Carlton's face dropped instantly into a grimace.

'What the hell are *you* smiling about?'

Fforde hesitated. 'I don't … I'm not sure. You were laughing so I suppose I was sort of joining in.'

'I was laughing at that,' she said, pointing at the corkboard on the floor between them. 'You're actually trying to make an evidence board, aren't you?'

Fforde was starting to feel affronted by this vicious assault from an officer of the law, unprovoked and undeserved as far as he was concerned. He was increasingly unwilling to let her have everything her own way – in his apartment, what was more. He decided to offer some resistance.

'So what if I am? I'm integral to this case, whatever you might think, and I'm perfectly entitled to pursue my own enquiries.'

'Pursue your own—?' Carlton laughed again. 'Is that what you think you're doing? You stick a crummy map on a piece of card and bung a few pins in, and you think you're doing something constructive towards solving a murder case?'

In spite of himself, Fforde bit back.

'Well, you're not making a very good job of it so far, so why shouldn't the rest of us have a go?'

It was, he had to admit, a mistake. Carlton took another step towards him and gritted her teeth.

'I'll tell you exactly the same thing that I told your pal, Professor Stone. If you and your chums put so much as one foot out of place while I'm investigating the murder of Felicity Penman, I'll have you up before a judge faster than you can say "contempt of court". And if by some miracle you happen to come across any more scraps of evidence, no matter how small or insignificant, and you fail to report it through the official channels, then you'll be up for obstruction. Got it?'

With her nose about six inches from his own, Fforde felt it prudent to agree.

'Right, you little scumbag.'

Fforde was sure she couldn't talk to him like that but he had no desire to challenge her on it.

'From now on you are not going to speak a word of this to anyone. Am I clear?'

Fforde nodded.

'To be completely transparent about it, not only does that include the list of people I mentioned at the bookshop the other night, it also encompasses any human being living on planet Earth, all constituent species of the lower orders of the animal kingdom, any plant life you might have knocking about your seedy little flat and, just to cover the absolute bottom of the evolutionary tree, *members of His Majesty's press*. Do you understand?'

Fforde nodded again.

'If I so much as get a sniff of you opening your trap to anyone or anything on any topic even remotely related to this investigation, unless Sergeant Muir or I am present at the time, I will personally see to it that you are charged, convicted and preferably hung, drawn and quartered. Now, can you repeat back what I have just said to you?'

Fforde had an overwhelming suspicion that she was talking bollocks – such a decision wouldn't be hers to make, would it? – but he didn't trust that the detective novels he'd read and the crime series he'd watched were sufficiently accurate on the legalities of witnesses in murder cases to back up his theory.

'You don't want me to speak to anyone.'

Carlton threw her head back, as if looking to the heavens.

'Hallelujah! He finally gets it.'

She turned away abruptly, catching the corkboard with her foot as she went. It scudded across the floor, coming to rest against the large Chinese vase that had gone down in family folklore as the receptacle in which his great-great-Uncle Cyril's ashes had been smuggled out of Mafeking after its relief in the Second Boer War for a decent British burial by his great-great-Aunt Hilda. Fforde had always harboured a secret belief that being scattered heroically to the Transvaal winds would have made for a much more glorious send-off than a muddy shrubbery in Beckenham Crematorium, but he'd kept that thought to himself for his grandfather's sake.

As Carlton passed Muir on her way to the door, he held out the stub of his pencil and waved it at Fforde. His attempt at intimidation was undermined somewhat by his fluting voice and Bristolian vowels.

'Don't go messing with what you don't understand. Understand?'

Half an hour later, his tail so far between his legs that he could almost feel it tickling his scrotum, Harrison Fforde realised who he could talk to about all this. DCI Carlton hadn't specifically ruled out speaking to the other members of the reading group, and surely she couldn't expect them not to confide in each other, now that they were all witnesses in a murder case? That would be just too unrealistic to hope for on her part. She must know that – especially given their propensity for detective fiction – they would be certain to pick over the facts as they knew them. No, he concluded, that couldn't possibly count as part of her moratorium.

Besides, he had important things to tell them. He might play down the telling-off he'd received for talking to the *Echo* – today's news famously being tomorrow's fish and chip paper – but a feeling of quiet elation was starting to grow inside him. Far from trashing the investigation, his quick thinking about putting on his driving gloves to handle the packages might just have preserved a vital clue in the murder enquiry, and he was desperate to let the others know that finally – *finally* – he'd done something right.

He rummaged about under the debris on the table for his phone and opened WhatsApp.

Chapter Ten

From his seat in the window of the Coco Café, Stone had a good view of the offices of the *Norcester Echo* and the little patch of green beside them that some inspired *bürgermeister* had designated a pocket park. As he held an outsize cup between two hands, idly blowing the contents to cool them, he watched a squirrel gambolling in a tree. It was definitely gambolling. He knew it was gambolling, even though he couldn't remember ever actually hearing the word defined. There was something about the squirrel's acrobatic insouciance; it lacked the purposefulness of running and the frivolousness of mere scampering.

It was definitely gambolling.

Stone sighed and wished he could bring the same kind of precision to his thinking about Felicity Penman's murder.

'Your tuna melt,' said the teenage girl in black leggings and a stained white shirt who deposited a plate in front of him and turned swiftly away before he had time to thank her.

Stone stared at the plate and sighed again. Tuna melt

should not, under any circumstances, contain chopped peppers. He lifted the lid of the ciabatta roll to see just how extensively the offending vegetables were distributed through the filling, then used the wrong end of his teaspoon to start fishing out the bits of red and green. The tuna melt was likely to be cold by the time he'd finished but that would be preferable to having warm chunks ruin its consistency. Maybe he should have trusted his first instinct and gone for lunch at one of the ubiquitous chains that scattered the High Street.

He'd never tried the Coco Café before. He was unlikely to again.

Stone took out his mobile phone and scrolled through the messages. Fforde had invited the reading group to yet another meeting at the bookshop, and he wondered what the point of getting together for a third evening on the trot would be, besides revisiting the same blind alleys as yesterday. But the tone of Fforde's text suggested some urgency, and given that there was precious little of that from the police, maybe the group was the best way to help Felicity. At least they would feel like they were doing something.

The thought of DCI Carlton and DS Muir prompted him to search further back in his messages.

Keep out of my way.

It was a strange threat, especially for a senior officer in the early stages of a murder investigation. Normally one might expect the police to be looking for cooperation and collaboration from the nearest thing they had to a witness, but Carlton had offered little but hostility since their first encounter in the bookshop's reading room. A few possibilities presented themselves. He wondered if she might be feeling pressure from higher up the ranks; maybe a superintendent or assistant chief constable was watching events unfold with particular interest and it was making her uncomfortable. But even if that were the case, she shouldn't be taking it out on innocent civilians.

He kept coming back to the thought that she suspected one of them wasn't innocent.

She'd certainly been especially incisive about her questioning of his career and his previous connections with Norcester, and Stone had spent a lot of time worrying about why. It had been clear that she knew more than she was letting on about his reasons for retiring, but why was she dropping such unsubtle hints – and what did it all have to do with Felicity's murder anyway? If Carlton knew the truth about him, she'd realise it was irrelevant to this case. Which left, in true Holmesian fashion, only one possibility: she *didn't* know the truth and was leaning on him in the hope of getting him to reveal something incriminating.

Either way, she was on to a loser. And it wasn't going to solve the case.

Stone abandoned the congealing mess of a sandwich and looked across at the front door of the *Echo* building, self-importantly entitled Newspaper Tower. At three storeys, the word 'Tower' was doing some heavy lifting, and Stone wasn't convinced that the other half of the epithet would be appropriate for long, given the parlous state of the newspaper industry at the hands of digital publishers and the departure of advertisers in droves for the rosier climes of social media. Then again, the death of newspapers had been predicted at every significant advance of technology, from radio and film to mass-market television and the advent of workplace computers, and yet they were still clinging on. Perhaps they would settle into a niche role aimed at hardy enthusiasts, like videotape. Or retired professors. They might even experience a resurgence in future years, like vinyl. What he couldn't imagine was their long-term survival in town centre locations such as this, fighting for life against a rising tide of unverified gossip or – worse – indifference.

Stone couldn't be the only one who still valued the truth. Could he?

The thought immediately brought him back to Felicity Penman, whose quest for accuracy had first appealed to his mathematical mind. Hers was usually focused on making sure books were filed in their correct place on the shelves or keeping the shop's mailing list up to date, but the same logical way of thinking had been evident from the outset, and Stone had warmed to her instantly.

'Professor, is it?' she'd asked teasingly when he filled out his customer details the first day he'd set foot in The Quaint Bookshop. There had been at least three other members of staff on duty and milling around the large main hall, but Stone had approached Felicity, attracted by her casual fashionability and the easygoing laugh she shared with a colleague nearby.

'Retired,' he'd replied, trying to put a note of modesty into his voice.

'Ah, professors never really retire, though, do they? They might go scuttling off to their study for some research or to write the definitive textbook on their subject, but you don't properly put your feet up and do nothing, do you?'

Stone had wriggled a little: she'd skewered him completely. The fact that he hadn't chosen retirement for himself merely added to the sense that his career was far from over, and

Felicity Penman could apparently tell that from a moment's acquaintance.

'I imagine bookshop owners are much the same,' he offered, feeling it was rather lame in comparison to her astute psychological insight.

'Depends on the bookshop,' she said. Was that a half-wink? 'And besides, I'm just the manager. You won't be able to separate us from books, that's true, but some of us would much rather do it in a remote location, far from civilisation, with a raging fire and a glass of whisky.'

Stone nodded approvingly. 'I'm all for raging fires. And whisky. And books,' he added hurriedly, gesturing expansively around the shop.

Felicity smiled warmly at him. 'I wouldn't expect anything less. Now, if you could just fill in your first name?'

Stone's pen hovered above the form. He looked hard at the blank window on the slip, then glanced up at Felicity, her eyes brimming with expectation.

He was about to explain when a noise from behind him drew attention from everyone in the shop. Someone was raising their voice in what sounded like an agitated fashion. Stone looked back at Felicity but the benign expression hadn't changed.

'Aren't you going to shush them?' he asked.

She offered an indulgent smile. 'Bit out of date, I'm afraid. We're a community resource. We welcome all and sundry. Bookshops haven't shushed anyone in years – a bit like libraries. Now, your first name?'

He put down the pen. 'I don't really use it. Most people call me Professor.'

'Oh, right. It's a bit unorthodox, but I suppose we don't have to have your first name. Not even an initial?'

Stone hesitated. 'E,' he said eventually.

Felicity scooped up the card containing Stone's personal details and popped it into a little box beside the till. 'Isn't there a policeman who doesn't have a first name? In literature, I mean.'

It was Stone's turn to smile: he'd faced this his entire working life. 'You're thinking of Inspector Morse. Goes almost the entire series of novels without ever admitting his first name. Then it's a big thing in the penultimate one when it's finally revealed.'

'As what?'

'I don't think I should tell you that. It's a massive spoiler.'

'I'm not sure I'll ever read them.'

'Even so.'

'All right, then … *Professor*. Have it your own way.'

From this flirtatious beginning had sprung an ongoing friendship, never straying beyond the bounds of appropriateness – or, indeed, the bookshop – but giving Stone a heartening feeling of welcome and relaxation every time he stepped inside the building. He'd made a point of talking to her on every visit, getting to know her reading preferences even as he divulged his own, and learning a few details of her life outside work. She told him she lived alone, was a Norcester native who'd been educated at a private school in a neighbouring town thanks to a scholarship she'd won at the age of eleven, and was an avid fan of Norcester United Football Club, where she'd held a season ticket for several years. It was a triumph of hope over experience, she claimed, but she maintained her optimistic fervour in deference to her father, who'd died when she was young but bequeathed her his own love of the club. It helped that their team colour was red (her own childhood favourite) but she'd have stuck with them if their strip had been lime-green and poo-brown stripes.

It had barely been eighteen months since they'd met, a mere year since the start of the reading group – set up at Felicity's suggestion, but eagerly administered by Stone – and now he had lost a friend.

Alongside the privilege of having been one of the few people he thought she opened up to, Stone felt a strong sense of duty towards her. He didn't know what DCI Carlton was up to – parts of his interview had even left him wondering if she was actually interested in solving the case at all – but he certainly was, and no amount of strong-arming from an unhelpful copper was going to stop him doing right by Felicity. The irony of what had evidently been a solitary existence was not lost on him: his own life was no more sociable than hers, but in his defence, crime fiction was littered with loners. He often felt he associated most closely with Hercule Poirot, another single man with a concealed past, although his own penchant for mysteries had not so far resulted in any real-life confrontations with criminals.

Perhaps that was about to change.

Stone pushed the remaining cold dregs of coffee away from him and stood up to put on his coat. During the entire hour he'd been sitting in the café there had been no sign of the reporter in a black jacket whom he'd seen outside the police station, and now he wrote off the whole lunchtime expedition as a waste of time. He'd hoped he might spot her going in or out of Newspaper Tower and be able to confirm her identity as a journalist, maybe even follow her to see what she was pursuing. It seemed incredible to him that she could be chasing anything other than the inside track on Felicity's murder. Norcester couldn't have seen a story this big in years, and there was no way her lurking outside the police station was a coincidence. Stone wondered if she had a source inside the force who'd tipped her off about Carlton interviewing the reading group. If so, he'd need to let the other group members know that there was a news hound sniffing around, and to repeat Carlton's warning about not talking to the press. Bella Bourton wouldn't dare, he guessed, and Lauren might be smart enough to stay away. Fforde, however, was a potential loose cannon. He needed to shut him down before he went shooting his mouth off to any pretty young face who asked him a question.

He left the café and crossed to the newspaper offices. As soon as he stepped inside, the headlines screamed at him from the copies of that day's edition that were lying on the counter for sale and he knew he was too late.

Back in his study, the offending article abandoned in disgust on the floor by his armchair, Stone stood in the middle of the room, staring at the desk that looked out onto the street. There, framed by neatly positioned officeware, a computer screen and keyboard, and his large leather-bound diary, lay two facsimiles of the contents of his anonymous package. He'd dug out his own copy of Archimedes's treatise when he'd first got back from the bookshop the previous evening, having surrendered the parcel itself to Fforde for safekeeping. Beside it on the desk was a page torn from a notebook, onto which he'd copied the line of text that had been typed on all their slips of paper: *The Secret of Father Brown.*

It was curious, Stone mused, that he had never read

Chesterton's famous short stories about the Roman Catholic priest whose intuitive and empathic methods made him one of the most revered among amateur detectives from the golden age. It was one of those strange gaps in his reading history that he'd never quite got round to filling, even though plenty of colleagues in numerous English departments had sung the cleric's praises and recommended his creator's elegant writing style. Stone hadn't even watched the television series, so his knowledge of the becassocked sleuth was severely limited. Within minutes of opening the package, he'd been knee-deep in initial research, discovering that *The Secret of Father Brown* was the overarching title and eponymous framing story for a collection of ten tales published by Chesterton in 1927. None of the titles in the anthology meant anything to him, or suggested anything worthy of further immediate investigation, but he'd recorded them nonetheless for future reference.

What puzzled him most was the fact that the Chesterton title was simply typed out on a sheet of paper – typed, he noted; not printed – whereas the other part of the parcel was an actual book.

Not that it was any more illuminating.

Stone had come across *On Floating Bodies* during his long-ago days as a student mathematician. The Archimedes text was as dry as the Sicilian sand he'd experimented with, even to the eyes of a young acolyte, but it was one of the most important documents in the ancient history of his subject, containing as it did the principle of hydrostatics that came to be named after its proponent. But while one notable Victorian translator had described the second volume as 'a veritable *tour de force* which must be read in full to be appreciated', Stone had never quite got round to it. Which was all very well, but more than two millennia after the assassination by Roman sword of the greatest thinker of his age, what on earth did it have to do with a modest bookshop manager in a Midlands backwater?

He considered the '*Floating*' part of the title and wondered if that might be hinting at something waterborne – was there another victim out there dumped in a canal or river, just waiting to be found? Did the perpetrator perhaps live on a houseboat? – but if so, Stone had nothing else to narrow down the search.

He returned to the armchair and sat with the volume in his hand, flicking through the dog-eared pages. He'd done it many times already, hoping he might find some chapter heading or glaring footnote to give him a clue, but there was nothing to implicate a killer or provide a motive for murder.

He was actually going to have to read the damn thing.

He was six arduous pages in when the mobile phone in his trouser pocket vibrated, making him start. Ripped from the gripping narrative of the academic tract, he took out the phone and looked at the message that had just dropped in from a number he didn't recognise.

The room was warm but Stone felt a sudden and soul-sapping chill.

I'm at your front door.

In the space of less than half a second, he convinced himself that Felicity's killer had decided he was next on the list, and he was mentally composing a message of dire warning to send to the others in the event of his brutal death when he checked himself.

He didn't have to let this person in. He could go to the

door, peer through the spy hole and, if he didn't like the look of them, barricade himself in and call the police. Even if they forced entry – which would take some time, he imagined – he could make his escape via the back door before they reached the hall.

There was no danger in at least looking, was there?

He tiptoed unnecessarily down the hall and cocked an ear superfluously.

When he leaned forward to inspect his unexpected visitor, who had already let themselves into the porch, his terror switched immediately to panic.

On the last occasion he had heard from Paula Grayson, things had not ended well. They had known each other for the best part of fifteen years, beginning when the illustrious Ms Grayson had taken a post as a lecturer in the Maths department of the university where Stone was already a professor. He had not been directly involved in her appointment but she arrived trailing a CV of impressive proportions, including a PhD from Manchester University, several fellowships at a variety of institutions and a selection of references from some of the biggest names in academia. He'd actually heard her name hailed at one conference as the rising star of British mathematics, and it did her career chances no harm at all to be almost six feet tall, wear three-inch heels and designer labels, and look like a cross between Audrey Hepburn and Kylie Minogue – a set of facts she acknowledged to close friends but would deny fiercely, to the point of threatening legal action, in public forums. When he finally met her for the first time, she'd given him the broadest smile, taken his hand in both of hers and gushed: 'I'm so thrilled to meet you, Professor Stone.' He'd been as smitten as the rest of the department and hated himself just a tiny bit for being so shallow.

Their mutual admiration had sparked something more than colleague status. Stone became one of those close friends to whom she admitted the effect of her natural charms. But his was not simply an affection rooted in her beauty: he had a genuine respect for her professional abilities, both as a mathematician and as a teacher. She seemed to have an innate talent for making students fall in love with the subject that went far beyond the surface attraction of an hour or two spent in one of her lectures, and her decision to specialise in one of his pet areas – probability – threw them together more frequently than the statistics of their shared module might have predicted. Perhaps inevitably, one drunk Christmas party saw them step over the poorly guarded frontier between esteemed collaborators and the murky territory of something vaguely lustful. While they had refrained from sharing most of their bodily fluids, they had unquestionably strayed into the sinister catacomb marked 'Physical Attraction', and there was no going back.

The predominant feeling between them after that was awkwardness, not for any reason of transgression – there were, at the time, no proscriptions on intradepartmental liaisons between consenting and unattached members of staff – but because Stone knew he had insufficient experience of grown-up relationships to be able to tell if this one could work successfully, and he suspected the same of Paula Grayson. In the absence of either of them being capable of leading the partnership to anything substantial or stable, it fizzled out and they retreated to a now-altered state of maladroit co-working that rendered any shared projects sterile and fruitless, and made employee meetings something of a nightmare. Other staff thought they had fallen out and began to avoid the increasingly frosty environment in their vicinity until things had finally come to a head one summer semester when a frustrated senior lecturer with, Stone suspected, his own agenda invited them to get on with it and have sex, or bugger off and put everyone out of their misery.

A fumbled and failed attempt at the former had been swiftly followed by Paula's adoption of the latter.

He hadn't seen Paula Grayson since.

Actually, that wasn't quite true. They had bumped into one another at a social event related to a symposium where Stone was giving the keynote address, and after a few terse words, Paula had upended her champagne flute down the front of Stone's shirt. He still wasn't sure if it had been deliberate.

'Paula,' he said, opening the door and putting as much warmth into his voice as he could while attempting to paste on a pleasant smile.

On the step, dressed to several integers past the nines, Paula Grayson was as stunning as he'd ever seen her. Middle age definitely suited her: she'd lost the waif-like thinness in her face and the slightly reserved stance of the *ingénue* and was now making the most of her height and imposing stature to look him straight in the eye. She'd changed both her hairstyle and her eyewear, both to significant advantage, and she wore an immaculately cut business suit in a fashionable shade of turquoise, the jacket's top button meticulously undone to reveal a cleavage either designed to intoxicate or reckless as to its effect – Stone didn't care which.

'I'm not here for small talk,' she said, wafting past him into the hall. 'I want a favour.'

Stone was unsurprised. She had never been one for chit-chat, even in their closest moments, and her text message from the other side of the door had already confirmed to Stone that little had changed in that regard.

'Come in and make yourself comfortable. Let me get you something to drink.'

She went ahead of him and turned into the living room, where she made for the nearest chair and sat down, looking relaxed and very much at home. Which was fine, mused Stone, except that it was someone else's home.

'Gin and tonic, if you have any lemons.'

Stone glanced at his watch before he could stop himself. Two-fifteen.

'Any problem with that?' she asked, an intimidating eyebrow raised towards him.

'No, no, of course not. You won't object if I don't join you – it's just that I've got work to do.'

Stone realised he still held *On Floating Bodies* in his hand. Paula looked at it as he waved it airily around.

'Archimedes? On a Thursday afternoon? As dedicated as ever, I see.'

'It's not research,' he began, then stopped. He didn't want to talk to Paula about Felicity's murder, the strange package or anything else, for that matter. As far as he'd been aware, this chapter of his life's book was scored through, closed and glued tightly shut. Only someone had just turned up with the solvent.

'Ooh, a mystery,' said Paula dangerously, the familiar twinkle emerging in her eye.

'Not really.'

'Come on, then – spill the beans.'

It wasn't a playful invitation: it felt to Stone like an order.

'There are no beans to spill. And even if there were, I don't think you'd be the most appropriate person to spill them to.'

Paula laughed but there was no mirth in it. 'Stranding a preposition? My God, it must be important.'

Stone put on his most pompous voice, the one he'd habitually reserved for latecomers in his lectures. 'There's nothing wrong with ending a sentence with a preposition. Only grammar pedants try to argue that, and you work in the wrong subject. Leave that to the English department.'

Paula leaned back in the chair and crossed her legs. 'If you say so.'

'I do.'

'Well, discussing linguistic semantics isn't going to get me that G and T, is it?'

Stone went into the kitchen and took out the ingredients he needed to make her extremely pre-prandial drink. Having assembled the spirit and the mixer, he roughly cut a chunk from the lemon he found in the fridge and dropped it into a tall glass. By the time he returned to the living room with her drink in one hand and a cup of coffee for himself in the other, she was more sprawled than sitting, leaning across towards one of the bookcases to inspect his collection.

'There seem to be an inordinate number of detective stories on these shelves. I don't remember you having quite such a fondness for the murder mystery.'

'A man needs a hobby,' he said cautiously, passing her the glass.

She laughed again, this time unveiling that delicate flutter he'd found so appealing all those years ago, and Stone felt the ice around his heart begin to soften.

'So, what's this favour you need?'

Chapter Eleven

When Bella entered the reading room at seven that evening, she was charmed to see the Professor stand up from the settee. Such a gentleman. And so clever. Why was she lumbered with an uncultured oaf like Trevor when there were articulate, appealing men like Professor Stone out there for the taking? She blamed her sister Ronnie. 'Grab him while you can,' she'd said when Bella had first told her about Trevor's proposal, offered romantically from beneath a Vauxhall Astra with a broken camshaft. 'With genes like ours, you can't afford to be fussy.' Foolishly, Bella had believed her. Subsequently, while Ronnie had decided that their sisterly tendency to plainness meant she was doomed to a life of spinsterhood, Bella had so far endured nineteen years and three months of unfussy marital servitude. She wasn't quite sure which of them had been dealt the worse hand.

Lauren looked up from the settee and gave Bella a brief smile, while Harrison Fforde was pacing from one side of the reading room to the other. He paused mid-flow to give her a welcome.

'Marvellous – the whole team is assembled,' he said.

'You make us sound like a secret society,' said Stone, sitting back down in one of the armchairs. 'All we need is a shed and a password and we could be the Famous Five.'

'Five?' queried Bella. 'But there's only four of us.'

Lauren seemed a little more upbeat than when Bella had last seen her almost twenty-four hours earlier. 'There were only four of them too – Julian, Dick, George and Anne. The fifth one was Timmy, the dog.'

'Still very much a part of the team,' said Fforde, resuming his pacing. 'Quite a nose for sniffing out trouble.'

'Oh, I see,' said Bella, confused. 'Does anyone have a dog?'

The two men shook their heads.

'I've got cats. Will they do?' said Lauren.

'Have they got noses?' asked Bella, surprising herself with the boldness required to make her small joke.

Stone cleared his throat pointedly.

'Yes, quite right,' said Fforde. 'Getting off track.'

Bella put down her handbag and took off her coat, preparing to settle down beside Lauren. As she did so, Fforde launched into what was obviously a prepared speech.

'Thank you all for coming tonight. I realise it's a little unorthodox meeting for a third night running but you must admit the circumstances are unusual.'

The Professor grunted. 'You could say that.'

'If I might be permitted to continue?' said Fforde. 'Maurice has restricted us to half an hour again.'

Bella thought he was settling into the role of amateur sleuth rather well: the gravity suited him. He was no Lord Quaint, of course, but then who was? She tried to think of an actor who might be sufficiently charismatic to handle the part but she came up short.

Fforde would have to do for now.

'Now, you may be wondering why I summoned you all here.'

'I'm not sure about "summoned",' said Bella, immediately revising her opinion of Fforde's skills. 'I thought we were invited.'

'Is it to talk about your starring role in today's *Norcester Echo*?' asked Stone.

'No, it isn't,' said Fforde, hurrying on. 'The answer lies – or at least it did until they took Felicity's body away – out there among the bookshelves. Out there is a real-life murder mystery. Out there is the tragic and senseless death of one of our little community. Out there—'

Stone coughed loudly.

'Anyway,' Fforde continued, moderating his tone from the melodramatic to the merely pontificating, 'you get my point. There's a murder to be solved. And we're precisely the right people to solve it.'

The room fell silent. Bella glanced around to see the Professor deep in contemplation, his brow furrowed in a way she'd often read about but didn't think she'd actually ever encountered outside the pages of a novel, and Lauren staring into the middle distance, clearly lost in thought. Fforde had stopped pacing and was posed, one hand on his chin, apparently awaiting the approval of his audience.

Am I missing something? Bella wondered. *What are they all thinking about?*

'Um ... isn't that what the police are for?' she asked eventually, when she felt the moment had lasted long enough.

Fforde exploded in a gale of laughter. 'The police? Oh please, spare me the *naïveté*.'

He pronounced it with the accents.

Bella shrank a little. Maybe Harrison was mistaking rudeness for gravity.

'No, my dear, if we've learned anything from our various encounters with Detective Chief Inspector Carlton over the past couple of days, then it's perfectly plain that that woman is not going to solve the murder of Felicity Penman. She has neither the wit nor the resources for such a task, and if her sidekick Muir is anything to go by, they'll be a positive hindrance to the case, rather than its solution.'

He turned towards Stone.

'Professor, how did you find them?'

Bella realised they hadn't shared details of their interviews at the meeting the previous evening. Maurice had been true to his word and thrown them out after thirty tear-stained minutes, giving them only enough time to pool their packages and ponder unproductively over their significance. Now she was keen to hear how the others had got on with their statements.

'Well, I think you might have a point about their competence,' Stone said reluctantly, 'especially Sergeant Muir. He seemed particularly slow on the uptake when they were interviewing me yesterday but, quite honestly, DCI Carlton wasn't much help either. She let him ramble on inanely and I'm not sure they believed anything I told them.'

Lauren looked confused. 'What do you mean? Why

wouldn't they believe you? Surely they don't think you've got something to do with it?'

'Me, you – probably even Bella here. Who knows what they think. Carlton's giving nothing away and treating everyone like a suspect.'

'She didn't treat me like a suspect.'

All eyes turned to Bella, who immediately blushed. She recalled her chat with the inspector the previous afternoon as a rather civilised affair, a gentle half-hour of explanation about how she'd stumbled across The Quaint Bookshop one chilly spring afternoon, been encouraged by Felicity Penman to sign up for the reading group some time later, and found her both pleasant and stimulating company in the short time that she'd known her. There had certainly been no sense from Miranda Carlton that she was anything other than a useful source of background information.

'She was quite nice to me, actually. Gave me tea and biscuits.'

'Biscuits?' Fforde was erupting again. 'You don't solve a case by giving your suspects biscuits!'

'I told you – she didn't treat me like a suspect.'

Lauren leaned forward and spoke carefully. 'Maybe it's a trap. Maybe she's lulling you into a false sense of security before springing some vital piece of evidence on you and catching you out.'

'But I haven't done anything. How could she catch me out?'

Lauren leaned back again. 'Good point. But Harrison's right – we can't trust her to solve the murder. And who better than a group of crime fiction fans to come to the rescue?'

Fforde stepped closer to his seated counterparts, a gleam in his eye. 'The reading room is our shed, Lauren's cats can be Timmy, and we can be—'

Stone lifted a hand to stop him.

'If you're going to start doling out the parts, then I'm definitely Julian. Lauren is George, Bella will have to be Anne, and you … well, Harrison, you've always struck me as a bit of a Dick.'

'All right, boys, that's quite enough of that.' Lauren had rather a firm tone when she needed it, Bella noticed.

'If we're going to work together on this, we have to be a team. Wouldn't you agree?' She turned to Bella, as if for support.

Bella was not sure about the type of support she was willing to give. When Felicity had first invited her to the reading group, she'd been pleased to be asked and moderately excited to be doing something beyond the purview of Trevor. What she hadn't signed up for was a trip into the unknown on a vessel of dubious seaworthiness with a captain and crew whose fitness for service were outside her sphere of experience to properly assess.

'Well, yes,' she said hesitantly. 'But I don't think we should be sticking our noses in where the police don't want us.'

'Nonsense!' said Fforde. 'That's exactly where we should be sticking our noses. If they're unwilling or unable to do the job themselves, then somebody's got to step up, haven't they?'

'I suppose…'

'Exactly. And we're in the perfect position to do the stepping. We all knew Felicity – some better than others, admittedly – we were all here on Tuesday night, and apparently we're all on the list of suspects for the police.'

'Actually, as I think I mentioned, I don't believe I am,' corrected Bella. But Fforde wasn't listening.

'Which brings me to the reason I asked you all to come tonight.'

Stone sighed. 'Finally.'

'I've been … busy.'

There was a pause. Bella imagined that Fforde was hoping it was a dramatic one.

'Better than not being busy, I suppose,' retorted Stone archly.

'Now, now, what did I just say?' Lauren gave Stone a stern glare.

'All right. I'm only teasing him. What have you been up to, Harrison?'

'Just before I texted all of you to come and meet me here, I had a visit at my apartment from Carlton and Muir.'

He stopped, presumably to enjoy the stir of interest this provoked, Bella thought. But he deserved it: this was new information, and maybe he was about to expand on it.

The Professor seemed marginally less impressed than the others. 'Was it to talk about your starring role in today's *Norcester Echo*?' he repeated mischievously.

Fforde hesitated. 'Initially, yes.'

'And what did they make of it?'

'That's not the point. The point is that when I gave them our packages—'

The Professor's exclamation made Bella jump.

'You did what?'

Fforde was on the defensive. 'I had to. She'd have murdered me for real if she found out we'd been sent them and hadn't handed them over. But you're missing the point again.'

'Which is?' The Professor seemed to have conceded that particular argument, Bella was pleased to see.

'Which is that DCI Carlton was very impressed with the way I'd handled them. I think she believed they might be able to get fingerprints off them, as I think I suggested last night.'

Bella wondered just how impressed the inspector had really been but allowed Fforde his moment. 'Oh, wouldn't that be good?'

Fforde grinned, evidently pleased with himself. 'I thought you might like that little nugget. But that's not all. Their visit also inspired me to get started on this.'

With a flourish, he drew out his mobile phone, already prepared for this moment with a photograph on its screen. 'A little something I've been working on.'

Bella half-rose from her seat, looking curiously at the screen, but sat down again after a moment.

'Sorry, Harrison – I can't make it out.'

'Well, you can't see it properly on here, but I couldn't really bring it into the shop and set the whole thing up.'

'What is it?' asked Stone wearily.

Fforde withdrew the mobile and looked at it again himself, checking the screen had not gone blank or frozen.

'It's the evidence. I've been collecting information and putting it up on this corkboard at home.'

'Oh, I've seen them do that on the telly,' said Bella, standing now and approaching Fforde. 'Let me have a proper look.'

Fforde used two fingers to pinch the photo open, enlarging the image for Bella to see more clearly.

'This is a map of Norcester, and these are the locations of

interest so far. There'll be more to add as we go along, no doubt – all of our homes, for starters.'

'Why do you need to put our homes on there?' Bella asked.

'Because that's where the parcels were sent to, of course,' he replied. 'Everything connected to the case has to go on here.'

'Seems a bit pointless to me,' muttered Stone from the depths of his chair.

'Oh, don't say that,' said Bella, tearing herself away from Fforde's mobile. 'He's put a lot of work into this. I think it could be very beneficial.'

Lauren gave Bella an interested look.

'You've changed your tune, Bella,' said the younger woman. 'A minute ago you were all for leaving it to the police and staying out of it.'

'Yes, well, as the old song says, a day can make quite a difference.'

Fforde put his hand on Bella's arm. 'It's not been a day, and that's not really how the lyric goes.'

'Isn't it? Well, you know what I mean. And anyway, your evidence board may be a lovely hobby but it doesn't change the fact that I still think the professionals are better placed to handle it.'

She sat down again next to Lauren and put her handbag on her knee. This needed proper consideration. She recalled that Basil Rathbone resorted to smoking a pipe for his Sherlock Holmes contemplations, and Bella knew exactly what she needed. From her bag, she took out a little parcel of greaseproof paper and unfolded its neat ends.

'Anybody like a sandwich?' she asked, offering the parcel around.

Nobody answered.

'There's just one problem,' Fforde said. From his tone, Bella thought she might have annoyed him with her refreshments interlude.

'What's that?' asked Stone.

'I don't know what else to put on it. It'll only be any good to us if we can fill it with clues.'

Lauren leaned forward, a keen look on her face. 'I've got that covered.'

'What do you mean?' asked Bella, trying to disguise the fact that her mouth was full of cheese and pickle. Honestly, she reflected, sometimes she reminded herself of Trevor. And not in a good way.

Lauren paused, apparently uncertain of whether to go on.

'Harrison's not the only one who's been speaking to someone else. I know Carlton told us not to, but I really wanted to do something to help. So I've called in my brother. He's a real tech whizz and I've put him to work on a deep dive into the internet to see if he can come up with any answers to the question that's been bothering me.'

'What question's that?' said Bella, her mouth now empty.

'The question we should probably have started with last night: who would want to kill her?'

'And why,' added Stone grimly.

'Anyway, Simon's found out a bit, although he's run into something of a dead end. Apparently he can't find any trace of Felicity Penman before she started working at the bookshop eighteen months ago. It's as if she's got no online footprint.'

'How is that possible?' asked Fforde.

'I don't know,' said Lauren, 'but I'll get Simon to send you what he's got so far. Maybe it'll give you something to add to your corkboard.'

'Thanks. It is looking a bit bare.'

A thought struck Bella. 'You could always add information about the contents of our packages.'

'Good idea,' said Fforde, and Bella glowed a little.

Lauren's look had mutated into one of seriousness. 'Yes, I wouldn't mind knowing a little more about those packages. Who sent them to us, and why? I've spent all day looking at strangers and wondering if I should be scared. Are we next on the killer's hit list?'

Professor Stone surfaced from what looked like a moment of deep cogitation to answer Lauren's question.

'Or are those packages something else entirely?'

Bella stared at him and realised he was looking at the floor beneath her feet. She glanced down herself and saw, to her shame, that she'd been making a mess with her sandwich.

'Maybe they aren't a warning at all,' Stone went on. 'Maybe they're breadcrumbs. Maybe someone is trying to point us in the direction of Felicity's murderer.'

Friday

Chapter Twelve

Lauren glanced up from her phone and looked over at Simon, still ensconced in the armchair across the room nearly forty-eight hours after he'd arrived at her house. He'd slept easily on the sofa, roughing it with the cats, and showed no signs of needing daylight. He'd assembled lots of background information about The Quaint Bookshop, the town's constabulary and even Sergeant Muir's personal life – another avid fan of Norcester United and a regular at the force's five-a-side sessions every Thursday evening – but that was all it was: background information. Felicity Penman's past remained stubbornly undiscovered, and the wealth of material offered little concrete assistance to any enquiries into her murder.

She picked up the copy of the *Norcester Echo* that she'd popped out for an hour earlier and flicked through its pages for the second time. If the reading group was having trouble finding out anything new about Felicity's tragic death, the local paper didn't seem to be doing any better. Lauren had read Fforde's misguided interview in the previous day's edition and had marvelled at his ability to make stuff up for dramatic effect, but there was nothing so salacious in the latest bulletins: the *Echo* had merely rehashed a lot of what Fforde had said twenty-four hours earlier, and there was clearly nothing new coming from the reporters' police contacts. Warmed-up tittle-tattle was the best they could muster.

She folded up the paper and dropped it onto the little table in front of her.

She was studying Simon's boyishly tousled hair and the rip in one knee of his jeans when her mobile pinged.

'Breakfast's here,' she said, and got up to open the front door.

'Morning,' said the delivery girl, not much younger than Lauren herself and more cheerful than she had any right to be, serving up tepid comestibles to lazy householders in the rain for minimum wage plus tips. Lauren added a couple of coins to the girl's takings and took the large brown paper bag from her in return.

'Bloody lovely,' said Simon, his face full of the first succulent mouthful of ground something-or-other.

'Wasted calories,' Lauren replied, and took a bite herself. A large dollop of ketchup snuck out of the back end and plopped into the flimsy cardboard box.

'Ha! How's the view from your high horse?'

'Spectacular, as always.'

Simon paused his chewing and studied Lauren from across the room.

'Not even a hint of irony?'

'Not if I can help it,' said Lauren, and shoved two fries into her mouth.

Ten minutes later, as she went out to the kitchen to collect some paper towels, Remus began sniffing around the paper bag.

'Keep the cats away from the rubbish,' she called over her shoulder.

In the kitchen, she grabbed the roll and topped up her coffee from the cafetière, returning to find both cats in the custody of Simon, who had one tucked under each armpit, where they were struggling to free themselves from his grasp.

'They're desperate to get into the bag,' he said, looking up at his sister.

She put the coffee on her writing table and tore off a piece of kitchen roll, which she handed to Simon.

'Wouldn't it have been easier to pick up the rubbish instead of the cats?'

He released the felines and laughed as they scuttled away from him across the floor.

'Oh yeah, probably.'

As he went back to his laptop, Lauren watched her brother closely, seeing shades of their father in his fierce concentration and echoes of their mother in his wavy hair and willowy frame. She hadn't spent this long in his company since she'd left home more than a decade earlier and she was beginning to find his lack of domesticity irritating. While it was heartening to see the boy she remembered behind all the nonsense that had happened in more recent times, she'd forgotten just how much of a boy he could be. As far as she could tell he hadn't bathed or even washed since he'd arrived and the living room was starting to pong of sweaty socks and ripe hormones. She'd managed to keep on top of the seemingly endless stream of dishes, mugs and glasses he got through but he'd have to change his clothes soon. Wouldn't he?

'Simon, you've hardly moved from that chair since the day before yesterday. You must need some fresh underwear, at least.'

'You know the four-day rule,' he said.

Lauren dragged up a memory from years ago, recalling their mother attempting an almost identical conversation with him. 'Forwards, backwards and same again inside out,' he'd said when she queried his ability to make his boxers last more than half the week.

'Do that in your own house if you like, but not here. For God's sake, Simon – go home and have a shower, at least.'

'What about the new lines of enquiry?'

'They'll have to wait,' said Lauren, and pulled his hand away from the laptop. 'Come on, I mean it – you stink.'

Simon struggled to his feet and began slipping on his battered old trainers. 'All right, sis. Don't get your knickers in a twist.'

'It's your knickers I'm concerned about,' she said, and dragged him towards the front door.

When she opened it to let him out, a young woman with platinum-blonde hair was standing in the drizzle with one arm outstretched, on the point of pressing the doorbell.

'Oh good, you're in,' she said, flashing a practised smile at Lauren before looking past her at the dishevelled figure in the hallway. 'I was hoping to catch you. Is this your boyfriend?'

Simon emerged into the light, blinking slightly but evidently impressed by the creature on the doorstep. He held out a hand.

'Simon Sherwood. I'm the brother.'

The woman, who seemed to Lauren to be aged about halfway between her and Simon, shook his hand and beamed.

'Delighted to meet you. I'm Nicki Bailey from the *Norcester Echo*.'

Lauren's heart sank. Immediately she connected the voice she'd heard on the phone the other night to this spectacle of youthful eagerness in front of her.

Of course this was Nicki Bailey.

Of course she'd tracked her down.

Of course Simon would fancy her.

'What can I do for you?' she asked the new arrival.

'We spoke on the phone the other night.'

'I remember.'

'But I think we got cut off.'

'I remember.'

Romulus brushed round Lauren's ankles, took one look at the weather and meandered back inside.

Nicki shuffled on the doorstep and looked up at the drizzle that was stiffening into actual rain.

'Look, do you mind if I come in? I've tried to leave you alone for a couple of days but I really want to ask you a few questions about the bookshop.'

'I can't talk to you, I'm afraid. I'm under strict instructions from the police.'

Nicki's face relaxed into another smile. 'DCI Carlton? Oh, you don't want to worry about her.'

'Don't I?'

'No, of course not. She comes across all tough-talking and intimidating but she's a pussycat underneath. Trust me.'

That was the last thing Lauren felt inclined to do, but Simon had other ideas.

'You'd better come in,' he said, physically manhandling Lauren to one side to let the reporter into the hallway. 'You're getting soaked out there.'

Lauren shoved Simon in the small of the back and he stumbled out of the door.

'Home, remember?'

As Nicki moved further into the hall, Lauren pulled a distasteful face at her brother, out of sight of the visitor.

'Right, yeah, OK,' he babbled, addressing himself more to Nicki than to his sister. 'I'm just popping out – I won't be long.'

'Take as long as you need,' Lauren called after him, then turned her attention back to Nicki Bailey, bedraggled and hopeful in her hall. It was too late to throw her out now: like a vampire, she'd been invited over the threshold and there was no going back, however uneasy she felt.

She could be polite. She could make her a cup of tea. But she didn't have to tell her anything.

Within five minutes, Lauren realised she'd been played. Nicki Bailey had slipped off her wet coat and shoes in the hall and was now sitting in Simon's vacated armchair with her feet up under her, making herself totally comfortable. Even Remus had wandered over to greet her. Lauren couldn't work out how she'd managed it, but clearly Nicki was very good at getting what she wanted.

Lauren was on high alert to avoid falling into the same trap that had lured Harrison into talking to the *Echo*. She'd wanted to ask him at the group meeting about how his front-page interview had gone down with the police, but she realised that Fforde had managed to dodge Professor Stone's question on the topic. She didn't imagine Fforde would have been flavour of the month with Carlton, that was for sure. She hoped she was made of stronger stuff than him, but she'd have to be on her guard nonetheless.

She tried making small talk.

'Have you been at the paper long?'

'About three years,' said Nicki, cradling the mug that Lauren had just given her and looking thoroughly soaked.

Don't get sucked in by her pathetic appearance, Lauren thought.

'And how did you become a journalist?'

'It's a tribute to my dad, really,' said Nicki, declining to expand on her answer in spite of Lauren giving her an additional few moments.

Don't be taken in by a sob story.

'You must enjoy it?'

'Mostly, yeah. There are some aspects you don't relish – death knocks, for instance – but on the whole it's good.'

'Death knocks?'

Nicki nodded. 'Calling on the relatives of people who've died. Trying to get them to talk to you. I hate that bit.'

'I can imagine. Sounds like a horrible job.'

'It can be. But then sometimes you get people who really want to talk about their loved one, like a proper obituary. That can be nice. I usually tell them it's a chance to pay their respects, to tell the world what the person meant to them. That often works.'

Lauren winced. Was she feeling particularly cynical towards this girl because of her own vulnerability in a situation she didn't know how to handle, or was she right to be wary of what seemed to Lauren to be manipulative techniques? The previous day's front page popped up again in her mind, followed by an imagined glimpse of Harrison Fforde being yelled at by a furious DCI Carlton.

'But you've suffered your own loss, haven't you?' Nicki went on.

'Nothing like losing a relative,' she said, sitting back in her chair opposite Nicki. The girl really did look rather damp.

'Don't underestimate the impact of grief. Catches people in strange ways, sometimes months down the line.'

Lauren decided to try and play down her involvement. 'I didn't really know Felicity Penman all that well.'

'Doesn't matter. The fact is you knew her, and her dying in such a brutal way is bound to have an effect on you.'

Brutal? Lauren realised with a jolt that she had no idea exactly how Felicity had been murdered. DCI Carlton had given nothing away at her interview, and Harrison's account in the paper was all made up anyway, so the actual details remained a mystery to her.

'Er, I'm afraid I don't know how she died.'

Nicki looked surprised.

'Really? But I thought you were there when it happened?'

'Well, in a way. We'd just finished our meeting of the reading group and Felicity had locked up behind us when we heard her scream.'

'What did it sound like?'

'Dreadful – like something out of a horror movie.'

'So you went back inside. And what did you find?'

'Only after the police broke in,' said Lauren, feeling her heart pick up pace as she recalled the events of Tuesday night. 'We went in straight after them to see what had happened but when they realised she'd been attacked, they kept the four of us away from the body.'

'Four of you? That's you, Harrison and who else?'

'Well, Professor Stone, of course – he's the leader of the group, really.'

'Ah, yes. The one with the secrets.'

'Sorry?'

Nicki checked herself, as if she'd given something away inadvertently. 'Oh, nothing. Just something my editor told me. So that's three – who's the fourth?'

Lauren made a mental note to get Simon on the case of Professor Stone's 'secrets'. He didn't seem like the type to have a dodgy past, but then you could never be sure, could you? I mean, just look at Simon: there was plenty in his background that he wouldn't want made public.

'We've just acquired a nice new member, Bella Bourton. She seems lovely. Goodness knows whether she'll want to carry on with the reading group after this.'

Lauren paused as she thought back to the previous evening, when Bella had once more been the odd one out. It had taken some persuading to convince her to go along with the rest of them in investigating Felicity's murder. In the end, it was only Stone's new line of thinking that had done it. The chance to follow the breadcrumbs and solve the case, in defiance of the rather arrogant DCI Carlton, had appealed to all of them. Now Lauren saw that Nicki Bailey might provide them with the opportunity to add something concrete to Harrison's corkboard.

'So how did Felicity die?'

Nicki didn't miss a beat.

'Bludgeoned to death with *The Complete Works of Ellery Queen*. Any chance of a refill?'

Lauren took the mug from Nicki's outstretched hand and wandered into the kitchen, turning over this new piece of information. *What a horrible way to go*, she thought at first, then began to wonder if it wasn't, perhaps, the worst way for a bookshop manager to meet their end. Obviously it would have been preferable not to die at all, but if it was going to happen, she could imagine far less appropriate murder weapons than a heavy hardback to the cranium.

'How do you know the cause of death?' she asked Nicki when she returned, the mug restored to a moderate state of fullness without running the risk of spilling over onto the pale carpet.

Nicki nodded sagely. 'Contacts.'

She wasn't giving much away, that was for sure. Lauren was pleased she could say the same about herself, then realised with a sinking feeling that that simply wasn't true at all. Somehow, this smart operator had managed to get her to give up loads of information about the reading group, the scene of the crime and even the details of her relationship to the victim.

Thank God she wasn't recording any of it.

But as she watched Nicki balance the mug on her knee, her feet tucked up cosily on the armchair, she saw for the first time a notebook stowed between Nicki's legs and the side of the chair, a pen lodged in the spiral wire at the top of its pages.

'Have you been taking notes?' she asked, horrified.

'What? Oh, this,' said Nicki, lifting up the notebook with her free hand. 'Just a few thoughts as an *aide-mémoire* – I've got a terrible memory.'

'You know you can't quote me on any of this,' said Lauren, her heart racing again at the thought of what she might have inadvertently divulged.

'Well, technically I can,' said Nicki. 'But let's not get into that. We were talking about your grief at losing someone you knew in such difficult circumstances. How do you feel about it now, after a few days of living with it?'

'No,' said Lauren decisively. 'I'm not telling you anything else. And I haven't given you my permission to take notes so you can't actually quote me.'

She had no idea if that was true but she had to try to bluff her way out of it. Otherwise DCI Carlton would be waiting for her on the far side of another newspaper article.

'Look, if you want to get into the technicalities, I made it perfectly clear when you first opened the door that I was a reporter from the *Norcester Echo*. You let me in, sat me down in front of the fire – God, you've even made me two cups of tea – so you'd be a bit hard-pressed to argue that you haven't consented to our interview.'

'It's not an interview, it's a conversation,' said Lauren, aware that her voice had risen at least half an octave.

'You say potato…' began Nicki.

'No, I bloody well don't say "potato",' Lauren erupted. 'I say you're a devious piece of work with a malicious streak a mile wide, and I'd like you to leave my house right now.'

Nicki looked completely unfazed as she got up and handed Lauren her mug, still hot with its refill. She gathered up her notebook and pen, slipped her shoes and coat back on and followed Lauren to the front door.

'It's a shame, though,' she said, tucking the notebook into a coat pocket.

'What is?'

'You, with this story. It's such a great first-hand account. You could probably make a few quid out of it if you wanted. I could show you how.'

Lauren applied much the same pressure to Nicki's back as

she had to Simon's on his departure, only without the accompanying filial affection.

Nicki lifted her coat up over her head to shield herself from the weather and headed for the gate. As she neared it, Simon appeared suddenly on the other side, popped open the latch and invited her to go through first.

'Are you leaving?' Lauren heard him say.

'Yes, she is,' she called into the rain.

She watched Simon add something else she couldn't quite make out, then saw Nicki smile and give a half-wave from under her coat before running off down the street.

Lauren held the door open for her brother and slapped his arm as he passed her into the hall.

'Don't encourage her,' she said, trying to sound stern. 'She's a snake.'

'She seems all right to me,' Simon replied, shaking himself so that droplets of water splashed up the wall. At least he'd got a fresh shirt on.

'She's under thirty with a pulse. Of course she seems all right to you. But you're not to talk to her again, do you understand?'

Simon looked like he was about to object but must have seen the alarm in her eyes because he backed off and went into the living room without saying anything else.

'You didn't take long,' said Lauren, following him in.

'I was hoping to catch your visitor before she left.'

'Well you did. Now leave it at that.'

'What did she want?' Simon asked.

'Never mind. Just take my word for it that she's not to be trusted. Now come on – we've got research to do.'

Lauren felt uneasy all over again as Simon sat down and

opened up his laptop. She knew she could exercise no real control over him and worried that he might try to contact Nicki again. Which could lead to all sorts of complications, especially given what he knew from Lauren about the case. Not for the first time – but this time for a rather different reason – she wondered if she'd made a mistake getting him involved.

She didn't want Simon to make a habit of becoming a liability.

She pushed the thought to the back of her mind and tried to refocus on the job in hand.

'If you can't get any further with Felicity, then I think it's time we looked at the packages. You start on *The Secret of Father Brown*, see if you can work out what relevance it has to the murder. I'll concentrate on the books.'

As Simon settled down to his new assignment, she went to the bookcase against the back wall and picked out a familiar volume. She wished she still had the copy from her package, but that was now under lock and key in some police evidence compound. Riffling through the pages, she remembered every twist and turn in the Victorian narrative. What she couldn't understand was why she'd been sent a copy of *A Study in Scarlet*.

She sat in the armchair by the fire and flicked to the first page. However well she remembered it, she'd always read it before as a punter. Now she was a sleuth herself. Was there something in its twists and turns that might reveal itself to her on a new reading?

A tremor of excitement shivered through her. Perhaps she held the answer to Felicity's murder in her hand.

Chapter Thirteen

Of all the members of the reading group, the last one Professor Stone expected to pay him a private visit was Bella Bourton. Lauren he could easily imagine – he had begun to see himself as rather a father figure for her, and guessed from her quiet respect towards him that she might feel much the same. As for Fforde, he could well believe the actor might want to call on him just for the opportunity to take the rise out of him: Fforde had engaged in what Stone refused to call 'banter' ever since they first met, nearly a year ago, and more recently it had taken on a rather sharper edge, as if Fforde had realised Stone didn't want to play his game and was therefore pushing the boundaries to see how far he could go with it. After more than three decades accommodating the playful testing of expanding young minds in academia, Stone had developed a considerable tolerance towards this kind of nonsense; in Fforde, still apparently not having outgrown the idiocy of youth, he found it increasingly aggravating.

So when Bella rang his doorbell a few minutes before

eleven that morning, while he was cutting himself a slice of bread for some mid-morning toast, it took him slightly longer than it might otherwise have done to invite her in out of the rain.

'What a nice surprise,' he said, ushering her into the hall and stepping back to allow her to take off her damp coat.

Two unexpected visitors in as many days. Anyone would have thought there was a mystery to solve.

'Oh, that looks lethal, Professor,' Bella said warily, handing him the dripping garment.

He looked down at his hand and saw that he was still holding the impressively crafted bread knife. He put it down on the little hall table he kept for just such eventualities and took the coat from her.

'How did you find me?' he asked.

Bella smiled. 'I did a bit of digging,' she said, evidently pleased with herself.

'Heavens. Two meetings of the reading group and you're a fully-fledged detective.'

'You're still in the phone book,' she said prosaically.

Stone hadn't heard of anyone using the phone book in years. He'd actually forgotten he was listed.

'Well, don't take this the wrong way but I wasn't expecting to see you this morning.'

'No. Likewise. But I didn't get a very good night's sleep last night.'

'Oh, I'm sorry to hear that,' said Stone, wondering if Bella realised that the 'Doctor' in his professional title had nothing to do with medicine and if she was after a cure for insomnia then she had very much come to the wrong place.

Unless she wanted him to bore her to sleep.

'Well, thank you – but that's not why I'm here.'

Stone was aware that they were still standing in the hall, where he could feel a draught from the porch whirling around his ankles.

'Shall we go through?' he asked, gesturing towards the nearest door.

Bella led the way into the room and stood uncertainly in the middle of it, apparently awaiting further instructions.

'Please, take a seat,' said Stone, indicating a variety of options from which Bella could make her choice.

She selected a low, padded chair with wooden arms and a knitted antimacassar, both of which Stone had inherited from a great-aunt on his mother's side. As a child, Stone had always sat in that chair whenever the family made its biannual visits to the Suffolk coast, where the elderly relative had lived, and she'd remembered the fact when it came to distributing her worldly goods in her last will and testament. The young Stone had appreciated the chair more for its comfortable contours around his childish frame than for its aesthetics, but he didn't feel able to dispense with it once it had been delivered from the old lady's estate, and it remained part of the mismatched collection of pieces that served as his furniture.

'Was there something you wanted to talk to me about?' he asked Bella from a standing position.

'There was actually,' she replied, putting her elbows on the arms of the chair and linking her hands together in front of her.

'Should I put the kettle on?'

'Oh, that would be lovely. Milk no sugar for me, please.'

As Stone swirled hot water around a comedy teapot with a cartoon face painted on the side and two oversized feet sticking out of the bottom, he wondered what might be on

Bella's mind to the point where she was losing sleep. Of course, the traumatic experience after Tuesday night's meeting was enough to cause anyone worry, but two factors mitigated against that as the reason: first, Bella knew Felicity Penman the least of all of them, and although any violent death was shocking, it seemed unlikely that it should hit her particularly hard; and secondly, why had it taken several days for her to be affected in this way? As he dropped two teabags into the pot and gathered up the only matching mugs he could find – plain white ones usually reserved for visiting workmen – he resolved to probe Bella on these two questions.

When he returned to the front room carrying a tray with all the necessary accoutrements, he found her standing by one of the large bookcases that were set into the alcoves either side of the fireplace, examining the titles intently.

'What an amazing collection of books,' she said, turning to face him. She had two in her hand.

'You're welcome to borrow those, if you'd like,' he said, nodding at the volumes she was holding.

'Oh, these? Could I?'

'Of course. What have you found?'

She held them up. 'This is that Agatha Christie book I got sent – *The Body in the Library*. I didn't have a chance to read it before Harrison gave it to the police. I'd like to have a look to see if I can find any clues.'

Stone reprimanded himself for not having thought of it himself, and suspected that if there were clues to be found in the Marple mystery, he was the more likely of the two to decipher them. But he could hardly withdraw his invitation now.

'Good idea. What's the other one?'

'*Criminal Law for Dummies*. I thought perhaps I should at least brush up on the basics.'

She moved back to the low chair and sat down again, adopting the same posture as before.

'I'm surprised you ever need to go to the bookshop. I should have thought you'd got everything you need right here.'

'A lot of dusty old things accumulated over a lifetime of study.'

He put the tray down on a coffee table to one side of the room, then picked the whole lot up and placed it halfway between their two chairs.

'I imagine so,' she said. 'I didn't understand a lot of the words in the titles, so goodness knows what they're like inside.'

'Mostly as dusty as they are on the outside,' said Stone, smiling. He decided he liked Bella for her unassuming modesty but guessed that it might conceal something more robust if push came to shove. He made a mental note not to shove her if he could possibly avoid it.

'We'll let the tea brew for a minute or two. Now, you were saying there was something you wanted to talk to me about.'

'Well, yes…'

She stopped, and Stone wondered if she was struggling to articulate something awkward, or even painful.

'I'm all ears,' he nudged.

A look of confusion passed over Bella's face.

'Felicity's murder, of course – what did you think I wanted to talk about?'

Was that it? He'd been expecting some great revelation or confession, when all Bella had wanted was to discuss the case.

'Oh, I see. I thought you might have something important to tell me.'

'You don't think Felicity being murdered is important?'

'No, of course I do,' stuttered Stone, feeling a little nonplussed by the whole situation. Bella had been the one, out of the four of them, who had been most reluctant to explore the crime outside the purview of the police's investigation, and yet here she was, sitting in his front room, treating this conversation as the most obvious thing in the world.

'Sorry, Bella – it's just that I didn't think you were particularly keen on the reading group investigating the case.'

Bella reached across to the tea tray, swirled the pot and began to pour dark brown liquid into the two mugs. Stone noted another point in his mental log: she was well capable of taking control of a situation if it suited her aims.

'And you were right. To begin with. But as we talked at the shop last night, I started to see things differently. And I'm feeling a lot better thinking of the packages as a clue rather than a threat.'

'Well, we don't know that for sure…' he began, then trailed off at the sight of Bella's hopeful face.

He accepted the mug that Bella offered him and settled back in his own seat, an off-the-shelf armchair with overstuffed cushions that he'd bought one December in one of those sales that were advertised interminably on the television and which never actually seemed to end. He'd wondered if he should wait for a further discount in January, but decided to treat himself to it as an early Christmas present. He'd been pleased to note that it had actually gone up in price after the holidays, and he'd felt a strange, illogical affection for the chair ever since.

Bella sat down and cradled her mug. 'So tell me everything you know.'

There was a vividness in Bella's eyes and it sparked something in him. He was the one who had known Felicity best, after all, and given the antagonism of the police – for reasons that still escaped Stone's mathematical logic – then why shouldn't the reading group take matters into their own hands? They had no real way of knowing where the police were with their enquiries, but his confidence in Detective Sergeant Muir's abilities was non-existent, while DCI Miranda Carlton had made it clear to them all that she deemed her investigation off limits. He'd considered telephoning her later today and asking her how things were going but he knew that she was under no obligation to tell him anything. Especially if she really did consider them suspects.

Now, if Bella was truly on board as well, maybe the four of them could pull something out of the bag. The only question was, where was the bag, and what did it contain?

'Why have you come to me, Bella? We all talked about this last night.'

The vividness deepened in her eyes.

'Because you really know what you're doing,' she said eagerly. 'Look at these books. You said it yourself: you've spent a lifetime gathering knowledge and information and insight into the human spirit. If any of us is equipped to use those kinds of skills to track down a murderer, then it's you. Oh, Lauren is bright enough and keen enough, but she's out of her depth, I can tell. And as for Harrison, his evidence board is all well and good but he's so wrapped up in it that he can't see the cork for the trees. We could have spent hours last night going round in circles again and again and still not got any closer.

But you, Professor – you're the one who can solve this case. I want to be around to watch that happen.'

It had been a long time since Stone felt adored.

Over the next hour, he went over the details of everything they knew about the case, from the discovery of Felicity's body in the bookshop after their meeting and the pointlessness of the police interviews that had revealed nothing at all except the officers' inadequacies, to the oblique packages that must contain some kind of message but which they had so far been unable to decipher. Every so often, Bella let out a little squeak of delight as Stone marked out the territory as they knew it: a mysterious attacker must have lain hidden in the shop as the reading group departed on Tuesday, killed Felicity in a vicious assault with an as-yet undiscernible motive, and was now evading justice. Someone else with insider knowledge of the crime was, potentially at least, trying to point the reading group in the direction of the murderer, for reasons unknown. But the identities of both these individuals were a closed book, to use an appropriate metaphor, and the clues that had been sent – if indeed they really were clues – seemed as opaque as the Perspex in the reading room's walls. There was, of course, the remote possibility that the killer and the package sender were one and the same person, but for the life of him Stone couldn't fathom any logical explanation for the murderer offering up clues to their own identity.

By midday, he had exhausted all the factual information he could muster.

He was still no nearer to a conclusion.

'You're just like that Lord Quaint,' said Bella as he finally sat back in his chair, his theories spent.

'Except that he comes up with a solution.'

'Oh, don't worry about that,' said Bella. 'The way you're tackling it, it won't be long before you can get everyone together in a room and point the finger at the killer.'

Stone smiled wanly. 'I don't think it works like that in real life.'

'Why not? It'd be just like *Delivery of Death,* with all the suspects lined up and the police hanging on your every word to solve their case for them.'

'There's one vital thing you've forgotten,' said Stone, leaning forward in his chair and lowering his voice.

'What's that?' asked Bella breathlessly.

'The bookshop doesn't have a milkman.'

Stone was enjoying the guffaw he'd drawn out of his guest when it was suddenly cut short by the doorbell.

Bella immediately looked contrite.

'Oh, I'm sorry, Professor. I didn't know you were expecting visitors.'

Stone was puzzled. 'I'm not,' he said, and went to the front door.

Paula Grayson was dressed more casually than she had been the previous day but there was no difference in her attitude.

'I don't take kindly to being ignored,' she said.

'What do you mean?' asked Stone. 'I haven't been ignoring you. We finished our conversation yesterday and that was that.'

'You might want to check your text messages,' she said, and pushed past him into the hall.

Stone hurried after her. The last thing he wanted was for her to run into Bella – that would create too many complications all round.

But Paula was already in the front room, staring at the mousy little creature in Aunt Edna's battered old chair with a look in her eye that would have put Bela Lugosi to shame.

'Er, Bella, this is Paula Grayson, an old colleague of mine.'

'Less of the "old", if you don't mind,' said Paula, not taking her eyes off Bella. 'And who are you?'

Bella stood up and held out a hand.

'I'm Bella Bourton. Pleased to meet you.'

Paula took the extended limb between a finger and thumb and held it at a distance as she looked back at Stone.

Her voice dripped with venom. 'Where did you find this one?'

'Paula—' Stone began.

'No, don't tell me. She's a mature student and you're treating her to some extracurricular tuition to bring her up to speed on the latest advances in mathematics.'

'Don't start,' said Stone, his mind racing for ways to get rid of Paula. Bella seemed lost for words in the face of this force of nature, a deer caught in the headlights of a particularly vindictive HGV driver with a craving for venison.

'Or is she another ex-colleague reacquainting herself with her old professor?'

She turned back to Bella and let go of her hand.

'You're not the first, you know, and you definitely won't be the last.'

'Paula, shut up!'

Stone had been unable to keep the anger out of his voice, and now the three of them stood surprised by it.

'I'm sorry about this, Bella. I told Paula yesterday that I couldn't help her with her little problem but she doesn't seem to be able to take no for an answer.'

Paula laughed a short, humourless laugh. 'Oh, the irony.'

Stone ignored her. 'And now she's leaving.'

Paula didn't move for a full five seconds, then turned on a sweet, superficial smile to face Bella, who smiled back in stunned reflection.

'It was lovely to meet you, Bella. I don't imagine our paths will cross again.'

She spun on the spot and marched for the door.

'You, on the other hand – *Professor* – will be seeing me again very soon, I'm sure. In case you'd forgotten, I'm at the Renaissance. I hope you're looking forward to it as much as I am.'

As the front door slammed, Stone found himself for once at a loss for words. How the hell was he going to explain all that to Bella?

Chapter Fourteen

There was a mustiness about the walls and high wooden shelves that made Harrison Fforde wonder how often the room was used. He had certainly never visited this part of the bookshop before, and it looked from the water damage to the ceiling and the peeling paint on the window frames that it was one of the lesser cared-for parts of the building.

He'd had to fight Maurice Stapleton to be allowed to access it. With The Quaint Bookshop's heavy disposition towards crime in all its fictional varieties, customers requesting visits to the section upstairs, in what used to serve as overspill galleries for chapel congregations, were rare and it was often closed completely. But Fforde, like the other trusted confidants Felicity had invited to join the reading group, knew what was hidden there: not exactly treasure, but an archive of old Norcester reference books and documents that the shop manager had rescued from a skip as the town's central library reinvented itself for the modern age by throwing out much of its past. Supplemented by back copies of the *Norcester Echo* and other sundry oddities, it was a trove that Felicity made available to academics, local historians and anyone else who might find it useful.

Such as detective fiction aficionados investigating a murder.

Now, having won over the stand-in manager with a mixture of flattery and vague threats, Fforde found himself alone in this rundown penthouse, surrounded by giant volumes of ancient documents, books of maps from centuries past and collections of records for subjects as varied as the Norcester Cricket Leagues (1951–54) and the town's annual eisteddfod, which had run for fifteen misguided years between the two world wars after a tuba player from the Valleys had decided the English shire counties were the perfect location for a transplanted version of his home country's cultural delights. Every year, for as long as Dafydd Jenkins had remained in his post as a conductor on the Norcester trams, he'd carved time out of his schedule to organise the week-long festival, cajoling and encouraging amateur musicians and performers to plumb their non-existent Welsh heritage in the name of art. It had all ended tragically in 1937 when an unattended candle had burned the sadly uninsured Jenkins bungalow to the ground and he'd decamped to his homeland in penury, taking his tuba with him. Astonishingly, nobody else stepped in to run the eisteddfod and it vanished into the mistiest of Welsh mists.

All this and more Fforde had discovered in his first half-hour in the reference section.

When he looked up from the gripping tale to discover from the clock on the wall that it was almost one-thirty, he dragged himself away from the tram timetables and turned his attention to the reason he was there.

The back copies of the *Echo* were stored on an accessible shelf near the door, conveniently placed next to an angled reading table, which would allow him to hoist the large bound volumes onto a surface where he could peruse them easily. He had been worried that he might have to scour every page of every edition of the paper, but fortunately for him, the bookshop had documented at least the last ten years' worth of papers by category, and cross-referenced them in an index system that was fully computerised. Maurice Stapleton had started to explain how it was a pilot project between the newspaper and the bookshop, funded by an obscure pot of money from a foundation devoted to media transparency and potentially to be replicated by independent bookshops across the country, but Fforde had lost interest quickly and manoeuvred the strange little man out of the room so he could get started. That was when the eisteddfod programmes had caught his eye and he'd given away the valuable time anyway.

Now he reckoned he had an hour or so to find what he was looking for before his stomach demanded he go out hunter-gathering. The computer terminal to the left-hand side of the door was reasonably easy to navigate and he used it to flick through the indexes, searching for references to Felicity Penman and The Quaint Bookshop.

He found a handful of articles relating to the shop, which he photographed on his phone for future exploration. For now, he was more interested in the manager herself. At home, his cursory search online had led him nowhere, although Lauren's brother Simon had made significantly more progress, according to the information Lauren had emailed Fforde that morning. Simon had tracked down her starting date at the shop, the address of the flat she rented in a converted paper mill half a mile from her work, and even a copy of her employment contract, along with the impressive CV she'd submitted to earn an interview for the post. Fforde had declined to pursue with Lauren the means by which her brother had managed to acquire all this information, but he was sure it couldn't be completely legal. The less Fforde knew about the details the better, he concluded, and if it came to it he could always deny he'd ever seen it. *An email from Lauren Sherwood, officer? With attachments? No, I never received that.*

Simon's research had been dynamite, with a side order of TNT.

He had already investigated the CV thoroughly – more thoroughly than the bookshop, in fact, since every role on it had proved to be fake. As a result, the computer whizzkid had uncovered a giant hole in Felicity's life before she came to Norcester, and everything Fforde thought he knew about her was suddenly in doubt. His knowledge of the bookshop manager and her past life was non-existent, and it threw him. Had he really known her at all? If she was prepared to rustle up a forged CV in order to land a moderately important role in the realms of Norcester's day-to-day routine, what else might she be capable of? And what of that previous existence, before her appearance at The Quaint Bookshop? Were there murky shadows that might be better left unexplored? Was she somehow involved in bigger, shadier things than the reading group had ever suspected? And had they led directly to her unpleasant demise?

Fforde had felt adrift at the bewildering questions that Simon's information had brought to the surface. But despite the colossal gap that had opened up in his understanding of

Felicity, nothing he had been able to find out so far had come anywhere near to plugging it.

Slippery, impossible to pin down, a mystery: just who was Felicity Penman anyway?

He had decided to explore Felicity's background on her home turf and caught the bus into town.

Now he discovered three pieces in the newspaper index catalogued with her name, and all were within the last eighteen months.

He found the relevant bound volumes and lifted them onto the reading table. He tracked down the earliest of the articles with ease, not least because it constituted a page lead accompanied by a large picture. In the image, Felicity was at the centre, surrounded by half a dozen other people, all in the traditionally corny local newspaper pose of a firing-squad straight line with their thumbs up and extended towards the camera. Someone on the picture desk staff clearly had a failure of imagination because as Fforde had flicked through the pages he'd spotted numerous other examples of the exact same pose.

The caption and story revealed that Felicity had arrived in Norcester as manager of The Quaint Bookshop and was to be welcomed by the town for her extensive experience and expert knowledge, gleaned from a past that was not specified in the article but was reported to be glowing and exemplary. She was even quoted as saying that she had always had a soft spot for Norcester, had relatives living there and was very much looking forward to leading the bookshop to a bright new future as a community hub and occasional arts venue.

Fforde doubted the relatives would be genuine – Felicity was proving a much trickier character than she'd fooled them into believing, complicating his feelings about her no end – but he made a note of them on his phone for future verification.

The second article, from around four months later, told of a special event hosted by the bookshop in which a famous author who had made her name as a panellist on television game shows was guest of honour at a mini literary festival, inaugurated by shop manager Felicity Penman and acclaimed for attracting such a luminary for a question-and-answer session with around two hundred interested readers.

In the most recent piece, dating back just six months, Felicity was more incidental. She was mentioned in a round-up of the top one hundred movers and shakers in the town, registering at number fifty-seven between the Norcester-born bassist of a punk band that had recently seen success in the Netherlands and a local architect whose design for a footbridge in Wisbech was creating a bit of a stir in structural engineering circles.

Fforde captured an image of each of the articles, even though he had serious doubts about their usefulness.

Then he phoned Lauren.

'You smell weird,' she said as Fforde walked past her into her hallway half an hour later.

'What do you mean, weird?' he asked.

Lauren sniffed.

'Like damp in a house.'

'That'll be the bookshop,' said Fforde. 'I've been in the reference section. I don't think anyone's been in there for weeks – maybe longer.'

'The reference section – why?'

'I've been trying to find out more about Felicity. Why and how she faked that CV.'

'Yes, odd, isn't it? She was clearly very good at her job, so why did she need to lie about it? How did you get on?'

'I didn't get very far.'

Lauren shepherded him into the living room, where Simon grunted at his laptop without looking up. 'My brother. Take no notice. So tell me more about what you've been up to in the reference section.'

She indicated a chair and Fforde sat obediently.

'I've been trawling through old copies of the *Norcester Echo* and she only appears in it three times, all of them recently.'

'And that's a surprise because…?'

'Well, apart from the fact that she's the fifty-seventh most important mover and shaker in Norcester, it means we still don't know anything about her. At least, not from before the beginning of last year.'

A shadow passed across Lauren's face. 'Another dead end, then. Simon's had the same.'

From behind her, the brother murmured something Fforde couldn't make out.

'If you've got something to say, share it with the whole room,' said Lauren tartly, and Fforde suddenly saw the teaching assistant in her. He could picture her in front of a class of eight-year-olds, commanding the room with that edge in her voice, and he decided he was glad he wasn't eight.

'I said, we're looking in the wrong place,' said Simon. 'Do you watch true crime documentaries, Mr Fforde?'

'Not if I can help it. There's more than enough misery right here in Norcester.'

'The thing is, the majority of murder victims are killed by someone they know.'

Fforde was surprised. 'Really?'

'I know – it's an incredible fact, isn't it?'

Fforde thought for a moment. 'Actually, no. Not when I think about the people I know.'

'I'll choose not to take that personally,' said Lauren.

'My point is,' Simon continued, 'if we knew more about the people around Felicity, we might be one step closer to finding her killer.'

'Brilliant, Miss Marple,' said Lauren. 'So get on with it.'

Fforde sighed. 'But there is nothing more to find out about her. You've reached a dead end online and I've uncovered everything the *Norcester Echo* has to tell us about our friendly neighbourhood bookshop manager. Aside from one mention of her having relatives here – which I don't believe for a moment – she's a blank page, if you'll pardon the pun.'

Simon's voice had a tone of determination in it now. 'That's just not possible. Not in this day and age. Nobody under about seventy-five can possibly exist without a digital footprint. It just can't be done. Even if you're not on Facebook or Instagram you leave traces of yourself everywhere. We have to be missing something.'

Fforde was working through the implications.

'Felicity was probably in her mid-thirties. But the only information about her dates from the last eighteen months. How can you go thirty years without appearing anywhere online? Unless…'

'Unless what?' asked Lauren.

'Unless she only started being Felicity Penman when she came to Norcester.'

Chapter Fifteen

Remus had pinned Fforde to his chair and Simon was uncharacteristically camped out in the kitchen, munching peanut butter sandwiches and dropping crumbs into his laptop, when Lauren spotted two figures striding in through the garden gate.

'Oh poo,' she said loudly, alarming Remus and prompting him to leap athletically from Fforde's lap to the floor, banging his head against a table leg in the process.

The cat pretended nothing had happened and strolled off with his nose in the air.

'What's up?'

'Visitors,' she said enigmatically, and hurried to the front door. She was unlocking it when the bell rang.

Under a battered umbrella held by the hapless DS Muir stood DCI Carlton, her make-up untroubled by the rain and her features set in a firm, mildly terrifying grimace of distaste. At least, it looked like distaste at first glance to Lauren. It could just as easily have been dyspepsia.

'Chief Inspector,' said Lauren, standing back to allow her visitors in. 'To what do I owe the pleasure?'

Her voice sounded much more casual than she felt: if she'd let her true emotions show, she'd have been warbling with a vibrato that would have inspired envy in Celine Dion.

'I doubt it's a pleasure, but ten out of ten for effort.'

Carlton marched through to the living room uninvited, leaving Lauren torn between following her to try to control where she sat or remaining where she was to supervise the sergeant's cack-handed attempts to fold up the umbrella without sending cascades of water all over the hall.

Rank won it.

When Lauren reached the living room, Carlton was already expressing surprise at finding Fforde there. Fortunately, that meant she was at the other end of the room from Lauren's computer and the paperwork lying beside it. Lauren wasn't worried about her frankly inconsequential notes on Felicity and her possible secret past, which were scribbled on a notepad alongside a transcript of the enigmatic Father Brown message. Fforde had suggested – and she'd agreed – that they keep the revelation of the fake CV to themselves for now at least, allow Simon to do his thing, then present a perfectly detected and documented theory to both their fellow group members and the police. For a moment she considered telling Carlton all about it right now, as the opportunity had so conveniently offered itself up in her own living room, but she held back as she wanted to know first why the chief inspector had paid her a call.

No, that was not the reason she wanted to maintain a distance between the officers and her desk. The thing that concerned her most was the printout of the latest chapter in her new work-in-progress, *The Book Bludgeoner*, which featured a decidedly frosty police officer and her dimwitted assistant vainly chasing a killer whose modus operandi involved beating his victims over the head with successive alphabetic volumes of the *Encyclopaedia Britannica*. So far, he'd reached *Conifer to Ear Diseases* with another fourteen to go, although nobody was quite sure how many of the eleven appendices he'd be looking to add to his roster.

Instead, the inspector sat in the large, cosy armchair that Lauren usually selected for herself, near the fireplace and with a good view of the front garden. Lauren opted for the chair by the window, hoping the presence of Fforde would help keep the officer's attention away from the computer.

Muir, however, turned out to be a law unto himself, ironically, and wandered aimlessly about the room with a notebook in one hand and pencil poised in the other. Lauren couldn't tell if he was recording their conversation or making a careful study of the premises, filing away vital information for later use. She had no idea what that use might be but his prowling made her even more uncomfortable than Carlton's steely eye.

'I won't have a drink, thanks for not asking,' said the inspector after surveying Lauren and Fforde for a long moment.

Lauren felt a pang of guilt for her omission but rejected it swiftly as she reminded herself that DCI Carlton's natural state appeared to be far ruder than she could ever be.

'How can I help?' she asked sweetly.

The inspector's reply was not what she was expecting. 'You can't. But I have some information that I think you'll be interested to hear. It's actually quite handy having Mr Fforde here as well – it saves me saying it twice.'

'Information?' repeated Lauren. She noticed Muir sidling towards the desk.

'Information.'

'And what information is that?' Fforde sounded genuinely interested, leaning forward in his chair, watching Carlton closely.

Muir had reached the desk now and was beginning to peer at the papers spread across it. Lauren badly wanted him to stop.

'Sergeant, if you don't mind, I'd prefer it if you didn't start rootling around in my private things, thank you.'

Carlton clicked her fingers irritatedly and Muir moved smartly away from the desk to park himself beside her armchair, where he looked for all the world like Herman Munster to Carlton's Lily.

'Now, listen to me,' said the senior officer. 'I'm under no obligation to tell you this, and there are people on the force who certainly wouldn't adopt the same course of action in my shoes. But I'm nothing if not empathetic.'

Lauren found herself biting her lip to stop herself responding. She wasn't one for making snap judgements, she hoped, but in the list of epithets she might hypothetically have compiled in relation to Miranda Carlton – whom she readily confessed she only knew by passing acquaintance and could therefore not make a reliable call on the subject – empathetic did not feature highly. Or at all, in fact.

The absence of both Romulus and Remus from the room served to confirm her assessment.

Cats know stuff.

The chief inspector went on, 'I realise Felicity Penman was very well-liked among the members of your book club.'

'Reading group,' murmured Fforde automatically. Carlton ignored him.

'And that's why I'm letting you know the latest development in our enquiry.'

Lauren's heart thumped a tiny bit faster. Had she misjudged the woman after all? Might she have to re-evaluate her in the light of this? Perhaps she wasn't entirely the chilly, officious robot she'd first seemed. And there was another thing: if Carlton was willing to take them into her confidence in this way, the implication was that not only had she ruled them out as possible suspects, but she might even be prepared to regard them as useful associates in the investigation. The imprimatur of the officer in charge of a murder case would add a supreme stamp of authority to their status. Did that make the reading group approved vigilantes? Like Batman to Carlton's Commissioner Gordon?

Of course, she didn't know what information the inspector was going to impart yet. But it must be important if she was making a house call to deliver it.

'We've had a significant breakthrough with your packages,' said Carlton.

Fforde leaned in a little further.

Carlton nodded at him as she spoke.

'You did well to use gloves when you gathered them all together.'

Lauren could see his mind perform a silent air-punch at the news.

'Forensics have found fingerprints on the books.'

Lauren had to give her credit: she could spin out a good tease.

'Well, don't keep us in suspense all day,' said Fforde. 'Do you know who they belong to?'

Lauren was keeping pace with his logic. If the police had an identity they could hang the fingerprints on, they must surely be one step away from nailing Felicity's killer.

'We do,' said the chief inspector. 'They belong to Felicity Penman.'

Lauren watched Fforde's expression mirror her own thoughts in real time. He moved from anticipation to bewilderment, taking minor detours via astonishment and disbelief, all in the space of half a second.

She was sure one of them was about to speak when there was a crash from the kitchen.

Instantly, Carlton was on high alert.

'Is there someone else here?'

Lauren's heart, thumping in time-and-a-half just a moment ago, came to an abrupt halt. She'd forgotten all about Simon, and his ham-fisted announcement of his presence in the house threatened to change everything. Already Carlton's demeanour had shifted from marginally warmer to deep permafrost.

'My brother's just popped in to say hello,' said Lauren. She knew it sounded pathetic. 'It's not against the law, is it?'

'No, Miss Sherwood, it's not against the law – as long as that's all it is. I seem to recall explicitly instructing you not to talk to anyone about the case.'

Lauren considered protesting her innocence, claiming that Simon's was a flying visit and they'd told him nothing about the investigation into Felicity's murder, but she knew that would be futile. It was bad enough that she and Fforde had been discovered sitting together in her living room with evidence of their digging around lying carelessly on the desk and floor. Under Carlton's strict interdiction, even that left them open to criticism.

Before she had a chance to reply, Simon appeared at the living room door.

To Lauren's amazement, DCI Carlton leaped to her feet.

'Bloody hell!' she exclaimed. 'Simon Sherwood.'

Simon interrupted the transit of his last morsel of peanut butter sandwich from his hand to his mouth and offered the inspector a broad grin. 'Inspector Carlton – what are you doing here?'

Carlton stared at Lauren. 'Simon Sherwood's your brother?'

Lauren was mystified. 'You didn't know?'

Carlton began busying herself, collecting Sergeant Muir and heading for the door. She turned back to find her subordinate blocking her view of the room. Pushing him brusquely to one side, she waved a warning finger at Lauren and Fforde in turn.

'What I told you before still applies.' She looked disdainfully at Simon. 'Especially to him. I've only told you about the fingerprints because it doesn't make any material difference to my enquiry whether you know or not. But as far as your little club is concerned, I have a strong suspicion that one or more of you is hiding something, and the presence of this toerag only makes me more suspicious of the lot of you. I don't know what the thing is that you're hiding, but somewhere in your little cabal of cosy crime there are secrets to be winkled out, and I'm the person who's going to do the winkling.'

Lauren tried to suppress the mental image that immediately popped up.

'You can't seriously suspect us, can you?'

Carlton looked down at the copy of *A Study in Scarlet* that was lying on the floor where Lauren had left it, then back at its owner.

'Big fan of our Sherlock, are you?'

Lauren nodded nervously, wondering where she was going with this.

'Thought as much. Bloody Conan Doyle. He was the first.'

'The first what?'

'The first writer to make out that coppers were just a useless bunch of jobsworths, and it took a genius amateur to really understand the criminal mind. But we've got our fair share of geniuses, haven't we, Sergeant Muir?'

Lauren looked at Muir, whose expression never flickered.

'So we'll be watching you closely. Got it? Now I'm sorry we can't stay to enjoy your company any longer but we have another house call to make. What's the name of that reporter, Muir?'

'Bailey, ma'am,' said the sergeant, tucking his pencil behind his ear.

'Nicki Bailey?' said Simon before Lauren could stop him.

Carlton turned slowly and stared at him suspiciously.

'And how do you know Nicki Bailey?'

Lauren couldn't believe Simon had fallen into the inspector's trap. Maybe not quite genius, but smart enough to catch him out.

'Er, her name's all over the *Echo*?' she offered tentatively, pointing at that day's edition on the coffee table.

Carlton was nodding again.

'If you say so, Miss Sherwood.'

As the officers went into the hall Lauren heard Muir open the umbrella, then watched through the front window as the pair marched to the gate and disappeared down the street.

It was only when they'd gone that she realised she'd forgotten to tell them about Felicity's CV.

'You didn't tell me she was on the case,' said Simon from behind her.

She turned back to the room. 'How was I to know you knew her?'

Fforde asked, 'How *do* you know her, incidentally?'

Simon looked a little sheepish. 'Let's just say our paths have crossed.'

'Professionally, you mean?' said Lauren.

Simon laughed. 'Well, I could hardly have dated her, could I? Although, thinking about it, she's not too shabby for an older woman.'

'Simon!' Lauren didn't know if she was more appalled at the casual sexism or the implication that her brother might fancy Miranda Carlton, who seemed to Lauren to be an impossibly distant and alien type of being.

'What? I'm just saying…'

'I daren't imagine what you're just saying. Besides, I thought you had the hots for Nicki Bailey.'

'Nicki Bailey?' said Fforde, the bewilderment returning to his face.

But the siblings were too engrossed in their habitual back-and-forth to notice.

'The hots – wow. Welcome to the nineteen-fifties, Daddy-o. You'll like it here with our hipsters and cool cats.'

Lauren lifted a cushion from the chair beside her and threw it at Simon.

'Shut up.'

He tossed it back and stared thoughtfully at the ceiling.

'You're right, though.'

'About what?'

'About me fancying Nicki Bailey.'

'I know I am. I've had to watch your animal impulses all your life, don't forget. Just don't go acting on it this time.'

Simon had an inane grin on his face.

'Sorry, sis. Might be a bit late for that.'

Chapter Sixteen

Bella Bourton was back at square one. The previous evening she had been unconvinced about the wisdom of the reading group pursuing their own investigation. All the arguments about the blinkers of DCI Carlton and the incompetence of her henchman had failed to persuade her either that they would have any more luck themselves, or that they should even risk trying their hand at solving Felicity Penman's murder. Harrison Fforde's corkboard notwithstanding, everything seemed to point to it being a terrible idea, and as she lay listening to Trevor snoring at five-thirty in the morning, she told herself that officers of the law were the correct people to be leading the enquiries, however much she might doubt their capabilities.

In the cold light of day, she'd found herself arguing the exact opposite, rerunning the other side of the debate in her head as she got on with the chores. Lauren had been influential, maybe because it was she who had extended the warmest welcome to the group, but also because her practicality could probably be counted on to bring a sensible perspective to the discussion. Despite seeming out of her depth, if Lauren thought it was a good idea to bypass the authorities, then maybe she had something.

But it had been the Professor's impeccable laying out of the facts of the case that morning which had been most compelling, and Bella had turned to his copy of *Criminal Law for Dummies* in an effort to prepare herself.

By four o'clock, though, she had put on her coat and was making her way through the wet streets to the central police station. She'd ploughed through the first three chapters of the book, found them exhausting, and decided to leave it to the professionals.

On reflection, she should have started with the Agatha Christie.

'I thought you should know that the reading group is also investigating Felicity's murder,' she told DCI Carlton nervously after being led to an interview room and supplied with a plastic cup of water.

The inspector sat opposite her with DS Muir inevitably at her side.

At their previous meeting two days earlier, Bella had been too preoccupied with the horror of her situation as a murder witness to take much notice of the senior officer and her sidekick. Now she studied them more closely, with the eye of a would-be competitor, and tried to weigh up the others' evaluation of them as an investigating team.

Miranda Carlton was making no secret of her opinion of the reading group. Although she had been pleasant enough to Bella at their last meeting, she had also made it plain that her view of the group's sleuthing abilities amounted to amused derision at best, outright contempt at worst. Privately, Bella feared this was a dangerously closed-minded attitude for a detective to entertain, let alone display freely, but that was a view she would never have expressed, to the reading group or anyone else.

She wondered what sort of hinterland Carlton occupied in her personal life – if indeed she had time for one, given the nature of her work. She found it hard to imagine a Mr Carlton traipsing round Tesco's with her on a Saturday morning, or hordes of little Carltons wiping snotty noses before being packed off to school. Much more likely was a stark but sleekly furnished apartment for one in one of those high-rise blocks that had gone up in the last few years to the south of the town centre, all steel and glass with no soul, and an existence that revolved exclusively around the job. And maybe a large glass of wine from a huge American fridge at the end of a shift.

Then again, she was prepared to be proved wrong: maybe the DCI's pockets were stuffed with germ-infested tissues as they spoke.

The sergeant gave off a very different vibe. That was the word, wasn't it? Vibe? He was just as scruffy as he had been when they first met on the night of Felicity's murder. Was it really only three days ago? His tie was askew, his top button undone and his lank hair looked like it hadn't seen a comb in days, possibly longer. He squinted at the notebook in front of him through a pair of thick spectacles, twitching his nose occasionally as they slid down it. She could picture him perhaps living with his ageing mother in the house he'd grown up in before flunking his exams and taking an entry-level job as a cadet with the local force because that seemed like a safer career than taking the King's shilling as a squaddie. Either way there were reasonable prospects and a decent pension; the police force probably offered fewer opportunities for violent death. As with his boss, Bella couldn't see him with a partner, but for very different reasons.

Bella tried to remember his first name. Jeremy? Jimmy? Geoffrey – that was it. She was impressed with her own powers of recollection and stored away the feeling for possible future use: remembering even the tiniest details could prove invaluable in an investigation like this.

'Ah, my mole on the inside,' said Carlton.

Bella couldn't tell if the inspector was being sarcastic but she bristled anyway, just in case.

'I'm not your mole,' she said defensively. 'I just thought you should know.'

Carlton gave a curt nod. 'Very public-spirited of you.'

'Not at all. It was just after what you said about withholding information, I didn't want you to think…'

'Much appreciated,' said Carlton, still nodding.

Bella suspected she might be mocking her.

She didn't like it.

Carlton stood up. She clearly considered the interview was over.

'Is that it? Because I'm a bit busy at the moment and I thought you had something important to tell me.'

'That was it,' said Bella. Really, somebody ought to teach the DCI a few manners when dealing with members of the public. It wasn't as if she was one of those villainous types Carlton could speak to in such a high-handed manner.

'Right, well I have to say I'm not overly concerned about the detective faculties of a book club.'

'Reading group,' said Bella, feeling suddenly sullen.

'Sorry?'

'We're a reading group, not a book club.' She'd heard Professor Stone say so, although she wasn't completely clear in her own mind about what the difference was. She made a mental note to ask him some time.

'All amounts to the same thing. A bunch of dabblers interfering with my investigation.'

Bella didn't hide her irritation at Carlton's cavalier attitude.

'There's a subtle difference between the two, actually.' She hoped Carlton wouldn't press her on it until she'd had that chat with the Professor. 'I should have thought that kind of detail was rather in your line, Inspector.'

Carlton stopped on her way out of the door, causing DS Muir to bump into her. She ignored him and turned back to lean across the table at Bella.

'If I were you, Mrs Bourton, I'd be inclined to leave the detective work to the professionals.'

'Actually, that's just what I told the others,' said Bella, holding her gaze in what felt to be an act of defiance.

'Oh good. At least somebody has a little sense. Mind you, I'd be surprised if they took much notice of you. Don't I remember you telling me you're the newest member?'

'That's right.'

'So not even an experienced bunch of amateurs,' muttered Carlton, and turned for the door.

As Sergeant Muir escorted her back to the front desk, Bella churned inside. On one hand, she knew DCI Carlton was quite right: what could a bunch of amateurs achieve compared to the resources and expertise of the Norcester Constabulary? On the other, there was much about Carlton's manner that rankled, and Bella could totally understand the desire of the other members of the reading group to solve this particular mystery in spite of the police investigation. The top priority had to be seeing justice done for Felicity, of course, by any means possible, but wouldn't it feel joyous to get one over on Chief Inspector Carlton in the process?

Bella glanced at DS Muir as they walked down a long, institutionally lit corridor with bare off-white walls and dark blue carpet tiles.

'Is she always like that?' she ventured.

Muir grunted.

'I'm not asking you to speak out of turn; it's just—'

Muir stopped and faced her. 'Look, Mrs Bourton, I know the boss can seem a bit, well, abrupt at times.'

'That's one way of putting it.'

'But she's got a lot on her plate. A murder enquiry is a massive deal, you know. There's tons of stuff goes on in the background that your average member of the public can't even imagine and she's got the whole force's eyes on her right now. Talk about stress. You should be honoured she even agreed to see you for five minutes this afternoon. Day three of a manhunt is about as stressful as it gets. So cut her a bit of slack, will you, and do as she asks: stay out of her way. You'll only be making it more difficult for everyone, and if you want to see someone in the dock for killing your friend, then you're best off letting us get on with our jobs. Understand?'

Bella understood. Muir's little soliloquy had given her plenty of food for thought – not to mention ammunition that the reading group should be taking seriously – and she boarded her bus with the sergeant's words playing over in her head.

Yes, she could 'cut some slack' to the DCI, as he'd put it; make allowances for her arrogance and disdain.

Yes, she could stay out of the way of the official investigation, and even do her best to persuade the others to do the same. It would be heartbreaking for all of them if their dabbling were to hinder – or, worse, destroy – the police's case against the perpetrator and Felicity's killer were somehow able to walk free.

And yes, she could begin to see things from the DCI's point of view, especially since, now she came to think of it, the officer had actually been rather complimentary towards her. *A little sense,* she'd said. *Very public-spirited.* And while she stopped short of thinking of herself as the inspector's mole, she certainly felt that she had, perhaps, a foot in both camps.

It was all for Felicity, after all.

The streets of central Norcester meandered past the window, spattered by a continuing drizzle that distorted the view and romanticised it with something approaching a soft filter. With her eyes defocused, Bella drifted off into a memory. The first time she'd met Felicity had been about six weeks earlier, when she'd carried a couple of romantasy novels to the counter at the bookshop and asked if she could sign up for the newsletter. A pleasant conversation about books had followed, with Felicity wrapping it up by introducing herself and inviting Bella to seek her out if she ever needed any bibliographical advice. Once a week since then, Bella had made a point of doing exactly that – not because she needed any particular help, but because the manager was so approachable, so friendly, so warm. All things Bella was in dire shortage of at home. Each week's chat had grown a little longer, the manager's questions a tad more searching and personal and

Bella's willingness to answer them more free and relaxed. By the time Felicity came to suggest she might enjoy the weekly Tuesday get-together of a few like-minded folk, Bella was ripe for agreeing.

But now Felicity was dead.

And the reading group was all Bella had left to remind her of Felicity: a random collection of readers with a nominal interest in murder mysteries.

Random.

Or was it?

As the bus jolted to a halt at her stop, Bella's vision came back into sharp focus and she was struck by a thought that shocked her with its thrilling potential.

Perhaps the reading group of The Quaint Bookshop was not, as she had supposed, a chance gathering of happy fiction-lovers. Perhaps they had been *assembled*.

As she scurried towards her front door, Bella's mind was teeming with competing recollections. She couldn't remember if any of the others had told her how they became involved with the reading group. She knew that in her case the invitation had come directly from Felicity and she badly wanted to know if the same had been true for the others. If so, then it seemed pretty clear that Felicity had cultivated the group. And if that were true, then the alarming possibility arose that Felicity Penman, charming and intelligent bookshop manager, had put together a team of people specifically designed to solve a mystery.

And that threw up a further tantalising, yet upsettingly awkward, question.

Had Felicity known she was going to die?

Bella slipped the key into the lock and let herself into the dark house. She had no idea what qualities Felicity had seen in her that might inspire the manager to include her in such an enterprise. But clearly Felicity felt she could trust her as a vital piece in the jigsaw, and even if Bella couldn't quite put her finger on what the overall image might look like, she knew she couldn't let Felicity down.

She'd summon up all the defiance she'd felt staring down DCI Carlton an hour before. She'd use the enthusiasm of the rest of the group to fire her courage in this grim new adventure. She'd take whatever quality Felicity had seen in her and stand squarely behind it to help solve the poor girl's murder and bring her killer to justice.

She would play a crucial role in the drama that was about to unfold.

Bella had reached her valiant conclusion even before the door clicked shut behind her.

She'd reckoned without Trevor.

Chapter Seventeen

It was already nearing five o'clock when Lauren reached the offices of the *Norcester Echo*. After Simon's revelation that he'd been in contact with the reporter again, she'd debated with herself about what the proper course of action should be under these circumstances. While Simon was his own man and perfectly entitled to sow his oats wherever he chose, this particular ploughed field was not a fallow one: the thought of him spending time with a newspaper journalist who had already proved she was salivating at the prospect of nailing down Lauren's story left her with a tangible and decidedly unpleasant lump in her gullet. In the interests of damage limitation, she couldn't let it go unaddressed.

In the end, she'd screwed her courage to the sticking place – wherever the hell that was, Lady Macbeth? – and made the trip into town.

'I'd like to speak to Nicki Bailey, please,' she announced to the receptionist in her bravest voice.

The woman looked up from her computer screen, boredom etched into every pore.

'Is she expecting you?'

Lauren winced internally at her thick Norcester accent, contorting the vowels into a nasal, sub-Brummie drawl.

'No, but I think she'll want to see me.'

'Everyone says that,' she replied, turning back to her screen and tapping the keyboard with fingers which, Lauren now saw, were extended by at least an inch and a half with huge, clawlike nails painted several hideous shades of green and pink and adorned with sparkling diamanté ornamentation. How on earth was she able to type, she wondered.

'No, I really think she'll want to see me,' Lauren persisted.

The receptionist sighed, stopped tapping and looked up at her again.

'Convince me,' she said.

Lauren decided the *Norcester Echo* could really do with some people-skills training for its front-of-house staff, but now was hardly the time to suggest it.

'It's about the murder at The Quaint Bookshop the other night. I was there.'

The woman gave her a look which made Lauren wonder if she'd completely misinterpreted her meaning: had she come in to confess to being the killer?

'I mean, I'm a witness,' she said hurriedly.

The look of horror passed swiftly from the woman's face and she almost smiled at Lauren.

'Oh, I see. Well, wait there a minute.'

Lauren had expected her to pick up the phone that lay on the counter beside her computer keyboard, but instead she made for a door in the wall behind her and disappeared through it. Lauren caught a glimpse of an open-plan field of desks, mostly unoccupied, then the door swung closed.

Five minutes later she was back, gesturing at Lauren to move to the end of the counter, where she lifted up a hinged section and allowed her through. She led her into the back office, which was much noisier than Lauren had anticipated, and towards a door in the far wall. Through this one, she found herself in another room, crammed tightly with a dozen or so desks arranged in a horseshoe shape around a central hub, the back wall painted bright red and partitioned off into a bank of glass-panelled offices. One side wall was emblazoned with a giant *Norcester Echo* masthead, the paper's promotional legend inscribed underneath: *Serious about news.* On the opposite side, in letters printed out singly on sheets of A4 paper, was sellotaped the word 'Editorial'.

From the centre office, a rotund man of about fifty emerged, a printout of a newspaper page in one hand and a large marker pen in the other. He headed straight for the hub of desks, where two men and a woman were poring over more printouts, and tossed his page down in front of them. As it landed, he trapped it with the marker pen and scored a thick black line across the middle of it.

'Hate that headline,' he announced to nobody in particular, and began walking away.

'What do you want, J?' called one of the men. 'Something lighter?'

'Something better,' he said, and disappeared into the office.

The receptionist tapped Lauren on the shoulder and pointed for her to follow.

'Nicki's not here at the moment but the editor's expecting you.'

As the clawed woman departed through the door they'd entered by, Lauren stood speechless. Her second thoughts were actually her fourth thoughts, but it was pretty much the same ones coming round again so she gave herself the benefit of the doubt. She'd used the murder as an excuse to speak to Nicki but the ruse had bitten back and now she was faced with the might of the *Echo*'s editor and nothing to say to him. Quite the opposite, in fact: he was the last person she wanted to talk to, about Felicity or anything else for that matter. In the inner sanctum of the journalists of the *Norcester Echo*, she felt wildly intimidated. What had she been thinking?

She was fast reaching the conclusion that she would just edge quietly from the room when the editor's voice boomed across at her.

'Are you the murder woman?'

All eyes turned to Lauren. There was no escape.

'Come on in. Don't be shy – we don't bite. Well, not often, anyway.'

A few half-hearted laughs went up from the troops and Lauren forced a smile to her lips.

The editor indicated a path she could negotiate to reach him, and she began picking her way through the piles of stacked newspapers, overflowing bins and general detritus of the office.

'Jerry Northover,' the editor said, holding out a hand as Lauren approached.

She shook it, noting a disconcerting dampness to the palm, and found herself being subtly guided inside.

The pillar-box paint on the rear wall of the editor's office was enough to induce a migraine, while down one side of the room ran a set of shelves that were mostly empty, except for a handful of journalism books and two or three heavy-looking trophies. Lauren noticed the words 'Press Gazette' engraved on one of the larger slabs of glass and mentally conceded that if she had ever won an award for excellence in assisting teachers, she'd have had it ostentatiously on display as well.

Northover pointed to an array of chairs surrounding a large table in the centre of the room, and Lauren sat at one of them. The editor moved round to the far side of the desk that spurred off the table at a T and deposited himself heavily in the large, padded seat behind it.

'You're looking for Nicki Bailey, aren't you?' he said without preamble.

Lauren nodded, still struggling to locate the voice that seemed to have scurried away down her oesophagus and was currently in hiding somewhere beneath her rib cage.

'I'm Lauren Sherwood. She came to see me this morning.'

The man's expression changed. Lauren couldn't tell what the new one meant.

'Sherwood? This is about the bookshop murder, isn't it?'

Lauren felt she could hardly admit to Nicki's editor that the real reason she was there was to tear a strip off the reporter for manipulating her brother's weakness for a pretty face.

'That's right,' she said.

'Well, look, you've made the journey to get here – we can't let you go without speaking to someone. As it happens, I'm about to knock off for the evening. Let me take you for a drink.'

Lauren certainly hadn't expected that. She was just about to turn down his offer in as sensitive a way as she could muster when he stood up suddenly, lifted a jacket from the back of his chair and thrust his arms into it in one practised movement, and made for the door.

'Look, Mr Northover—' she began.

'It's Jerry. We don't go in for the formalities these days.'

'Jerry, then. Listen, I don't want to take up your valuable time.'

'Not at all. I'd love to sit down with you and hear your story. So far we've only had that actor chappie's version, and after all the flak we've had from the cops I'm starting to wonder if it wasn't more trouble than it was worth. Exclusives are much-coveted things but they can come back to haunt you if you're not careful.'

Lauren felt an uneasy churning sensation in her chest. 'I don't want to talk about the murder,' she said, hesitating as Northover edged her towards the door.

'Really? Then why are you here?'

It was a good question, and one that Lauren didn't feel able to answer. Not honestly, at least.

'I just wanted to have a quiet word with Nicki.'

Northover pushed open the door and planted a hand on her back to guide her out.

'Why don't we talk about it over that drink? There's a lovely new bar in the Renaissance Hotel and they make a cracking cocktail. As the saying goes, it's five o'clock somewhere, and by happy coincidence, that somewhere happens to be right here.'

Which is how Lauren Sherwood found herself, piña colada in hand, discussing the death of Felicity Penman in the Serendipity Bar of the Renaissance Hotel with the editor of the *Norcester Echo*.

She had established, before they even sat down at a table looking out at the river, that their conversation would be off the record. At least, she was fairly sure that she had.

'Let's see what you've got to say for yourself and then we can work all that out,' Northover had said, hurrying on to ask what she'd like to drink before strolling over to the bar and launching into a very amicable-looking conversation with the barman.

That meant it was off the record. Didn't it?

Anyway, she concluded, there could be real advantages to talking to someone like Jerry Northover. He was the man in charge, which meant he would make the ultimate decisions about which stories were covered by the paper, and how. Given his position of authority – not to mention status in the community – he would be much less likely than a fresh young reporter to do anything irresponsible. Yes, there were definite positives to chatting to Jerry Northover, especially if he was paying for the cocktails.

And, with his experience ferreting out stories and information, he might even be able to help the reading group's investigation.

'So, what time did you say you all left the building?' asked Northover, his phone out on the table between them, recording the conversation 'just to be on the safe side', he'd said.

Lauren hadn't believed a word of it.

'A little after nine. And it was only a couple of minutes after that that we heard Felicity scream.'

'Must have been terrifying. Or horrific? Or chilling? What word would you use, exactly, Lauren?'

'I didn't really think about it at the time.'

'OK, but now – what word would you use?'

'I don't know. Yes, chilling is probably good.'

'Chilling. Great.'

Lauren looked across at the *Echo*'s editor, flabby around the jowls and ruddy in the broken veins of his cheeks. Close up, she put him at mid-fifties, maybe a little older, and definitely divorced, probably with a drink problem; the stereotype of a hardened newspaper hack. He was weathered and wily and there was something steely in his eyes that left her feeling slightly queasy. She hadn't fallen for the phone recording thing for a second: she knew she was being set up.

But two could play at that game.

'So if it was your investigation into the murder, how would you go about it?'

Northover put down the incongruous martini glass he was holding and seemed to size her up. Was he deciding whether to open up to her, or simply working out how to get the next meaty quote?

'Well, in a way we are investigating the murder. It's just that we don't have the resources – or the authority – of the Norcester Constabulary at our disposal, so we have to make use of the sources we can reach. Which right now is you, Lauren. I take it the police have questioned you?'

'Oh yes, extensively,' said Lauren, remembering the drab twenty minutes she'd spent with DCI Carlton and DS Muir trying to recall every detail of Tuesday night, from the merits of Lord Quaint's *dénouement* to the moment she'd screamed down Professor Stone's phone at the 999 dispatcher that something terrible had happened inside The Quaint Bookshop and they needed to send help.

'And what about your colleagues in the reading group, Harrison Fforde and the others?'

'Yes, they were interviewed too. I think Harrison was first, then Bella.'

'Bella? I don't know about Bella. What's her surname?'

Clearly Nicki Bailey hadn't communicated everything to her editor.

'Bourton. She's our newest recruit. Lovely, but a little shy.'

'And Professor Stone?'

So he knew about the Professor. She was certain that she hadn't mentioned him by name. Maybe Harrison had, although she couldn't recall seeing it in the *Echo*'s story, when Harrison had given them such an overblown account of what had happened.

'Do you know him?'

Was that a hesitation? Had the editor let something slip that he hadn't intended to?

'No, I don't know him personally. But his name cropped up once or twice when I was news editor of the *Pittingham Times*. He used to work at the university there.'

'Oh, right,' said Lauren, filing the information away as mildly interesting but not especially useful. It was hardly a glaring coincidence that the two men should have been employed in the same nearby town before moving to the metropolitan hub that was Norcester.

'Were you in Pittingham long?' she asked after a moment.

'About two years.'

Lauren was surprised and said so.

'You don't stick around in one place for too long if you want to climb the greasy pole in journalism,' he explained.

'Really? I'd have thought once you were in a comfortable job on a comfortable salary you might be tempted to put down some roots.'

Northover laughed. 'Comfortable salary? This is regional newspapers we're talking about. There's no such thing as a comfortable salary. No, if you want to get on, you have to get out. Unlike professors.'

Lauren studied the editor over the rim of her glass. Was that a look of resentment lurking behind the strong blue eyes? Was he jealous of Professor Stone?

'What did you hear about him?' she asked eventually.

'He had something of a reputation in certain circles,' Northover went on.

That was more interesting. 'What circles are those?'

'Oh, you know – academic, social, that kind of thing.'

Lauren had serious doubts that Jerry Northover moved in the same circles as Professor Stone. One of them was suave and sophisticated; the other was a journalist. Then again, the editor of the town's newspaper was sure to have plenty of podgy fingers in lots of different pies, and she could well imagine his path crossing everyone's from mayoralty to the mafia. On reflection, it was quite likely that Stone's name had come up somewhere on Northover's radar.

'And what have you heard?'

Northover smiled indulgently and picked up his drink. He toyed with the stick that held an olive, swishing it about in the almost colourless liquid as he studied Lauren.

'I'm not sure who's interviewing who here.'

'I always thought it was "whom",' said Lauren primly. She was rather enjoying teasing him.

'Quite right in correct grammatical English,' said Northover, not missing a beat. 'But in colloquial conversation, I think you'll find most people perfectly willing to accept the absence of the accusative case in a sentence such as that.'

Teasing only worked if you could spar with your opposite number on equal terms, Lauren realised. The arrival of the accusative case took the discussion into a realm where she couldn't compete.

She cut her losses.

'I'll take your word for it. Now, you were telling me about Professor Stone.'

The smile vanished from Northover's face and he put down his drink again.

'This may sound a strange question, Lauren, but how well do you know him?'

Lauren was rather taken aback. Was the editor implying something untoward about their relationship?

'I don't know what you mean,' she said.

'All right, let me put it like this. There are certain things in Professor Stone's background that might lead an upright member of the community to think twice about spending too many of their leisure hours in his company.'

'What things?' Lauren was vaguely appalled but didn't quite understand why.

'Well, that's where it gets a bit murky,' said Northover. 'The libel laws of England and Wales being what they are, I can't really go into too much detail.'

Lauren was not sufficiently acquainted with libel laws to be able to respond with any degree of authority. And she had no idea what Wales had to do with it.

'Can you give me a clue?'

'Let's just say that Professor Stone's record in the world of academia is not completely untarnished.'

'What do you mean? Has his research been questioned? Were his methods unsound?'

Northover held her gaze for a moment.

'Nothing as lofty as that,' he said eventually. 'More things of a personal nature.'

He stopped, clearly unwilling to volunteer any further information.

'You can't leave me hanging with that,' said Lauren, aware that her voice had risen in pitch by several semitones. She hoped she didn't sound over-eager.

'My point is, maybe you don't know your book club colleague as well as you thought you did. Now, I understand that one's past may not be something you blurt out among relative strangers in a bookshop, especially elements of the fruitier variety, but it does seem to me that the Professor has kept certain things about himself hidden from the rest of you.'

Lauren sat in silence as she turned over the news she'd just received. She wasn't entirely sure what Northover was getting at, with his unsubtle hints at private indiscretions from Stone's past, but it couldn't be good if even the mention of them in a conversation over cocktails had the potential to land the editor with a libel suit. Lauren's knowledge of the legalities of defamation may have been as flimsy as her knowledge of IT but she didn't need a Masters in Slander to be worried about what she was hearing.

And then the Big Thought struck her.

When it did, it rendered all of her other thoughts about Professor Stone and his possible secret past puny and insignificant. In the way that fertile minds occasionally do, hers had catalogued in a fleeting moment every possible transgression from exam cheating to thumping a truculent student, taking in a diversion to a cul-de-sac of sexual impropriety along the way. All were swept aside in an instant.

None had the thrilling horror of the Big Thought.

'Are you saying Professor Stone had something to do with Felicity's murder?'

Northover's eyes didn't move from hers as he reached forward, picked up the olive and slowly took it from the stick with his teeth.

'But he couldn't have. He was with the rest of us when Felicity was attacked.'

Northover raised a single eyebrow and munched on his olive.

Lauren glazed over as she cast her mind back to Tuesday night; waving goodnight to Felicity, hearing the bolts being shot home, standing outside the bookshop chatting to Bella for a few moments after Fforde and the Professor…

And then she remembered, clear as the martini in front of Jerry Northover: the Professor had left them at least two minutes earlier, departing up the alleyway next to the shop, where a side entrance allowed ramp access to those who couldn't manage the front steps.

Was that enough time to go back inside?

And if so, what did he do in there?

Like a mouse dropping in a bowl of French onion soup, a memory surfaced of something the Professor had said in the minutes following the attack, when they'd been herded into the reading room and were waiting to be seen by DCI Carlton.

Something about getting their story straight.

Before she could come to any conclusion about exactly what he'd meant – let alone share her fears with the editor of the *Echo* – the object of her thoughts appeared in the flesh. With timing that would have prompted envy in Harrison Fforde, Professor Stone made his entrance through the revolving doors of the Renaissance Hotel, a brown scarf concealing much of his face, crossed the foyer in plain sight of the Serendipity Bar and breezed past the concierge towards the lifts in the far wall.

Even Jerry Northover had the grace to look surprised.

Chapter Eighteen

At least the rain had stopped. That was something.

Stone realised his desperation to find something positive about this visit had led him inexorably to the tediously British subject of the weather, but he couldn't for the life of him come up with anything better. He certainly hadn't trudged the streets of Norcester, his scratchy brown scarf wrapped tightly round his chin, for his own amusement. It had taken him six hours of wrangling to reach the conclusion that he had no choice.

Of course, empirically and philosophically speaking, he had a choice. No one was holding a gun to his head, and even if they were he still technically would have had a choice, however unappealing the options might be. There was always a choice.

Except that, in this instance, he really didn't have a choice.

'Good evening, sir,' said the man at the concierge desk as Stone marched past on his way to the hotel lifts at the back of the lobby.

Stone attempted a Cockney accent.

'Wotcher, mate,' he muttered from behind the scarf, burying his nose into the fabric along with his chin. He'd already failed dismally in his bid not to be seen; the last thing he wanted was to be recognised.

He had visited this hotel on numerous occasions – the ground-floor Serendipity Bar, with its expansive views over the river, had a particularly fine selection of malt whiskies – so it had added substantially to his annoyance that his current mission required him to jeopardise one of his favoured drinking spots.

'I'm glad you finally decided to see sense,' said Paula, blocking his entrance at the door of her room.

Stone's edginess rose a notch. Paula was dressed in a thigh-length silk nightie in pale blue, all cleavage and legs, with a diaphanous white robe draped over the top. He supposed that was intended as a superficial nod to decorum, but if so, decorum had ignored the gesture and left the building.

'It's barely six o'clock,' he said, brushing past her into the luxurious room. 'Put some clothes on.'

He noted that an ice bucket stood on a low table near the window, the lipped neck of a champagne bottle revealing that it was already open and chilling. Two flutes flanked the bucket, one drained almost to the bottom, the other so far unused.

'I'm not stopping,' he said, pointing at the glasses.

Paula allowed the door's weighted mechanism to swing it softly shut behind her as she took two paces into the room.

'That's a bit presumptuous, isn't it? What makes you think it's for you?'

Stone sighed. Still those childish games that had left them

in such limbo the last time they'd tried to establish any kind of relationship.

'I'm only here to sign a piece of paper.'

Paula moved over to the bed and sat on the crisp white linen where it had been turned down. She patted the dark red faux fur runner beside her and offered Stone what he took to be an alluring smile.

'Why are you in such a hurry?' she purred. 'At least have a drink with me.'

Against all his instincts, Stone sat. In a chair by the window. He glanced outside, where the strings of lights decorating trees in the park opposite twinkled their reflections into the water below him.

'How long are you here for?' he said, not really wanting to make conversation.

'A couple of weeks, maybe more. I've been doing a little sightseeing and now I've got a few things to sort out.'

'Mixing business with pleasure.'

'Nothing changes,' she said, and stood up.

Stone watched her pour two full glasses of champagne. As she handed one to him, he asked, 'Where is it then?'

'Where's what?'

'The paperwork.'

'Oh, relax, will you?' she said, waving a dismissive hand in his direction before tipping a sizeable draught of fizz into her mouth. She let it rest there before swallowing. Stone spotted the ploy, but then he was meant to.

He put his glass down on the table, the bubbles untasted.

'Not like you to pass up a drink,' she said.

'Well, maybe some things do change,' he said. 'Now, I'd like to get this over and done with, if you don't mind.'

Professor Stone's approach to references had always been pragmatic, largely dependent on the likelihood of ever needing something in return from the subject of the recommendation. He justified the cynicism required for such an enterprise by convincing himself that everybody knew and understood the rules of the game, and nobody ever requested a reference except for form's sake. The contents were generally anodyne, and the more functional he could make them, the happier he was. Of course, if he could find a way of refusing the request in the first place, that was even better.

In this instance, he could see no way of avoiding it. Paula had him over a barrel.

Oh, sod it. Call it what it is, he thought.

It's blackmail.

Paula went back to the bed, this time to the side nearest Stone, and sat down again. She crossed her legs, allowing the robe to fall either side of the impeccably shaped limbs that Stone remembered so well, even from his brief acquaintance with them.

He remembered how they looked when she first unveiled them to him.

He remembered how they felt wrapped round him.

But no – he must resist. It was bad enough that her knowledge of his Pittingham secrets meant she could lean on him to provide her with a reference. With further leverage of the sexual variety, she would have a field day, even if there was no longer a field to have a day in. He might have left the world of academia, but Stone was too careful of his reputation, especially in a town where he had built himself a nice, quiet retirement with the respect and admiration of a couple of clubs devoted to social activities in which his title and bearing afforded him the kind of status he revelled in.

He wasn't about to give that up for a five-minute fumble in a blackmailer's boudoir.

'I'd like to ask you something first,' she said, leaning forward provocatively.

Stone sighed again.

'That woman who was at your house this morning…'

'Bella?'

'Bella, yes. Tell me all about Bella.'

Stone shrugged. He supposed he shouldn't have been surprised at Paula's line of questioning, but it was clear she hadn't been interested in listening earlier on, so why was she interested now?

'There's nothing to tell. As I tried to explain, she's just another member of the reading group I go to at a bookshop.'

'Just? How belittling.'

'I was introduced to her for the first time less than a fortnight ago and I've met her less than half a dozen times since.'

'Nothing you want to confess, then? No little peccadilloes to report to your old friend?'

Paula took another gulp of her drink.

'Nothing at all. In fact, if you want to know the truth, I haven't been with anyone since we broke up.'

A weight deadened inside Stone as he spoke. While it was perfectly true, it was not something he'd intended to reveal to Paula. Evidently she still had the craft to get him to do things he didn't want to do.

Well of course she did. That was why he was here, wasn't it?

Paula feigned surprise.

'Goodness! The renowned Professor Stone unable to find himself a mate. There's something I never imagined possible. Or perhaps I've spoiled you for womankind. Maybe after me it's just not worth going to bed with anyone else.'

Stone pursed his lips at her. 'Given our rather unfortunate experience when we attempted what I shall magnanimously call sex but everyone else in the world would doubtless class as an utter failure, I think you know exactly what my response to that suggestion is.'

He reached for his glass and emptied it down his throat in one violent movement.

'Yes, well,' she said. 'You are familiar with the concept of karma, I believe?'

'It takes two to tango. Or not, in this case,' said Stone uncharitably.

Paula fell silent.

Stone leaned across to pick up the bottle and poured himself another drink.

'How is retirement suiting you?' she asked eventually.

Stone looked back from the view of the river that he'd been staring at. The lights were mesmerising.

'You don't really want to know.'

'Don't I? It sounds positively thrilling, as far as I can make out. The usual Stone chaos following you about wherever you go.'

He stared at her, trying to work out what she was playing at now.

'What on earth are you talking about?'

She ran a teasing finger around the rim of her glass and kept her eyes averted from his.

'Murder is in a different league from what you used to get up to, I'll give you that.'

Stone felt a lump rise in his gullet. He tried to keep his voice even.

'I repeat, what on earth are you talking about?'

'I'm talking about your little bookstore friend. Felicity Penman. Such a sad story.'

'You think I—? Don't be ridiculous.'

Paula looked at him, alarm suddenly etched onto her face.

'No, of course not! That's not what I meant at all.'

'Then what?'

'I just meant that you seem to have got embroiled in a murder case, that's all. Of course I don't think you did it. What do you take me for?'

Stone felt it wisest not to answer that particular question. He put down his glass and stood up.

'Paula, why do you play these games? All you do is wind people up.'

'I'm sorry,' she said, and he thought she might actually mean it.

'Anyway, what could you possibly know about Felicity's murder?'

'I read about it in the local paper – the *Echo*, is it?'

Stone snorted his contempt. 'Don't believe what you read in that rag,' he said with feeling.

'It only caught my eye because of her – the victim.'

Stone was wary again. 'What about her?'

'Well, you know.'

'No, I don't. That's why I'm asking.'

'You know, the fact that we both knew her.'

The bombshell hit Stone with considerable force. He'd only

known Felicity since coming to Norcester, and Paula had only been in town for a few days; for all he knew, it was quite possible she had not even arrived until after the bookshop manager met her unfortunate demise several days earlier.

How could she possibly have known Felicity?

'What do you mean, we both knew her?'

Paula looked confused. 'The girl. Her name didn't ring any bells but as soon as I saw her photograph in the paper I realised who she was at once.'

The cogs started turning in Stone's mind, but it quickly became apparent to him that they hadn't been properly oiled.

What did Paula know that he didn't?

'And who was she?'

'A student at our old university.'

'She was? How do you know? I certainly didn't teach her.'

'Neither did I, but do you remember the girl who got thrown out for dealing drugs to research fellows from the junior common room?'

Stone screwed up his face as he tried to recall the incident. It had been a number of years but Paula's description was raising a faint memory at the back of his mind. He tried to drag it forwards but it clung on annoyingly.

'That wasn't Felicity, though? I'm sure I'd remember her if that were the case.'

Paula shook her head. 'No, it wasn't her. But Felicity was her best friend. For a while it looked as though she might be found guilty by association and thrown out as well, but she managed to persuade the Dean that she knew nothing about it, and she was allowed to finish her degree.'

Stone wasn't surprised he hadn't remembered her. Professors could see hundreds of students every year, and only the truly outstanding or miserably awful tended to stick in the mind. And if she hadn't even been in the Maths department, then the chances of his recalling her were next to zero, no matter how badly she or her friends had behaved.

Probability and all that.

'If it really was Felicity, I'm sure she was telling the truth. The girl I knew wouldn't have been involved in anything like that.'

'Oh, it was her all right.'

'How can you be so sure?'

'I ran into her the other day.'

The news came as a shock. 'But I thought you said you only arrived in Norcester recently.'

'Monday,' said Paula. 'I walked past her outside the bookshop, on my way here from the station. She recognised me for some reason – we had quite a little reminiscence together. It must have been the day before she was killed.'

If Felicity's murder was a puzzle, then several new pieces had been unexpectedly thrown onto the pile that was mounting in Stone's brain. But they were blurred and fuzzy and he couldn't make them out at all, let alone see how they might fit into the overall picture.

He needed time to think. Time away from Paula Grayson.

Stone turned towards the door.

'Where are you going?'

'Home,' he said, furrowing his brow.

'Hang on a minute. We've still got unfinished business.'

He stopped and looked at her. 'Show me it, then. Where do I sign?'

Paula stood up and slinked over to him, resting one hand

on his shoulder and weaving the fingers of the other across his chest.

'I thought you might like to write it yourself – in your own words. A handwritten reference these days is so much more unusual. Adds a certain old-school credibility, I think.'

He grasped her fingers and removed them from his chest.

'Fine. I'll let you know when it's ready.'

Paula peered at him from under long, dark eyelashes. Without taking her eyes off him for a moment, she shrugged off the robe and let a stringy strap of the nightie fall off one shoulder.

'I'm really incredibly grateful, you know,' she said, purring again.

Chapter Nineteen

Trevor had railed at her for almost two hours, barely pausing to draw breath. To begin with, Bella had been frightened. Now she was bored.

'Where have you been?'

He'd been waiting for her in the hall, red-faced and glowering. All Bella's musings about Felicity assembling the group, knowing she was going to die and trying to point them towards the solution to the mystery, vanished like optimism on her wedding day.

'I had to pop out,' she said, scrabbling for an explanation. She couldn't very well tell him she'd been talking to the police. For the second time in two days.

'I ran out of onions.'

'Really?' he said, his voice wavering as if he were trying to control his temper. 'So where are they?'

'Where are what?'

'The onions you popped out for.'

She stared at him inscrutably.

'They didn't have any.'

'Oh, right.'

She could tell he didn't believe her. She was about to attempt a change of subject when Trevor dropped his bombshell.

'This is what happens when you join a book club,' he said sneeringly.

So he'd found out. She didn't know how, but she suddenly realised she didn't care. Bolstered by the same irritation that DCI Carlton had triggered before DS Muir had softened her stance, she stood her ground.

'It's not a book club, it's a—'

'I don't care what it is,' shouted Trevor. 'It's the principle that matters. You've been going behind my back and lying to me about it. After nineteen years of marriage, this is the thanks I get.'

Bella couldn't stifle a relieved chuckle. Was that all he was worked up about? She remembered that she'd dreaded him finding out, with all the arguments and recriminations that would doubtless follow. But now that he knew, it felt much less significant than she'd feared.

'Don't laugh at me!' he thundered, and Bella stopped instantly.

'I'm not laughing at you, Trev, it's just that you're taking this far too seriously. It's not like I'm having an affair.'

How could he be feeling so affronted by the thought of her going out to meet a few like-minded people for a harmless discussion about books? Surely that wasn't enough to prompt this over-the-top reaction?

'It's exactly like that,' he yelled.

The two of them stood breathing heavily at either end of

the hall. It crossed Bella's mind that they must resemble a pair of gunslingers from the old Wild West, facing each other down in a dusty street while the terrified townsfolk hid among the hay bales and barrels. In the depths of English suburbia, on a threadbare carpet runner that really did need replacing now she came to look at it, the image didn't quite hold together: not so much *High Noon* as *High Tea*.

She smiled again.

It pushed Trevor over the edge.

'Don't think for one minute that you're ever going back there.' There was real spite in his tone now. 'It's over – understand? Finished.'

And in Bella's head, suddenly it was. It took another ninety minutes for him to run out of steam but when he did she was ready to take her opportunity.

Finally, after nineteen years, three months, four days and roughly three-and-a-half hours, Bella Bourton had had enough.

Now, in the seclusion of their bedroom, with Trevor having banged angrily out to the pub and some easy-listening music on the Alexa speaker, Bella couldn't remember the last time she'd had so much fun with his clothes. In the past, the limit of her enthusiasm for his wardrobe extended to the jeopardy of the washing instruction labels, wondering whether she could get away with tumble-drying a pullover that clearly displayed the little symbol advising against it. She'd risked it successfully on two separate jumpers and only abandoned the practice when she managed to shrink his favourite cardigan from a baggy comforter to a tight sausage skin, incurring his insipid wrath followed by a few days of sulky silence.

Now she was having a ball.

This was how to spend a damp Friday evening. Maybe

later she'd watch back-to-back episodes of *Dancing on Ice* on catch-up, just to spite him. He'd always disliked Holly Willoughby. In fact, that should have been a red flag years ago: nobody dislikes Holly Willoughby.

There were three piles: the decent stuff, such as it was, was going into a suitcase for him, the ones of questionable taste in a bag for the charity shop, and the downright ugly or offensive were heading for the dump. The latter pile mounted up quickly, and Bella marvelled at the extraordinary range of unpleasant clothes her husband had managed to acquire over their years together. Of course, she realised, if she'd emerged earlier as this powerful butterfly from the chrysalis of suppression and gloom to which she'd been subjected, then nothing she was chucking out would have made it into the wardrobe in the first place. She would have made him wear brighter colours, better-fitting shirts and smarter shoes. As it was, she was embarrassed to give most of his dull, plain stuff to anywhere other than the tip.

She was emptying his underwear drawer, taking particular delight in binning the dark brown Y-fronts she'd always hated but had never dared mention, when her eye fell on something bright red, tucked into a corner and only visible because she'd already moved a whole bunch of other distasteful items. She was moderately convinced that Trevor had never worn anything red in his life – except, of course, his Norcester United replica shirt and the MAGA cap he'd bought on the internet specifically to upset the neighbours – and this had the distinct look of something that had been deliberately hidden, so she was intrigued to find out what was stashed away behind the grunties.

When she pulled out a skimpy pair of bikini bottoms,

edged with white fur and tied at the sides with lacy bows, she gasped.

Then she remembered they were hers, bought by her for their first Christmas together in an attempt to warm up the chilly winter nights with a bit of festive frivolity. He'd ridiculed her at the time – 'You look ridiculous' had been his exact words, she vividly recalled – but he'd evidently kept them. Bella had never worn them again, had forgotten all about them in fact, so to discover them hidden in a place she was unlikely to come across them seemed bizarre. Not to say a little discomforting.

She held the bikini up to her waist and instantly regretted it. The passage of nineteen years was kind to few people, she told herself, but she couldn't imagine trying them on, even for old times' sake.

And then a surprising thought struck her.

She found herself wondering whether Professor Stone might find her attractive in them.

The thought was not quite random. Since the arrival of Paula Grayson to interrupt her meeting with the Professor earlier in the day, Bella's mind had gone wandering on several occasions. Paula had clearly believed she was visiting Professor Stone for some kind of hook-up – a notion which made her smile to begin with, but as she mulled it over, caused her to consider her current position.

Trevor might only have been gone half an hour, but their relationship was over. Bella had decided. Now she sat on the edge of the bed, fur-lined bikini bottoms in hand, wondering if she had any kind of romance in her future. What did the stars hold for her love life? Thanks to Trevor's overblown outburst and her own growing confidence, she had pronounced herself freshly single and, while perhaps not in the prime of her life, could at least still catch sight of her prime in the rear-view mirror. At first she entertained no unrealistic expectations of the Professor – that was several bridges too far for her imagination to contemplate – but the fact that Paula had even conceived of it as a possibility began to pose intriguing questions in Bella's mind.

Why shouldn't she take a lover?

Why shouldn't she raise her sights higher than a council roadmender with a bad back and an iffy line in flatulence?

Why, in the end, shouldn't she be with someone like Professor Stone?

And why – more to the point – had he popped into her mind when she found the furry pants?

As she reflected on their last encounter, another question began to gnaw at her: why had Professor Stone turned inexplicably coy about the accusations Paula had alluded to? He had clammed up like a mantrap after Paula left, and no amount of coaxing could persuade him to open up to her. It seemed that the Professor had a secret he didn't want her to know about. Or anyone else, for that matter. Bella considered trying to contact Paula to find out more, but she seemed an unlikely confidante – she'd suggested that she didn't expect to meet Bella again – so for now, Stone's mystery remained his secret.

Then again, she hardly knew him. There were other people who had known him for a lot longer. Maybe they were aware of his secret? Maybe they would tell Bella if she asked them?

Questions. So many questions.

Most telling of all, Bella realised with a jolt, was that none of them related to Trevor.

Chapter Twenty

When the Professor got home from the Renaissance Hotel, his thoughts were a little fuzzy from champagne and ethical conundrums. How on earth Inspector Morse managed to down all those pints of real ale and still keep a clear head for his crosswords – let alone his murder cases – was beyond him. Come to think of it, quite a few fictional detectives had what could be described as an interesting relationship with alcohol. Sam Spade loved his bourbon. Rebus even had a scotch named after him. And while private eye Mike Hammer drank mainly beer, that was only because his creator, Mickey Spillane, joked that he couldn't spell cognac.

The Professor made it all the way to the front door before realising that it stood very slightly ajar.

He stared at the lock which, judging by the raw wood gouges in the frame and the splinters on the floor below, had clearly been jimmied open. With one finger he eased the door further and peered into the darkness.

There was no sign of activity inside. With a rising fury in his throat at his home having been broken into, Stone stepped over the threshold and marched into the hall. He suppressed a warning voice in his head that he should be calling the police and instead conducted a thorough search of the premises himself, striding from room to room, blithely turning on each light as he came to it and ready to strike at any straggling burglars who might be lurking within.

It took him five minutes to search the whole house.

There was nobody there.

'I'd like to speak to DCI Carlton,' he proclaimed on getting through to the central police station's switchboard. 'I don't care what time of night it is – I need you to put me through to her.'

It took a little negotiation with the call handler and a rather larger softening of his tone and attitude to persuade the girl to connect him. Eventually, it was the mention of a possible connection to the murder of Felicity Penman that swung it, and after a few moments of frustrating waiting, during which he paced the front room and stared out into the night through unclosed curtains, Carlton's voice came on the other end of the line.

'Professor Stone. How can I help?'

She sounded weary, Stone thought, but then three days into a murder investigation, with precious little in the way of evidence – if the *Echo* had it right – she was bound to be feeling the pressure. Things wouldn't have been helped, either, by the incompetence of her team: Detective Sergeant Muir made for a poor second-in-command.

'My house has been burgled,' he said simply.

If he'd been expecting sympathy he was in for a shock.

'And?'

Stone paused, rather taken aback by her disinterest.

'I thought you might want to know.'

'Have you reported it?'

'That's what I'm doing now.'

Exasperation crept into her voice. 'No, I mean have you reported it through the usual channels, got a crime number for your insurance company and so on?'

Stone couldn't understand why she was palming him off like this. 'I'm sorry – I thought a break-in at the house of a prime witness in your murder case might be of more interest to you.'

'Why?'

'Well, don't you think it might be relevant?'

'I doubt it. Plenty of people's houses are broken into. I can't really see anything special about yours.'

'Bit of a coincidence, don't you think?'

'Not really. It's days since Felicity was murdered, hardly anybody knows that you were there – you've done a great job of keeping your name out of the paper, by the way – and what would be gained by the murderer burgling your house anyway? Coincidence seems like just the right word.'

When she put it like that, Stone's own insistence on the probabilities started to work on his brain.

'I can transfer you back to the switchboard, if you want that crime number?'

With the chief inspector's cold logic still chilling his thoughts, Stone began tidying up the mess left by his uninvited intruders. As far as he could tell, nothing of any value had been stolen, which merely added to his confusion and rendered his registering the break-in rather superfluous. Why would a common-or-garden burglar decline to avail himself of a laptop or camera lying in plain sight? And if you're going to pull out drawers from desks and bedside tables, why not then follow up with the theft of some of the more valuable contents?

Stone tried, and failed, to make sense of it.

Then he poured himself a medicinal quantity of brandy and forced himself to start at the beginning of *On Floating Bodies*.

Again.

Saturday

Chapter Twenty-One

For the first time in ages, Harrison Fforde was feeling good about his stage name. Ever since the last Indiana Jones movie had repopularised the Hollywood star – in spite of (or perhaps because of) the CGI magic that had made him look even younger than his British copycat – Fforde had found his alter ego an increasingly heavy burden on his non-existent career. His agent had told him his pseudonym had become a standing joke in casting circles and not in a good way, while the use of it by people he regarded as friends, such as the nice folk at the reading group, struck him these days as inauthentic, verging on fraudulent. His ex-wife was the last remaining stalwart who insisted on using his old forename, and he was starting to feel that he rather liked its informality. He'd even considered reverting to the identity his wistful parents had bestowed on him, only to discover from the actors' union Equity that they now had a Harry Monkton on their books, and his real name was no longer any good to him either.

But now that he had formed the notion that Felicity

Penman might be an invented persona, he had suddenly become an expert in false identities. He'd lived most of his life as someone else, he realised, and while that had started to become tiresome in the real world, here in the fantasy land of sleuthing, it made him the pre-eminent authority on fakery.

There were more impressive things to be an expert on than lying but at this point in his career he was happy to take what he could get.

'What we really need to know is what her name was before she was Felicity Penman,' he said, pacing Lauren's living room and stroking his chin in what he imagined to be a thoughtful fashion. He'd been turning theories over in his mind most of the night and arrived on Lauren's doorstep painfully early to share them. To her credit, she'd been surprisingly willing to let him in.

'How on earth are we going to do that?' she asked, aiming her question as much at her brother as at Fforde, he noticed.

But Harrison Fforde wasn't going to let any young upstart steal his limelight.

'There's a whole industry devoted to new identities,' he said, beginning to enjoy his self-appointed status as a guru. 'Some of it's quite above board – like changing your name for Equity, for instance – but there's also a world of subterfuge and intrigue, full of shadow personas and parallel lives. You've just got to know where to look.'

Lauren gave him a glance that he thought might almost have been admiration.

'How do you know all this stuff?'

'Research for roles, mostly. I once had to play a character who assumed several different identities depending on who he was with at the time. I learned quite a lot about social masking and that kind of thing.'

'That's not the same as taking on a new identity, though, is it?'

'No, but you've got to be good at one if you're going to do the other.'

'Deception, you mean?'

'Not necessarily.'

Fforde moved over to where Simon was staring at his laptop and leaned in close, jabbing a finger at it.

'Do you mind if I—?'

'Well, I was in the middle of researching Pittingham, after what Lauren told us about Professor Stone.'

Simon had been asleep on the settee when Lauren got in from her drinks with the editor the night before, so it had only been when Fforde rang the doorbell that morning, waking him up from a twelve-hour nap, that she'd been able to divulge the intriguing information she'd gleaned about Professor Stone. Simon had wanted to get to work on the new lead straight away, but Lauren ordered him to wash, change his underwear and – importantly – brush his teeth before she would contemplate sharing the room with him. In the half-hour or so of digging he'd undertaken since then, he'd managed to confirm Professor Stone's twenty-year tenure in the Maths department at Pittingham University, Jerry Northover's rather shorter stint on the *Pittingham Times*, and the salacious story of the naked calendar produced by the women's varsity rowing team that had outsold every textbook in the student union bookshop before being withdrawn following a complaint from a particularly prudish parent about their daughter's rowlocks being on display for all and sundry to gawp over.

'I shan't be too long,' replied Fforde, reaching for the device without further discussion.

Whether in surprise or out of simple obedience, Simon blinked at him and meekly surrendered the laptop. Fforde took it to the chair that had become comfortably familiar with his contours and began tapping keys until a formal home page flashed up, topped with a royal crest, announcing the website of the official public record.

'What's that?' asked Lauren, standing behind him now for a better look.

'The *London Gazette*,' he said proudly.

'Of course,' said Simon from across the room. 'Why didn't I think of that?'

'A newspaper?' asked Lauren.

'No, not a newspaper,' said Fforde, 'although the name might lead you to believe so.'

'Then what is it?'

'This, my little murder mystery compadre, is the Holy Grail for identity tracers.'

Lauren looked blankly at the screen. 'What do you mean?'

'The *London Gazette* is the official public record,' her brother explained. 'All kinds of notifications get posted there. Companies going bust, the executors of wills looking for beneficiaries, people being given honours – all listed in the *London Gazette*.'

'And most importantly for us,' added Fforde, a triumphant note creeping into his voice, 'whenever anybody wants to change their name officially, by deed poll, they have to announce it publicly. And the way they do that is by a notice—'

'—in the *London Gazette*,' Lauren said, nodding her head.

'Exactly. Of course, it's all digital these days, but that gives us a real advantage.'

'It does? How?'

Fforde finished scrolling and clicked purposefully into a little window on the screen.

'We can search for a name.'

Lauren stared at him. 'You think Felicity Penman could be on this website?'

Fforde grinned. He liked having the upper hand. It was so rare.

'If she's done it by the book, then it's more than likely.'

It took Simon less than five minutes to find his way round the website. By their own ready admissions, neither Lauren nor Fforde was a tech expert and there were elements to the site that they found decidedly confusing. Fforde suspected it was more about their abilities than the website's user-friendliness, but whatever the reason, they were grateful for the tech wizard's presence and they left him to it while they sat silently opposite each other in front of the fireplace.

When he finally found what they were looking for, Fforde felt completely vindicated and totally useless at the same time.

'There she is,' he shouted, pointing at the page Simon had just called up.

He had no idea what to do next.

'That's what we've got Tim Berners-Lee here for,' said Lauren.

'Who?'

'Tim Berners-Lee? The man who invented the internet?'

A grunt came from Simon. 'He didn't.'

Lauren looked at him. 'Yes, he did.'

'No, he didn't. He invented the worldwide web. Two completely different things.'

Lauren tutted and turned back to Fforde.

'Honestly, he could start an argument in an empty room.'

Ten minutes after that, Fforde was staring at page after page of search engine results that Simon had traced.

'It's always much easier when you have a name. There are thousands of mentions of her going back years.'

'Surely they're not all about the same person?' said Lauren, peering over her brother's shoulder on one side while Fforde watched from the other.

'Lucy Eastwood – they're all about Lucy Eastwood.'

'But that's a pretty common name, isn't it? There could be loads of Lucy Eastwoods.'

'I've asked specifically for the one with the location that was on the name change.'

'Even so, there might be more than one there.'

'It's possible. But I'm cross-referencing them and ruling out the ones that aren't our Lucy Eastwood.'

Even as they watched, Simon clicked on and discarded a succession of Lucy Eastwoods, including a dog groomer in Macclesfield, an enthusiastic amateur baker from Grimsby whose delicious-looking scones were all over Pinterest, and a female American Footballer with a dodgy sideline in foot photographs on OnlyFans.

It was Lauren who spotted the first picture of Felicity Penman, albeit much younger and looking very different from the assured professional they had all known.

'That's her!' she shouted into Simon's ear, causing him to recoil uncomfortably.

'All right. I'm sitting right here,' he said.

When he clicked onto the image, a page appeared with a bold blue strip across the top announcing, 'Pittingham University Board Games Club'. The top picture showed Felicity with three other students crowded round a Cluedo board, with a brief caption: 'Club members at a recent social event.'

'Bit of a DIY website,' said Simon disparagingly.

'Never mind that,' said Lauren. 'We've already found out much more about her as Lucy Eastwood than we ever knew as Felicity Penman.'

'Including,' said Fforde ominously, 'the fact that she was a student at Pittingham University.'

They all paused while they considered the implications.

'Do you think she knew Professor Stone there?' asked Lauren eventually.

'Must have done, surely,' Fforde replied. 'It would be too much of a coincidence otherwise, wouldn't it?'

'I don't know. In all the time I've been part of the reading group, they've never given any indication that they knew each other before. And it would be very difficult to keep up the pretence of her new persona if he'd known her before as Lucy Eastwood.'

'Unless they had a secret connection that they were both trying to hide,' said Fforde. The information Lauren had given them about Stone's mysterious appearance at the Renaissance Hotel the previous evening, coupled with Jerry Northover's dark hints about things from his past that he might prefer stayed there, were playing on his mind.

'I don't understand why Felicity changed her name when she came to Norcester,' said Lauren.

'Neither do I. That's got to be the key to the case, though, hasn't it?'

'But how are we going to find that out? We can't exactly ask her, can we?'

'Wait a minute,' said Simon, sitting up suddenly and looking keenly at the screen. 'This is interesting.'

'What have you found?' asked Lauren.

'Another photograph.'

Fforde peered closer. 'What are we looking at? That's not Felicity – or Lucy Eastwood.'

Simon clicked again and the board game photograph appeared beside the new one. Fforde saw immediately what Simon had noticed. Beside Lucy Eastwood at the Cluedo board was another girl, heavily made up and with a white streak dyed into otherwise jet-black hair. The two had their arms wrapped round each other. In the second picture, the same face stared straight out at the camera, like a police mugshot, in the middle of a newspaper report that was too zoomed in to be readable.

'It's the same girl,' said Fforde slowly. 'What's the article about?'

Simon manipulated the trackpad on the laptop and the focus pulled out to reveal the entire report from the *Pittingham Times*, together with its headline in a bold, sans-serif typeface: 'Drug dealer in suicide after uni kicks her out'.

Lauren's hand went to her mouth. 'Oh,' she said, looking nauseous. 'Felicity's friend killed herself.'

Simon scrolled slowly through the text, allowing all three of them to read the ins and outs of the tragic story of Mariella Brown. Unsurprisingly, the newspaper cutting concentrated on her misdemeanours – the touting of illegal substances to her peers on university premises, her subsequent hauling across the coals by the institution's authorities and inevitable removal under its zero-tolerance policies – before revealing that she'd taken her own life three days later. The cause and effect were not explicitly linked by the report, although one unnamed interviewee hinted heavily that she must have decided on the brutally terminal option rather than return home to an unsympathetic family.

When they finished reading, Lauren went back to her chair and sat down heavily.

'I don't care what she did; nobody deserves that kind of end,' she said sadly.

'I still don't get it,' said Fforde, continuing to stare at the laptop screen and wrangling his thoughts into some kind of order. However culpable Mariella Brown might have been, Lucy Eastwood had done nothing wrong – unless the very fact of her friendship was enough to damn her in the eyes of the university authorities.

'Why did Lucy Eastwood feel the need to move to a new town and assume a new identity – and a new look? I mean, she wasn't the one thrown out of uni, was she?'

'Maybe she just wanted a new start,' said Lauren. 'As somebody new.'

Simon was still tapping at the laptop. Marvelling at its raw power – his own regularly crashed if you opened more than three tabs – Fforde watched in awe as the young man clicked on tabs to reveal a succession of information. Within minutes he'd found a number of online reports into Mariella's death, some more lurid than others; there were newsletters, social media pages and other links to the poor girl, and Felicity made the occasional appearance in some of them too, although it was always under her old name. Then came a batch of tabs relating to Lucy Eastwood herself, and finally a Facebook feed that seemed to have been dormant for the best part of two years.

Simon began scrolling back through the feed, which featured the usual array of photographs – many of them filtered, Fforde assumed – revealing a school prom, family occasions and various other events and anniversaries in which Lucy and a rotating pool of friends dressed up or down according to venue, age and personal style. Lucy herself seemed to have gone through a minor Goth phase in her late teens, possibly coinciding with winning a place at the university where Mariella began to make increasingly frequent appearances in the photos. Mariella was much more flagrant in her tastes, and Fforde could see her influence extending over Lucy as time went by, from spiky haircuts and heavy eyeliner in their first year to sharp-cut outfits and brighter colours as they neared the date of Mariella's expulsion. Fforde wondered if the transition to a more grown-up, classy look had anything to do with a rise in income from Mariella's extracurricular activities, but he couldn't convince himself that Felicity – or Lucy, as she had been then – was involved in that particular enterprise.

'It doesn't make any sense,' said Lauren when Simon finally stopped scrolling and sat back in his chair, stretching his hands behind his head. 'What's all this got to do with Felicity changing her name? And if it is something to do with Professor Stone, why all the secrecy?'

'And,' said Fforde, the wheels spinning fast now, 'if it was a secret before, why is she trying to tell us about it now, from beyond the grave?'

Another silence descended.

'It's got to be connected to the university,' said Lauren eventually.

Fforde felt a sudden surge of bravery. 'Well then, there's only one thing to do.'

'What's that?'

'We go to the organ grinder. I know we've met three times this week already, but I think we should have another session of the reading group. It's time we confronted Professor Stone.'

Chapter Twenty-Two

Bella was fast losing patience with the odd man in the bow tie. She'd been the first to arrive for the reading group, wanting to get there early and prepare the room for the announcement she was about to break to them. Ever since Trevor had arrived home late from the pub to find what was left of his things standing in two suitcases and a cardboard box in the hall, she'd been desperate to tell someone. She'd have phoned Ronnie that morning had it not been for the fact that her sister was away in Chichester for a weekend of recorder-playing with her Tudor ensemble and Bella knew she would not take kindly to being interrupted, no matter how monumental the news. She had acquaintances, of course, but Bella's sheltered life and lack of real friendships had meant that she considered none of them worthy of hearing about it first. The only other option she was willing to contemplate was Trevor's sister Bridget – their shared animosity towards him meant they'd always got on well – but she was pretty sure he'd have slunk off there last night to wheedle a bit of familial sympathy and a cooked breakfast out of her. When Harrison had messaged with a request for the reading group to meet again that evening, she knew she'd found her audience, and her eagerness to tell the others had grown steadily during the course of a day in which she'd slept in, had a long, hot bath – with a glass of white wine – ordered junk food on an app she downloaded specifically for the purpose, and watched the lovely Jasmine Harman attempt to relocate a succession of would-be Mediterranean property buyers in four consecutive episodes of *A Place in the Sun*.

Now Bella was bursting with anticipation.

And here was the strange, rather creepy substitute manager trying to stand in her way.

'No, I'm sorry, Mrs Burton—'

'Bourton.'

'Mrs Bourton. I am given to understand that your membership of the reading group only commenced two weeks ago, and last week was, of course, the occasion of the unhappy demise of our manager, so you have technically only really been a member for one meeting. I couldn't possibly allow you access to our special services – and by that I mean the private reading room – without your being chaperoned by someone of much longer standing with the group.'

His voice quivered with the self-imposed authority of the natural jobsworth, and his bottom lip trembled to match.

Bella wondered exactly what unfortunate incidents in his past had led Maurice Stapleton to become such a pastiche of officialdom. Surely nobody set out to develop such a nauseatingly priggish character by design? Something must have happened to him during his developmental years, or possibly in early adult life, to turn him into this objectionable obstacle to her intentions. For a moment, she mused on what that something might have been – an overbearing parent? a childhood bully? a romantic rejection? – then realised it made no difference to her right now. She still needed to get past this gatekeeper and no amount of psychoanalysis on her part would get beneath the surface of his high-handedness.

She tapped into her growing reserves of inner strength and took the forthright approach.

'Don't be silly, Maurice,' she said, and marched past him.

The flustered bluster that followed her down the nave of the bookshop reminded her of a panicked chicken trying to evade the farmer's clutches. Maurice trailed after her, clucking vaguely outraged expressions of fury and affront, but Bella knew he could not touch her, literally or metaphorically. As she sailed gracefully across the dark blue carpet tiles, she allowed his warnings and threats to merge into a wash of sound that lifted her spirits and carried her on a wave of blissful indifference to the door of the reading room.

A door that was locked.

Bugger. Now she would have to listen to Maurice droning on until one of the others arrived.

'Eureka!' he said when she stopped with her hand on the doorknob, unable to progress any further. 'Now who's holding all the cards? Let this be a lesson to you: you can't just take the law into your own hands, Mrs Burton.'

'Bourton.'

But Maurice was in full flow.

'There are procedures in place, and they're in place for a reason. If we all just decided to do our own thing, live life our own way, there'd be chaos. Anarchy. Nothing would get done.

All the systems that society has developed for smooth functioning would fall apart, and then where would we be?'

Bella resisted the temptation to answer '*Inside the reading room*' and zoned out from his monologue.

She had more important things on her mind than Maurice Stapleton.

In the short time that she'd been a member of the reading group, she'd lost a shop manager to murder, a husband to eviction and a drab life of drudgery to a new, Technicolor world of excitement and mystery. She felt as though she was properly alive for the first time in years – possibly since she married Trevor – and she wanted to play a full part in the group's ongoing investigation into Felicity Penman's murder.

'Everything all right?'

Harrison Fforde's best actor voice boomed down the nave, cutting through Bella's thoughts and stopping Maurice Stapleton mid-flow. She turned to see him marching across the shop, with Lauren half a step behind him, almost cantering to keep up.

'Just being given a lecture on the correct procedures for using the facilities,' she said, smiling at Fforde in gratitude for rescuing her. 'Apparently I'm not sufficiently trustworthy to be permitted access to the reading room without a more senior member of the group accompanying me.'

Fforde arrived at the locked door, Lauren a moment later, and gave Maurice a look which Bella thought was intended to convey disapproval but actually looked more like thunderous hostility. She certainly wouldn't have wanted to be on the receiving end of it.

The odd little man began to bluster again.

'I was simply explaining to Mrs Burton—'

'Bourton,' said Fforde.

'—that I can't just allow any old Tom, Dick or Harry access to the facilities without proper approval. I have regulations that need to be followed.'

'Firstly,' said Fforde, drawing his shoulders back to tower over the bureaucrat, 'I think you might be stretching the term "regulations" beyond its acceptable limits. Letting Mrs Bourton into the reading room on her own is hardly a matter of GCHQ-level significance. And secondly, I don't think Mrs Bourton will take too kindly to being described as "any old Tom, Dick or Harry".'

He turned to her.

'Would you, Bella?'

She felt a warm glow at being so publicly included in his entourage. He was on her side, not Maurice's, and seemed willing to make a point of it.

'It's not so much the "Dick" that I object to as the "old",' said Bella, flashing Fforde a glint of amused appreciation.

He appeared to pick it up.

'Quite. Barely middle-aged, I'd guess.' He looked back at the bewildered shop assistant. 'Which makes your insinuations about both her character and her age decidedly ungentlemanly. I'm surprised at you, Maurice.'

The four of them stood in a circle of stunned silence for a moment before Maurice Stapleton finally found his voice.

'Well, I'm sure I didn't mean to cause offence,' he said, delving into his trouser pocket to bring out a bunch of keys.

Bella tried to analyse his tone, uncertain whether he was sounding defensive, apologetic or simply put out. She abandoned the attempt to figure it out and watched him flick through the keys before settling on a shiny silver one, sliding it into the lock at the centre of the doorknob.

'I'm perfectly happy to allow you access to the reading room now that Mr Fforde and Miss Sherwood are here,' he said, pushing open the door and standing back before nodding ingratiatingly at Bella.

She moderated her tone to one of exaggerated politeness, hoping it might be taken as the sarcasm she intended. 'That's so kind of you.'

Lauren and Fforde followed her into the room, Fforde swinging the door closed without looking at the forlorn figure behind him with its face contorted into a toadying grimace.

Bella couldn't contain her laughter.

'Isn't that rather risky?' she asked. 'I've got a feeling Maurice might be a rather dangerous enemy to make.'

'Oh, don't worry about him,' said Fforde. 'All mouth and no trousers. He's been lurking around the shop for years, just waiting for an opportunity to get his hands on the top job, but everyone knows he isn't up to it.'

'Must have put his nose out of joint when Felicity arrived?'

'It certainly did,' said Lauren, sitting on the sofa beside Bella. 'He's got twenty years on her at least, and would definitely have thought his experience would count in his favour. But you saw what Felicity was like. Who in their right mind would choose him over her to be the manager?'

Bella could see that made complete sense.

It also set her mind racing.

Fforde took his place in one of the armchairs and leaned in towards the others.

'I'm glad the Professor's not here yet. We've got things to talk about.'

Bella waved him down. 'Before we get into anything else, I'd like to make an announcement.'

Fforde looked mildly disgruntled at having the wind removed so efficiently from his sails. But Bella wasn't going to let anyone steal her big moment: she'd started with Maurice Stapleton and she was quite prepared to take on Harrison Fforde as well, if it came to it.

'What is it, Bella?' asked Lauren. 'Tell us what's happened.'

A beaming smile broke out on Bella's lips.

Fforde interjected. 'I believe these days the young people call it spilling the tea.'

'Why?' Lauren looked confused.

'No idea,' he confessed. 'Move on.'

'Well,' said Bella, lowering her voice as if about to divulge the riddle of the sphinx. In this case a big, grinning sphinx. 'I threw Trevor out last night.'

'No way!' said Lauren, a look of genuine shock on her face.

'Yes way,' said Bella. 'I packed his things and left them in the hall for him.'

'How are you feeling now?'

'A bit giddy, if I'm honest,' Bella giggled. 'Actually, I feel better than I have done in years.'

'Well, good for you!' said Lauren, looking at Fforde as if for encouragement. 'That's terrific news, isn't it?'

'Is it?'

'Of course it is, Harrison. Bella's just thrown off the shackles of patriarchal imperialism and feels great. We should all be celebrating.'

'Oh yes,' Fforde said, a cheery tone forced into his voice. 'Let's all celebrate smashing the patriarchy.'

'So that's my news,' said Bella, leaning back and clasping

her hands together on her lap. 'Now what did you want to talk about?'

More than ever she wanted to be a part of this enterprising group of investigators and she put aside Harrison's momentary disgruntlement, conceding that it was he, after all, who had called the meeting. But why didn't he want to wait for Professor Stone before talking about his 'things'?

'We think we've got a breakthrough,' said Lauren conspiratorially.

'What do you mean?'

Fforde delayed for effect, casting a glance at his audience like the professional actor he purported to be.

'We have a trail,' he announced at last.

'A trail?'

'A trail,' Fforde repeated. 'Leading us back from Felicity Penman's body, out there in the bookshop, to a mystery worthy of Ruth Rendell, involving false identities, dodgy pasts and who knows what else.'

Bella felt irritation alongside her curiosity. And it wasn't just the mention of Ruth Rendell, whose name Bella recognised from the old television series but whose literary work Fforde must know was beyond her sphere. The pair of them had clearly stumbled across something new since they'd last gathered two nights earlier. Now she desperately wanted to know what it was, and why they'd kept it from her. She had her own theories to put to them, but for now she felt on the back foot.

It was Fforde's turn to sit back, a satisfied look on his face.

'Lauren and I have been working on it all afternoon – along with her brother, who turns out to be surprisingly accomplished for such an unassuming young man – and we made quite a discovery.'

He paused again.

'Felicity Penman was not Felicity Penman.'

Bella looked from one to the other, their faces a mixture of trepidation and triumph.

'Excuse me?'

'She wasn't even a bookshop manager. She faked her CV to get the job here. We've seen it, and Simon's researched it. It doesn't hold water.'

Bella's head was beginning to swim. So they *had* been conducting their own private investigations on the side. Well, she supposed, that was not terribly surprising – they hardly knew her, after all – but she couldn't help feeling more than a little left out, especially since they'd clearly been totally fine about involving someone from outside the group completely.

Resolving to convert her put-outedness into determination, she pushed Fforde again.

'But what do you mean, Felicity wasn't Felicity?'

He looked almost gleeful. 'In a previous life, Felicity Penman was'—he paused again—'Lucy Eastwood.'

This was not the revelation he'd thought it was going to be.

'And who exactly is Lucy Eastwood?'

By the time Fforde and Lauren had unfolded the details of what they had uncovered, Bella was convinced that everyone had got everything wrong. According to Fforde, this Lucy Eastwood had changed her name eighteen months previously, to Felicity Penman, and moved to Norcester to start a new life under a new identity. In his excitable rush to get the story out, he skipped over vital information that would have helped Bella enormously in the hearing, and Lauren had to keep interjecting to fill in gaps that predated Felicity's move, when she was still Lucy Eastwood. In this haphazard way, Bella learned that a university friend of Lucy's had been dealing drugs and got thrown out for it, with Lucy's own involvement bringing her reputation into severe question.

None of it tallied with the sweet, intelligent girl who had introduced Bella to the reading group in the first place.

'No, I'm sorry,' she said when Fforde finally reached the end of his narrative. 'I know people sometimes live secret lives, and I realise that I didn't know Felicity as well as the rest of you, but I simply can't believe that she'd be caught up in anything like drug-dealing. She was far too smart for that. I think you must have got it wrong.'

Fforde shook his head. 'There's no arguing with the *London Gazette*.'

'What's the *London Gazette*?'

'The official record. That's who Lucy Eastwood was, and Felicity Penman is who she became.'

'I can't believe it,' said Bella and slumped back on the sofa. 'I thought I'd got a breakthrough of my own but it doesn't feel like much now.'

Lauren leaned towards her. 'What sort of breakthrough?'

'Oh, it's nothing really. I just had an idea that maybe Felicity had an ulterior motive for starting the reading group.'

'What do you mean, motive?'

'I'm not sure. It just seems a little too … planned, if you know what I mean. I think she brought us all together deliberately.'

Lauren and Fforde stared into the middle distance, turning this new notion over. Eventually, Fforde let out a long 'Mmm' and scratched his head.

'Sounds plausible,' he said, nodding slowly. 'Although I've no idea why.'

'Well, could it be something to do with solving the mystery of her murder?'

As soon as she said it, she realised how unlikely it sounded.

'Even if that's true,' Fforde said, 'how does it help us with our investigation?'

Bella thought hard, trying to put the pieces together.

'Well, it doesn't, does it? As far as I can see, the fact that Felicity Penman used to be somebody else and put together a group of readers after lying about her CV brings us no closer to finding her killer.'

Lauren leaned forward again and touched Bella on the arm. 'We haven't told you the most worrying bit yet.'

Bella felt a shock of alarm. 'What's that?'

'The university Felicity's friend got thrown out of was in Pittingham,' said Fforde. 'That's where Stone was a professor before he retired.'

Bella could hardly take in what they were telling her. It was all too bizarre.

'Just a coincidence, surely?'

'Is it?' said Lauren. 'Think about it, Bella. Felicity was a student at Pittingham University, where Professor Stone was teaching and her friend got thrown out. Then she turns up with a fake identity in the same town where he's living in retirement, only to be killed eighteen months after arriving. You've got to admit that sounds a little suspicious.'

Bella wasn't sure what Lauren was implying but she didn't like it. In the vaults of her memory, something someone had said at the fateful reading group meeting on Tuesday was taunting her; if only she could get a handle on what it was.

'I don't think that sounds suspicious,' she said, feeling suddenly protective towards the Professor. 'The fact that Felicity was a student at his old university is not so small a chance – it's not that far away, is it? There must be thousands of students there and the likelihood of at least one of them moving to Norcester is hardly implausible.'

'There's more,' said Lauren.

Five minutes into her explanation of what she'd seen and heard at the Serendipity Bar the previous evening, Bella cut her off.

'No,' she said flatly. 'I refuse to believe that Professor Stone had anything to do with Felicity's murder. It's too preposterous. This Jerry person must have got the wrong end of the stick or something.'

Fforde nodded slowly. 'I'm sure you're right, Bella. The Professor might be many things but he's not a killer.'

Bella wasn't sure he sounded convincing, even to himself.

He went on, 'I'd love to know what the big secret is that he's hiding, though. If nothing else, that might give us a steer towards what happened to Felicity. Or Lucy. Where is he, anyway?'

He got up and went to the door, poking his head out and peering around. He obviously saw what he was looking for as he shouted across the shop.

'Maurice, have you got a minute?'

The strange little man arrived moments later in a flurry of recrimination.

'This is a bookshop, Mr Fforde. People are reading. You can't go shouting the odds whenever you feel like it.'

'Oh, sorry. Didn't think. Look, you haven't seen Professor

Stone on your travels, have you? He was supposed to be here twenty minutes ago.'

Maurice Stapleton blanched.

Then he gulped.

Then he blanched some more.

'You haven't heard?' he said timidly. 'I thought that was why you were meeting again tonight.'

'Heard what?' asked Lauren quickly.

'Tell us, man.' Fforde's voice was getting louder again.

'Let him speak,' said Bella. She felt no protectiveness towards the weaselly character but she figured it was the quickest way to get him to talk.

Maurice looked from one to another; then, apparently registering that he held the balance of power in the room, he breathed out slowly and broke into a grim, ghastly smile.

'Your Professor has been arrested. By the police.'

It was Fforde who broke the silence that descended on the room. 'Well, it's hardly going to be by the overpriced books squad, is it?'

Bella was horrified. 'Arrested? What for?'

'I'll show you,' said Maurice, and disappeared as quickly as he'd arrived. Less than a minute later he was back, a copy of the *Norcester Echo* in his hand. He held it up before the three of them, the grimace as grotesque as before.

The headline answered Bella's question. It also posed a dozen more.

Professor held over double murder.

'Double murder?' said Lauren. 'What are they talking about? They didn't have that story when I spoke to the editor last night.'

She grabbed the paper from Maurice and started reading aloud.

'*A retired professor is being held by police tonight for questioning about two murders in Norcester over the past few days. Professor E. Stone, who taught Maths at Pittingham University until two years ago, was arrested early this morning by detectives investigating the killing of bookshop manager Felicity Penman and a former colleague of the professor's, Paula Grayson.*'

'Who the hell is Paula Grayson?' said Fforde, taking the paper out of Lauren's hands and staring at it in disbelief.

Bella's horror stepped up a notch.

'I know who Paula Grayson is. I – I've met her. She called round at the Professor's house while I was there yesterday.'

'Well, now she's dead,' said Fforde, still clutching the *Echo*. 'Stabbed in her hotel room with a bread knife. Here – they've got a picture of it.'

He thrust the newspaper in Bella's direction and she took it reluctantly, an intense feeling of dread almost paralysing her. Without even looking at the photograph, she knew what it was going to show.

'That's not just a bread knife,' she said slowly. 'That's Professor Stone's bread knife.'

Sunday

Chapter Twenty-Three

'Won't this thing go any faster?'

Fforde's intervention was unhelpful. Lauren's trusty Mini had served her well for several years now, even though she'd bought it second-hand and it had, she suspected, more miles under its belt than the odometer suggested, used car salesmen in her experience being less concerned with accuracy in that regard than the customers they were selling to. The little orange beast was perfectly capable of a decent top speed in three figures, although she had never – and would never – put the manufacturer's claims about that to the test, and she knew it was completely roadworthy, having put it through its mandatory checks and received the appropriate documentation from her friendly mechanic less than a month previously. For Fforde to impugn either its capabilities or its functionality was simply ill-informed, bordering on rude.

Which left her driving. It was, she concluded, most likely that he was having a go at her own skills, rather than the car's technical abilities, and that made her even more grumpy than any potential slight on the vehicle. She recalled the BMW that had overtaken her on the way home from the bookshop on the night of Felicity's murder, with its young passenger leaning out of the window making what she'd assumed was an obscene gesture, and she wondered if she could remember it clearly enough to repeat it into the rear-view mirror for Fforde's benefit now.

Sadly, she couldn't.

'Shut up, Harrison,' she settled for instead.

'It's just we could probably walk to Pittingham quicker than this if we set our mind to it,' he complained, staring dolefully out of the window at the passing countryside.

'Leave her alone,' said Bella affably from beside Lauren. 'Better five minutes too late in this world than twenty years too early in the next.'

Lauren smiled and stored Bella's aphorism away for future use.

'Besides,' Bella continued, 'we're not on a schedule, are we?'

As Fforde fell into a sullen silence, Lauren considered again the wisdom of their present mission. It had been she who suggested the road trip the previous night at the bookshop, when the full drama of Professor Stone's situation was revealed to them by the strange little man in a bow tie. Maurice Stapleton had seemed jubilant not only that he'd been the one to impart the vital information to what was left of the reading group, but also that the weight of evidence was pointing incontrovertibly towards the Professor. Evidently there had been some history to the animosity he'd displayed, and Lauren wondered how far Felicity's enthusiasm for the group had been at odds with her colleague's apparent disapproval;

perhaps he'd tried to oppose its inception but been overruled. That would certainly provide a motive for his frostiness since her death, although from Lauren's standpoint it seemed sparse enough reason to dislike the group. Then again, people had gone to war over not much more – a football match in one central American example, she vaguely recalled, or the notorious War of Jenkins' Ear, in which Britain and Spain fought for almost a decade after the seafaring Captain Jenkins's unfortunate appendage was severed by Spaniards in the Caribbean. And then there was the absurd case of the 1859 Pig War, which Lauren had read about only recently, when a pig sparked conflict after straying onto neighbouring land and munching through a garden. The fact that the land was disputed territory between Canada and America raised the stakes somewhat and hundreds of troops were deployed on both sides for twelve tetchy years. The scale of that particular dispute rather put Maurice's antipathy into perspective, but it did demonstrate amply how the most ridiculous disagreements could escalate beyond all reason.

Lauren pulled her mind back to the present, swerving slightly to avoid a wayward tandem in the custody of two elderly cyclists in bright yellow Lycra.

'Do you think he'll see us?' she asked Bella, glancing to her left.

'Why wouldn't he?'

Lauren feared she might know the answer to that. If Jerry Northover had been correct in his assessment of the Professor's reputation back in Pittingham, a journey to seek out a former colleague in the hope of finding a witness to his good character – and therefore the unlikelihood of his being a double-murderer – was starting to look foolhardy at best.

It had been Simon who'd tracked down the erstwhile head of the Maths department at Pittingham University the previous afternoon, but the idea of actually paying him a visit hadn't occurred to Lauren until the reading group meeting, when Bella had been categoric in her defence of the Professor's innocence.

'I don't care what the *Echo* says, I don't care what Chief Inspector Carlton says: I refuse to believe that Professor Stone is a killer,' she'd insisted as Lauren and Fforde had debated the newspaper's article in their reading room.

'You've got to admit the evidence is pretty damning,' Fforde had argued, stabbing the *Echo* with his finger.

'Circumstantial at best,' Bella had said, and Lauren wondered if she'd been reading up on legal jargon in her spare time.

Privately, she'd found herself agreeing with Fforde's assessment of the *Echo*'s latest reporting: Nicki Bailey appeared to have some excellent anonymous contacts within the force, fortuitously overshadowing Lauren's own recent conversations with both the journalist and her editor in the process. Saturday's edition had ignored those interviews entirely and seemed instead to have concluded that the mystery of the murdered bookshop manager was all but solved, and that police would be charging their suspect at any moment. She couldn't really see how Professor Stone, for all his eminence and authority, was going to wriggle out of it.

What Bella had said next was the real clincher, though, and Lauren winced at the recollection of it.

'We're supposed to be his friends, aren't we? If the papers and the police are determined to shoot him down, then it's up to us to prevent a wrongful conviction.'

She'd definitely been at the textbooks, Lauren decided.

'We might not have been able to save Felicity, but we can still help Professor Stone. And the only way to do that is to find the real culprit.'

Her words had cut Lauren instantly, and she felt bloody that she'd been so willing to take the so-called evidence at face value. Heaven knew there were enough people in the town who'd be quite prepared to have the Professor convicted, judged and sent away for a very long time without even hearing the facts, so the least the reading group could do was try to find some balancing material for the other side of the scales of justice. Simon's discovery that Derek Carmichael, former head of the Maths department and therefore Professor Stone's old boss, still lived in a quiet street not far from the university campus in Pittingham had triggered the thought in Lauren's head that he might be able to give them something useful. As well as a character reference, there was the slight chance that he could shed some light on the incident that had led ultimately to the death of Felicity's classmate and friend, Mariella Brown.

She had no idea how that might help them, but at least it felt like doing something.

Derek Carmichael turned out to be a sweet, inoffensive-looking giant of a man with a propensity for weak puns and strong drink. His tweed jacket and knitted waistcoat seemed to Lauren like something from a bygone era and he could easily have passed for an extra in one of those gentle afternoon murder mysteries among the higher-numbered channels on the

TV guide. *Rosemary and Thyme*. Or *Darby and Joan*. Or *Mary, Mungo and Midge*.

No, hang on: that was something else entirely, wasn't it?

It was barely midday when they reached his house, neatly perched behind a laurel hedge with its 1950s brick façade presenting orderliness and respect to the outside world, but he was already drinking scotch and soda before his Sunday lunch. The appealing smells of a roast dinner wafted through from the kitchen at the back of the house and Lauren was disappointed that they never got any closer to it than the book-lined lounge just inside the front door.

They introduced themselves and Lauren explained their quest to learn more about Professor Stone, taking care to keep the gorier details of their motivation out of her synopsis. They had yet to gauge his personal feelings towards the Professor and discretion, as she knew only too well from her brother's embarrassing history, was not just the better part of valour; it was tantamount to the whole damn thing.

In response, Derek Carmichael shook each proffered hand warmly and vigorously, then indicated a large leather sofa in front of the window.

And if he was unwilling to share his redolent repast with three uninvited guests, he was more liberal with the libations.

'There's gin, whisky, vodka or sherry,' he told them. 'I've got chocolate and Turkish delight too but you know what Dorothy Parker said about the respective merits of candy and liquor. At least I believe it was Dorothy Parker.'

'You're thinking of Ogden Nash, I suspect,' ventured Fforde, who sat upright on the sofa with his hands on his knees, while Lauren and Bella adopted more reclining reposes either side of him.

'Ah yes, of course!' erupted Carmichael, a great guffaw welcoming Fforde's correction of his attribution. 'Marvellous – a fellow aesthete.'

With the former academic towering above them, the trio on the sofa were disinclined to refuse his offer of a drink. Bella accepted a weak gin and tonic, Fforde took a neat shot of whisky, while Lauren opted for 'something soft, if you have it' on the grounds that she was driving. Secretly, she found Bella and Fforde's willingness to imbibe at this time of day moderately scandalous, especially given the nature of their assignment, but she refrained from commenting. Perhaps it was best to humour their host, after all.

'All too frequently soft these days, my dear,' replied Carmichael, instantly belying Lauren's first impression of him as inoffensive. She sighed inwardly and wondered how this man had survived the last years of his departmental headship if this was where his misogynistic bar was set. Presumably the #MeToo movement had not completely passed Pittingham University by, but if his willingness for priapic punning to three strangers in his own home on a quiet Sunday morning was anything to go by, its natural history students would have had no shortage of dinosaurs to dissect.

Several scotch-and-sodas later, and with the aroma from the kitchen growing increasingly charred by the minute, Carmichael had happily divulged his longstanding friendship with Professor Stone: their easy working relationship and plentiful mellow nights spent in their cups, the occasional word he'd had to have with him about rumours of indiscretions ('just make sure you don't get caught' appeared to have been his strongest advice), and the final sad farewell when Carmichael opted for early retirement rather than endure the latest round of diversity training that was being forced on the university's leadership team. He had left several years before Stone's own departure and could shed no light on those circumstances. As for any secrets the Professor might have been harbouring, Carmichael either didn't know or he wouldn't be giving them up to a trio of unexpected visitors on a bibulous Sunday morning.

Lauren decided she could bear his faux affability and ill-disguised prejudices no longer – they would undoubtedly fare better by not calling Carmichael as a character witness on the Professor's behalf – and was about to make their excuses to leave when Bella slipped in one final question.

'This might seem a bit random, Mr Carmichael, but do you remember a girl called Mariella Brown?'

The expression on the old man's face changed in a moment.

'God, yes. How could I forget? Worst moment in my time at the university.'

Lauren suddenly wanted to hear more from the old fossil. 'What do you mean?'

He looked at each of them in turn, his eyes glassy with remembrance or booze, and seemed to be sizing them up.

'Now listen, I'm as tolerant as the next man,' he began.

Lauren was damn sure she didn't want to meet the next man.

'But you can't go around flogging grade-A narcotics to the student body from a university building. It's just not proper. Unfortunately for me, I had the bad luck to be on the disciplinary committee that decided her fate.' His face came into sharper focus and he gave them a pleading look. 'We had no choice in the matter. She had to go. You can see that, can't you?'

Fforde edged forwards. 'You weren't to know what she was going to do, Mr Carmichael. It wasn't your fault.'

Lauren was glad Fforde had stepped in: she was far from sure that she would have been so generous.

'Try telling that to the poor girl's mother,' said Carmichael. 'She still holds me responsible.'

Lauren was aghast. 'Her mother?'

'Kathy, yes. I see her most weeks in Sainsbury's.'

'Mariella Brown's mother still lives in Pittingham?'

Lauren wasn't sure how but she knew immediately that this was a lead they had to follow. Any light that Mariella's mother could shed on the story – and in particular, Lucy Eastwood's involvement in it – might well give them a clue as to why she had changed her name, fabricated a CV and applied for the job of manager at The Quaint Bookshop in Norcester.

Within five minutes, they had gleaned Kathy Brown's address from Derek Carmichael and were back in the Mini and on the road.

Chapter Twenty-Four

In his younger days, it was beer. Over the last twenty years or so, it had been cheap whisky. Now Professor Stone had discovered a new weapon in the arsenal of things to leave him with a massive headache in the morning: a night in a police cell.

It was one he was anxious never to repeat.

And yet the prospect of several thousand more of them loomed in his mind as he dragged it from tenuous slumber, disturbed by the clangings and shouts of the underground complex that was hidden from public view and knowledge beneath the central police station. It stretched out almost half a mile in all directions, including under the High Street, so that blissfully ignorant shoppers frequently walked above the heads of some of the town's most hardcore criminals without ever realising it. Stone had, in fact, been down here once before, on a heritage day tour that took visitors on an unlikely journey through Norcester's legal history, and he remembered thinking then that it was not an environment in which he would care to be held against his will. Established more than three centuries earlier, when professional 'thief-takers' would apprehend innocent men and women for capital crimes from stealing food to witchcraft, the cells had a grim and gruesome past and, judging by his nocturnal incarceration, probably about the same number of vermin.

Stone shook off the night's fug and reviewed the past thirty-six hours.

The overriding notion that crowded his brain to the exclusion of pretty much every other idea was that he'd made a huge blunder. When he'd returned to Paula Grayson's hotel room in the early hours of Saturday morning to deliver his handwritten reference, and found her body, blood drenching the sheets and a massive, jagged blade hinting provocatively at the cause of death, his first thought had not been *How can I evade the misdirected forces of justice when they see my kitchen knife and assume me to be a double-murderer?*

No. Despite his horror at the scene in front of him, Stone had been more prosaic than that.

Stone's first thought was to call 999.

It was something he regretted deeply.

While he waited for the police to arrive, he'd considered a few options. Given the gruesome nature of the scene that greeted him, he'd stepped outside the room and there found himself thinking both rationally and unemotionally about his situation. He felt more than a little guilty that he had not been more deeply affected by the murder of someone he'd once had feelings for, but the urgency of his plight and the logical domains of his prefrontal cortex overrode any inclination to the kind of mental distress that would interfere with basic functioning.

He could get upset later. For now, he needed to think.

It crossed his mind to contact DCI Carlton and let her know directly that she had another person to add to her roster of Norcester murder victims. He'd ruled that out as bordering on collaborating with the enemy. Carlton would find out about the latest attack soon enough. And she had, after all, expressly forbidden the reading group from talking about the case, even among the four of them, so really she only had herself to blame if he declined to mention this development to her.

He'd thought about vacating the premises in the hope of absenting himself from a second crime scene before it was even identified as such by the local constabulary. That one was even simpler to veto: his DNA would be all over the place from his visit the previous evening, and forensics would have him named, catalogued and in the frame for Paula's murder faster than you could say 'prime suspect'. Nothing shouts 'perpetrator' louder than running away, however innocent you are.

The other thing he'd mulled over, shuffling from foot to foot in the corridor outside Paula's room, was whether or not to notify the hotel's own staff. This had presented something of a conundrum, since he had purported to be her husband in order to gain access to the room and if he now reported her demise, then he might find himself catastrophically lured into continuing the charade. That would have caused even greater complications when the time came to explain himself to the police, and added considerable circumstantial weight to the case they were likely to want to build against him. Then again, he felt there was something rather sinister and underhand about not at least tipping off the receptionist, giving him fair warning about the imminent invasion of a murder squad and allowing the staff time to prepare themselves for what was bound to be a trying few days of police interviews, media intrusion and local notoriety. On balance, he'd settled on keeping the news to himself, and would have got away with it entirely if it hadn't been for the housekeeper, who passed him as she went down the corridor one way carrying a bundle of towels and came back five minutes later with a Henry Hoover to find him still inexplicably loitering there. He'd thrown her a forced smile but she hadn't returned it, and he could only guess at how the conversation might have gone when she got home after her shift.

'We had a murder at work today.'

'Oh yes?'

'I saw the man who did it. Shifty-looking bastard. I walked right past him. Twice.'

This putative domestic *tête-à-tête* had been driven forcibly from Stone's mind six hours later when he heard a heavy iron key clanking in the lock of his cell. He leaped involuntarily to his feet, realised the movement could be interpreted as a sign of jumpiness, and therefore possibly guilt, and sat down quickly again on the emaciated strip of woven fabric that passed for a mattress.

When the custody sergeant stuck his large red head in through the door, Stone tried to look nonchalant. He wasn't sure why.

'Five-minute warning,' the sergeant grunted, and Stone presumed he was getting special treatment. He'd seen enough episodes of *Z-Cars* to know that not every prisoner would be given the same advance notice of their impending questioning by investigating officers. In addition, the sergeant could have delivered his message much more quickly, and with less inconvenience to himself, by simply sliding back the peephole in the door and grunting it to him without ever setting foot inside the cell. Maybe Stone's professional status had swung something in his favour among the custodial staff.

Time would tell if the same applied to the detectives awaiting him in the interview room somewhere above his head.

Within five minutes of the interview beginning, Stone knew it was a false hope.

Detective Chief Inspector Miranda Carlton was no easier to communicate with as a suspect than she had been when he was a mere witness. The promotion had done nothing to ease his predicament. Half a week had gone by since he'd first faced her and he thought she looked tired, but her eyes were lucid and, in depressing contrast to his previous encounter, her line of enquiry seemed to Stone to be razor-sharp and precision-tooled.

A bit like the knife that had killed Paula.

'You're not denying this is your knife?' she'd said, nudging the bagged and bloodied weapon towards him across the table.

Stone looked at her, then at the duty solicitor to his left. He didn't bother looking at DS Muir, who sat diagonally across from him with a thick brown folder of papers in front of him, an open notebook beside it and his trusty pencil stub poised to inscribe his every utterance, even though a tape was clattering noisily through the recording device at the end of the table.

'It'd be a bit pointless to try, wouldn't it?'

'And you're aware, since you were there, that this was the weapon used to murder Paula Grayson.'

'I imagine it was stolen when my house was burgled. I'd foolishly left it on a table in the hall.'

Carlton snorted. 'Very convenient. Rather like the burglary itself. You wouldn't like to tell me now that you staged the whole thing, would you? It would save everyone an awful lot of time.'

The duty solicitor – a man who'd introduced himself to Stone with a limp handshake and a muttered 'Digby' – leaned towards his new client, shielding his mouth from the police officers to whisper in Stone's ear.

'You don't have to answer that.'

Stone sat upright again without looking at the lawyer.

'My solicitor's advising me that I don't have to answer that,' he told Carlton.

Digby let out a frustrated splutter. 'You didn't have to tell them.'

Stone raised an eyebrow towards the senior officer.

'I think this could be a long morning.'

Carlton's eyes narrowed, she shifted her gaze to Digby, then returned to Stone.

'You know you're allowed to appoint your own solicitor, don't you? I'd be happy to wait an hour or two. It won't make much difference to the investigation. It's all pretty clear-cut. I can't imagine we'll need too long to wrap things up.'

'No point,' said Stone, his hopes sinking. Carlton had already made up her mind. 'I won't be taking their advice anyway, so it might as well be him.'

'All right. If you insist.' She half-turned to Muir. 'Make a note of that, would you, Sergeant? Professor Stone has declined our generous offer of instructing his own brief.'

Muir didn't reply but scratched furiously into his notepad, his tongue sticking out between his lips like a studious schoolboy.

'Now, Professor, perhaps we could start with the formalities. Your full name.'

'Stone,' he said, his face impassive.

'No,' she said. 'Full name, please. For the record.'

'*Professor* Stone.'

She sighed. 'I think you might be right about it being a long morning. An initial, then?'

Stone thought about it. An initial wasn't the end of the world.

'E.'

'E?'

'E.'

'Like Morse.'

'Not really. His first name was Endeavour. Mine isn't.'

Carlton leaned forward, putting both her elbows on the table and clasping her hands under her chin.

'I could do you for obstructing justice, you know.'

'But you won't.'

'Really? Why's that?'

'No point,' repeated Stone. 'You believe you've got a rock-solid case, so it doesn't matter what happens in this interview. It doesn't matter if I tell you everything I know or if I don't say anything at all. It won't make a blind bit of difference to your case one way or the other.'

'Maybe,' she said. 'Maybe not. But I would like to hear your version of events. For the record.'

Stone had spoken the truth: it wouldn't make any difference to the way things played out. But he told Carlton everything he knew anyway. He told her about visiting Paula at her hotel the previous evening; about Paula's sordid blackmail to which he, even more sordidly, had submitted, returning in the small hours to deliver the handwritten testimonial; about Felicity Penman's previous life in the town where he'd last worked in academia, and the improbable but factually correct circumstance of their paths having crossed in both places, albeit tangentially; even about her drug-dealing friend, whose story was completely unrelated to current events, as far as Stone could tell, but who helped him to form a complete narrative for his inquisitor.

Carlton listened without interrupting until, after almost twenty minutes of non-stop divulgence, Stone came to a halt.

She leaned forward from the relaxed posture she'd adopted while he was speaking and pulled her shoulders back as if flexing her official muscles. It seemed it was her turn now.

'So, we've got three women, all of whom were connected to you via the university in some way,' she said. 'And all dead, coincidentally.'

The news came as a shock to Stone.

'Felicity's friend is dead too?'

Carlton stared at him for a long moment. Stone suspected she was trying to work out if his confusion was genuine.

'Contrary to what your little group seems to think about the police, we haven't just been sitting here idly waiting for a killer to walk in and surrender themselves. We've been doing a little investigating of our own. Does the name Lucy Eastwood mean anything to you?'

She stopped and stared again, presumably watching to see if the name registered any flicker of recognition in him.

It didn't.

'Or Mariella Brown?'

Another blank.

'Would you be surprised to learn, Professor, that Lucy Eastwood was the girl you knew as Felicity Penman?'

'I certainly would,' he said, trying desperately to figure out the mangled threads of the chief inspector's narrative.

'She changed her name when she came to Norcester.'

'And this Mariella Brown...?'

'The best friend. Until she died.'

Stone knew that the pause which followed was Carlton allowing the unspoken implication to land.

'Let me ask you another question, Professor. How many of these three women did you sleep with?'

In his head it felt like a fortnight but it couldn't have taken more than half a second for him to regain his composure.

'Just the one,' he said evenly. 'And just the once.'

'Let me guess: Paula Grayson.'

Stone didn't bother replying.

'Was this before or after you moved to Norcester?'

'Look, Chief Inspector, if you're trying to suggest some kind of sexual intrigue that might provide me with a motive to murder, then I'm afraid you're going to be sorely disappointed. What little *frisson* that existed between me and Ms Grayson was extinguished long before I retired. In fact, I hadn't seen Paula for nearly ten years before she showed up on my doorstep the other day.'

'So the CSI boys aren't going to find intimate traces of your DNA on her body?'

With nothing likely to make any difference to the outcome of the interview, Stone decided he wasn't going to play any more.

'This is the twenty-first century, Inspector,' he said, deliberately under-ranking her. 'Surely you have women among your crime scene investigators these days?'

She ignored his blocking tactics.

'You're telling me there was nothing untoward about your relationship with Felicity Penman or her friend?'

He stared disbelievingly at her, then at Muir, who was still scribbling without looking up. Stone wondered what was going on behind his shiny pate at that exact moment.

'Untoward? My God, maybe we are back in the nineteenth century. No, Inspector. There was nothing untoward. As far as I'm aware, I never even met this Mariella Brown, and I didn't know Felicity Penman before she moved to Norcester. Now, if you don't have anything more concrete to put to me, perhaps I could request a cup of tea?'

She ignored him again. He was getting a bit annoyed with it.

'Let me tell you what I think happened,' she said, leaning back and slowing her pace to let her words sink in. 'I think you and Mariella Brown had something going on at your old university. It wasn't nice, it certainly wasn't permitted, and maybe you came to your senses and broke it off with her. I think that's why she killed herself. Or maybe it wasn't suicide at all? Maybe that was your first murder. Anyway, it was chalked up as a tragic tale of youthful transgression gone horribly wrong and nobody was any the wiser.'

She paused and leaned forwards again.

'Except somebody was. Mariella's best friend Lucy knew

the whole sorry story, and she followed you to Norcester to make you pay. She invented a new persona, Felicity Penman, and found a way to get close to you. The bookshop was a stroke of genius – she guessed it was one of the likeliest places you'd get involved with, and she was right. As it happens, by all accounts she also found her calling. Everyone tells me she was a brilliant shop manager.'

Stone couldn't argue with that.

'And then, finally, she confronted you about Mariella. On Tuesday of this week, in fact. After the reading group meeting.'

She paused in her monologue and extended a hand to DS Muir without looking at him. He shuffled through a few sheets in his brown folder and placed a piece of paper in her hand. When she slid it across the table towards Stone, he looked down at it in curiosity.

He was staring at a grainy CCTV image of a nighttime scene in a location he vaguely recognised but couldn't quite place. In the centre of the picture was an indeterminate figure in dark clothing, almost completely obscured by an open umbrella.

'That's a photograph taken from CCTV in the street behind The Quaint Bookshop,' said DCI Carlton as if that would make everything obvious. 'Captured about three minutes before Felicity Penman was murdered. Now, perhaps you can save me the bother of getting a warrant to search your house by telling me now whether you own an umbrella like that?'

Stone peered closer. As far as he could tell from the poor-quality photograph, it was a bog-standard black umbrella with no distinguishing features. He thought he might have three in the coat rack by his front door.

'Of course I do. But so does half of Norcester. You're not trying to tell me you think that's me under the umbrella?'

'Aren't I?' said Carlton slowly.

'Well, if you do, you're more of a fool than I took you for. I was inside the bookshop five minutes before that, with at least three witnesses as an alibi.'

'But if I have the details right, you left them by the front door and went up the side alley.'

'That's right. And if I wanted to go back inside to murder Felicity, why on earth would I bother going up to the street at the back, putting up an umbrella and showing off to a CCTV camera? It makes no sense.'

Carlton smiled and leaned back, folding her arms. 'You've just said it yourself, Professor. An alibi. If you ever came under suspicion, you could claim you had exited the alleyway under your umbrella and there'd be no way to prove you wrong. Except it's backfired on you and become a crucial piece of evidence against you. Odd, isn't it, that we haven't got you in plain sight on CCTV leaving the scene.'

Stone was trying hard to resist the temptation to laugh.

'Not odd at all, in fact, Inspector, since I returned to the front of the bookshop when I heard Felicity's scream and rejoined the others.'

'Thus creating what you believed was a perfect alibi. But I think there was just enough time for you to nip out the back, have your picture taken under the umbrella, then slip back in through the side door, kill Felicity and be back at the front with the others to raise the alarm.'

Stone was starting to feel fidgety.

'And why exactly would I do that?'

Carlton shifted in her seat, evidently getting a second wind.

'All right, Professor Stone, let's play that game. Why would you kill Felicity Penman? I think it's straightforward enough. You had no idea that anyone knew the truth about you and Mariella, but when Felicity confronted you, you were confident that she was the only one who did. So it was a simple matter of removing the last obstacle to your freedom, once and for all. It must have been quite a shock when Paula Grayson turned up, bringing up all those painful memories and letting it slip that she'd actually spoken to Felicity. How long did it take you to realise that you'd have to kill her too?'

Stone had listened to Carlton's narrative with an increasing sense of horror. Of course it was full of holes wide enough to drive a tractor through but none of that mattered. Even the insipid lawyer sitting next to him would have been able to make a case in court that sounded plausible enough, from Carlton's 'facts', to prompt a verdict on three charges of murder, and the verdict wouldn't be falling Professor Stone's way.

'You're wrong,' he said simply, a black aura descending around the periphery of his vision.

'Yes, well, you would say that, wouldn't you?' said DCI Carlton, and smiled.

All that had taken place yesterday, but it was seared into Stone's memory as clearly as if it had happened a quarter of an hour ago. In the intervening twenty-four hours he hadn't even seen Carlton or Muir but he knew they'd be hard at work securing the evidence they needed to back up their theory. She'd informed him before she left that she would be seeking an extension to his incarceration, and that a friendly magistrate was already lined up for a hearing on Monday morning to go through the legal niceties.

The slow, plodding footwork of building a methodical, watertight case would already be well under way.

Stone could see the attraction for DCI Carlton of not bothering to look any further than her obvious suspect. Him.

What he couldn't understand was that it flew in the face of all the real facts.

Chapter Twenty-Five

It took less than five minutes for Fforde to reduce Kathy Brown to tears.

He wasn't proud of it.

'I'm really sorry, Mrs Brown,' he said, attempting to rest a comforting arm round her shoulders. She shook it away and buried her face in her hands.

Bella shimmied herself between the two of them and gave him a pointed nudge with her hip.

Go away, Harrison, she seemed to be saying.

'Go away, Harrison,' she said, and led Kathy over to the little table in the corner of her kitchen.

Fforde moved as far as the fridge and watched in silence as Bella and Lauren began fussing around the bereaved mother. As Bella sat beside her and put a gentle hand on top of Kathy's, Lauren went to the kettle and started brewing up.

'Sorry about him,' he heard Bella say. 'These men just don't get it, do they?'

Fforde didn't know – couldn't begin to understand – what alchemical magic Bella was weaving but it was working. Five minutes after that, with a strong cuppa clasped between her hands and two clucking hens flanking her solicitously, Kathy Brown was pouring her heart out.

She wept as she relived the traumatic events from several years earlier, when her only child Mariella – the first in her family to win a place at university – was ejected from Pittingham, with tragic consequences. The tears dried and her voice softened as she recalled the happy friendship Mariella had enjoyed with Lucy Eastwood, and what a lovely, uplifting girl Lucy had been until the drama played out, then how she'd isolated herself, kept away from Kathy and her husband Jay, apparently unable to bear the pain of staying close to the family. But her tone hardened again as she recounted how that same husband – a workaholic who was never particularly good at forging familial bonds – had also separated himself, first emotionally and then physically, abandoning Kathy three months after the funeral and leaving Pittingham for good soon after that. She hadn't seen him since that day and had no desire to do so.

That chapter of Kathy Brown's life was firmly closed.

'I'm so sorry you've been through such a terrible time,' said Bella. 'I can't imagine the agony you've suffered.'

'Thank you,' said Kathy, sniffling into a crumpled tissue. 'And it's Ms.'

'Sorry?'

'It's Ms, not Mrs. Doesn't matter.'

'No, thank you for putting me straight. And thank you for telling us all that. It can't have been easy.'

Kathy nodded. 'You bottle stuff up – you know? I've got friends who I've talked to a bit, but it's really hard. They try to be supportive but I know they don't really want to hear me whingeing on. Especially after all this time. It's actually quite nice to be able to talk to someone who didn't have anything to do with it.'

'Well, that's not entirely the case,' said Bella, looking nervously at Lauren.

Fforde wondered if she was weighing up how much to divulge to this already fragile woman, and whether she could risk mining her for information about Professor Stone. It would be good to know if Mariella's path had ever crossed with his.

'What do you mean?' asked Kathy, although Fforde could detect no sense of suspicion in her voice.

'Oh, we don't know anything about Mariella's friendship with Lucy,' Bella went on quickly, 'but a friend of ours is in trouble and we think it might have something to do with what happened to Mariella.'

Kathy looked at Bella, then Lauren, and finally up at Fforde.

'Trouble?'

Bella spoke evenly and slowly. 'Ms Brown, have you ever had any dealings with Professor Stone?'

Fforde's heart hesitated…

'Who?'

…and resumed the beat.

'Stone. He's a professor in the Maths department at Pittingham University – at least, he was until he retired.'

'Stone?' Kathy turned the name round in her mouth.

'Stone? I don't think so. I know Mariella had dealings with the head of that department, Derek Carmichael. He chaired her disciplinary hearing, made the decision to throw her out. But I don't recognise the name Stone.'

'Are you sure?' pressed Fforde, earning him a stern look from Bella.

'Look, I don't know why you're here asking me all these questions but if there's something you want to know, just come out and say it. Please.'

Bella took a deep breath. 'Professor Stone is our friend and he's been accused of murder.'

'Murder?' Kathy looked utterly shocked.

'Yes,' said Fforde from beside the fridge. The performer in him couldn't resist grabbing the limelight. 'The murder of Lucy Eastwood.'

'What? Lucy's dead?'

Bella shot Fforde a furious look. 'I'm sorry we had to break it to you so bluntly, Ms Brown—'

But Kathy had already dissolved into tears again.

As Lauren concentrated on pulling out of their tight parking spot a few minutes later, Fforde punched some numbers on his phone in the back.

'Yes?' barked DCI Carlton when the call was put through to her.

'It's Harrison Fforde here,' he said, trying to put some confidence into his tone in the face of the scary senior officer. He'd once worked with an older actor who'd played a double-crossing East End nark in *The Sweeney* and had confessed to being genuinely terrified as the full wrath of Regan and Carter was unleashed on his character. Play-acting could sometimes tap into the deepest emotions.

'I thought you might like to know that we've confirmed some information about Professor Stone which should go some way towards exonerating him.'

'Oh yes?' The inspector sounded incredulous. 'And what's that?'

'We've established that he didn't know Felicity Penman when she was a student at Pittingham University.'

'And why might that exonerate him?'

It was a good question and, like the nark in *The Sweeney*, Fforde had nothing. While Kathy Brown's evidence was promising, it could hardly be construed as conclusive.

'Even if you're right,' Carlton went on, 'it means nothing. He didn't have to know Felicity in Pittingham for him to have killed her in Norcester. And he didn't have to know Felicity to have killed Mariella Brown. We might not have pinned those murders on him yet but he's bang to rights over Paula Grayson, and it's only a matter of time before he coughs to the others. Is that all you've got?'

Fforde realised it was, and it didn't amount to much at all.

The detective didn't wait for an answer.

'I don't know what you're up to but I've given you plenty of warnings about digging around in my investigation. Stay out of it. We've got our man, thank you very much: I don't need you lot trampling about leaving your muddy footprints all over my pristine case.'

'She's right,' said Lauren after Fforde hung up the call. 'Kathy Brown doesn't change a thing.'

'So what do we do now?' asked Bella.

Fforde stared out of the windscreen at the road in front of them. It was going to be a long, depressing drive home to Norcester.

'Back to the drawing board, I suppose,' he said.

Chapter Twenty-Six

The board in question was a lot fuller than the last time Bella had seen it. Then it was merely an out-of-focus image on Harrison's phone containing a few pins that indicated nothing of any real import. Now it seemed to have everything.

'That's come on a long way,' she said. 'We must be able to do something useful with it.'

Fforde didn't seem so sure. 'I've added everything I can think of,' he said, pointing at the multitude of headshots, variously coloured pins identifying different locations and the bright red twine that he'd used to link connected elements to each other. It reminded Bella of a scarf she'd once started knitting but abandoned three-quarters of the way through when a visiting toddler got his hands on the skeins and decided to make himself a giant bowl of woollen spaghetti, unravelling three weeks of work in one destructive playtime.

'It still doesn't seem like much.'

'Nonsense,' said Bella, trying to sound upbeat. 'It's very … thorough. It's a bit like the one they have on *Broadchurch*.'

'Thank you!' he shouted, his face lighting up for the first time that day. 'That's exactly the look I was going for.'

Fforde cleared a space for her on the settee – she would have to come back another day and tidy up properly for him, she decided – and she sat back, staring at the corkboard dangling precariously on the wall.

'Drink?' he asked, heading towards the counter over to one side which presumably passed for a kitchen. It had a sink with a little water heater attached to the wall above it, and Bella could see a toaster and kettle under the single cupboard in the corner.

'I suppose the sun's over the yardarm, isn't it?' she said, looking at the bottle of vodka that Fforde had picked up. She was still a little woozy from her lunchtime gin and tonic at Derek Carmichael's: another drink now wasn't going to make much difference.

'I've no idea what a yardarm is or where the sun is in relation to it but I'm ready for a drink,' he replied, nodding at the clock on the mantelpiece. 'It's gone six.'

'Goodness, is it really?'

Bella was surprised at how quickly the day had gone. Their jaunt to Pittingham, with its unusual interviews, background information of varying degrees of usefulness and subdued return to Norcester while three minds silently whirred in contemplation, had left her exhausted. On any normal Sunday, she'd have been cooking a roast of her own, trying and failing to persuade Trevor to join her on a bracing walk and curling up in front of the *Antiques Roadshow* to hazard wild guesses at the value of some obscure trinket an optimistic viewer had dragged along for the consideration of one of the eccentric experts. Her favourite episode ever had been the one where she'd correctly identified a doll she'd owned as a child and was astonished to discover its rarity put it in the 'eight to twelve thousand' category of valuations. Her own example had been much-loved and thoroughly worn and had long since been consigned to history but she felt the thrill of sympathetic joy as the woman on the telly gasped at the expert's pronouncement.

Today, of course, there'd been no roast, no Trevor and now little prospect of the *Antiques Roadshow* as she and Fforde summoned all their powers of detection and a large vodka and tonic in front of the corkboard.

Lauren had declined Fforde's invitation to inspect the board at his apartment, pleading tiredness and the need to check on Simon, who had been left alone that morning with his laptop and free access to Lauren's drinks cupboard. While she was keen to continue their perambulations through the evidence, she'd agreed when she dropped them both off that she would pick things up with them again next morning, when she'd had the benefit of a good night's sleep. Bella suspected she'd had enough of Fforde for one day – he could be pretty bombastic if you didn't keep him in his place, she'd realised – but there was a side to him that she found endearing and he was entertaining company when there was no danger of his putting his foot in anything delicate. She was fascinated to see him on his home turf and wondered if he would relax a little when his defences were down.

She hadn't quite anticipated the extent of the flat's slovenliness, which seemed very at odds with the theatrical flamboyance of Fforde's wardrobe, but then she guessed that in his line of work he would pay considerably more attention to his public persona than his domestic orderliness. In any case, she was willing to put it to one side in the interests of pursuing the investigation.

'I see you've included all the players in the drama,' she said, waving her glass towards the board.

Besides Felicity and the four members of the reading group, the array of passport-sized photographs encircling the Indian takeaway's map included DCI Carlton, DS Muir, Mariella Brown and even bit-players such as Maurice Stapleton, whose blurry image looked like a candid snap taken from a distance and blown up: his face was contorted into a weird grimace that seemed to mix stifled fury with constipation.

'Where on earth did you get all those pictures?'

'Oh, it was easy enough,' said Fforde, sitting next to her and taking a large swig of his drink. 'Carlton was on the police website and Muir I found by accident in a picture on the force's newsletter to Neighbourhood Watch groups. Mariella was in all those newspaper reports, of course, and I sneaked one of Maurice the other night at the bookshop. Makes him look like a proper villain, doesn't it?'

Bella had to admit it did.

'Who are those two?' she asked, leaning forward to point at two photos in the top right-hand corner of the board.

'See if you can work it out. Where does the string go?'

Bella noticed that a single piece of yarn joined the two images together before stretching across the map to a location in the heart of the town centre. She struggled to disentangle the thread from the mass of others that were swamping it but eventually established that it led to the *Norcester Echo*.

'That's the reporter I spoke to and her editor,' said Fforde, smiling. 'I was quite pleased with them, I must say.'

Bella couldn't see what relevance the newspaper and its staff might have to the murder investigation, but she couldn't fault Fforde on his diligence.

'I don't want to knock what you've done here, Harrison. It looks amazing.'

'Thank you,' said Fforde, completely missing the implication that there was more to come.

'You don't think you might have gone a bit … over the top, do you?'

The smile on Harrison's face dimmed a little; the corners of his mouth dropped by a good thirty degrees.

Bella felt bad.

'No, no. Don't listen to me. It really is amazing – you've done a fantastic job. And that picture of Maurice, well, it should be framed and hung over the door of the bookshop.'

Bella looked at it again, the weaselly creature's eyes dark and strangely angry even in their blurriness. His mouth formed an ugly gash across his face, the glasses were slightly askew and his side parting and combover rendered his appearance unfortunately totalitarian.

But it wasn't his comically grotesque look that struck Bella now. It was his officiousness.

'Harrison,' she mused, still staring at the picture.

'Mmm?'

'How well do you know Maurice Stapleton?'

'Maurice? Oh, I don't know. He's always been lurking in the shadows somewhere for as long as I've been going to the bookshop.'

'Has he always been such a jobsworth?'

'How do you mean?'

'You know, ordering people about, acting like the shop is his own personal kingdom, that kind of thing.'

Fforde paused, looking contemplative.

'I don't suppose he has, really. Up until this week he hasn't had the rank to pull, so I've never paid him that much attention.'

'No. That's precisely it – rank.'

'Sorry, Bella. I'm not entirely sure what you're getting at.'

Bella didn't have to cast her mind too far back to recall the last time she'd run up against the objectionable acting manager of The Quaint Bookshop.

'Do you remember when I was trying to get into the bookshop last night?'

'Of course.'

'He wouldn't let me into the reading room on my own – kept going on about regulations and chaperones.'

'And you said he'd be a dangerous enemy to make.'

'I did, didn't I? Maybe I'm smarter than I give myself credit for.'

'No. Still not with you.'

Bella moved forward to the front edge of her seat and put her vodka down on the floor beside the settee.

'He's been hiding in plain sight from the start,' she said, feeling her senses heighten as she started to put the pieces together.

'Maurice? You mean harmless little Maurice Stapleton?' Fforde was looking from the photo on the corkboard to Bella and back again, trying to understand what she was telling him.

'That's my point,' she said, finally taking her eyes off the image and looking keenly at Fforde. 'What if Maurice Stapleton isn't as harmless as he makes out?'

Fforde slumped back on the settee, a look of confusion shrouding his face.

'Think about it, Harrison.' Bella stood up and began pacing up and down in front of the corkboard. 'You'll know better than me, because I've only recently joined the group, but if Maurice's behaviour over the past few days is anything like his normal character then he really could be a danger. He's been obstructive to our investigation from day one, he's barely shown any feelings of upset at Felicity's murder, and he was positively overjoyed to break the news to us about Professor Stone's arrest. Don't you think that's all a bit suspicious?'

The frown on Fforde's face deepened.

Bella was on a roll. 'And there's another thing. In fact, you said it yourself – you told me he'd been hanging around for years waiting for a shot at the top job but nobody would even give him a look-in.'

'That's true,' said Fforde slowly. 'But it's one thing wanting the job and not being given it; it's quite another bumping off the competition to get it.'

Bella stopped in front of the board and began examining it in minute detail. She'd got as far as the printouts of the four book covers when she let out a small cry of surprise.

'*The Body in the Library*.'

'What about it?'

She turned and stared at Fforde, appalled and shaken by the thought that had just revealed itself to her.

'If we're right about Felicity using the packages to send us a message of some sort, then I think I might have cracked the code for my book.'

'Go on.' Fforde was on her line and she was going to enjoy reeling him in.

'I spent most of last night reading it. Trevor came round about half past nine and was trying to wheedle his way back in but I bolted the doors and told him to go back to his sister's. Anyway, my point is that although I didn't get more than about halfway through, I've just realised that I didn't need to finish it.'

'Why's that?'

'Because the clue isn't *in* the book. The clue *is* the book.'

Fforde's eyebrows lowered in confusion, then lowered some more.

'Sorry, I'm not with you.'

'I think *The Body in the Library* is pointing us to … well, not a library, but maybe it was the closest thing Felicity could come up with. I don't suppose Agatha Christie wrote a book called *The Body in the Bookshop*, did she? Oh, come on, Harrison, do keep up. I think my book is pointing us towards Maurice Stapleton.'

'Bloody hell, Bella – you might be right.' He took another slug of vodka and stared at the corkboard. He was silent for a long minute. 'But what about the other books?'

Bella was already ahead of him, although she knew her thinking was little more than wild guesswork.

'When Maurice refused to let me in last night he said something strange. I found the door locked and he said "Eureka!"'

'So?'

'It seemed an odd word to use under the circumstances. But what if Maurice is a fan of Archimedes, like Professor Stone?

What if Felicity's breadcrumb to the Professor was meant to indicate Maurice too?'

Fforde's brow was creasing again. 'And the other books – the Holmes and the Stieg Larsson?'

Bella wondered why it was she who was having to do all the work.

'I don't know, Harrison. Maybe she was just telling Lauren to think like Sherlock. And maybe Maurice has a tattoo of a dragon on him somewhere.' She could hear the sarcasm in her own voice. 'Would you like me to pin him down while you check?'

Fforde seemed not to notice.

'But why all the subterfuge with the packages? Why not just tell us what she wanted us to know?'

'I've no idea. But we've got to be on the right track, haven't we?'

She could see that Fforde was beginning to run with the theory. He switched his attention back to the corkboard and she watched his eyes follow different strands of wool as he formulated new connections and tested new hypotheses.

'We need to go to the bookshop,' he said at last.

'You're not thinking of confronting him, are you?' said Bella, alarmed that his enthusiasm might lead them into a lethal situation.

'Not yet. But if we can lull him into a false sense of security – he loves a bit of flattery – then we might be able to get him to incriminate himself. We could also try to get a look at the manager's office. It'll be his now, so there could be evidence in there.'

Bella decided she needed to bring the heat down a little: it was all getting a bit too James Bond for her liking.

'It's closed on a Sunday, so we can't do anything until tomorrow morning at the earliest. I'll give Lauren a ring and fill her in with our thinking, and maybe we can meet up early and talk it through. We've got to tread carefully, though. If we're right, then we could have found Felicity's killer.'

'Maurice Stapleton,' Fforde muttered to himself in amazement. Then he looked up again at Bella.

'Are you serious about this?'

'Deadly,' she said.

Chapter Twenty-Seven

Professor Stone knew, as soon as the sergeant consented to meet him in his cell alone at eleven o'clock at night, that something was amiss.

His request to speak to DS Muir had been unorthodox, to say the least. The chief – and, indeed, only – suspect in a murder case had severely restricted rights, carefully delineated by the law, and while Stone had no specialist training that gave him particular insight into what those rights were, he had at least read *Criminal Law for Dummies* and could safely predict that an off-the-record chat with one of the officers conducting the investigation did not qualify as one of them. Especially if the chat were to take place without that officer's superior officer being involved.

Or aware.

So Professor Stone knew that something was amiss.

When he saw DS Muir's demeanour – somewhere between mildly apprehensive and positively jittery – he concluded that whatever the thing was that was amiss was almost certainly amiss by a wider margin than he'd originally imagined. Were there degrees of amissness, he wondered? On a scale of one to amiss, this thing seemed to have nudged Muir into double figures at least.

Muir came into the cell gingerly and stood by the door, which he pushed to. He gave a quick glance through the remaining crack, as if checking there was nobody waiting for him outside, then looked back at Stone.

The Professor had known him for less than a week, interacted with him only a handful of times, and yet he was sure he could see a difference in him. The pencil stub was still tucked behind his ear, the dishevelment still reminiscent of an empty bin bag being blown about in a back alley, the expression one of permanent inferiority. But there was a new element in Sergeant Muir's appearance that Stone couldn't place.

It was tiny, almost imperceptible, but he'd spotted it in Muir's uncharacteristic reserve during his interview with Carlton earlier in the day. There'd been no flashes of misplaced bravado from the sergeant, no snide comments piggybacking off the chief inspector's putdowns. He'd been noticeably reticent and it was enough to convince Stone to put everything he had on this slimmest of chances.

Not that he had much.

'Was there something you wanted?' asked the figure by the door, the flat vowels squashing his words into servility.

Uriah Heep. That was it. Stone vividly conjured up an image of Dickens's 'far too 'umble' legal clerk, leaning lankily over a desk and rubbing his hands together sycophantically.

'Geoffrey,' said Stone, dredging the man's forename from the stagnant ditches of his memory.

'You know I can't talk to you about the investigation,' Muir jumped in. It seemed to Stone that his defensiveness was a little too eager.

'No, I understand that.'

'Then how can I help? If you need anything practical, the custody staff are here to assist. I know it's not exactly the Renaissance Hotel, but they won't let you starve.'

'Thank you. The service is exemplary,' said Stone, trying not to sound too sarcastic. 'But it was you that I wanted to speak to.'

Muir's eyes dropped to the floor. He shifted his weight from one foot to the other.

'Something's up, isn't it?'

Muir didn't reply.

'Your boss, DCI Carlton. Does she always run her investigations like this?'

Muir chewed his cheek.

'All right, answer me this: is she pursuing any other lines of enquiry, apart from me?'

Was that a hint of a shrug?

'No need, is there?' said Muir, still not making eye contact.

'Isn't there? If you were in my shoes, wouldn't you be hoping she was keeping every avenue open?'

Muir seemed to make a decision.

'I can't talk to you about this. I'm not even supposed to be here.'

He turned and opened the door.

'Geoffrey,' said Stone before he could leave. 'There's something you should know.'

The underling stopped but didn't look back.

'The reason I wanted to speak to you. While I've been lying

here stewing, I've gone back over every conversation I can possibly remember with Felicity and I've had what I can only really call a revelation. Do you know what that revelation was?'

Muir didn't answer. He stood resolutely by the door, refusing to look at Stone.

'I remembered that she once told me about a police officer she'd come across when she was a student. It was only tangentially relevant to the conversation Felicity and I were having – something esoteric about the dangers of unchecked authority, I think – but I distinctly recall her bringing up this officer as an example of too much power held in hands that weren't as accountable as perhaps they should have been. It's taken me until just now to realise it, but the name of the officer concerned was something like Chorlton, or Carling, or Charlton. Or maybe Carlton.'

He watched intently to see if there was any reaction from the sergeant.

He thought he spotted the merest hint of a twitch in his cheek before Muir left the cell.

Lying on his lumpy bunk, staring out of the grilled slot that passed for a window high above him, Professor Stone felt the walls narrow. He cut a lonely figure these days, adrift from his former colleagues and reliant on the reading group for his primary company, but in the depth of the night he felt even more alone than usual. He could have asked about visitors and tried to get Fforde or Lauren or even Bella to go scouting for evidence of his innocence but he suspected he knew what the answer to a request like that would be, at least until he'd been up before the magistrates for a preliminary hearing. Something in him clung to the possibility that the trio were exercising their detective skills more successfully than he'd been able to, but as the hours wore on the hope diminished. Whatever they managed to find – and he had not the first inkling of what that might be, or how they might have gone about it – they would still be up against the might of the Norcester Constabulary and its fixation on one man as the perpetrator of, perhaps, three murders.

It didn't ease his nocturnal meanderings to know that the one man was him.

The sergeant had told him nothing – and everything. Carlton was on the attack; that much he knew from his interview. She also seemed to be betting everything on Stone being her culprit, and if he was reading Muir correctly, he seemed as mystified by that as Stone himself was. Unless Felicity's ancient history anecdote really had been about Miranda Carlton. He'd been fishing a little with that, chancing his arm to see if it sparked a reaction; he couldn't, in all honesty, swear that Carlton was the name she'd mentioned, and he certainly wouldn't want to repeat it in a court of law. But Muir's rapid departure was telling nonetheless.

As he drifted into a fitful sleep, Stone felt as if he was edging towards something meaningful. What was DCI Carlton up to? Was she trying to conceal something by throwing the blanket of suspicion over Stone? If so, what was it that she wanted to hide? He could hardly bring himself to believe that she might be involved in a deliberate cover-up.

But if she was, then his future looked very grim indeed.

Monday

Chapter Twenty-Eight

Harrison Fforde was feeling disappointed in his fellow reading group members. Professor Stone was, at this moment, being held somewhere in the depths of Norcester's main police station, beyond the reach of visiting associates. Paraphrasing Oscar Wilde, Fforde reckoned that to be charged with one friend's murder may be regarded as a misfortune; to be arrested for two looked like carelessness. Lauren, meanwhile, had found the whole theory of Maurice Stapleton's candidacy for suspicion utterly ridiculous and was, even now, driving over to Fforde's house to pick him up and take him to The Quaint Bookshop, where she intended to make a point of exposing Maurice as completely innocent, no matter how objectionable Fforde found him. And Bella, having faced the full weight of Lauren's dismissiveness about their hypothesis on the phone the previous evening, had decided to opt out entirely from the morning's expedition, preferring to stay at home and do some quiet detective work on her own.

Was he the only one committed to finding Felicity's killer and exculpating the Professor?

'I'm sorry but it just makes no sense,' Lauren said without preamble.

Fforde declined to respond and clicked his seatbelt into place.

'I know he's had his eye on the manager's job but there's no way a man like Maurice Stapleton would stoop to murder to get it. He's just not the type.'

'Is that the best defence you've got?' asked Fforde. 'Because I'm not sure how well it would stand up under cross-examination from a decent prosecution barrister. "No, your Honour, it can't have been Mr Stapleton – Lauren Sherwood thinks he's just not the type."'

'Oh, stop being so pompous, Harrison,' said Lauren, her eyes fixed on the road ahead. 'Look at the facts. Was he even in the bookshop last Tuesday? I certainly can't remember him being there – can you? And Felicity was bludgeoned to death with *The Complete Works of Ellery Queen*. Maurice Stapleton could barely have picked that up, let alone hit someone over the head with it. Plus, you're forgetting one crucial factor.'

Fforde was already feeling browbeaten. 'What's that?'

'Paula Grayson. Is Maurice supposed to have killed her too?'

'Could be two entirely separate murders,' said Fforde morosely, even though he didn't really believe it himself.

'No – forget Maurice. He's not our man. We've got to focus on the packages we were sent. Those four books are the key to the mystery.'

'Sounds like you might have a plan.'

'Not really. But they did all have Quaint stickers on them,

so I'm thinking we should find where they came from on the bookshelves. If Felicity really was trying to guide us, then perhaps we'll find something in the gaps to give us a clue as to what happened after we left on Tuesday night. Who knows – maybe Felicity left us a series of handwritten notes that point unequivocally to the perpetrator.'

Whatever clues might lie in the bookshop, unnoticed or unappreciated by the police, Lauren seemed on a mission to find them.

Except that Maurice Stapleton stood in their way.

Literally.

'Sorry, Mr Fforde, but that area is still out of bounds to anyone without official permission.'

Fforde thought again how hard a man Maurice was to like and he hoped to God he wouldn't end up getting the manager's job permanently. In sharp contrast to the delightful Felicity, he was a man with ideas not just above his station but so far above it as to be almost invisible to the naked eye.

'We only want to look at the Noir shelves,' Fforde said, vainly trying to sidestep him in the main nave of the shop. For a brief moment he considered simply picking him up, a hand under each armpit, and depositing him to one side, but he realised that would only provide short-term relief alongside its undoubted satisfaction. 'The police can't still be investigating?'

'No. It's a matter of internal store policy. You wouldn't understand.'

Fforde felt his irritation rising. Maurice's condescension was matched only by his priggish pout and Fforde was fast reaching the conclusion that violence might be the only answer.

Lauren tapped him on the arm and shot him a look.

'Come on. Obviously Mr Stapleton has important matters to attend to, and we're just getting in his way.'

Fforde was about to object and have another go at remonstrating with the man when Lauren gripped his elbow tightly and manoeuvred him away.

'Leave him alone,' she hissed, taking Fforde to the far side of the nave. 'He can't stand guard for ever.'

They sat at a table and waited, making casual conversation and flicking through the old copies of *The Bookseller* that lay there. Fforde could feel Maurice's eyes boring into the back of his head from his sentinel post near Noir, but Lauren was right: he couldn't stay there all day, could he? He'd have other work to do besides guarding his fiefdom against snoopers. He'd have to leave the section at some point. And when he did, perhaps they could sneak in and hunt down the four critical locations before Maurice realised they were even there. They wouldn't need long: just a few minutes should do it.

They waited ten minutes before Lauren came up with another plan. She went back over to the archway and engaged the imperious manager in animated conversation, gesticulating towards the front door. Fforde pretended to read his magazine. When he looked back, Maurice Stapleton was gone.

'I don't know what you did but I love you,' he said as he passed Lauren on his way into Noir.

'Don't ask,' she said, a glint in her eye. 'I'll wait here in case he comes back. Just don't be too long.'

The Christie section was enormous. Fforde hadn't expected so many titles to be ranged across so many shelves. There were hardbacks, paperbacks, large print, CD audiobooks and even a weathered old box that appeared to contain a twelve-cassette recording of Poirot stories. The copy of *The Body in the Library* that Bella had been sent had been in hardback and he quickly found the spot on the shelf that it had occupied. He pulled out four or five books to either side of the gap and peered into the darkness behind, fully expecting to see a slip of paper or some other kind of clue.

There was nothing. The back of the shelf was empty.

Archimedes would not be in this section, he knew, so he turned his attention next to Stieg Larsson. This was a more modest selection, but again had a telltale gap where Fforde's book had previously stood. *A Study in Scarlet* was also absent, even though Fforde checked assiduously under both Conan and Doyle.

Maurice Stapleton had clearly done an excellent job of keeping people out of this area.

As he reached the place where Felicity had been attacked, Fforde stopped for a moment and thought of his friend. With the shelves of fiction staring down all around him, he felt a sudden chill in the air and wondered what exactly had happened on this spot almost a week earlier. Who was it who had stepped out of the shadows among these bookcases and beaten her with one of her own tomes – the ultimate fate for a bookseller? Was it someone she knew, meeting her out-of-hours for an assignation that had gone disastrously wrong? Had she expected her assailant? Or perhaps they'd got it all arse-about-face and the crime had been nothing more than an opportunist burglary gone awry. Someone waiting in the darkness until the shop had been locked up for the night before they went searching through drawers and lockers for any valuables left carelessly on show, and who had been discovered, through devastating ill luck, by the manager herself and accosted with lethal consequences. But if that were the case, then surely the forensics officers would have found something incriminating: it was only those perpetrators acting with malice aforethought who could make sure they covered their tracks well enough not to be given away by a stray chewed fingernail or a discarded bit of nose-picking.

No, Felicity's murder had to have been deliberate and planned. He was convinced of it.

Fforde was making his way out of the forbidden shelves, deciding whether to ask at the till where he might find translations of the ancient Greek mathematicians, when a voice hailed him from across the nave.

'Hey there! Mr Fforde!'

The reedy tones were unmistakable: Maurice had spotted him. Lauren was nowhere to be seen.

'I thought I told you that area was out of bounds.'

'Did you?' he asked innocently as the man showed surprising sprightliness in his approach.

'You know very well I did.'

His face was darkening and Fforde wondered if he had the power to impose any sanctions on him. The last thing he wanted was to be banned from the bookshop when the reading group was in the middle of something really meaty.

'I still don't understand why, though,' he said, standing his ground as Maurice circled behind him and blocked his return to Noir.

'I told you – it's store policy.'

Fforde conjured up an image of some dusty shareholders sitting in a dusty office making careful rules about precisely who can go where when a murder takes place on the premises. He seriously doubted his mental picture matched reality.

'Who decided it?' he asked.

Maurice Stapleton hesitated.

'It doesn't matter who decided it. The fact remains that you are not allowed in there.'

Fforde wondered if he'd actually been seen emerging from the section or merely loitering in its vicinity. It was possible that Maurice didn't know he'd already done what he set out to do.

'All right, Mr Stapleton,' he said in a placatory tone. 'You're the boss.'

This made the acting manager pause as much as any of the objections Fforde had put up, and he realised he might have hit upon a winning formula. Appealing to Maurice's sense of superiority might just get him further than challenging it.

'While I'm here, I'd like your advice.'

'As long as it's not got anything to do with the tragic events of last week,' he said, looking to Fforde as if he'd drawn himself up an extra inch or two.

'Nothing at all,' he lied. 'I've been asked to audition for a role in an Archimedes biopic and I'd like to read up on him a bit. I don't suppose you've got any of his work in the non-fiction section, have you?'

The look on Maurice's face told Fforde all he needed to know: he had no idea of the relevance of Archimedes to the murder investigation.

'Er, well, yes … I think we might have. If we do, it'll be upstairs in the reference section, with science and engineering.'

He jabbed a stubby hand in the direction of the stairs.

Fforde marched away, wondering what had happened to Lauren.

'Er, thank you, Mr Fforde,' came the reedy voice from behind him. 'I appreciate your cooperation.'

It was the work of minutes to establish that *On Floating Bodies* should have been on the Mathematics shelf but wasn't. Instead, a gap in the spines taunted Fforde once more.

As he entered the main hall at the bottom of the steps, wondering whether he should just go home, a door in the far wall opened and Lauren stepped out. In her hand she clutched a plastic bag and, catching Fforde's eye as she crossed the hall, she made an urgent signal for him to turn and leave.

'What's going on? Where did you get to?' he asked as they hurried down the High Street towards the car park.

'The manager's office,' she said as if it was the most normal thing in the world. 'I saw an opportunity and I took it.'

Fforde was impressed. And also intrigued. Lauren was still clutching the bag.

'You found something in there?'

'In the bottom drawer, buried under a bunch of leaflets.'

She thrust the bag at Fforde, freeing her hands to search for the car keys in her pockets. As she unlocked the Mini, he rummaged through the contents.

Lauren had clearly not had time to sift anything. She'd lifted paper clips, rubber bands, even the little ink stamp thingy that was supposed to have been superseded by barcodes and computers but was surely the only reason anyone ever went into bookselling in the first place. And then, under a sheaf of creased A5 leaflets about a long-distant open day on the theme of Dungeons and Dragons, he found what Lauren had unknowingly been searching for.

A brown envelope. Exactly like the ones they had been sent.

Inside the car they explored their treasure further. In the envelope, tucked into the bottom corner, was a scrap of paper folded in half. Fforde pulled it out and opened it up.

The Secret of Father Brown.

Lauren was delving into the bag again and came up with something else.

A notepad. With names on it.

But not just any names: this was a list of people Fforde knew. At the top of the list, in blue ballpoint, he read 'Professor Stone', alongside an address in a pleasant part of town near the park. Below him was Lauren Sherwood, her address less salubrious but equally clearly written.

Third on the list was his own name, with his apartment details inscribed neatly beside it.

A gap of two lines followed, then – in a different-coloured ink, suggesting a later addition – Bella Bourton, with what Fforde assumed was her home address. Another two-line gap and a final name, this one in bright red.

Nicki Bailey, c/o the *Norcester Echo*.

With a sudden vehemence that took him completely by surprise, Lauren threw all the bag's contents onto Fforde's lap and powered up the engine.

'Is everything all right?' he asked as she reversed recklessly out of the parking spot and shoved the car into first gear.

'I can't believe we've been so stupid,' she said, forcing the Mini into a gap between two cars that both blared their horns at it.

'I can't believe we ever doubted the Professor. Of course he didn't murder Felicity or Paula Grayson. DCI Carlton's not just barking up the wrong tree – she's barking in the wrong forest.'

Fforde found he was quickly reminiscing about her old way of driving, like she had when they'd gone to Pittingham the day before. This Lauren was fast, she was wayward, she was dangerous. She also seemed to have solved the case.

'You were sent *The Girl with the Dragon Tattoo*, weren't you, Harrison?'

'Yes.'

'What does it mean to you?'

'Not much. I've read it, of course—'

'Really? Or have you just seen the Daniel Craig film?'

That smarted. 'No, thank you very much, Hetty Wainthropp. I have actually read it.' He paused. 'Saw the film as well…'

'All right, then. So what's it about?'

Fforde realised he remembered the film much better than the book.

'It's about a teenage girl who's disappeared. There's a serial killer … a journalist…'

'There you go – a journalist. Felicity was definitely sending us clues.'

Lauren couldn't, under closer questioning on the way back to her house, quite explain why the perpetrator had selected Felicity as her first victim, nor Paula Grayson as her second, nor what connection she might have had to either of them, nor how she could physically have carried out the murders, nor what her possible motive could be.

But none of that mattered. The point was that she knew who had done it. Now she had to act on that knowledge.

Once inside the house, she shouted for her brother but was met with only silence. Following her uncertainly into the living room, Fforde saw her go to Simon's laptop, which stood open on the chair, and start clicking and scrolling heavily, as if it held some secret that could only be divined by thumping it into submission.

When she stopped abruptly, uttering an oath Fforde had

never heard her use before, he knew something was seriously wrong.

Peering over her shoulder at the laptop screen, he realised they were looking at Simon's emails.

The message at the top of the inbox was from Nicki Bailey.

Its subject field read: 'Meet-up?'

Lauren clicked on the email and they watched it spring open. In just two lines, Nicki – writing from her work address – was responding to an invitation from Simon to get together for coffee and a chat. He had a strong hunch about the killer and as she was writing about the murders he wanted to check some facts with her before floating his ideas with Lauren. Her affirmative reply, really rather keen in tone, suggested both a venue and a time. The venue was the Coco Café. The time was now.

Despite his misgivings about Lauren's latest theory, Fforde could see that she was frantic. He took out his mobile and searched for the café, quickly discovering that it was opposite the offices of the *Norcester Echo*.

Lauren, meanwhile, was pushing buttons on her own phone. Fforde could hear that the call rang out, going to voicemail.

'Simon, listen to me. You mustn't go to the café. Call me as soon as you get this – it's vitally important.' She paused, then added as an afterthought: 'I mean it. I'm not messing around.'

She was halfway towards the front door when Fforde stopped her with a hand on her arm.

'Shouldn't we think about calling the police?'

Lauren thought for no more than five seconds.

'There's no point. Carlton wouldn't believe us and if we called 999 we'd probably be dismissed as time-wasters. To be fair, we can hardly expect Norcestershire's finest to drop everything and go chasing a random lead on the say-so of one potentially crank caller. How would you react if you were on the receiving end of a call like that?'

Fforde realised she was probably right.

'What are we going to do then?'

A look of incomprehension passed across Lauren's face.

'What do you think we're going to do? We're going to go to the *Echo*. I think my brother's in mortal danger.'

Chapter Twenty-Nine

It was the previous week's copies of the local paper that had done it. Bella was glad she'd inherited her parents' habit of buying the *Echo*, even though it had become considerably slimmer, less entertaining and more crammed with typographical errors than in their day. Now, fortuitously the morning before she'd be putting them out for recycling, the back copies were paying real dividends.

She'd been quite content to leave Lauren and Fforde to their jaunt. Lauren had been more than a little dismissive the previous evening, rejecting Bella's suspicion of Maurice Stapleton out of hand, and Bella had, for the first time since meeting the girl, felt unvalued by her. If she wanted to prove a point by making a trip to the bookshop, then let Harrison take the brunt of it. She might be overreacting, Bella thought, but a morning away from the others might help her to think clearly.

Besides, she had other things to be doing.

Bella had come to the conclusion that the best way to promote Professor Stone's innocence was to have it declared on the pages of the town's newspaper. A week ago, she wouldn't have had the first clue how to go about doing that. Now, however, she was a seasoned veteran in the world of investigation, with corkboards, internet searches and a crime-fighting gang to match Scooby-Doo's under her belt. Inevitably she would take the role of Velma, Lauren being far more Daphne-like in her youth and glamour; among the boys, of course, Stone was a natural Freddie, while Fforde bore more than a passing resemblance to Shaggy.

In many ways.

Gathering the *Echo*s from the pile beside the back door awaiting collection, she flicked through the editions since the day after Felicity's murder. She read report after report, from an overblown account of the crime itself, written in sub-tabloid sensationalist language, to Fforde's dramatically misguided interview, no less hyperbolic and quoting phrases that sounded exactly like him. Every article carried the same byline: Nicki Bailey.

It was to Nicki Bailey that Bella needed to make her pitch.

And Maurice Stapleton was going to be her accusee.

The walk from her home to the offices of the *Echo* would, on a pleasant summer's day, be one of some charm and appeal. On a blustery, rain-spitting, lowering afternoon, Bella could only think of it as miserable. With no bus route connecting the two locations, she fought her way up the hill to the top end of town, gusts prompting her to wrap her coat even tighter around her and clamp her woolly hat firmly onto her head.

Under the building's portico, she stood with her back to the front door and gazed out at the view across the town below her, the town she called home. In recent years, it had managed to avoid the worst excesses of high-rise construction, although one or two cranes on the skyline suggested that might be in the process of changing. In the far distance, a second hill rose up on the opposite side of town, cradling the settlement between them, where the meandering River Nore provided a focus for the industry and trade that had gathered around its useful features. Bella remembered her mother once telling her as a child that if the river had been a little wider and deeper, allowing for larger waterborne freight in medieval times, then Norcester might have found itself as the capital city, instead of a Midland non-entity more bypassed than adored. It had carved itself a moderate reputation over the centuries as a centre for paper-making – Norcester stationery still carried a certain cachet in some quarters – but the more the world shifted to a digital axis, the more niche its output became. Now, only one paper mill remained along the banks of the Nore and the citizens' chief employment came from the extensive call centres that had made their home way over to Bella's left, under the giant grey rectangles that lined the river valley on its way to the North Sea.

Inside the offices, she went to the back of a queue of people waiting to be seen. The unkempt man in front of her fidgeted as he clutched in his fingerless-gloved hand a sheet of paper tightly packed with green-inked, handwritten capital letters. Bella wondered what had upset him, for upset he clearly was.

Her attention was drawn away from the twitching wretch by her mobile phone, which vibrated in her coat pocket, causing her to start. She pulled out the device and tapped the icon for WhatsApp to see who had messaged her.

It was Harrison Fforde. He'd sent a picture and a single line of text to the group chat.

The picture appeared to show a list of names and addresses

on a notepad. Without her glasses she couldn't make it out clearly. But she could read the line of text.

Found in Felicity's office drawer, it said.

Bella sighed at Fforde's ambiguity. Why did he have to be so cryptic? If he had something to tell her, couldn't he just come out and say it? At best it looked like he'd managed to come up with half a solution to the origin of the packages; but half a solution was no solution at all, when you came to think about it.

She was composing a reply to the effect that she was busy at the *Echo* and would respond later when the man in front of her started shouting.

'I've been waiting four and a half hours to speak to someone. Why won't anyone talk to me?'

He waved his missive in the air as if to prove his point.

One of the three girls behind the desk called out to him.

'No you haven't, Rodney. I saw you come in less than five minutes ago.'

'It's a bloody disgrace,' Rodney yelled, and stormed off towards the door.

'Let me have your letter, at least,' the girl shouted after him.

In a swerve that would have outfoxed Diego Maradona, Rodney diverted to the desk, slammed his sheet of paper down without making eye contact with the girl, and exited the building.

'Next, please.'

The girl caught Bella's eye and waved her over.

'Is he all right?' Bella asked, looking over her shoulder as the front door banged shut behind Rodney.

'Don't worry about him,' the girl said. 'He's a regular.

Comes in every Monday, Wednesday and Friday on his way to the Rose and Crown, demanding we print his latest letter.'

'About what?'

'Who knows? Could be anything. Escaped lions roaming the High Street, aliens stealing his Bee Gee albums, the Eurovision Song Contest being fixed by Michael Gove – you name it.'

'Do they ever get printed?'

'Never. But it doesn't matter. He doesn't read the paper anyway. Now, what can I do for you?'

She flashed a smile revealing pristine dentistry that was surely well beyond the pay scale of an office receptionist.

Bella had to think for a moment. With everything that was going on, she momentarily forgot why she was at the *Norcester Echo* in the first place.

'Oh yes,' she said, remembering. 'Would it be possible to speak to one of your reporters?'

'I should think so. I'll see if anyone's free.' She reached for the large phone propped up in front of her and picked up the receiver. 'Can I ask what it's about?'

'Oh, sorry,' said Bella. 'I should have been clearer. I don't want to speak to just any reporter. I want to speak to Nicki Bailey. It's about the murder at the bookshop.'

The girl behind the desk replaced the phone in its cradle and adopted a serious-looking face.

'Are you connected in some way? It's a terrible story, isn't it?'

Bella wasn't sure how to answer. She looked down as she thought, noting the long, pink-painted nails that Bella would have found infuriatingly cumbersome on the ends of her own fingers.

'I suppose I am really,' she said, looking the girl in the eye once more.

'I'm so sorry,' the girl said.

'It's all right,' said Bella cheerfully. 'I'm not family or anything. I just have some information that I think Nicki might be interested in. I believe the police have arrested the wrong man.'

The girl looked shocked and intrigued at the same moment.

'Goodness. That does sound like something Nicki would want to hear.'

She picked up the phone again and punched three digits on its keypad, her nails proving no impediment. Bella nodded appreciatively.

'Hello? Is Nicki there, please? I've got someone at the front desk she's going to want to speak to.'

Bella watched the girl listen intently for a few moments, taking the opportunity to read the name badge that was pinned to her cream blouse. She recalled doing something similar with Felicity six weeks earlier.

Ariana.

'I'm so sorry,' Ariana said, putting the phone down a second time. 'Nicki's not in right now. Apparently she's got the morning off.'

Bella was surprised: she'd thought the continuing pursuit of a double-murderer in Norcester would have kept the paper's crime correspondent busy round the clock.

'Would you mind having a word with the editor instead?'

It seemed like a step up to Bella; if she could persuade the editor himself to run a story declaring that Professor Stone was innocent, she would count that as an extremely good morning's work. In her mind's eye she could already see the

Professor giving her a grateful hug after his release, with the real culprit safely locked away thanks to Bella's ingenuity and tenacity.

As she was led by Ariana through one open-plan office and into the busy editorial department, Bella pressed 'Send' on the message she'd been posting back to Fforde. Through the second door, the first thing she noticed was the bright red wall at the far side, where a stocky, ruddy-faced man was just coming out of a room separated from the main one by an opaque glass panel and door. It reminded Bella a little of the bookshop's reading room – minus the vivid décor, of course – and she remembered again why she was here: this was for her newfound friends.

She put a determination into her step and began making her way through the sea of desks.

The editor wouldn't know what had hit him.

Chapter Thirty

'Get away from my brother, you bitch!' Lauren shouted, crashing through the door of the Coco Café and lurching in the direction of Simon's table.

The whole place fell instantly silent. A lady over to Lauren's left stopped with a scone just inches from her gaping mouth and another customer let out a terrified squeal before dropping her cup. Even before it had smashed into tiny pieces on the floor, Lauren had reached her brother, with Fforde stumbling a few paces behind.

It was only then that she realised she had no idea what to do next.

She stood lamely beside their table, staring angrily at Nicki Bailey. The rest of the café minded its own business in tones markedly more hushed than they had been when Lauren first rushed in, although she suspected that surreptitious eyes were on her, wondering what craziness she was going to come out with next.

Simon looked utterly bewildered.

'What the hell is wrong with you, sis?' he asked in a low voice.

She turned on him.

'I thought I told you to stay away from her?'

He had the good grace to look a little guilty. Then he pushed back.

'I don't have to do everything you say, though, do I?'

'Oh, for God's sake, Simon – you're not twelve any more.'

'Then let me live my own life for once. I'm perfectly entitled to come into town on my own and meet someone for coffee.'

Lauren's emotions bubbled over.

'Not when they're a murderer, you're not,' she shouted, and burst into tears.

The café stopped minding its own business and started minding theirs again.

'What are you talking about?' said Simon, leaping to his feet to put a comforting arm round his sister and usher her onto his chair.

Lauren struggled to hold back the churning feeling in her throat. She couldn't believe that she was sitting opposite the woman who'd killed Felicity Penman and Paula Grayson and was even now calmly enjoying a cup of what looked like a rather delicious iced macchiato with her naïve little brother.

The naïve little brother squatted next to her chair and rested a hand on her arm.

'Calm down, sis, and tell me what on earth is going on?'

Lauren delved into her coat pocket for a tissue and dabbed at her nose. Then she waved the damp item across the table.

'It's her, Simon. She's the killer.'

A buzz of horrified excitement sprang up across the café.

One or two people started putting on their coats, and the lady who'd dropped her cup scurried over to the counter, waving a ten-pound note. She seemed in a hurry to leave.

Even through her blurry vision, Lauren could make out the impassive face of Nicki Bailey staring back at her across the teacups. Was that a hint of a smirk on her lips?

'Don't try and deny it,' Lauren said. 'We know it was you. We've found Felicity's evidence.'

She signalled to Fforde, who oddly seemed to be keeping his distance from the table. Now was the time for him to step up.

'Show her, Harrison.'

Nicki seemed remarkably calm for someone who'd just been collared for double murder. She picked up the teaspoon from her saucer, dropped a cube of sugar into the cup and stirred it slowly. Lauren wondered if she was considering using the spoon as an offensive weapon. She might have rescued Simon from immediate danger but there was still a killer to be dealt with, and Fforde was so far proving less than useless. Lauren had serious doubts about her capacity to restrain a psychopath on her own.

Because that's what Nicki Bailey clearly was.

'I'm sorry, Lauren, but you've got it all wrong,' Nicki said eventually. 'I don't know what this evidence is that you claim to have found, but whatever it is, you've misinterpreted it.'

'See?' said Simon, patting Lauren's arm in a feeble display of comfort. 'Nicki's not the killer. In fact, she did you a big favour by not running that interview she did with you. Of course, I had to ask her nicely.'

He gave Nicki a sweet smile.

'Don't listen to her, Simon. She's lying to you.'

She turned to the whole room, everyone staring openly at them now.

'Somebody call the police. This woman is a killer.'

Nobody moved.

'Lauren, you're embarrassing yourself,' said Nicki, and leaned forwards.

When she spoke again, her voice was lower, although Lauren expected most of the neighbouring tables would still be able to hear. Good – she wanted them to.

'I didn't even know Felicity Penman, I'd never heard of Paula Grayson until after she was killed, and Simon and I have been discussing the real identity of the murderer. You can't seriously think I had anything to do with it?'

Nicki summoned up a faint smile that Lauren assumed was meant to convince her of her innocence, but she was determined not to be fooled again. She'd already been wrong about Professor Stone, and look where that had left the old man. The least she could do was make sure the real perpetrator was arrested: she might never get over her guilt for believing the Professor was capable of murder but she could at least try to do right by him now.

She was starting to feel angry again. She turned to Fforde and gestured for him to hand over the contents of Felicity's desk. When he passed her the notepad, she thrust it under Nicki's nose.

'There. Look at that. Felicity made that list of people to send clues to. We all got packages containing books that were designed to point us in the direction of her killer. And look – there it is, your name at the bottom. In red.'

She placed heavy emphasis on the last two words, as if that would add extra weight to her argument.

Nicki smiled more broadly.

Wow, Lauren thought. *She really is a psychopath.*

'There's a good reason why my name is on that list,' she said.

'Yes – because she knew you were out to kill her.'

'No, Lauren. My name is on that list because I got a package as well.'

It took a moment for Lauren to comprehend what she'd just said. When she did, it felt like the wind had been punched out of her.

'You?'

'Me.'

It made no sense. If Felicity believed Nicki was trying to kill her, why would she include her on the list of people to send clues to?

'What was in your package?'

'A slip of paper with a book title on it—'

'*The Secret of Father Brown,*' said Simon.

'Yes. And a copy of *The Prodigal Daughter.*'

Fforde piped up. 'The Jeffrey Archer novel?'

'Exactly. And I think I know what it means.'

Simon stood up and rubbed his thighs, bringing the circulation back.

'So you see, sis – Nicki's on our side.'

Lauren wasn't listening to him.

'You think you know what it means?'

'The book title and *The Prodigal Daughter* – they're basically the same clue. I think Felicity was trying to point us all to Mariella Brown's father.'

For the second time in less than a minute, Lauren felt punchdrunk. The entire case she'd built to identify Nicki

Bailey as the murderer had collapsed like a house of cards. Admittedly, the cards had been poorly made and the house was standing in an industrial-level wind tunnel, but it still hurt.

Simon grabbed a chair from a nearby table and sat down. Fforde followed suit. As usual, Simon had his phone in his hand and was busy scrolling on the edge of Lauren's peripheral vision.

She stared at Nicki, trying to wrap her head round the latest development and reframing the reporter as an ally instead of a nemesis. If she was honest with herself, she'd rather enjoyed having a nemesis: it had made her feel significant, like the heroine in a psychological thriller rather than a secondary character in a cosy crime novel. If all she could bring to the narrative was mistaken identity and a comic interlude in a coffee shop, then what good was she?

It was just like her novels all over again.

Lauren had a changeable relationship with her unfinished manuscripts, she would readily admit. On one hand, they were a much-needed outlet for her inner emotional life, which she had refused to allow to the surface since the age of thirteen on account of her innate vulnerability and raging imposter syndrome. On the other, she could rarely convince herself that they were anything better than childish ramblings, destined never to see the light of day or another reader's eyes. Either way, she had used her lack of faith in them to prevent herself from approaching agents and publishers, certain in the knowledge that she would be rebuffed and her confidence knocked irreparably. She had once pseudonymously entered a competition requiring the submission of the first three chapters of a romantasy novel, and her fourth-place result had briefly boosted her self-esteem to the point of writing the next three chapters. But then the momentum had gone off the boil – rather like the relationship between the werewolf and the succubus in the story – and *The Darkening Heart* remained uncompleted somewhere in her computer's memory banks.

And then the obvious question struck her and she jumped back on the psychological thriller horse.

'So who *is* Mariella Brown's father?'

'That's just what we were trying to work out when you blundered in,' said Simon. 'And I think I might have the answer.'

With a flourish, he turned his phone round to face them and gestured at it with his free hand, like a magician's assistant displaying the inexplicably empty box.

There on the screen was a social media feed, a photograph of a group round a restaurant table visible beneath a post that contained only emojis of balloons, party hats, popping champagne bottles and hearts.

'What are we looking at?' Lauren asked.

'Mariella Brown's Facebook page. Photos from her eighteenth birthday.'

Lauren took the phone from Simon and peered hard at the photograph. It was difficult to make out any individual faces but it certainly looked like a celebration.

'Are there more?'

'Flick to the next one.'

Lauren swiped and found herself staring at a close-up image of a smiling young woman and an older man embracing her, captioned with just five words: 'Me and my lovely dad.' But the young woman's smile wasn't quite right – there was nothing going on behind the eyes – and she wasn't returning the man's embrace.

He, by contrast, looked triumphant.

But Lauren didn't care how he looked. All she cared about was that she knew him.

Where had her doubts about Professor Stone originated? Who, besides Nicki, had a connection that could be surmised from the book in Fforde's parcel? And who was in a perfect position to manipulate the public narrative around a double murder in the town through the pages of the *Norcester Echo*?

With a gasp, Lauren flashed the image in Nicki's direction and watched the colour drain from her face. In unison, they both looked out of the window, across to the newspaper offices, then back at each other.

'Will he be there now?' Lauren asked.

Nicki nodded.

Lauren grabbed her phone where it lay on the table, starting to get up. Then she stopped, horrified. WhatsApp was showing her a new message.

From Bella.

> Reply later. I'm at the Echo. Telling the editor I know who did it.

They crashed through the front door of the newspaper, Nicki leading the way with her official pass in her hand. She ran over to the desk, ignoring the affronted woman who was being dealt with, and waved her phone at the girl on the other side, whose name tag revealed her to be Ariana.

'Have you seen this woman today?'

Ariana sized up the little group in front of her, recognised

Nicki and leaned in to look at the photograph of Bella from the WhatsApp group.

'She came in a few minutes ago.'

'And then left?'

'No. She wanted to speak to you but they told me you were on a half-day.'

'I was,' said Nicki. 'So where is she now?'

'I took her through. She's in with the editor.'

Lauren felt a sudden burst of responsibility for Bella, whom she'd tried to welcome into the reading group but whose theory she'd been less than charitable about the previous evening. To be fair, Bella had been miles off the mark, but there'd been no need to be quite so cavalier about it. If anything were to happen to Bella now, Lauren knew she would never be able to forgive herself.

She grabbed the pass from Nicki's hand, vaulted the reception desk and ploughed through the door into the open-plan offices.

She could sense the other three just yards behind her but she had the edge on them. She made straight for the door marked 'Editorial', flashing the pass on the digital entry pad and barging it open with her shoulder. On the other side, all eyes turned to look at the noisy intruder but Lauren took no notice.

'Is the editor in his office?' she shouted to nobody in particular.

Nobody in particular answered. They all looked terrified at the appearance of a windswept, screaming banshee in their midst.

'Straight ahead,' said a voice from behind her, and she felt Nicki push her in the direction of the far wall, where she remembered the opaque glass door labelled 'Editor' and the warm red glow within.

Heaving her shoulder against the glass, she let out a rebel yell of fear and rage.

The momentum took her across the room, passing Bella – whose face was frozen in astonishment – and thundering into the form of Jerry Northover, standing behind Bella with his hands raised above his head, clutching a heavy-looking piece of glassware.

The collision sent them both sprawling, the glassware shattering in a corner and Lauren winded temporarily. But Fforde was right behind her and leaped on top of Northover, sitting heavily on his chest and pinning his arms down with his knees.

'I'm terribly sorry,' he said to his captive. 'I've no idea what's happening but I think it's best if you stop wriggling.'

Lauren caught her breath and sat upright, staring at the unfortunate editor between Fforde's knees.

Fforde looked curiously at her.

'What's going on, Lauren?'

'Felicity was too clever for all of us,' she said, waving a hand vaguely at the décor. 'How's this for a clue?'

'What clue?' Fforde asked.

'This room, Harrison.'

'It's a red office. So what?'

'No, Harrison. It's not a red office. It's a study in scarlet. And you're currently sitting astride Jerry Northover – or should I call you "J"? Everyone, meet Mariella Brown's father. Father Brown, you might say.

'A man with a secret.'

Chapter Thirty-One

Police chases were even more exciting in real life than they appeared on television, Fforde decided as they threaded through the streets of Norcester crammed into Lauren's little orange Mini. Her driving seemed to have gone up yet another notch, with amber lights jumped, cyclists capably dodged and even the brakes being soundly tested at a pedestrian crossing to avoid an elderly lady walking a dog over to the park. Fforde couldn't be sure if Lauren had actually broken any traffic laws – she maintained a steady thirty miles an hour, he could see from his seat behind her – but she was certainly managing to rile the pursuing officers.

Unlike their counterparts in movies where law enforcement are raiding a newspaper's office, there had been precious little resistance from the staff of the *Norcester Echo* when the intrepid trio from the reading group paraded their glorious leader out of the building, his arm held in a half-nelson by Fforde and the two lady members flanking him with severe expressions on their faces. One thin man in a striped tie and thick-rimmed spectacles had attempted to block their path through the outer office but Nicki Bailey had moved him aside magisterially and they had been allowed to leave by everyone else. Someone in the Editorial department must have phoned the police as soon as they left, however, for there were blue flashing lights and sirens on their tail within a minute of regaining Lauren's car for the journey across town.

Fforde didn't know why the boys in blue had bothered turning out: the Mini was heading for the central police station, after all.

Maybe they'd guessed that and had decided not to go for a full-scale pursuit. That was disappointing: Fforde would have enjoyed helicopters overhead, bullhorns yelling their names with a warning to stop, even the deployment of a stinger to shred the car's tyres and bring them to a dramatic halt.

As it was, they pulled up on the forecourt of the police station and waited.

Not even any armed police.

Jerry Northover had started fidgeting again. Once they'd got him inside the car, firmly wedged into the back seat between Nicki and Fforde, he'd wriggled and writhed in the confined space until Fforde decided enough was enough and elbowed him pointedly in his plenteous gut. That, coupled with the surreal nature of their drive across town, had kept him moderately quiet, but as they waited in the station car park for officers to come and deal with them, he was off again.

'I'm going to have you all for this,' he said. Fforde imagined he was trying to sound threatening.

'For what, exactly?' asked the actor.

'Wrongful imprisonment, kidnap, assault – I'll make sure they throw the book at you.'

Bella turned round from the front seat and looked at the bulky journalist, his hands bound behind his back with a pair of jump leads from Lauren's boot.

'Oh, I doubt that, Mr Northover. You see, according to … well, pretty much every crime book I've ever read, justifiable force is a perfectly acceptable way of capturing a known criminal.'

'Known criminal? What are you talking about? I'm a respectable member of society – tell them, Nicki – and I know people in this town.'

'That sounds suspiciously like a threat to me,' said Fforde, enjoying tormenting the man.

Northover seemed to switch tactics, appealing to Lauren in the driver's seat.

'I thought we had an understanding, Lauren. I thought at least you might have had an idea of the real culprit after our drinks the other night.'

Fforde couldn't see Lauren's face but he heard a smile in her voice.

'It certainly opened my eyes to a few things, Mr Northover. Yes, I'll admit I spent half the weekend following a blind trail that you sent me down. Foolishly, I doubted my friend Professor Stone, based on the poison you poured into my ear on Friday night. But Bella here was a better friend and dragged us all back from the cul-de-sac.'

Bella preened a little. *Well, quite right too,* Fforde thought.

By now the Mini was totally blocked in by police cars with their lights still flashing, and a small huddle of people was gathering outside, some in uniform, others civilians. Nobody seemed quite sure what to do next.

Fforde activated the button on his window and waited while it slid slowly down.

'I wonder if someone would mind taking this gentleman into custody?'

They were all being escorted into the building – Fforde knew he shouldn't have been surprised that the three of them would also be wanted for questioning – when DCI Carlton appeared in the vaulted lobby, her voice echoing round the marble. To one side and slightly behind her trotted DS Muir, his face dark and impenetrable.

'What the hell is going on here?'

'Ah,' said Fforde. This was the one copper he hadn't wanted to confront.

'I have no idea what you think you're doing but you're way off track.'

'No, I don't think they are,' said Sergeant Muir, stepping for the first time out of the shadow of his boss.

All eyes turned on the scruffy man in the tan raincoat. For once, he didn't have the stub of a pencil in his hand, and he looked a few inches taller next to Carlton than Fforde remembered.

'There's been something wrong with this investigation from the start, ma'am, and I'd like to hear what these people have got to say about it.'

'Don't be ridiculous, Muir,' she began, but he cut her off.

'*And* I'd like to hear what Professor Stone has to say about it too.'

He motioned to a couple of uniforms nearby and his meaning was plain: they were to fetch the Professor from his cell.

In the two minutes that followed, Fforde called to mind the

impasses between the characters in *Reservoir Dogs, Pulp Fiction* and *The Good, the Bad and the Ugly*, only without the guns. If he hadn't worried that it might be considered somehow offensive to somebody, he might have called it a Mexican stand-off.

Carlton refused to move: maybe she felt in a stronger position surrounded by fellow officers who would be more likely to take her side than theirs.

Northover was unable to move: he was now handcuffed to a lean, athletic young man perhaps thirty years his junior.

And the reading group were not going anywhere: like Sherlock Holmes, Hercule Poirot, Jane Marple and Jane Tennison, they'd cracked their case.

It might be a rather ramshackle case, with holes that wanted plugging and in dire need of a polish, but Fforde reckoned it would hold fast under scrutiny.

He was about to find out.

Stone seemed tired and haggard when the custody sergeant appeared with him at the top of the stairs leading to the basement. Fforde couldn't be sure if he looked surprised or simply relieved to see the three of them there but his expression definitely brightened.

'All right,' said DS Muir, looking more professional than Fforde could remember seeing him. 'What have you got?'

Over the course of the next ten minutes, each of the four members of the reading group provided fragments of evidence, dollops of speculation and one compelling theory about the murder of Felicity Penman. They were unanimous on the motive: to silence Felicity from spilling the beans about the tragedy she'd watched unfold back at Pittingham University, when her best friend Mariella Brown was thrown out with lethal consequences. It was Felicity who had known that Mariella was being forced to deal drugs to her fellow students, and they guessed that the pusher behind that dealing was her own father. From the safety of his post as news editor on the *Pittingham Times,* he could both mastermind his daughter's distribution of the narcotics – supplementing what he'd confessed to Lauren was a meagre income from the paper – and also control any negative publicity if the story of a drug-taking student were ever to emerge. But when Mariella took the most drastic way out of her situation, either he couldn't handle the pain or he decided he'd be safer in another location and had abandoned Mariella's mother to her grief. It had taken Felicity several years to track him down, and when she did she had no idea of what to do next. They couldn't fathom why she hadn't simply gone to the police and told them all about him, but for whatever reason, he'd remained in place at the now lofty position of editor of the *Norcester Echo*. Felicity, it seemed, had hatched a different plot to expose him.

'And that's where the reading group came in,' said Fforde, spreading his arms as if everything would suddenly make sense.

'Where's that?' asked Northover, disdain dripping from his lips.

'She recruited us as her private detectives – only we didn't know it. Unbeknownst to the killer, she sent us clues before she died. He thought getting rid of her would put an end to the trail that led to him, but he was wrong.'

Fforde thought he'd made a pretty good case. So he was more than a little put out when Northover laughed.

'So what you've actually got is nothing,' he said eventually. 'All you've done is slander me in front of all these police officers. You can't stand up a word of this nonsense.'

Professor Stone took a step forward, into the middle of what had become a circle of keen interest. As well as the reading group, Northover, Nicki Bailey, Carlton and Muir, a little knot of intrigued onlookers had formed and were hanging on the participants' every word.

'We might not be able to, but I suspect DCI Carlton can,' he said.

He looked at the detective's sidekick. 'Sergeant Muir. Perhaps you'd like to do the honours of arresting the chief inspector?'

Fforde had heard stories of people turning purple with rage, of course: he'd just never actually seen it for himself.

'If you're looking for charges,' the Professor went on, 'you could start with aiding and abetting a murderer, fraud, misconduct in a public office—'

Carlton looked like she was about to explode.

'Oh, and conspiracy to pervert the course of justice. I take it I'm still technically under arrest?'

DS Muir turned squarely to face her, his expression one of nervous anticipation. 'How about it, boss? Are you going to come clean?'

She stared blankly at him for a full thirty seconds before finally crumpling under his accusatory gaze. Instead of her usual commanding assertiveness, a tremble was audible to the whole lobby. 'All right, Geoffrey. I can't keep up this charade any longer. I admit it.'

Suddenly all hell broke loose.

Jerry Northover let out a roar of rage, something unearthly from the depths of his being that Fforde could only applaud for its diaphragmatic projection.

And then he ran.

Handcuffed as he was to the athletic police officer, he somehow found a strength in his core that propelled him towards the front door of the police station. The young copper was dragged involuntarily in his wake but by the time he found his feet and had stopped stumbling crazily, Northover's momentum was taking him headlong towards the exit. In every direction, uniforms sprang to life and Fforde gazed in wonder at the whirlwind of black and white and neon yellow that filled the lobby. But it was a single voice, echoing powerfully across the space, that brought the editor of the *Norcester Echo* to an abrupt halt. The officer he was attached to crashed heavily into him as he stopped. Puffing and sweating profusely, the bulky figure of Jerry Northover turned back to the source of the shout.

DCI Miranda Carlton had not moved from the spot.

'No, Jerry,' she said as the hubbub of the crowd caved into silence. 'It's over.'

Tuesday

Chapter Thirty-Two

Professor Stone put his coffee cup on the table, tapped out a code on his phone to switch it off and turned his back to the Perspex wall. In the hushed stillness of the room, he could feel the ghost of Lord Quaint at his shoulder, urging him on to the *dénouement*, and the expectant faces on the seats in front of him were curiously reminiscent of the assembled household of Crompton Hall.

Only this time, there was no killer to unmask.

Jerry Northover had been in police custody for almost twenty-four hours and, if DS Muir were to be believed, charges would be brought before the day was out. What the reading group was interested in now was the way the jigsaw was pieced together. Stone knew he didn't possess all the little cutout bits on his own but he was confident that between them they could finish the picture.

'Ladies and gentlemen,' he began.

'Yes, yes,' said Fforde, wafting a hand as if in

encouragement to move on. 'Cut the preamble and tell us everything.'

Stone saw Lauren's elbow dig into Fforde's ribs from her position beside him on the battered old sofa.

'Oh, let him have his moment,' she said, glancing across at Bella Bourton in one of the armchairs. 'He has had to put up with being wrongfully imprisoned.'

Stone indulged her with a grateful smile.

'I don't intend to delay us all for very long. We do have our next book to decide on, after all.'

'Sod the next book,' said Fforde. 'This is much more exciting.'

'All right, then,' said Stone. 'Let's wrap it up.'

'Start with the packages,' said Bella, sounding eager. She pointed at the pile of five volumes on the coffee table between them, gathered from the bookshop stock to replicate the copies that were being held by the police. 'What do they all mean?'

Stone picked up the stack and lifted them off one by one, dropping them back on the table in turn as he discussed them.

'*A Study in Scarlet* – that one Lauren has explained quite adequately. It was a reference to the editor's office at the *Norcester Echo*.'

Thunk.

'Now, *On Floating Bodies* is a little more obscure, but I believe Felicity was targeting me with my specialist subject. Archimedes, as I think I mentioned last week, was known as the father of mathematics, so there was another clue to Mariella Brown's relative there, alongside the Father Brown title.'

'Nothing to do with a body floating somewhere?' said Fforde.

'Nothing at all.' Stone declined to mention that his own thought process had followed exactly the same path for a long time, leading only to a dead end.

Thunk.

'Thanks to Nicki Bailey, we've got a fifth book to add to our clues. *The Prodigal Daughter*. I don't imagine that needs much explanation now, does it?'

'But why send it to someone outside the reading group?' asked Lauren.

'Back-up, I suppose. Just in case Felicity's carefully selected team of detectives wasn't up to the job.'

He dropped the book onto the growing pile.

Thunk.

'As the new girl in the reading group, Bella was sent *The Body in the Library* partly as an introduction to detective fiction and partly to make the link with Felicity herself. In the absence of a Christie novel about bookshops, the library was the next best thing. Of course, at the time she was posting packages, I don't think she expected to actually become the body in the library. Or the bookshop. It turned out to be much more literal than she ever intended.'

Bella looked confused. 'But if she wasn't sending us clues to her murderer, what was she doing?'

'I'll come to that.'

Thunk.

'As for *The Girl with the Dragon Tattoo,* I haven't got my head round that one. Any ideas?'

Lauren said, 'It's about a cynical journalist and a man with a secret past. Surely that's a straightforward pointer to Jerry Northover.'

'But why send it to me?' asked Fforde.

Stone shrugged. 'Had to go to somebody, and you were the only one without a book.'

Fforde looked a little crestfallen. 'Thanks for that. Makes me feel really special.'

Stone noticed Lauren nudge him again. He guessed this time it was more in sympathy. But then Lauren looked up at him, something inexplicable behind her gaze, as if she had something she wanted to confess to him.

He couldn't imagine what.

Thunk.

'You should feel special, Harrison,' he said, deliberately using Fforde's first name. 'Your corkboard was a stroke of genius. It certainly got Bella thinking in a new direction.'

'Just the wrong one,' she said ruefully.

'Doesn't matter. In a case like this, as so many crime authors are at pains to point out, it takes a bit of lateral thinking to come up with the real solution. And I believe Bella has proven herself well suited to fully-fledged membership of our little group, don't you?'

The enthusiasm from Lauren and Fforde was palpable and genuine.

'So, back to Bella's biggie,' said Fforde after the mutual congratulations had died down. 'Why was Felicity trying to draw our attention to the editor of the *Norcester Echo*?'

'Ah,' said Stone, raising a finger in what he hoped was a decisive gesture. 'That's where Felicity's secret past comes into play. We know she was best friends with Mariella Brown, and we also know that Mariella got kicked out of my university for dealing drugs.'

'Hang on,' said Fforde. 'Just clear up the question of names for me. How could Jerry Northover be the father of Mariella Brown?'

'Easy,' said Bella. 'She used her mother's maiden name instead of her father's surname. Do you remember Kathy telling us she was *Ms* Brown, not Mrs? I'm thinking of going back to my maiden name, actually. It happens more often than you might think.'

'And if you check out her Facebook page you can see why,' said Lauren. 'In those photographs of her eighteenth birthday, she looks like she wants nothing to do with him.'

Stone was about to resume his narrative when there was a tentative knock at the door. Fforde went to it and threw it open, revealing the cowering figure of Maurice Stapleton hovering beyond, an envelope grasped in his spindly fingers.

'Yes?' boomed Stone from inside the room.

'I've got something for you,' said the acting manager, proffering the envelope to Fforde.

'What is it?'

'I don't know,' he said as if the question had been the most affronting thing he'd encountered all day. 'But it's got Felicity's handwriting on it.'

Fforde snatched it from him and looked at the front of the envelope. The writing matched perfectly the addresses on the front of their anonymous packages.

'*To the Reading Group*,' he read aloud.

Bella was on her feet. 'What? Where did you get this?' she demanded.

Maurice took half a step backwards.

'She gave it to me before last week's meeting,' he said, the affront paling into nervousness. 'Asked me to give it to you at this week's meeting if she wasn't here.'

Stone felt something like anger begin to stir in him.

'And you didn't think to give it to us before now? I can't begin to guess what it says but I imagine you could have saved us a whole lot of trouble – and possibly at least one life.'

Maurice looked like he was about to crumple like the envelope he'd been clutching.

'I was asked to hand it over at the next scheduled meeting. That's what I'm doing.'

'But the murder, the investigation,' said Lauren incredulously. 'Why didn't you take it to the police?'

'How do you know it has anything to do with the murder? For all you know, it might be a list of forthcoming dates for your meetings.'

Fforde began tearing open the envelope, his brow furrowed.

'He's right, you know. And besides, it's probably just as well he didn't give it to DCI Carlton. It would never have seen the light of day.'

He extricated the contents of the envelope and cast a glance at the top sheet of several that were folded together. After a moment, he passed them to Stone.

The Professor looked down at the papers and breathed in slowly.

'Close the door, Harrison.'

Fforde did as he'd requested, leaving Maurice spluttering on the outside.

Dear Friends of the Reading Group,

You will by now have realised that Felicity Penman is not entirely what she seemed. She is, in fact, a fictional character –

something you're all very familiar with. And that's why I've chosen you. Over the past weeks and months, you have each in turn shown yourselves to possess particular skills, characteristics and attitudes that lend themselves perfectly to the undertaking I'm currently pursuing.

It's probable, if you are reading this, that you will also know the background to Felicity's invention, her arrival in Norcester and her single-minded mission to expose Jerry Northover as the man responsible for the death of my friend Mariella Brown.

I have no doubt that you are aware of Mr Northover's criminal past in Pittingham, his horrible treatment of Mariella in forcing her to deal drugs to what he saw as a captive audience at the university, and her subsequent decision to take the most final of ways out of her hellish situation. When I first tried to hold him to account, I met with only resistance from the police. Indeed, I thought the whole thing had died with her when her father disappeared from Pittingham soon afterwards and that he was never going to be brought to justice. You can imagine how I felt, then, when I discovered by chance a couple of years ago that the same Jerry Northover was now editor of the Norcester Echo and living an apparently blameless life as an upright member of the community.

Without evidence of any actual crime I was unable to expose him. So I had to find another way to bring him down. You'll know, I'm sure, that I indulged in a little subterfuge for the next part of my plan, fabricating a CV that fortunately landed me the job of manager of The Quaint Bookshop, where I began assembling my team. I hope you won't resent me for selecting you for a different purpose from the overt objective of forming the reading group. It was your skills as sharp-eyed, clear-thinking human beings that I required rather than your literary criticism, but you are no less valuable for that.

Professor Stone: you have been the foundation of my plan from the start, with your analytical brain and indomitable logic leading invariably to the correct answer. Lauren, you have brought empathy and character insight to the team, just as I'm sure you do to your manuscripts. Harrison's passion and optimism in the face of significant challenges have been a constant source of inspiration to me while planning my little puzzle, and the arrival of Bella, with your quiet resilience and lack of ego making you the ideal team player, has given me the last elements I was seeking. Between you, you embody all the qualities of the great fictional detectives, and I have never doubted your ability to solve my mystery.

If you are reading this, rather than hearing it from me in person, then I will have misjudged Jerry Northover once again. I didn't believe him capable of inflicting actual physical harm – although maybe Mariella's stories about her upbringing should have rung more alarm bells for me – so if he has taken things to a conclusion I'm not anticipating, then I can only apologise for putting you all through such an ordeal. I wish my subterfuge had not been necessary in the first place.

By the same token, I also want to thank you all – for your friendship, short or long, for your intelligence and diligence in pursuing this game, and for being the remarkable detectlves I always suspected you were.

With all my affection,

Lucy Eastwood

They were silent for some minutes after Stone finished reading. It was Fforde who broke the atmosphere.

'I still can't get my head round the editor of the local paper being a drug-dealer. Seems a bit implausible.'

'He wasn't the editor in Pittingham,' Stone explained.

'And he was short of cash too,' said Lauren. 'He told me. Said there was no money in local newspapers. I guess that's why he saw an opportunity to make some extra via Mariella.'

'Sounds dangerously close to being a *deus ex machina* if you ask me,' said Fforde. 'And I don't care whether the "c" is hard or soft.'

Stone puffed out his chest and resumed his air of authority. '*Deus* or not, those are the facts. Remember your Sherlock Holmes, Harrison: when you have eliminated all which is impossible, then whatever remains, however improbable, must be the truth. And at least it wasn't the milkman. Jerry Northover had both the pull and the contacts to run a mini empire directly from his desk at the *Pittingham Times*.'

'Professor, I have a confession,' said Lauren.

Ah, so this was what she'd been building herself up to.

'He made me doubt you,' she went on apologetically. 'I suppose that was all part of a smokescreen to cover up his activities.'

Stone nodded forgivingly. 'Don't worry about it, Lauren. Regret is a wasted emotion – and I should know. If I was in your shoes I'd probably have doubted me too.' He wasn't sure he really believed that but now was not a time for recriminations. 'Any deflection away from him was useful. That's why he encouraged Nicki to pursue the reading group. He wanted to fill the paper with fake news about the murder.'

Fforde grunted. 'He did that all right.'

Stone wondered if Fforde registered even the slightest hint of irony and decided he probably didn't.

He wasn't about to point it out.

'Poor Mariella,' said Bella. 'A horrible childhood, a horrible father and a horrible end.'

The room fell silent again, each face frowning.

Finally, Lauren said, 'I wonder why the police weren't interested when she first went to see them.'

'I think I can answer that,' said a voice from behind her.

Stone looked up to see Geoffrey Muir standing in the doorway in a smart new double-breasted jacket. Columbo was gone; Remington Steele had appeared in his place. He carried a heavy plastic bag.

'The problem was that we didn't believe her. Or should I say, we chose not to believe her.'

Muir stepped into the room, deposited his bag on the table and surveyed the assembled company. Stone's position as Lord Quaint had been usurped, albeit temporarily, by his very own Chief Inspector Watkins, who brought with him, at Stone's invitation, the missing pieces of the jigsaw.

'Lucy Eastwood made the unfortunate error of telling her story to a particular officer on the local force, at the time a mere uniformed inspector, by the name of Miranda Carlton. And nobody else bothered to check it out. Well, why would they? Look at it from their point of view. A young woman comes in with a wild story about her friend being driven to suicide by her drug-dealing journalist father. The first officer she speaks to makes a brief record in her notebook and files it under "Bin". It wouldn't cross anyone's mind to question Inspector Carlton's judgement, so Lucy's complaint ended there.'

Fforde looked keenly at Muir. 'But I don't understand. Why would Carlton want to sweep it under the carpet?'

Stone took a step forward. It felt important to reassert his position.

'If I may, Sergeant? Stop me if I get anything wrong.'

Muir backed off slightly, allowing Stone the floor.

'I think Miranda Carlton went off the rails a long time before she met Lucy Eastwood. My guess is she's been taking backhanders from criminals for years – you know, making sure evidence is conveniently lost before cases come to court, that kind of thing. And I think Jerry Northover found out about it somehow. Maybe his contacts in that world were just as good as hers; maybe someone let something slip over a pint in a pub. But as soon as he had the story of a corrupt police officer, he also knew he had leverage. It meant that when it came to dealing drugs to students, he could do it without worrying about the local constabulary breathing down his neck.'

He turned to Muir. 'How am I doing so far?'

Muir nodded. 'As a *quid pro quo* for burying the story, she turned a blind eye to his activities. Then later, after he'd come to Norcester as editor of the *Echo*, she could call on him to put in a good word with the chief constable when she was looking for promotion.'

Fforde grunted. 'You scratch my back, I'll give you a full body Thai massage with all the extras.'

'Something like that,' said Muir.

'How much of this did Felicity know?' asked Bella.

It was a question Stone himself had been pondering. Since he'd dropped the suggestion to DS Muir late on Sunday night in his prison cell, he'd been trying to work out if Felicity had been aware of DCI Carlton's involvement in the Northover affair, or if it had simply been a coincidence that her name had come up in that conversation he'd had with her about the abuse of power.

'I don't think she can have known,' he said. 'Not about Carlton's corruption. It would have given her a completely different story to take to the police, and we all know how honest officers don't take kindly to corruption in their ranks.'

He looked again at Muir, whose face had hardened into a gritted-teeth sneer.

'But then, like Felicity, I don't think Miranda Carlton expected things to go as far as they did, either,' Stone continued.

'Murder, you mean?' asked Lauren.

'Exactly.'

Fforde asked Muir, 'Do we know precisely what happened here last Tuesday night?'

Muir fidgeted uncomfortably. 'Do you really want all the details?'

'Spare us the blood and guts,' said Bella. 'But I think I'd like to know a bit more about how things played out.'

Muir coughed and shifted his weight. 'It's taken a bit of piecing together – Mr Northover hasn't exactly been forthcoming – but we've established he'd been drinking that night in the Serendipity Bar of the Renaissance Hotel. The barman said he'd been hitting the whisky pretty heavily. He left about nine o'clock and our assumption is that he came here to confront Felicity. He must have arrived at the side door just as you lot were leaving. There's no CCTV coverage in the alley but we found a figure under an umbrella from footage behind the shop.'

Stone winced. 'And put two and two together to make a case against me.'

Muir looked embarrassed. 'Sorry about that, Professor.'

'Wait a minute,' said Bella. 'It wasn't raining last Tuesday night.'

'Which is exactly what makes an umbrella suspicious,' said Fforde.

'Anyway,' said Muir, apparently anxious to move his narrative on, 'forensics found evidence of a scuffle, so I'm thinking he grabbed the nearest big book he could find in a drunken rage and lashed out at her.'

'How did he know she was on to him?' asked Lauren.

Muir smiled a small smile.

'Barmen make very good witnesses – those that don't drink their own bars dry, that is. Serendipity Bar again. He'd seen them together a couple of nights earlier, thought it was a bit odd given the age difference and the fact that he seemed much angrier than she did. Initially he wondered if she was touting for business and asking too much money.'

'Oh no,' exclaimed Bella, looking horrified.

Muir ignored the interruption. 'But then he decided she wasn't the type and filed it away as strange but interesting. He's been a mine of useful information, has that barman.'

'And yet none of his information could influence DCI Carlton to drop her pursuit of a case against me,' said Stone. He still wasn't quite ready to let Muir off the hook.

'It's become apparent that she had her own agenda,' said the sergeant stiffly. 'I couldn't make sense of some of her actions this last week, so your comment on Sunday night really got me thinking, Professor. What if she had got it all wrong? What if this reading group was indeed the key to the mystery of Felicity Penman's murder? But it was only after your little escapade yesterday that we were able to identify all the elements – Northover's previous questioning, Lucy Eastwood's crazy claims, the truth about DCI Carlton – and put together a coherent case.'

'Too late to help Felicity,' said Bella sadly.

'And Paula Grayson,' said Stone.

'Yes,' said Lauren, a baffled look on her face. 'Paula Grayson – how does she fit into this?'

Muir shrugged. 'Unfortunately for her, she just happened to be in the wrong place at the wrong time. She'd come to Norcester looking for you'—he pointed at Stone—'and ran into Felicity quite by chance. Jerry Northover already knew Felicity was on to him, so when another face from the old university turned up, he jumped to a huge conclusion.'

'He believed Paula was part of Felicity's plan to bring him down?' asked Stone.

'So he had to remove her too.'

A light went on in Lauren's eyes as she looked at Stone. 'And then he took the chance to frame you for it. When he and I saw you at the hotel on Friday night, he filled me with horror stories about your past life in Pittingham and made it look like you'd gone to the Renaissance to find Paula.'

A sickening thought struck Stone.

'And what's the betting he went to my house, broke in and stole my bread knife, then went back to the hotel to kill Paula with it?'

Muir nodded again. 'Sounds about right. He's all over the CCTV in the hotel.'

Fforde looked doubtful. 'Will it stand up, though? Without any concrete evidence tying him to the knife?'

'He's stuck with the traditional defence so far,' said Muir. 'No comment. But it's only the hardened criminals who can keep that up for long. I have a strong sense that Mr Northover won't be able to stand a full-blown murder interrogation, even if we do it strictly by the book. Which we do every time, of course,' he added quickly.

Stone reflected that the manhunt for Jerry Northover had been all-consuming for Felicity: to uproot from one town, inveigle her way into a job for which she was not technically qualified, wait months for the right team of unwitting collaborators to present themselves, then set in motion a plan which had no guarantee of success. She was certainly playing the long game.

'So you were right about one thing: Felicity did come to Norcester to confront the man responsible for Mariella's death. You just got the wrong man.'

'Can't get it right every time,' Muir said. 'And at least you're in the clear now.'

'No thanks to you. It took a bunch of amateur sleuths from the reading group to solve the case.'

'Looks like a good call on Felicity's part. She couldn't do it on her own – she'd already tried that route. On the other hand, she couldn't risk telling you the whole story up front in case you didn't believe her, like DCI Carlton hadn't. She needed you to work it out for yourselves.'

Stone noted Muir's graceful acknowledgement of the reading group's role in the *dénouement* to the whole business. It couldn't have been easy for him.

'And what about Jerry Northover trying to bash me over the head yesterday?' asked Bella. 'What had I done to deserve that?'

Muir laughed ruefully. 'I suspect you said the wrong thing to him, that was all.'

'I only told him I knew who the murderer was – but I was wrong. I thought it was Maurice Stapleton.'

'Did you identify the killer before he attacked you?'

Bella looked thoughtful. 'No, now you mention it, I don't think I did.'

'Another conclusion jumped,' said Stone grimly. 'When you told him you knew who the murderer was, he assumed you were about to name him, and obviously decided you had to go too. It was a bit brazen in his own office, and he'd never have got away with it, but by that stage he wasn't thinking straight. That's if he ever had been.'

The room fell into thoughtful contemplation. Stone had heard the others tell of Bella's lucky escape and he felt a sudden affection for the woman he'd previously dismissed as less erudite than the rest of them. Perhaps he needed to recalibrate his analysis. And anyway, perhaps erudition wasn't everything.

'I've got a question for you,' said Fforde, eyeing the sergeant cautiously.

'Fire away.'

'That list in Felicity's drawer. Why didn't the police find it?'

'We did. Only it didn't seem to be important. Mr Stapleton said that kind of thing was nothing unusual.'

'Shifty so-and-so,' said Bella.

'Oh, he's harmless enough,' said Muir. 'He's got delusions of grandeur, I'll grant you, but he was quite useful to our investigations.'

'It was him who told you we'd been holding extra meetings, wasn't it?' said Lauren.

'Couldn't help himself,' said Muir. 'Fundamentally he's a jobsworth. If it's any consolation, I don't imagine he'll be in post very long.'

Fforde pushed again. 'And the empty envelope with *The Secret of Father Brown* in it? Who was that intended for?'

'That we'll never know,' said Muir. 'There were no more names on the list, but clearly Felicity had another package in mind when she died. Maybe she was going to send something a bit more obvious, just in case her crack team let her down.'

Fforde bristled. 'If you recall, we didn't even receive her packages until after she'd been murdered.'

'Besides,' Stone said pointedly, 'we weren't the only detectives on the case.'

'Touché,' said Muir, and pointed at the plastic bag on the table. 'That's why I've brought you these. Let's call it an apology, shall we?'

Stone reached forward and pulled two bottles of champagne from the bag.

'I wonder if we can get Maurice Stapleton to find us some glasses.'

'I must admit you haven't done too badly for a book club,' Muir offered approvingly.

'Reading group,' said four voices in unison.

Bella looked at Stone. 'I meant to ask you about that, Professor. Why do you insist on calling it a reading group?'

A malevolent little creature inside Stone turned over and yawned. 'Ancient history, Bella. Something that happened in a book club I belonged to years ago. I swore then that I would never be part of a book club again.'

The pricking-up of Fforde's ears was almost comical.

'Oh, do tell us more.'

Stone shook his head gravely. 'Sorry, Harrison. That's a story for another time. Maybe.'

After Sergeant Muir had left, the four members of the reading group poured the fizz and stood in a circle.

'Do you think we could make our next book a little less … dangerous?' asked Bella.

'No murders,' said Lauren.

'A comedy, perhaps,' said Fforde.

With the mood shifting unmistakably towards a toast, everyone turned deferentially to Professor Stone, who raised his glass.

'To Felicity Penman,' he said. 'And Lucy Eastwood.'

As his three friends drank their toasts, Stone looked from one face to another, torn between pride and poignancy. Felicity had been right in her assessment of each of them – Bella the eager new recruit, Lauren the smart young sage, even the well-intentioned Harrison with all his amiable faults.

Stone would never be able to thank Felicity for bringing them together.

But he was very glad she had.

Acknowledgments

You can't make an omelette without breaking eggs, the saying goes, and it's fair to admit I've broken quite a few in the preparation of this particular omelette. Fortunately, there's been a whole kitchen's worth of chefs, sous chefs, chefs de partie, commis chefs and – essential for the writing process – a sommelier to rescue the resulting concoction.

Murder by the Book wouldn't have happened in the first place had it not been for the extraordinary support of HarperCollins publisher David Brawn, with whom I originally worked on Desmond Bagley's 'lost' novel *Domino Island* and its Davies sequels, *Outback* and *Thin Ice.* Without David's enormous experience and judicious care for the Bagley legacy, I might never have made it into print at all. The fact that he was astute enough to introduce me to another HarperCollins division, One More Chapter, is a reflection of his acumen and generosity, for it was here that *Murder by the Book* found its true home.

If you haven't spotted it already, One More Chapter is a bit different in the world of publishing, and it's been both enlightening and a whirlwind of plate-spinning to bring the first of this new series to fruition.

Publisher Charlotte Ledger's enthusiasm for the project has been inspirational and helped carry one uncertain author through to a complete first draft. Editor Helen Williams saw the raw ingredients, offered brilliant advice and considerable encouragement to the cook, and contributed enormously to the finished feast. I am hugely indebted to them both.

Along the way, a small army of dedicated and talented people have added their own *soupçon* of finesse to the recipe: line and copy editors Victoria Oundjian and Simon Fox; proofreaders Linda Joyce and Janet Marie Adkins; managing editorial assistant Kara Daniel, responsible for setting the book; cover designer Lucy Bennett, whose stunning work makes it look so tasty on the bookshelves; and a marketing team led by Katie Sadler and including Chloe Cummings and Grace Edwards, who work so hard to reach those all-important people, the readers.

On which subject, if you're still with me, there are a few more thanks to convey.

First, it's you, the person currently in possession of this book. Unless you've stolen it or skipped to the back without actually reading it. Even then, you're reading this now, so I'll take that as a win. The point is, without you, the reader, there would be no published books, and whether you loved it or hated it, I really appreciate your taking the time to explore *Murder by the Book*. Of course, if you hated it, I'd prefer it if you didn't mention it to anyone. By contrast, five-star reviews always go down well.

Elsewhere, my trusty pal and beta-reader Richard Howarth deserves all the Star Baker aprons for once again casting his eagle eyes over the completed manuscript. Now that's what I call a good friend.

In a book that's fundamentally about books and the folk who value them, it's only right and proper that I should pay tribute to those wonderful people who sustain our bookshops and libraries in the face of increasing social and financial pressures. Booksellers – whether part of international chains or dogged independents carving out a tough niche – are the lifeblood of the book industry, and I urge you to use them or lose them, as the cliché goes. As for libraries, from my first childhood library in Abington, Northampton, to the delights of Blackpool's Carnegie-funded emporium of literature, where the staff are enormously welcoming and supportive to readers and writers alike, they provide a vital service that should be treasured and preserved for the generations that are following on. It's the least we can do for them.

Finally, no list of acknowledgements and thanks would be complete without the one who keeps me going: my muse, my confidante, my co-conspirator, Tricia. Not only do you make it all possible, you make it all worthwhile. The icing on the cake, you might say.

So that was *Murder by the Book*. Now, what does a bookshop reading group do after it's solved one murder…?

READ THE NEXT INSTALMENT IN THE COSY CRIME CLUB MYSTERY SERIES: *A GAME OF MURDER*
PERFECT FOR FANS OF RICHARD OSMAN!

A remote country house. An unexpected death.
Any *clue* who did it?

As guests of honour at a remote country house weekend, The Quaint Bookshop reading group are forced to put their detective skills to the test once more when the chef plunges to her death from the tallest tower.

But did she throw herself off – or is there a killer on the loose? As heavy snow cuts them off from the outside world, the group squares up to a cast of characters worthy of a certain board game. There's just one hitch: they don't have any clues.

The author and One More Chapter would like to thank everyone who contributed to the publication of this story...

Analytics
Imogen Wolstencroft

Audio
Fionnuala Barrett
Ciara Briggs

Contracts
Laura Amos
Inigo Vyvyan

Design
Lucy Bennett
Fiona Greenway
Liane Payne
Dean Russell

Digital Sales
Laura Daley
Lydia Grainge
Hannah Lismore

eCommerce
Laura Carpenter
Madeline ODonovan
Charlotte Stevens
Christina Storey
Jo Surman
Rachel Ward

Editorial
Janet Marie Adkins
Rosie Best
Kara Daniel
Simon Fox
Linda Joyce
Charlotte Ledger
Victoria Oundjian
Jennie Rothwell
Sofia Salazar Studer
Helen Williams

Harper360
Emily Gerbner
Ariana Juarez
Jean Marie Kelly
emma sullivan
Sophia Wilhelm

International Sales
Peter Borcsok
Ruth Burrow
Bethan Moore
Colleen Simpson

Inventory
Sarah Callaghan
Kirsty Norman

Marketing & Publicity
Chloe Cummings
Grace Edwards
Katie Sadler

Operations
Melissa Okusanya
Hannah Stamp

Production
Denis Manson
Simon Moore
Francesca Tuzzeo

Rights
Ashton Mucha
Alisah Saghir
Zoe Shine
Aisling Smyth
Lucy Vanderbilt

Trade Marketing
Ben Hurd
Eleanor Slater

The HarperCollins Distribution Team

The HarperCollins Finance & Royalties Team

The HarperCollins Legal Team

The HarperCollins Technology Team

UK Sales
Isabel Coburn
Jay Cochrane
Sabina Lewis
Holly Martin
Harriet Williams
Leah Woods

And every other essential link in the chain from delivery drivers to booksellers to librarians and beyond!

YOUR NUMBER ONE STOP
ONE MORE CHAPTER
FOR PAGETURNING BOOKS